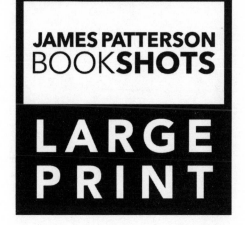

BOOK**SHOTS**

BY JAMES PATTERSON
AVAILABLE NOW

Cross Kill

Zoo 2

The Trial

Little Black Dress

Chase

Let's Play Make-Believe

Hunted

113 Minutes

$10,000,000 Marriage Proposal

French Kiss

Learning to Ride

The McCullagh Inn in Maine

The Mating Season

Sacking the Quarterback

NONFICTION

Trump vs. Clinton: In Their Own Words

BOOK**SHOTS**
STORIES AT THE SPEED OF LIFE

What you are holding in your hands right now is a collection of BookShots.

BookShots are page-turning stories by James Patterson that can be read in one sitting.

Each and every one is fast-paced, 100% story-driven; a shot of pure entertainment guaranteed to satisfy.

Available as compact paperbacks, ebooks, and audio, everywhere books are sold.

BookShots—the ultimate form of storytelling.

From the ultimate storyteller.

KILL OR BE KILLED

THRILLERS

JAMES PATTERSON

BOOK**SHOTS**
LARGE PRINT EDITION

Little, Brown and Company
New York Boston London

Copyright © 2016 by James Patterson

BookShots / Little, Brown and Company
Hachette Book Group
1290 Avenue of the Americas, New York, NY 10104
bookshots.com

The Trial and Little Black Dress were first published in July 2016
Heist was first published in the UK by Random House in June 2016

First Edition: October 2016

BookShots is an imprint of Little, Brown and Company, a division of Hachette Book Group, Inc. The Little, Brown name and logo are trademarks of Hachette Book Group, Inc. The BookShots name and logo are trademarks of JBP Business, LLC.

The publisher is not responsible for websites (or their content) that are not owned by the publisher.

The Hachette Speakers Bureau provides a wide range of authors for speaking events. To find out more, go to hachettespeakersbureau.com or call (866) 376-6591.

ISBN 978-0-316-50559-8
LCCN 2016944256

10 9 8 7 6 5 4 3 2 1

LSC-C

Printed in the United States of America

CONTENTS

JAMES PATTERSON
BOOKSHOTS

THE WOMEN'S MURDER CLUB
TRIAL

WITH
MAXINE PAETRO

THE TRIAL

BY JAMES PATTERSON
WITH MAXINE PAETRO

CHAPTER 1

IT WAS THAT CRAZY period between Thanksgiving and Christmas when work overflowed, time raced, and there wasn't enough light between dawn and dusk to get everything done.

Still, our gang of four, what we call the Women's Murder Club, always had a spouse-free holiday get-together dinner of drinks and bar food.

Yuki Castellano had picked the place.

It was called Uncle Maxie's Top Hat and was a bar and grill that had been a fixture in the Financial District for 150 years. It was decked out with art deco prints and mirrors on the walls, and a large, neon-lit clock behind the bar dominated the room. Maxie's catered to men in smart suits and women in tight skirts and spike heels who wore good jewelry.

I liked the place and felt at home there in a Mickey Spillane kind of way. Case in point: I was wearing straight-legged pants, a blue gabardine blazer, a Glock in my shoulder holster, and flat lace-up shoes. I stood in the bar area, slowly turning my head as I looked around for my BFFs.

"Lindsay. Yo."

Cindy Thomas waved her hand from the table tucked under the spiral staircase. I waved back, moved toward the nook inside the cranny. Claire Washburn was wearing a trench coat over her scrubs, with a button on the lapel that read SUPPORT OUR TROOPS. She peeled off her coat and gave me a hug and a half.

Cindy was also in her work clothes: cords and a bulky sweater, with a peacoat slung over the back of her chair. If I'd ducked under the table, I'm sure I would have seen steel-toed boots. Cindy was a crime reporter of note, and she was wearing her on-the-job hound dog clothes.

She blew me a couple of kisses, and Yuki stood up to give me her seat and a jasmine-scented smack on the cheek. She had clearly come from court, where she worked as a pro bono defense attorney for the poor and hopeless. Still, she was dressed impeccably, in pinstripes and pearls.

I took the chair across from Claire. She sat between Cindy and Yuki with her back to the room, and we all scooched up to the smallish glass-and-chrome table.

THE TRIAL

If it hasn't been said, we four are a mutual heart, soul, and work society in which we share our cases and views of the legal system, as well as our personal lives. Right now the girls were worried about me.

Three of us were married—me, Claire, and Yuki—and Cindy had a standing offer of a ring and vows to be exchanged in Grace Cathedral. Until very recently you couldn't have found four more happily hooked-up women. Then the bottom fell out of my marriage to Joe Molinari, the father of my child and a man I shared everything with, including my secrets.

We had had it so good, we kissed and made up before our fights were over. It was the typical: "You are right." "No, you are!"

Then Joe went missing during possibly the worst weeks of my life.

I'm a homicide cop, and I know when someone is telling me the truth and when things do not add up.

Joe missing in action had not added up. Because of that I had worried almost to panic. Where was he? Why hadn't he checked in? Why were my calls bouncing off his full mailbox? Was he still alive?

As the crisscrossed threads of espionage, destruction, and mass murder were untangled, Joe finally made his curtain call with stories of his past and present lives that I'd never heard before. I found plenty of reason not to trust him anymore.

Even he would agree. I think anyone would.

It's not news that once trust is broken, it's damned hard to superglue it back together. And for me it might take more time and belief in Joe's confession than I actually had.

I still loved him. We'd shared a meal when he came to see our baby, Julie. We didn't make any moves toward getting divorced that night, but we didn't make love, either. Our relationship was now like the Cold War in the eighties between Russia and the USA, a strained but practical peace called détente.

Now, as I sat with my friends, I tried to put Joe out of my mind, secure in the knowledge that my nanny was looking after Julie and that the home front was safe. I ordered a favorite holiday drink, a hot buttered rum, and a rare steak sandwich with Uncle Maxie's hot chili sauce.

My girlfriends were deep in criminal cross talk about Claire's holiday overload of corpses, Cindy's new cold case she'd exhumed from the *San Francisco Chronicle*'s dead letter files, and Yuki's hoped-for favorable verdict for her client, an underage drug dealer. I was almost caught up when Yuki said, "Linds, I gotta ask. Any Christmas plans with Joe?"

And that's when I was saved by the bell. My phone rang.

My friends said in unison, "NO PHONES."

It was the rule, but I'd forgotten—again.

I reached into my bag for my phone, saying, "Look, I'm turning it off."

But I saw that the call was from Rich Conklin, my partner and Cindy's fiancé. She recognized his ring tone on my phone.

"There goes our party," she said, tossing her napkin into the air.

"Linds?" said Conklin.

"Rich, can this wait? I'm in the middle—"

"It's Kingfisher. He's in a shoot-out with cops at the Vault. There've been casualties."

"But—Kingfisher is *dead*."

"Apparently, he's been resurrected."

CHAPTER 2

MY PARTNER WAS DOUBLE-PARKED and waiting for me outside Uncle Maxie's, with the engine running and the flashers on. I got into the passenger seat of the unmarked car, and Richie handed me my vest. He's that way, like a younger version of a big brother. He thinks of me, watches out for me, and I try to do the same for him.

He watched me buckle up, then he hit the siren and stepped on the gas.

We were about five minutes from the Vault, a class A nightclub on the second floor of a former Bank of America building.

"Fill me in," I said to my partner.

"Call came in to 911 about ten minutes ago," Conklin said as we tore up California Street. "A kitchen worker said he recognized Kingfisher out in the bar. He was still trying to convince 911 that it was an emergency when shots were fired inside the club."

"Watch out on our right."

Richie yanked the wheel hard left to avoid an indecisive panel truck, then jerked it hard right and took a turn onto Sansome.

"You okay?" he asked.

I had been known to get carsick in jerky high-speed chases when I wasn't behind the wheel.

"I'm fine. Keep talking."

My partner told me that a second witness reported to first officers that three men were talking to two women at the bar. One of the men yelled, "No one screws with the King." Shots were fired. The women were killed.

"Caller didn't leave his name."

I was gripping both the dash and the door, and had both feet on imaginary brakes, but my mind was occupied with Kingfisher. He was a Mexican drug cartel boss, a psycho with a history of brutality and revenge, and a penchant for settling his scores personally.

Richie was saying, "Patrol units arrived as the shooters were attempting to flee through thefront entrance. Someone saw the tattoo on the back of the hand of one of the shooters. I talked to Brady," Conklin said, referring to our lieutenant. "If that shooter is Kingfisher and survives, he's ours."

CHAPTER 3

I WANTED THE KING on death row for the normal reasons. He was to the drug and murder trade as al-Baghdadi was to terrorism. But I also had personal reasons.

Earlier that year a cadre of dirty San Francisco cops from our division had taken down a number of drug houses for their own financial gain. One drug house in particular yielded a payoff of five to seven million in cash and drugs. Whether those cops knew it beforehand or not, the stolen loot belonged to Kingfisher—and he wanted it back.

The King took his revenge but was still short a big pile of dope and dollars.

So he turned his sights on me.

I was the primary homicide inspector on the dirty-cop case.

Using his own twisted logic, the King demanded that I personally recover and return his property. Or else.

It was a threat and a promise, and of course I couldn't deliver.

From that moment on I had protection all day and night, every day and night, but protection isn't enough when your tormentor is like a ghost. We had grainy photos and shoddy footage from cheap surveillance cameras on file. We had a blurry picture of a tattoo on the back of his left hand.

That was all.

After his threat I couldn't cross the street from my apartment to my car without fear that Kingfisher would drop me dead in the street.

A week after the first of many threatening phone calls, the calls stopped. A report came in from the Mexican federal police saying that they had turned up the King's body in a shallow grave in Baja. That's what they said.

I had wondered then if the King was really dead. If the freaking nightmare was truly over.

I had just about convinced myself that my family and I were safe. Now the breaking news confirmed that my gut reaction had been right. Either the Mexican police had lied, or the King had tricked them with a dead doppelganger buried in the sand.

A few minutes ago the King had been identified by a kitchen worker at the Vault. If true, why had he surfaced again in San Francisco? Why had he chosen to show his face in a nightclub filled with people? Why shoot two women inside that club? And my number one question: Could we bring him in alive and take him to trial?

Please, God. Please.

CHAPTER 4

OUR CAR RADIO WAS barking, crackling, and squealing at a high pitch as cars were directed to the Vault, in the middle of the block on Walnut Street. Cruisers and ambulances screamed past us as Conklin and I closed in on the scene. I badged the cop at the perimeter, and immediately after, Rich backed our car into a gap in the pack of law enforcement vehicles, parking it across the street from the Vault.

The Vault was built of stone block. It had two centered large glass doors, now shattered, with a half-circular window across the doorframe. Flanking the doors were two tall windows, capped with demilune windows, glass also shot out.

Shooters inside the Vault were using the granite doorframe as a barricade as they leaned out and fired on the uniformed officers positioned behind their car doors.

Conklin and I got out of our car with our guns

drawn and crouched beside our wheel wells. Adrenaline whipped my heart into a gallop. I watched everything with clear eyes, and yet my mind flooded with memories of past shoot-outs. I had been shot and almost died. All three of my partners had been shot, one of them fatally.

And now I had a baby at home.

A cop at the car to my left shouted, *"Christ!"*

Her gun spun out of her hand and she grabbed her shoulder as she dropped to the asphalt. Her partner ran to her, dragged her toward the rear of the car, and called in, "Officer down." Just then SWAT arrived in force with a small caravan of SUVs and a ballistic armored transport vehicle as big as a bus. The SWAT commander used his megaphone, calling to the shooters, who had slipped back behind the fortresslike walls of the Vault.

"All exits are blocked. There's nowhere to run, nowhere to hide. Toss out the guns, now."

The answer to the SWAT commander was a fusillade of gunfire that pinged against steel chassis. SWAT hit back with automatic weapons, and two men fell out of the doorway onto the pavement.

The shooting stopped, leaving an echoing silence.

The commander used his megaphone and

called out, "You. Put your gun down and we won't shoot. Fair warning. We're coming in."

"WAIT. I give up," said an accented voice. "Hands up, see?"

"Come all the way out. Come to me," said the SWAT commander.

I could see him from where I stood.

The last of the shooters was a short man with a café au lait complexion, a prominent nose, dark hair that was brushed back. He was wearing a well-cut suit with a blood-splattered white shirt as he came out through the doorway with his hands up.

Two guys in tactical gear grabbed him and slammed him over the hood of an SUV, then cuffed and arrested him.

The SWAT commander dismounted from the armored vehicle. I recognized him as Reg Covington. We'd worked together before. Conklin and I walked over to where Reg was standing beside the last of the shooters.

Covington said, "Boxer. Conklin. You know this guy?"

He stood the shooter up so I could get a good look at his face. I'd never met Kingfisher. I compared the real-life suspect with my memory of the fuzzy videos I'd seen of Jorge Sierra, a.k.a. the King.

"Let me see his hands," I said.

It was a miracle that my voice sounded steady, even to my own ears. I was sweating and my breathing was shallow. My gut told me that this was the man.

Covington twisted the prisoner's hands so that I could see the backs of them. On the suspect's left hand was the tattoo of a kingfisher, the same as the one in the photo in Kingfisher's slim file.

I said to our prisoner, "Mr. Sierra. I'm Sergeant Boxer. Do you need medical attention?"

"Mouth-to-mouth resuscitation, maybe."

Covington jerked him to his feet and said, "We'll take good care of him. Don't worry."

He marched the King to the waiting police wagon, and I watched as he was shackled and chained to the bar before the door was closed.

Covington slapped the side of the van, and it took off as CSI and the medical examiner's van moved in and SWAT thundered into the Vault to clear the scene.

CHAPTER 5

CONKLIN AND I JOINED the patrol cops who were talking to the Vault's freaked-out customers, now milling nervously in the taped-off section of the street.

We wanted an eyewitness description of the shooter or shooters in the *act* of killing two women in the bar.

That's not what we got.

One by one and in pairs, they answered our questions about what they had seen. It all came down to statements like *I was under the table. I was in the bathroom. I wasn't wearing my glasses. I couldn't see the bar. I didn't look up until I heard screaming, and then I ran to the back.*

We noted the sparse statements, took names and contact info, and asked each person to call if something occurred to him or her later. I was handing out my card when a patrolman came over, saying, "Sergeant, this is Ryan Kelly. He

tends bar here. Mr. Kelly says he watched a conversation escalate into the shooting."

Thank God.

Ryan Kelly was about twenty-five, with dark,
spiky hair. His skin was pale with shock.

Conklin said, "Mr. Kelly, what can you tell us?"

Kelly didn't hesitate.

"Two women were at the bar, both knockouts,
and they were into each other. Touching knees,
hands, the like. The blonde was in her twenties,
tight black dress, drinking wine coolers. The
other was brunette, in her thirties but in great
shape, drinking a Scotch on the rocks, in a white
dress, or maybe it was beige.

"Three guys, looked Mexican, came over. They
were dressed right, between forty and fifty, I'd
say. The brunette saw their reflections in the
backbar mirror and she jumped. Like, *Oh, my
God.* Then she introduced the blonde as 'my
friend Cameron.'"

The bartender was on a roll and needed no en-
couragement to keep talking. He said there had
been some back-and-forth among the five people, that the brunette had been nervous but the
short man with the combed-back hair had been
super calm and played with her.

"Like he was glad to meet her friend," said
Kelly. "He asked me to mix him a drink called

a Pastinaca. Has five ingredients that have to be poured in layers, and I had no open elder-flower. There was a new bottle under the bar. So I ducked down to find it among a shitload of other bottles.

"Then I heard someone say in a really strong voice, 'No one screws with the King.' Something like that. There's a shot, and another right after it. Loud *pop, pop.* And then a bunch more. I had, like, a heart attack and flattened out on the floor behind the bar. There was screaming like crazy. I stayed down until our manager found me and said, 'Come on. Get outta here.'"

I asked, "You didn't see who did the shooting?"

Kelly said, "No. Okay for me to go now? I've told this to about three of you. My wife is going nuts waiting for me at home."

We took Kelly's contact information, and when Covington signaled us that the Vault was clear, Conklin and I gloved up, stepped around the dead men, their spilled blood, guns, and spent shells in the doorway, and went inside.

CHAPTER 6

I KNEW THE VAULT'S layout: the ground floor of the former bank had been converted into a high-end haberdashery. Access to the nightclub upstairs was by the elevators at the rear of the store.

Conklin and I took in the scene. Bloody shoe prints tracked across the marble floors. Toppled clothing racks and mannequins lay across the aisles, but nothing moved.

We crossed the floor with care and took an elevator to the second-floor club, the scene of the shooting and a forensics investigation disaster.

Tables and chairs had been overturned in the customers' rush toward the fire exit. There were no surveillance cameras, and the floor was tacky with spilled booze and blood.

We picked our way around abandoned personal property and over to the long, polished bar, where two women in expensive clothing lay dead. One, blond, had collapsed across the bar top, and the other, dark-haired, had fallen dead at her feet.

The lighting was soft and unfocused, but still, I could see that the blond woman had been shot between the eyes and had taken slugs in her chest and arms. The woman on the floor had a bullet hole through the draped white silk across her chest, and there was another in her neck.

"Both shot at close range," Richie said.

He plucked a beaded bag off the floor and opened it, and I did the same with the second bag, a metallic leather clutch.

According to their driver's licenses, the brunette was Lucille Alison Stone and the blonde was Cameron Whittaker. I took pictures, and then Conklin and I carefully cat-walked out of the bar the way we had come.

As we were leaving, we passed Charlie Clapper, our CSI director, coming in with his crew.

Clapper was a former homicide cop and always looked like he'd stepped out of a Grecian Formula commercial. Neat. Composed. With comb marks in his hair. Always thorough, never a grandstander, he was one of the SFPD's MVPs.

"What's your take?" he asked us.

"It was overkill," I said. "Two women were shot to death at point-blank range and then shot some more. Three men were reportedly seen talking to them before the shooting. Two of them are in your capable hands until Claire takes them. We have one alive, being booked now."

"The news is out. You think he's Kingfisher."

"Could be. I hope so. I really hope this is our lucky day."

CHAPTER 7

BEFORE THE MEDICAL EXAMINER had retrieved the women's bodies, while CSI was beginning the staggering work involved in processing a bar full of fingerprints and spent brass and the guns, Conklin and I went back to the Hall of Justice and met with our lieutenant, Jackson Brady.

Brady was platinum blond, hard bodied, and chill, a former narcotics detective from Miami. He had proven his smarts and his astonishing bravery with the SFPD over the last couple of years and had been promoted quickly to run our homicide squad.

His corner office had once been mine, but being head of paperwork and manpower deployment didn't suit my temperament. I liked working crime on the street. I hadn't wanted to like Brady when he took the lieutenant job, but I couldn't help myself. He was tough but fair, and now he was married to my dear friend Yuki

Castellano. Today I was very glad that Brady had a history in narcotics, homicide, and organized crime.

Conklin and I sat with him in his glass-walled office and told him what we knew. It would be days before autopsies were done and guns and bullets were matched up with dead bodies. But I was pretty sure that the guns would not be registered, there would be no prints on file, and law enforcement might never know who owned the weapons that killed those women.

I said, "Their car was found on Washington— stolen, of course. The two dead men had both Los Toros and Mala Sangre tats. We're waiting for ID from Mexican authorities. One of the dead women knew Kingfisher. Lucille Alison Stone. She lived on Balboa, the thirty-two hundred block. Has a record. Shoplifting twice and possession of marijuana, under twenty grams. She comes up as a known associate of Jorge Sierra. That's it for her."

"And the other woman? Whittaker?"

"According to the bartender, who read their body language, Whittaker might be the girl-friend's girlfriend. She's a schoolteacher. Has no record."

Brady said, "Barry Schein, ADA. You know him?"

"Yes," Conklin and I said in unison.

"He's on his way up here. We've got thirty-six hours to put together a case for the grand jury while they're still convened. If we don't indict our suspect pronto, the FBI is going to grab him away from us. Ready to take a crack at the man who would be King?"

"Be right back," I said.

The ladies' room was outside the squad room and down the hall. I went in, washed my face, rinsed out my mouth, reset my ponytail. Then I walked back out into the hallway where I could get a signal and called Mrs. Rose.

"Not a problem, Lindsay," said the sweet granny who lived across the hall and babysat Julie Anne. "We're watching the Travel Channel. The Hebrides. Scotland. There are ponies."

"Thanks a million," I told her.

I rejoined my colleagues.

"Ready," I said to Brady, Conklin, and Barry Schein, the new rising star of the DA's office. "No better time than now."

CHAPTER 8

WHEN KINGFISHER BEGAN HIS campaign against me, I read everything I could find on him.

From the sparse reports and sightings I knew that the five-foot-six Mexican man who was now sitting in Interrogation 1 with his hands cuffed and chained to a hook on the table had been running drugs since before he was ten and had picked up the nickname Martin Pescador. That was Spanish for *kingfisher*, a small, bright-colored fishing bird with a prominent beak.

By the time Sierra was twenty, he was an officer in the Los Toros cartel, a savage paramilitary operation that specialized in drug sales up and down the West Coast and points east. Ten years later Kingfisher led a group of his followers in a coup, resulting in a bloody rout that left headless bodies from both sides decomposing in the desert.

Los Toros was the bigger loser, and the new

cartel, led by Kingfisher, was called Mala Sangre, a.k.a. Bad Blood.

Along with routine beheadings and assassinations, Mala Sangre regularly stopped busloads of people traveling along a stretch of highway. The elderly and children were killed immediately. Young women were raped before execution, and the men were forced to fight each other to the death, gladiator style.

Kingfisher's publicity campaign worked. He owned the drug trade from the foot of Mexico to the head of Northern California. He became immensely rich and topped all of law enforcement's "Most Wanted" lists, but he rarely showed himself. He changed homes frequently and ran his business from a laptop and by burner phones, and the Mexican police were notoriously bought and paid for by his cartel.

It was said that he had conjugal visits with his wife, Elena, but she had eluded attempts to tail her to her husband's location.

I was thinking about that as I stood with Brady, Conklin, and Schein behind the mirrored glass of the interrogation room. We were quickly joined by chief of police Warren Jacobi and a half dozen interested narcotics and robbery inspectors who had reasonably given up hope of ever seeing Kingfisher in custody.

Now we had him but didn't own him.

Could we put together an indictable case in a day and a half? Or would the Feds walk all over us?

Normally, my partner was the good cop and I was the hard-ass. I liked when Richie took the lead and set a trusting tone, but Kingfisher and I had history. He'd threatened my life.

Rich opened the door to the interrogation room, and we took the chairs across from the probable mass killer.

No one was more primed to do this interrogation than me.

CHAPTER 9

THE KING LOOKED AS common as dirt in his orange jumpsuit and chrome-plated bracelets. But he wasn't ordinary at all. I thought through my opening approach. I could play up to him, try to get on his side and beguile him with sympathy, a well-tested and successful interview technique. Or I could go badass.

In the end I pitched right down the center.

I looked him in the eyes and said, "Hello again, Mr. Sierra. The ID in your wallet says that you're Geraldo Rivera."

He smirked.

"That's cute. What's your real name?"

He smirked again.

"Okay if I call you Jorge Sierra? Facial recognition software says that's who you are."

"It's your party, Officer."

"That's Sergeant. Since it's my party, Mr. Sierra it is. How about we do this the easiest and best way.

You answer some questions for me so we can all call it a night. You're tired. I'm tired. But the internet is crackling. FBI wants you, and so do the Mexican authorities, who are already working on extradition papers. They are salivating."

"Everyone loves me."

I put the driver's licenses of Lucille Stone and Cameron Whittaker on the table.

"What were your relationships to these two women?"

"They both look good to me, but I never saw either one of them before."

"Before tonight, you mean? We have a witness who saw you kill these women."

"Don't know them, never saw them."

I opened a folder and took out the 8½ x 11 photo of Lucille Stone lying across the bar. "She took four slugs to the chest, three more to the face."

"How do you say? Tragic."

"She was your lady friend, right?"

"I have a wife. I don't have lady friends."

"Elena Sierra. I hear she lives here in San Francisco with your two children."

No answer.

"And this woman," I said, taking out the print of the photo I'd taken of the blond-haired woman lying on the bar floor.

"Cameron Whittaker. I counted three or four bullet holes in her, but could be more."

His face was expressionless. "A complete stranger to me."

"Uh-huh. Our witness tells us that these two, your girlfriend and Ms. Whittaker, were very into each other. Kissing and the like."

Kingfisher scoffed. He truly looked amused. "I'm sorry I didn't see them. I might have enjoyed to watch. Anyway, they have nothing to do with me."

I pulled out CSI's photos of the two dead shooters. "These men. Could you identify them for us? They both have two sets of gang tats but have fake IDs on them. We'd like to notify their families."

No answer, but if Kingfisher gave a flip about them, you couldn't tell. I doubted a lie detector could tell.

As for me, my heart was still racing. I was aware of the men behind the glass, and I knew that if I screwed up this interrogation, I would let us all down.

I looked at Richie. He moved his chair a couple of inches back from the table, signaling me that he didn't want to insert himself into the conversation.

I tried a Richie-like tack.

"See it through my eyes, Mr. Sierra. You have blood spatter on your shirt. Spray, actually. The kind a person would *expel* onto you if she took a shot to the lung and you were standing right next to her. Your hands tested positive for gunpowder. There were a hundred witnesses. We've got three guns and a large number of slugs at our forensics lab, and they're all going to tell the same story. Any ADA drawn at random could get an indictment in less time than it takes for the judge to say 'No bail.'"

The little bird with the long beak smiled. I smiled back, then I said, "If you help us, Mr. Sierra, we'll tell the DA you've been cooperative. Maybe we can work it so you spend your time in the supermax prison of your choice. Currently, although it could change in the near future, capital punishment is illegal in California. You can't be extradited to Mexico until you've served your sentence here. Good chance that will never happen, you understand? But you will get to *live*."

"I need to use the phone," Kingfisher said.

I saw the brick wall directly up ahead. I ignored the request for a phone and kept talking.

"Or we don't fight the extradition warrant. You take the prison shuttle down to Mexico City and let the *federales* talk to you about many mass murders. Though, frankly, I don't see you surviving long enough in Mexico to even get to trial."

"You didn't hear me?" our prisoner asked. "I want to call my lawyer."

Richie and I stood up and opened the door for the two jail guards, who came in and took him back to his cell.

Back in the viewing room Conklin said, "You did everything possible, Linds."

The other men uttered versions of "Too bad" and left me alone with Conklin, Jacobi, Brady, and young Mr. Schein.

I said, "He's not going to confess. We've got nothing. To state the obvious, people are afraid of him, so we have no witnesses. We don't know if he's the killer, or even if he is the King."

"Find out," said Brady. He had a slight southern drawl, so it came out "Fahnd out."

We all got the message.

Meeting over.

CHAPTER 10

IT WAS JUST AFTER 8:00 p.m. when I walked into the apartment where Julie and I live. It's on Lake Street, not too far from the park.

Mrs. Rose, Julie's nanny, was snoozing on the big leather sofa, and our HDTV was on mute. Martha, my border collie and dear old friend, jumped to her feet and charged at me, woofing and leaping, overcome with joy.

Mrs. Rose swung her feet to the floor, and Julie let out a wail from her little room.

There was no place like home.

I spent a good hour cuddling with my little girl, chowing down on Gloria Rose's famous three-protein meat loaf, downing a couple of glasses of Pinot Noir, and giving Martha a back rub.

Once the place was tidy, the baby was asleep, and Mrs. Rose had left for the night, I opened my computer and e-mail.

First up, Charlie Clapper's ballistics report.

"Three guns recovered, all snubbies," he wrote, meaning short-barreled .38 Saturday night specials. "Bullets used were soft lead. Squashed to putty, every one of them, no striations. Fingerprints on the guns and shells match the two dead men and the man you booked, identity uncertain. Tats on the dead men are the usual prison-ink variety, with death heads and so forth, and they have both the Los Toros bull insignia and lettering saying *Mala Sangre*. Photos on file."

Charlie's report went on.

"Blood on the clothing of the dead men and your suspect is a match to the blood of the victims positively identified as Cameron Whittaker, white, twenty-five, grade-school substitute teacher, and Lucille Stone, white, twenty-eight. ID says she was VP of marketing at Solar Juice, a software firm in the city of Sunnyvale.

"That's all I've got, Lindsay. Sorry I don't have better news. Chas."

I phoned Richie, and Cindy picked up.

My reporter friend was a cross between an adorable, girly journalist and a pit bull, so she said, "I want to work on this Kingfisher story, Linds. Tell Rich it's okay for him to share with me."

I snorted a laugh, then said, "May I speak with him?"

"Will you? Share?"

"Not yet. We'll see."

"Fine," Cindy huffed. "Thanks."

Richie got on the phone.

He said, "I've got something that could lead to motive."

"Tell me."

"I spoke with the girlfriend's mother. She says Lucy was seeing Sierra but broke it off with him about a month ago. Right after that Lucy believed that Sierra was dead. I mean, we all did, right?"

"Correct."

"According to Lucy Stone's mother, Sierra went to Lucy's apartment yesterday and Lucy wouldn't let him in. Mrs. Stone said her daughter called her and told her that Sierra was angry and threatening. Apparently, Lucy was afraid."

"He could have staked her out. Followed her to the Vault."

"Probably, yeah. I asked Mrs. Stone if she could ID Sierra. And she said—"

"Let me guess. 'No.'"

"Bingo. However..."

"Don't tease me, Richie."

He laughed. "Here ya go. Mrs. Stone said that the King's wife, Elena Sierra, has been living under the name Maura Steele. I got her number and address on Nob Hill."

A lead. An actual lead.

I told Richie he was the greatest. He laughed again. Must be nice to have such a sunny disposition.

After hanging up, I checked the locks on the door and windows, double-checked the alarm, looked in on my darling Julie, and put my gun on my night table.

I whistled for Martha.

She bounded into the bedroom and onto the bed.

"Night-night, sweet Martha."

I turned off the light and tried to sleep.

CHAPTER 11

WE MET IN THE squad's break room the next morning: Conklin, Brady, ADA Schein, and me.

Schein was thirty-six, married, and a father of two. He reported directly to DA Len "Red Dog" Parisi, and he'd been pitching no-hitters since he took the job, sending the accused to jail every time he took the mound. Putting Kingfisher away would be Schein's ticket to a five-star law firm if he wanted it. He was suited up for the next big thing even now, close shaved and natty in this shabby setting, and he was all business. I liked it. I liked him.

Schein said, "Summarizing what we have: A 911 tape of a male with a Spanish accent reporting that he's seen Kingfisher at the Vault, and we presume that that's the man we arrested. The tipster said he was a kitchen worker but could have been anyone. He called from a burner phone, and this witness hasn't stepped forward."

Conklin and I nodded. Schein went on.

"We have a witness who saw the run-up to the shooting but didn't see the actual event."

I said, "We've got blood on the suspect's shirt."

"Good. But a juror is going to ask if he could have gotten that blood spray if he was near the victim but he didn't fire the weapon."

Schein shrugged. "What can I say. Yeah. Bottom line, twenty-four hours from now we get a 'proceed to prosecution' from the grand jury, or our suspect goes out of our hands and into the lap of a higher or different jurisdiction."

"Spell out exactly what you need," said Brady. He was making a list with a red grease pencil on a lined yellow pad.

"We need legally sufficient evidence and probable cause," said Schein. "And I can be persuasive up to a point."

"We have to positively ID our man as Jorge Sierra?"

"That's the price of admission. Without that, no hearing."

"Additionally," said Brady, "we get a witness to the shooting or to Sierra's intent to kill."

"That would nail it."

When the coffee containers and doughnut box

were in the trash and we were alone at last, Rich said, "Cindy should run it in the *Chron* online."

"Like, 'SFPD needs info from anyone who was at the Vault on Wednesday night and saw the shooting'?"

"Yep," said Rich. "It's worked before."

CHAPTER 12

RICH WENT BACK TO the crime scene for another look, and I called the former Mrs. Jorge Sierra, now Ms. Maura Steele. She didn't answer the phone, so I signed out a squad car and drove to her address in Nob Hill.

I badged the doorman and asked him to ring up to Ms. Sierra-a.k.a.-Steele's apartment.

He said, "You just missed her."

"This is important police business," I said. "Where can I find her?"

"She went to the gym. She usually gets back at around ten o'clock."

It was quarter to. I took a seat in a wingback chair with a view of the street through two-story-tall plate-glass windows and saw the black limo stop at the curb. A liveried driver got out, went around to the sidewalk side of the car, and opened the rear door.

A very attractive woman in her late twenties or

early thirties got out and headed toward the lobby doors while she went for the keys in her bag.

Ms. Steele was slim and fine boned, with short, dark, curly hair. She wore a smart shearling coat over her red tracksuit. I shot a look at the doorman and he nodded. When she came through the door, I introduced myself and showed her my badge.

"Police? What's this about?"

"Jorge Sierra," I said.

She drew back. Fear flickered in her eyes, and her face tightened.

She said, "I don't know anyone by that name."

"Please, Ms. Steele. Don't make me take you to the station for questioning. I just need you to ID a photograph."

The doorman was fiddling with papers at the front desk, trying to look as though he wasn't paying attention. He looked like Matt Damon but didn't have Damon's talent.

"Come upstairs with me," Ms. Steele said to me.

I followed her into the elevator, which opened directly into her sumptuous apartment. It was almost blindingly luxurious, with its Persian carpets, expensive furnishings, and what looked to me like good art against a backdrop of the Golden Gate Bridge and San Francisco Bay.

I'd looked her up before getting into the car.

Ms. Steele didn't have a job now and had no listing under Sierra or Steele on LinkedIn, Facebook, or Who's Who in Business. Odds were, she was living on the spoils of her marriage to one of the richest men west of the Rockies.

Steele didn't ask me to sit down.

"I want to be absolutely clear," she said. "If you quote me or depose me or in any way try to put me on the record, I will deny everything. I'm still married. I can't testify."

I took the mug shot out of my pocket and held it up for her to see. "Is this Jorge Sierra?" I asked. "Known as Kingfisher?"

She began nodding like a bobblehead on crack. I can't say I didn't understand her terror. I'd felt something like it myself.

I said, "Thank you."

I asked follow-up questions as she walked with me back toward the elevator door. Had her husband been in touch with her? When was the last time she'd spoken with him? Any idea why he would have killed two women in a nightclub?

She stopped moving and answered only the last question.

"Because he is *crazy*. Because he is *mental* when it comes to women. I tried to leave him and make a run for the US border, but when he caught me, he did this."

She lifted her top so that her torso was exposed. There was a large scar on her body, about fifteen inches wide by ten inches long, shirring her skin from under her breasts to her navel. It looked like a burn made by a white-hot iron in the shape of a particular bird with a prominent beak. A kingfisher.

"He wanted any man I ever met to know that I belonged to him. Don't forget your promise. And don't let him go. If he gets out, call me. Okay?"

"Deal," I said. "That's a deal."

CHAPTER 13

EARLY FRIDAY MORNING CONKLIN and I met with ADA Barry Schein in his office on the second floor of the Hall. He paced and flexed his hands. He was gunning his engines, which was to be expected. This was a hugely important grand jury hearing, and the weight of it was all on Barry.

"I'm going to try something a little risky," he said.

Barry spent a few minutes reviewing what we already knew about the grand jury—that it was a tool for the DA, a way to try out the case with a large jury in an informal setting to see if there was enough probable cause to indict. If the jury indicted Mr. Sierra, Schein could skip arraignment and take Sierra directly to trial.

"That's what we want," said Barry. "Speed."

Rich and I nodded that we got that.

Schein said, "There's no judge, no attorney for the defense, as you know. Just me and the jury,"

Schein said. "Right now we don't have sufficient evidence to indict Sierra on a murder of any degree. We can place him at the scene of the crime, but no one saw him fire his gun, and the forensics are inconclusive."

I said, "I'm ready to hear about your 'risky' move."

Schein straightened his tie, patted down his thinning hair, and said, "I've subpoenaed Sierra. This is rarely done, because the putative defendant is unlikely to testify against himself.

"That said, Sierra *has* to take the stand. Like most people in this spot, he'll plead the Fifth. So I'm going to try to use that to help us."

"How so?" I asked.

Schein cracked his first smile of the day.

"I'll lay out my case to the jury by asking Sierra: 'You had a plan in mind when you went to the Vault on the fourteenth, isn't that right? Lucille Stone was your girlfriend, correct, sir? But she rejected you, didn't she? You followed her and learned that she was involved with a woman, isn't that right, Mr. Sierra? Is that why you murdered her and Cameron Whittaker?'"

I didn't have to ask Schein to go on. He was still circling his office, talking from the game plan in his head.

"The more he refuses to answer," Schein said,

"the more probable cause is raised in the jurors' minds. Could it backfire? Yeah. If the jury doesn't hold his refusal to testify against him, they'll hand me my hat. But we won't be any worse off than we are now."

An hour later Rich and I were in the San Francisco Superior Court on McAllister Street, benched in the hallway. Sierra had been brought into the courtroom through a back door, and as I'd seen when the front doors opened a crack, he was wearing street clothes, had shackles around his ankles, and was sitting between two hard-boiled marshals with guns on their hips.

Sierra's attorney, J. C. Fuentes, sat alone on a bench ten yards from where I sat with my partner. He was a huge, brutish-looking man of about fifty wearing an old brown suit. I knew him to be a winning criminal defense attorney. He wasn't an orator, but he was a remarkable strategist and tactician.

Today, like the rest of us, he was permitted only to wait outside the courtroom and to be available if his client needed to consult with him.

Rich plugged into his iPad and leaned back against the wall. I jiggled my feet, people-watched, and waited for news. I was unprepared when the courtroom doors violently burst open.

I jumped to my feet.

Jorge Sierra, still in chains, was being pulled and dragged out of the courtroom and into the hallway, where Mr. Fuentes, Conklin, and I stood, openmouthed and in shock.

Sierra shouted over his shoulder through the open doors.

"I have all your names, stupid people. I know where you live. Street addresses. Apartment layouts. You and your pathetic families can expect a visit very soon."

The doors swung closed and Fuentes rushed to Sierra's side as he was hauled past us, laughing his face off.

It was twenty past twelve. Rich said to me, "How long do you think before the jury comes back?"

I had no answer, not even a guess.

Fourteen minutes later Schein came out of the courtroom looking like he'd been through a wood chipper.

He said, "Sierra took the Fifth, and the jurors didn't like him. Before he got off the stand, he threatened them, and he didn't quit until the doors closed on his ass. Did you hear him? Threatening the jurors is another crime."

Rich said, "When do they decide, Barry?"

Schein said, "It's done. Unanimous decision. Sierra is indicted on two counts of murder one."

THE TRIAL

We pumped Schein's hand. The indictment gave us the time we needed to gather more evidence before Sierra went to trial. Conklin and I went back to the Hall to brief Brady.

"There is a God," Brady said, rising to his feet.

We high-fived over his desk, and Conklin said, "Break out the Bud."

It was a great moment. The Feds and the Mexican government had to step back. Jorge Sierra had been indicted for murder in California.

The King was in our jail and he was ours to convict.

CHAPTER 14

JOE AND I WERE dancing together close and slow. He had his hand at the small of my back, and the hem of my low-cut slinky red gown swished around my ankles. I couldn't even feel my feet because I was dancing on cotton candy clouds. I felt so good in Joe's arms—loved, protected, and excited, too. I didn't want this dance to ever end.

"I miss you so much," he said into my ear.

I pulled back so I could look into his handsome face, his blue eyes. "I miss you—"

I never got out the last word.

My phone was singing with Brady's ring tone, a bugle call.

I grabbed for the phone, but it slipped out of my hand. Still half under the covers, I reached for it again, and by that time Martha was snuffling my face.

God!

"Boxer," I croaked.

Brady's voice was taut.

"A juror was found dead in the street. Gunned down."

I said, "No."

He said, "'Fraid so."

He told me to get on it, and I called Richie.

It was Saturday. Mrs. Rose was off, but I called her anyway. She sounded both half asleep and resigned but said, "I'll be right there."

She crossed the hall in her robe and slippers and asked if I wouldn't mind taking Martha out before I took off.

After a three-minute successful dog walk I guzzled coffee, put down a PowerBar, and drove to Chestnut Street, the main drag through the Marina District. This area was densely lined with restaurants and boutiques, normally swarming with young professionals, parents with strollers, and twentysomethings in yoga pants.

All that free-spirited weekend-morning traffic had come to a dead halt. A crowd of onlookers had formed a deep circle at the barrier tape enclosing a section of street and the victim's body.

I held up my badge and elbowed my way through to where Conklin was talking to the first officer, Sam Rocco.

Rocco said, "Sergeant, I was telling Conklin, a

911 caller reported that one of the grand jurors in the Sierra jury had been 'put down like a dog.'

"The operator said the caller sounded threatening. She got the street and cross street before the caller hung up," Rocco continued. "Feldman and I were here inside of five minutes. I opened the victim's wallet and got her particulars. Sarah Brenner. Lives two blocks over on Greenwich Street. From the coffee container in the gutter, looks like she was just coming back from Peet's on Chestnut."

"Anyone see the shooting?" I asked.

"None that will admit to it," said Officer Rocco.

"Cash and cards in the wallet?"

"Yep, and she's wearing a gold necklace and a watch."

Not a robbery. I thanked Rocco and edged around the dead body of a young woman who was lying facedown between two parked cars. She wore jeans and a green down jacket with down puffing out of its bullet holes, and nearby lay the slip-on mules that had been blown off her socked feet by the impact or the fall. Shell casings were scattered on the asphalt around the body, and some glinted from underneath the parked cars.

I lifted a strand of Sarah Brenner's long brown hair away from her face so that I could see her features. She looked sweet. And too young. I touched her neck to be sure she was really gone. *Goddamnit.*

Putting Sarah Brenner "down like a dog" was a crude term for a professional hit meant to scare everyone connected with Sierra's trial. Inciting fear. Payback. Revenge.

It was just Kingfisher's style.

I thought he might get away with killing this young woman as he had done so many times before. He would hit and run again.

CHAPTER 15

MONDAY MORNING RICH AND I reported to Brady what we had learned that weekend.

Rich said, "Sarah was twenty-five, took violin lessons at night, did paperwork for a dentist during the day. She had no boyfriend, no recent ex, and lived with two other young women and an African gray parrot. She had a thousand and twenty dollars in the bank and a fifty-dollar credit card balance for a green down jacket. No enemies, only friends, none known to have a motive for her killing."

"Your thoughts?" Brady asked me.

"Maybe the King would like to brag."

Brady gave me a rare grin. "Knock yourself out," he said.

I took the stairs from our floor, four, to maximum security on seven. I checked in at the desk and was escorted to Sierra's brightly lit, windowless cell.

I stood a good five feet from the bars of the King's cage.

He looked like someone had roughed him up, and the orange jumpsuit did nothing for his coloring. He didn't look like the king of anything.

He stood up when he saw me, saying, "Well, hello, Officer Lindsay. You're not wearing lipstick. You didn't want to look nice for me?"

I ignored the taunt.

"How's it going?" I asked him.

I was hoping he had some complaints, that he wanted a window or a blanket—anything that I could use to barter for answers to questions that could lead to evidence against him.

He said, "Pretty good. Thank you for getting me a single room. I will be reasonably comfortable here. Not so much everyone else. That includes you, your baby girl, even your runaround husband, Joseph. Do you know who Joseph is sleeping with now? I do. Do you want to see the pictures? I can have them e-mailed to you."

It was a direct shot to the heart and caught me off guard. I struggled to keep my composure.

"How are you going to do that?" I asked.

Sierra had an unpleasant, high-pitched laugh.

I'd misjudged him. He had taken control of this meeting and I would learn nothing from him about Sarah Brenner—or about anyone else. The flush rising from under my collar let both of us know that he'd won the round.

I left Jorge Sierra, that disgusting load of rat dung, and jogged down the stairs to the squad room, muttering, promising myself that the next point would be mine.

Conklin and I sat near the front of the room. We'd pushed our desks together so that we faced each other, and I saw that Cindy was sitting in my chair and Conklin was in his own. There were open Chinese food cartons between them.

I said hello to Cindy. Conklin dragged up a chair for her and I dropped into mine.

"Nice of you to bring lunch," I said, looking at the containers. I had no appetite whatsoever. Definitely not for shrimp with lobster sauce. Not even for tea.

"I've brought you something even nicer," she said, holding up a little black SIM card, like from a mobile phone.

"What's that?"

"This is a ray of golden sunshine breaking through the bleak skies overhead."

"Make me a believer," I said.

"A witness dropped this off at the *Chron* for me this morning," Cindy said. "It's a video of the shooting at the Vault's bar. You can see the gun in the King's hand. You can see the muzzle aimed at

Lucy Stone's chest. You can see the flare after he pulled the trigger."

"This is evidence of Sierra shooting Stone on film?"

She gave me a Cheshire cat smile.

"The person who shot this video has a name?"

"Name, number, and is willing to testify."

"I love you, Cindy."

"I know."

"I mean I *really* love you."

Cindy and Rich burst out laughing, and after a stunned beat I laughed, too. We looked at the video together. It was good. We had direct evidence and a witness. Jorge Sierra was cooked.

FOUR MONTHS LATER

CHAPTER 16

NO MATTER WHAT KIND of crappy day life dealt out, it was almost impossible to sustain a bad mood at Susie's Café.

I parked my car on Jackson Street, buttoned my coat, and lowered my head against the cold April wind as I trudged toward the brightly lit Caribbean-style eatery frequented by the Women's Murder Club.

My feet knew the way, which was good, because my mind was elsewhere. Kingfisher's trial was starting tomorrow.

The media's interest in him had been revived, and news outlets of all kinds had gone on high alert. Traffic on Bryant and all around the Hall had been jammed all week with satellite vans. None of my phones had stopped ringing: office, home, or mobile.

I felt brittle and edgy as I went through the front door of Susie's. I was first to arrive and claimed "our" booth in the back room. I signaled to Lorraine and she brought me a tall, icy brewski, and pretty soon that golden anesthetic had smoothed down my edges.

Just about then I heard Yuki and Cindy bantering together and saw the two of them heading toward our table. There were kiss-kisses all around, then two of my blood sisters slid onto the banquette across from me.

Cindy ordered a beer and Yuki ordered a Grasshopper, a frothy green drink that would send her to the moon, and she always enjoyed the flight. So did the rest of us.

Cindy told me that Claire had phoned to say she would be late, and once Cindy had downed some of my beer, she said, "I've got news."

Cindy, like every other reporter in the world, was covering the Sierra trial. But she was a crime pro and the story was happening on her beat. Other papers were running her stories under her byline. That was good for Cindy, and I could see from the bloom in her cheeks that she was on an adrenaline high.

She leaned in and spoke only loud enough to be heard over the steel drums in the front room and the laughter at the tables around ours.

She said, "I got an anonymous e-mail saying that 'something dramatic' is going to happen if the charges against Sierra aren't dismissed."

"Dramatic how?" I asked.

"Don't know," Cindy said. "But I could find out. Apparently, the King wants me to interview him."

Cindy's book about a pair of serial killers had swept to the top of the bestseller lists last year. Sierra could have heard about her. He might be a fan.

I reached across the table and clasped Cindy's hands.

"Cindy, do not even think about it. You don't want this man to know anything about you. I oughta know."

"For the first time since I met you," Cindy said, "I'm going to say you are right. I'm not asking to see him. I'm going to just walk away."

I said, "Thank you, God."

Lorraine brought Cindy her beer, and Yuki took the floor.

She said almost wistfully, "I know Barry Schein pretty well. Worked with him for a couple of years. If anyone can handle the King's drama, it's Barry. I admire him. He could get Red Dog's job one day."

None of us would ever forget this very typical night at Susie's. Before we left the table, it would be permanently engraved in our collective memories. We were chowing down on Susie's

Sunday-night special, fish fritters and rice, when my phone tootled. I had left it on only in case Claire called saying she wasn't going to make it. But it was Brady's ring tone that came through.

I took the call.

Brady gave me very bad news. I told him I was on my way and clicked off. I repeated the shocking bulletin to Cindy and Yuki. We hugged wordlessly.

Then I bolted for my car.

CHAPTER 17

FROM THE LOOK OF it, the Scheins lived in a classic American dream home, a lovely Cape Cod on Pachecho Street in Golden Gate Heights with a princely view, two late-model cars, a grassy yard, and a tree with a swing.

Today, Pacheco Street was taped off. Cruisers with cherry flashers marked the perimeter, and halogen lights illuminated an evidence tent and three thousand square feet of pavement.

The first officer, Donnie Lewis, lifted the tape and let me onto the scene.

Normally cool, the flustered CSI director, Clapper, came toward me, saying, "Jesus, Boxer, brace yourself. This is brutal."

My skin prickled and my stomach heaved as Clapper walked me to the Scheins' driveway, which sloped down from the street to the attached garage. Barry's body was lying faceup, eyes open, keys in his hand, the door to his silver-blue Honda Civic wide open.

I lost my place in time. The pavement shifted underfoot and the whole world went cold. I covered my face with my hands, felt Clapper's arm around my shoulders. "I'm here, Lindsay. I'm here."

I took my hands down and said to Clapper, "I just spoke with him yesterday. He was ready to go to trial. He was ready, Charlie."

"I know. I know. It never makes sense."

I stared down at Barry's body. There were too many holes punched in his jacket for me to count. Blood had outlined his body and was running in rivulets down toward the garage.

I dropped enough f-bombs to be seen on the moon.

And then I asked Clapper to fill me in.

"The little boy was running down the steps right there to greet his father. Daddy was calling to the kid, then he turned back toward the street. Must have heard the shooter's car pull up, or maybe his name was called. He turned to see — and was gunned down."

"How old is the child?"

"Four. His name is Stevie."

"Could he describe what he saw?" I asked Clapper.

"He told Officer Lewis that he saw a car stop about here on the road at the top of the driveway.

He heard the shots, saw his father drop. He turned and ran back up the steps and inside. Then, according to Lewis, Barry's wife, Melanie, she came out. She tried to resuscitate her husband. Their daughter, Carol, age six, ran away to the house next door. Her best friend lives there.

"Melanie and Stevie are in the house until we can get all of them out of here."

"What's your take?" I asked Clapper.

"Either the driver tailed the victim, or he parked nearby, saw Schein's car drive past, and followed him. When Barry got out of the car, the passenger emptied his load. Barry never had a chance."

We stepped away from the body, and CSIs deployed in full. Cameras clicked, video rolled, and a sketch artist laid out the details of the crime scene from a bird's-eye point of view. Techs searched for and located shell casings, put markers down, took more pictures, brought shell casings to the tent.

Conklin said, "Oh, my God."

I hadn't heard him arrive but I was so glad to see him. We hugged, hung on for a minute. Then we stood together in the sharp white light, looking down at Barry's body lying at our feet. We couldn't look away.

Rich said, "Barry told me that when this was

over, he was taking the kids to Myrtle Beach. There's family there."

I said, "He told me he'd waited his whole career for a case like this. He told me he was going to wear his lucky tiepin. Belonged to his grandfather."

My partner said, "Kingfisher put out the hit. Had to be. I wish I could ask Barry if he saw the shooter."

I answered with a nod.

Together we mounted the brick front steps to the white clapboard house with black shutters, the remains of the Schein family's life as they had known it.

Now a couple of cops were going to talk to this family in the worst hour of their lives.

CHAPTER 18

WE RANG THE FRONT doorbell. We knocked. We rang the bell again before Melanie Schein, a distraught woman in her midthirties, opened the front door.

She looked past us and spoke in a frantic, disbelieving voice. "My God, my God, this can't be true. We're having chicken and potatoes. Barry likes the dark meat. I got ice cream pie. We picked out a movie."

Richie introduced us, said how sorry we were, that we knew Barry, that this was our case.

"We're devastated," Richie said.

But I don't think Barry's wife heard us.

She turned away from the door, and we followed her into the aromatic kitchen and, from there, into the living room. She looked around at her things and bent to line up the toes of a pair of men's slippers in front of a reclining chair.

I asked her the questions I knew by heart.

"Do you have a security camera?"

She shook her head.

"Has either of you received any threats?"

"I want to go to him. I need be with him."

"Has anyone threatened you or Barry, Mrs. Schein?"

She shook her head. Tears flew off her cheeks.

I wanted to give her something, but all I had were rules and platitudes and a promise to find Barry's killer. It was a promise I wasn't sure we could keep.

I promised anyway. And then I said, "Witness Protection will be here in a few minutes to take you and the children to a safe place. But first, could we talk with Stevie for just a minute?"

Mrs. Schein led us down a hallway lined with framed family photos on the walls. Wedding pictures. Baby pictures. The little girl on a pony. Stevie with an oversized catcher's mitt.

It was almost impossible to reconcile this hominess with the truth of Barry's still-warm body lying outside in the cold. Mrs. Schein asked us to wait, and when she opened the bedroom door, I was struck by the red lights flashing through the curtains. A little boy sat on the floor, pushing a toy truck back and forth mindlessly. What did he understand about what had happened to his father? I couldn't shake the thought that an hour ago Barry had been alive.

With Mrs. Schein's permission Richie went into the room and stooped beside the child. He spoke softly, but we could all hear his questions: "Stevie, did you see a car, a truck, or an SUV?... Car? What color car?...Have you seen it before?...Did you recognize the man who fired the gun?...Can you describe him at all?...Is there anything you want to tell me? I'm the police, Stevie. I'm here to help."

Stevie said again, "Was a gray car."

Conklin asked, "How many doors, Stevie? Try to picture it." But Stevie was done. Conklin opened his arms and Stevie collapsed against him and sobbed.

I told Mrs. Schein to call either of us anytime. Please.

After giving her our cards, my partner and I took the steps down to the halogen-lit hell in front of the lovely house.

In the last ten minutes the street had thickened with frightened neighbors, frustrated motorists, and cops doing traffic control. The medical examiner's van was parked inside the cordoned-off area of the street.

Dr. Claire Washburn, chief medical examiner and my dearest friend, was supervising the removal of Barry Schein's bagged body into the back of her van.

I went to her and she grabbed my hands.

"God-awful shame. That talented young man. The doer made damned sure he was dead," said Claire. "What a waste. You okay, Lindsay?"

"Not really."

Claire and I agreed to speak later. The rear doors to the coroner's van slammed shut and the vehicle took off. I was looking for Conklin when an enormous, pear-shaped man I knew very well ducked under the tape and cast his shadow over the scene.

Leonard Parisi was San Francisco's district attorney. He wasn't just physically imposing, he was a career prosecutor with a long record of wins.

"This is...abominable," said Parisi.

"Fucking tragedy," Conklin said, his voice cracking.

I said, "I'm so sorry, Len. We're about to canvass. Maybe someone saw something. Maybe a camera caught a license plate."

Parisi nodded. "I'm getting a continuance on the trial," he said. "I'm taking over for Barry. I'm going to make Kingfisher wish he were dead."

CHAPTER 19

A WEEK HAD PASSED since Barry Schein was killed fifteen hours before Sierra's trial had been scheduled to begin. We had no leads and no suspects for his murder, but we had convincing direct evidence against Sierra for the murders of Lucille Stone and Cameron Whittaker.

Our case was solid. What could possibly go wrong?

The Hall of Justice was home to the offices of the DA and the ME, as well as to the county jail and the superior court of the Criminal Division. For his security and ours, Sierra was being housed and tried right here.

Rich, Cindy, Yuki, and I sat together in the back row of a blond-wood-paneled courtroom that was packed with reporters, the friends and families of Sierra's victims, and a smattering of law students who were able to get in to see the trial of the decade.

At 9:00 a.m. Sierra was brought in through the rear door of Courtroom 2C. A collective gasp nearly sucked up all the air in the room.

The King had cleaned up since I'd last seen him. He'd had a nice close shave and a haircut. The orange jumpsuit had been swapped out for a gray sports jacket, a freshly pressed pair of slacks, a blue shirt, and a paisley tie. He looked like a fine citizen, except for the ten pounds of shackles around his ankles and wrists that were linked to the belt cinched around his waist.

He clanked over to the defense table. Two marshals removed the handcuffs and took their seats in the first row behind the rail, directly behind Sierra and his attorney, J. C. Fuentes.

Sierra spoke into his lawyer's ear, and Fuentes shook his head furiously, looking very much like a wild animal.

At the prosecution counsel table across the aisle, Red Dog Parisi and two of his ADAs represented the side of good against evil. Parisi was too big to be a snappy dresser, but his navy-blue suit and striped tie gave him a buttoned-up look and set off his coarse auburn hair.

He looked formidable. He looked loaded for bear.

I was sure of it. Kingfisher had met his match. And my money was on Red Dog.

CHAPTER 20

THE BUTTERFLIES IN MY stomach rose up and took a few laps as the Honorable Baron Crispin entered the courtroom and the bailiff asked us all to rise.

Judge Crispin came from Harvard Law, and it was said that he was a viable candidate for the US Supreme Court. I knew him to be a no-nonsense judge, strictly by the book. When he was seated, he took a look at his laptop, exchanged a few words with the court reporter, and then called the court to order.

The judge said a few words about proper decorum and instructed the spectators in what was unacceptable in his court. "This is not reality TV. There will be no outcries or applause. Cell phones must be turned off. If a phone rings, the owner of that phone will be removed from the courtroom. And please, wait for recesses before leaving for any reason. If someone sneezes, let's just *imagine* that others are saying 'God bless you.'"

While the judge was speaking, I was looking at the back of Kingfisher's head. Without warning, the King shot to his feet. His attorney put a hand on his arm and made a futile attempt to force him back down.

But Kingfisher would not be stopped.

He turned his head toward DA Parisi and shouted, "You are going to die a terrible death if this trial proceeds, Mr. Dog. You, too, Judge Crispy. That's a threat and a promise. A death sentence, too."

Judge Crispin yelled to the marshals, "Get him out of here."

Parisi's voice boomed over the screams and general pandemonium. "Your Honor. Please sequester the jury."

By then the marshals had charged through the gate, kicked chairs out of their way, and cuffed Sierra's wrists, after which they shoved and pushed the defendant across the well and out the rear door.

I was also on my feet, following the marshals and their prisoner out that back door that connected to the private corridor and elevators for court officers and staff.

Attorney J. C. Fuentes was at my heels.

The door closed behind us and Sierra saw me. He said, "You, too, will die, Sergeant Boxer. You are still on my list. I haven't forgotten you."

I shouted at Sierra's guards, "Don't let him talk to anyone. *Anyone.* Do you understand?"

I was panting from fear and stress, but I stayed right on them as they marched Sierra along the section of hallway to the elevators, keeping distance between Sierra and his lawyer. When Sierra and his guards had gotten inside the elevator, the doors had closed, and the needle on the dial was moving up, I turned on Fuentes.

"Remove yourself from this case."

"You must be kidding."

"I'm dead serious. Tell Crispin that Sierra threatened your life and he will believe you. Or how does this sound? I'll arrest you on suspicion of conspiring to murder Barry Schein. I may do it anyway."

"You don't have to threaten me. I'll be glad to get away from him. Far away."

"You're welcome," I said. "Let's go talk to the judge."

CHAPTER 21

CHIEF OF POLICE WARREN Jacobi's corner office was on the fifth floor of the Hall, overlooking Bryant.

Jacobi and I had once been partners, and over the ten years we had worked together, we had bonded for life. The gunshot injuries he'd gotten on the job had aged him, and he looked ten years older than his fifty-five years.

At present his office was packed to standing room only.

Brady and Parisi, Conklin and I, and every inspector in Homicide, Narcotics, and Robbery were standing shoulder to shoulder as the Kingfisher situation was discussed and assignments were handed out.

There was a firm knock on the door and Mayor Robert Caputo walked in. He nodded at us in a general greeting and asked the chief for a briefing.

Jacobi said, "The jury is sequestered inside the jail. We're organizing additional security details now."

"Inside the actual jail?" said Caputo.

"We have an empty pod of cells on six," Jacobi said of the vacancy left when a section of the women's jail was relocated to the new jail on 7th Street. He described the plan to bring in mattresses and personal items, all of this calculated to keep the jury free of exposure to media or accidental information leaks.

"We've set up a command center in the lobby, and anything that comes into or out of the sixth floor will go through metal detectors and be visually inspected."

Jacobi explained that the judge had refused to be locked down but that he had 24/7 security at his home. Caputo thanked Jacobi and left the room. When the meeting ended, Brady took me aside.

"Boxer, I'm putting two cars on your house. We need to know where you are at all times. Don't go rogue, okay?"

"Right, Brady. But—"

"Don't tell me you can take care of yourself. Be smart."

Conklin and I took the first shift on the sixth floor, and I made phone calls.

When I got home that evening, I told my protection detail to wait for me.

I took my warm and sleepy Julie out of her bed and filled Mrs. Rose in on my plan as we gathered toys and a traveling bag. When my bodyguards gave me the all clear, I went back downstairs with my still-sleepy baby in my arms. Mrs. Rose and I strapped her into her car seat in the back. Martha jumped in after us.

Deputy sheriffs took over for our beat cops and escorted me on the long drive to Half Moon Bay. I waited for their okay, and then I parked in my sister's driveway.

I let Martha out and gently extricated my little girl from the car seat. I hugged her awake. She put her hands in my hair and smiled.

"Mommy?"

"Yes, my sweets. Did you have a good nap?"

Catherine came out to meet me. She put her arm around me and walked me and Julie inside her lovely, beachy house near the bay. She had already set up her girls' old crib, and we tried to put a good spin on this dislocation for Julie, but Julie wasn't buying it. She could and did go from smiles to stratospheric protests when she was unhappy.

I didn't want to leave her, either.

I turned to Cat and said, "I've texted Joe. He's

on call for whenever you need him. He'll sleep on the couch."

"Sounds good," she said. "I like having a man around the house. Especially one with a gun."

"Don't worry," Cat and I said in unison.

We laughed, hugged, kissed, and then I shushed Julie and told Martha that she was in charge.

I had my hand on my gun when I left Cat's house and got into my car. I stayed in radio contact with my escorts, and with one car in the lead and the other behind me, we started back up the coast to my apartment on Lake Street.

I gripped the wheel so hard my hands hurt, which was preferable to feeling them shake. I stared out at the taillights in front of me. They looked like the malevolent red eyes of those monsters you see in horror movies. Kingfisher was worse than all of them put together.

I hated being afraid of him.

I hated that son of a bitch entirely.

CHAPTER 22

AN HOUR AFTER I got home to my dark and empty apartment, Joe's name lit up the caller ID.

I thumbed the On button, nearly shouting, "What's wrong?"

"Linds, I've got information for you," he said.

"Where are you?"

"On 280 South. Cat called me. Julie is inconsolable. I know I agreed that it was safe to take her there, but honestly, don't you think it would have made more sense for me to come over and stay with the two of you on Lake Street?"

I was filled with complex and contradictory rage.

It was true that it would have been easier, more expeditious, for Joe to have checked into our apartment, slept on our sofa instead of Cat's. True that along with my security detail, we would have been safe right here.

But I wasn't ready for Joe to move back in for

a few nights—or whatever. Because along with my justifiable rage, I still loved a man I no longer completely trusted.

"I had to make a quick decision, Joe," I snapped. "What's the information?"

"Reliable sources say that there's Mexican gang activity on the move in San Francisco."

"Could you be more specific?"

"Hey. Blondie. Could you please take it easy?"

"Okay. Sorry," I said. The line was silent. I said, "Joe. Are you still there?"

"I'm sorry, too. I don't like anything about this guy. I've heard that Mala Sangre 'killer elites' have come to town to deliver on Kingfisher's threats. Los Toros activity has also been noted."

"Gang war?"

"I've told you all I know."

"Thanks, Joe. Drive safe. Call me if Julie doesn't settle down."

"Copy that," said Joe. "Be careful."

And the line went dead.

I stood with the phone pressed against my chest for a good long while. Then I called Jacobi.

CHAPTER 23

I WATCHED FROM THE top of the steps up to the Hall the next morning as hundreds of people came to work, lined up to go through the metal detectors, and walked across the garnet-marbled lobby to the elevator banks.

They all looked worried.

That was both unusual and understandable. Kingfisher's presence on the seventh floor felt like a kryptonite meteor had dropped through the roof and was lodged in the jail. He was draining the energy from everyone who worked here.

I went inside, passed through metal detection, and then took the stairs to the squad room.

Brady had called a special early-morning meeting because of the intel from Joe. He stood at the head of the open-space bull pen, his back to the door, the muted TV hanging above his head.

Cops from all departments—the night shift, the swing shift, and our shift—were perched on the edges of desks, leaned against walls. There were even some I didn't recognize from the northern station crammed into the room. I saw deputy sheriffs, motorcycle cops, and men and women in plain clothes and blue.

Brady said, "I've called y'all together because we could be looking at a citywide emergency situation."

He spoke about the possibility of drug gang warfare and he answered questions about Mala Sangre, about Kingfisher, about cops who had been killed at the King's order. They asked about the upcoming rescheduled trial and about practical issues. The duty rosters. The chain of command.

Brady was honest and direct to a fault. I didn't get a sense that the answers he gave were satisfying. But honestly, he had no idea what to expect.

When the meeting was over, when the dozen of us on the day shift were alone with our lieutenant, he said, "The jurors are having fits. They don't know what's going on, but they can see out the windows. They see a lot of cops.

"The mayor's coming over to talk to them."

The mayor was a great people handler.

I was in the sixth-floor dayroom when Mayor Caputo visited the jurors and explained that they were carrying out their civic duty. "It's not just that this is important," he said. "This could be the most important work of your entire lives."

That afternoon one of the jurors had a heart attack and was evacuated. A second juror, a primary caregiver for a dependent parent, was excused. Alternates, who were also in our emergency jury lockup, moved up to full jurors.

When I was getting ready to leave after my twelve-hour day, Brady told me that an ambitious defender, Jake Penney, had spent the last four days with Jorge Sierra and had said that he was good to go.

The countdown to Sierra's trial had begun again.

CHAPTER 24

I WAS SLEEPING WHEN Joe called.

The time on my phone was midnight, eight hours before the trial was to begin.

"What's wrong?" I asked.

"Julie's fine. The SFPD website is down. The power is out at the Hall."

I turned on the TV news and saw mayhem on Bryant Street. Barricades had been set up. Reporters and cameramen shouted questions at uniformed officers. The Hall of Justice was so dark it looked like an immense mausoleum.

I nuked instant coffee and sat cross-legged in Joe's chair, watching the tube. At 1:00 a.m. fire could be seen leaping at the glass doors that faced the intersection of Bryant and Boardman Place.

A network reporter said to the camera, "Chet, I'm hearing that there was an explosion inside the lobby."

I couldn't take this anymore. I texted Brady. He was rushed. He typed, *Security is checking in with me up and down the line. Don't come in, Boxer.*

Then, as suddenly as they had gone out, the lights in the Hall came back on.

My laptop was on the coffee table and I switched it on. I punched in the address for the SFPD site, and I was watching when a title appeared on our own front page: *This was a test.*

It was signed *Mala Sangre.*

Kingfisher's cartel.

This had been their test for what? For shutting down our video surveillance? For sending out threatening messages? For disabling our electronic locks inside the jail? For smuggling bombs into the Hall?

It would have been a laughable threat if Kingfisher hadn't killed two people from the confines of his windowless cell. How had he pulled that off? What else could he do?

I called Cat. She said, "Lindsay, she's fine. She was in sleepy land when the phone rang."

I heard Julie crying and Joe's voice in the background saying, "Julie-Bug, I'm here."

"Sorry. Sorry," I said. "I'll call you in the morning. Thanks for everything, Cat."

I called Jacobi. His voice was steady. I liked that.

"I was just going to call you," he said. "The bomb was stuck under the lip of the sign-in desk. It was small, but if it had gone off during the daytime…" After a pause Jacobi began again. "Hounds and the bomb squad are going through the building. The trial is postponed until further notice."

"Good," I said. But I didn't feel good. It felt like anything could happen. That Kingfisher was in charge of it all.

My intercom buzzed. It was half past one.

Cerrutti, my designated security guard, said, "Sergeant, Dr. Washburn is here."

Tears of relief filled my eyes and no one had to see them. I buzzed my friend in.

CHAPTER 25

CLAIRE CAME THROUGH MY door bringing hope, love, warmth, and the scent of tea roses. All good things.

She said, "I have to crash here, Lindsay. I drove to the office. It's closed off from both the street and the back door to the Hall. It's too late to drive all the way home."

I hugged her. I needed that hug and I thought she did, too. I pointed her to Joe's big chair, with the best view of the TV. On-screen now, a live report from Bryant Street.

Wind whipped through the reporter's hair, turning her scarf into a pennant, making her microphone crackle.

She squinted at the camera and said, "I've just gotten off the phone with the mayor's office and can confirm reports that there are no fatalities from the bomb. The prisoner, Jorge Sierra, also known as Kingfisher, remains locked in his cell.

"The mayor has also confirmed that Sierra's trial has been postponed until the Hall is cleared. If you work at 850 Bryant, please check our website to see if your office is open."

When the segment ended, Claire talked to me about the chaos outside the Hall. She couldn't get to her computer and she needed to reach her staff.

Yuki called at two. "You're watching?"

"Yes. Is Brady with you?"

"No," she said. "But three cruisers are outside our apartment building. And I have a gun. Nothing like this has ever happened around a trial in San Francisco. Protesters? Yes. Bombs? No."

I asked her, "Do you know Kingfisher's new attorney?"

"Jake Penney. I don't know him. But this I do know. He's got balls."

Claire made soup from leftovers and defrosted a pound cake. I unscrewed a bottle of chilled cheap Chardonnay. Claire took off her shoes and reclined in the chair. I gave her a pair of socks and we settled into half a night of TV together.

I must have slept for a few minutes, because I woke to my cell phone buzzing on the floor beside the sofa.

Who was it now? Joe? Cat? Jacobi?

"Sergeant Boxer, it's Elena."

It took me a moment to put a face to a name. It came to me. Elena, a.k.a. Maura Steele, was Jorge Sierra's reluctant wife.

I bolted into an upright position. Had we thought to protect her? *No.*

"Are you okay?"

"I'm fine. I have an idea."

"I'm listening," I said.

CHAPTER 26

WHEN I'D MET WITH Elena Sierra, she had let me know that she wanted nothing to do with her husband. I had given her my card but never expected to hear from her.

What had changed her mind?

I listened hard as she laid out her plan. It was brilliant and simple. I had made this *same* offer to Sierra and utterly failed to close the deal. But Kingfisher didn't love *me*.

Now I had reason to hope that Elena could help put this nightmare to bed.

The meeting between Elena and her husband was arranged quickly. By late afternoon the next day our cameras were rolling upstairs in a barred room reserved for prisoners and their attorneys.

Elena wore a belted vibrant-purple sweater-dress and designer boots and looked like a cover girl. She sat across the table from Sierra. He wore orange and was chained so that he couldn't stand or move his hands. He looked amused.

I stood in a viewing room with Conklin and Brady, watching live video of Elena's meeting with Sierra, and heard him suggest several things he would like to do with her. It was creepy, but she cut him off by saying, "I'm not here for your pleasure, Jorge. I'm trying to help you."

Sierra leaned forward and said, "You don't want to help me. You want only money and power. How do I know? Because I created you."

"Jorge. We only have a few more minutes. I'm offering you the chance to see your children—"

"Mine? I'm not so sure."

"All you have to do is to plead guilty."

"That's all? Whose payroll are you on, Elena? Who are you working for, bitch whore?"

Elena got to her feet and slapped her husband hard across the face.

Joy surged through my body. I could almost feel my right palm stinging as if I had slapped him myself.

The King laughed at his wife, then turned his head and called out through the bars, "Take me back."

Two guards appeared at the cage door and the King was led out. When he was gone, Elena looked at the camera and shrugged. She looked embarrassed. She said, "I lost my temper."

I pressed the intercom. "You did fine. Thank you, Elena."

"Well, that was edifying," said Brady.

"She tried," I said to Brady. "I don't see what else she could have done."

I turned to Rich and said, "Let's drive her home."

CHAPTER 27

ELENA SIERRA HAD CURLED up in the backseat and leaned against the window. "He's subhuman," she said. "My father warned me, but I was eighteen. He was…I don't remember what the hell I was thinking. *If* I was thinking."

There was a long pause, as if she was trying to remember when she had fallen in love with Kingfisher.

"I'm coming to the trial," Elena said. "I want to see his face when he's found guilty. My father wants to be there, too."

Then she stared silently out the window until we pulled up to her deluxe apartment building on California Street. Conklin walked Elena into the lobby, and when he came back to the car, I was behind the wheel.

I switched on the car radio, which broke into a cacophony of bleats and static. I gave dispatch our coordinates as we left Nob Hill and said that we were heading back to the Hall.

At just about half past six we were on Race Street. We'd been stuck behind a FedEx truck for several blocks, until now, when it ran a yellow light, leaving us flat-footed at the red.

I cursed and the gray sedan behind us pulled out into the oncoming lane, its wheels jerking hard to the right, and the driver braked at an angle twenty-five feet ahead of our left front bumper.

I shouted, "What the hell?"

But by the time the word *hell* was out of my mouth, Conklin had his door open and was yelling to me, *"Out of the car. With me."*

I got it.

I snapped mental images as four men burst from the gray sedan into our headlight beams. One wore a black knit cap and bulky jacket. Another had a gold grille plating his teeth. The one coming out of the driver's side was holding an AK. One with a black scarf over half his face ducked out of view.

I dropped below the dash and pulled myself out the passenger side, slid down to the street. Conklin and I hunched behind the right front wheel, using the front of the car as a shield. We were both carrying large, high-capacity semiautomatics, uncomfortable as hell to wear, but my God, I was glad we had them.

A fusillade of bullets punched holes through the door that had been to my left just seconds before. Glass crazed and shattered.

I poked my head up during a pause in on-coming gunfire, and using the hood as a gun brace, Conklin and I let loose with a fury of return fire.

In that moment I saw the one with the AK drop his weapon. His gun or his hand had been hit, or the gun had slipped out of his grasp. When the shooter bent to retrieve it, Conklin and I fired and kept firing until the bastard was down.

For an eternal minute and a half curses flew, and shots punctured steel, exploded the shop windows behind us, and smacked into the front end of our car. If these men worked for the King, they could not let us get away.

Conklin and I alternately rose from behind the car just enough to brace our guns and return fire, ducking as our attackers unloaded on us with the fury of hell.

We reloaded and kept shooting. My partner took out the guy with the glittering teeth, and I wasn't sure, but I might have winged the one with the scarf.

The light turned green.

Traffic resumed, and while some vehicles streamed past, others balked, blocking cars behind them, leaving them in the line of fire.

There was a lull in the shooting, and when I peeked above our car, I saw the driver of the gray Ford backing up, turning the wheel into traffic, gunning the engine, then careening across the intersection at N17th.

I took a stance and emptied my Glock into the rear of the Ford, hoping to hit the gas tank. A tire blew, but the car kept going. I looked down at the two dead men in the street as Conklin kicked their guns away and looked for ID.

I got into the car, grabbed the mic, shouted my badge number, and reported to dispatch.

"Shots fired. Two men down. Send patrol cars and a bus to Race and N17th. BOLO for a gray Ford four-door with shot-out windows and flat right rear tire heading east on Race at high speed. Nevada plates, partial number Whiskey Four Niner."

Within minutes the empty, shot-riddled Ford was found ditched a few blocks away on 17th Street. Conklin and I sat for a while in our shot-to-shit squad car, listening to the radio snap, crackle, and pop while waiting for a ride back to the Hall. My right hand was numb and the aftershock of my gun's recoil still resonated through my bones.

I was glad to feel it.

I said to Richie, as if he didn't already know, "We're damned lucky to be alive."

CHAPTER 28

TWO HOURS AFTER THE shoot-out Conklin and I learned that the Ford had been stolen. The guns were untraceable. The only ID found on the two dead men were their Mala Sangre tats. Had to be that Kingfisher's men had been following us or following Elena.

We turned in our guns and went directly down the street to McBain's, a cross between a place where everyone knows your name and the *Star Wars* cantina. It was fully packed now with cops, lawyers, bail bondsmen, and a variety of clerks and administrators. The ball game was blaring loudly on the tube, competing with some old tune coming from the ancient Wurlitzer in the back.

Rich and I found two seats at the bar, ordered beer, toasted the portrait of Captain McBain hanging over the backbar, and proceeded to drink. We had to process the bloodcurdling firefight and there was no better place than here.

Conklin sat beside me shaking his head, probably having thoughts like my own, which were so vivid that I could still hear the *rat-a-tat-tat* of lead punching through steel and see the faces of the bangers we'd just "put down like dogs." I stank of gunpowder and fear.

We were alive not just because of what we knew about bad guys with guns, or because Conklin and I worked so well together that we were like two halves of a whole.

That had contributed to it, but mostly, we were alive and drinking because of the guy who'd dropped his AK and given us a two-second advantage.

After I'd downed half of my second beer, I told Conklin, "We weren't wearing vests, for Christ's sake. This is so unfair to Julie."

"Cut it out," he said. "Don't make me say she's lucky to have you as a mom."

"Fine."

"Two dirtbags are dead," he said. "We did that. We won't feel bad about that."

"That guy with the AK."

"He's in hell," said Rich, "kicking his own ass."

Oates, the bartender, asked if I was ready for another, but I shook my head and covered the top of my glass. Just then I felt an arm go around my shoulders. I started. It was Brady behind us, all white blond and blue-eyed, and he had an arm around Conklin, too.

He gave my shoulder a squeeze, his way of saying, *Thanks. You did good. I'm proud of you.*

"Come back to the house," Brady said. "I've got your new weapons and rides home for both of y'all."

"I've only had one beer," Rich lied.

"I've got rides home for *both* of y'all," Brady repeated.

He put some bills down on the bar. Malcolm, the tipsy dude on my left, pointed to the dregs of my beer and asked, "You done with that, Lindsay?"

I passed him my glass.

It was ten fifteen when I got to Cat's. I took a scalding shower, washed my hair, and buffed myself dry. Martha sat with her head in my lap while I ate chicken and noodles à la Gloria Rose. I was scraping the plate when the phone rang.

"I heard about what happened today," Joe said.

"Yeah. It was over so fast. In two minutes I'd pulled my gun and there were men lying dead in the street."

"Good result. Are you okay?"

"Never better," I said, sounding a little hysterical to my own ears. I'm sure Joe heard it, too.

"Okay. Good. Do you need anything?"

"No, but thanks. Thanks for calling."

I slept with Martha and Julie that night, one arm around each of my girls. I slept hard and I dreamed hard and I was still holding on to Julie when she woke me up in the morning.

I blinked away the dream fragments and remembered that Kingfisher would be facing the judge and jury today.

I had to move fast so that I wasn't late to court.

CHAPTER 29

CONKLIN AND I WERE at our desks at eight, filling out the incident report and watching the time.

Kingfisher's trial was due to start at nine, but would the trial actually begin? I thought about the power outage that had occurred two days ago, followed by the bomb explosion and the threatening message that had read *This was a test. Mala Sangre.* And I wondered if Kingfisher had already left the Hall through the drain in his shower, El Chapo style.

His trial had been postponed three times so far, but I had dressed for court nonetheless. I was wearing my good charcoal-gray pants, my V-neck silk sweater under a Ralph Lauren blazer, and my flat-heeled Cole Haan shoes. My hair gleamed and I'd even put on lipstick. *That's for you, Mr. Kingfisher.*

Conklin had just dunked his empty coffee

container into the trash can when Len Parisi's name lit up on my console.

I said to Conklin, "What now?" and grabbed the phone.

Parisi said, "Boxer, you and Conklin got a second?"

"Sure. What's up?"

"Counsel for the defense is in my office."

"Be right there." I hung up, then said to Conklin, "I'm guessing Sierra wants to change his plea to insanity."

He said, "From your lips to God's ears."

It was a grim thought. In the unlikely event that Kingfisher could be found guilty because of mental disease or defect, he would be institutionalized and one day might be set free.

"There's just no way," said Conklin.

"Wanna bet?"

Conklin dug into his wallet and tossed a single onto the desk. I topped his dollar bill with one of mine and weighed down our bet with a stapler.

Then we booked it down the stairs and along the second-floor corridor at a good pace, before entering the maze of cubicles outside the DA's office. Parisi's office door was open. He signaled for us to come in.

Jake Penney, the King's new attorney, sat in

the chair beside Parisi's oversized desk. He was about thirty-five and was good-looking in a flawless, *The Bachelor* kind of way. Because Cindy researched him and reported back, I knew he was on the fast track at a topflight law firm.

Kingfisher had hired one of the best.

Conklin and I took the sofa opposite Parisi, and Penney angled his chair toward us.

He said, "I want to ask my client to take Elena's offer. He changes his plea to guilty, and he goes to a maximum-security prison within a few hours' drive of his wife's residence. That's win-win. Saves the people the cost of a trial. Keeps Mr. Sierra in the USA with no death penalty and a chance to see his kids every now and again. It's worth another try."

Parisi said to Conklin and me, "I'm okay with this, but I wanted to run it by you before I gave Mr. Penney an okay to offer this deal to Sierra."

I said, "You'll be in the room with them, Len?"

"Absolutely."

"Mr. Penney should go through metal detection and agree to be patted down before and after his meeting."

"Okay, Mr. Penney?"

"Of course."

There was a clock on the wall, the face a hand-drawn illustration of a red bulldog.

The time was 8:21.

If the King's attorney could make a deal for his client, it had to be now or never.

CHAPTER 30

CONKLIN AND I WAITED in Parisi's office as the second hand swiped the bulldog's face and time whizzed around the dial.

What was taking so long? Deal? Or no deal?

I was ready to go up to the seventh floor and crash the conference when Parisi and Penney came through the door.

"He wouldn't buy it," Parisi said. He went to his closet and took out his blue suit jacket.

Penney said, "He maintains his innocence. He wants to walk out of court a free man."

It took massive willpower for me not to roll my eyes and shout, *Yeah, right. Of course he's innocent!*

Parisi shrugged into his jacket, tightened the knot in his tie, glanced at the clock. Then he said, "I told Sierra about the attack on you two by Mala Sangre thugs. I said that if the violence stops now, and if he is convicted, I will arrange for him to do his time at the prison of his choice,

Pelican Bay. He said, 'Okay. I agree. No more violence.' We shook on it. For whatever that's worth."

Pelican Bay was a supermax-security prison in Del Norte County, at the very northwest tip of California, about fifteen miles south of the Oregon border. It was a good six-and-a-half-hour drive from here. The prison population was made up of the state's most violent criminals and rated number one for most gangs and murders inside its walls. The King would feel right at home there.

"I'll see you in court," Parisi said to Penney.

The two men shook hands. Conklin and I wished Parisi luck, then headed down to the courtroom.

Kingfisher had agreed to the safety of all involved in his trial, but entering Courtroom 2C, I felt as frightened as I had when I woke up this morning with a nightmare in my mind.

An AK had chattered in the King's hands.

And then he'd gotten me.

CHAPTER 31

KINGFISHER'S DAY IN COURT had dawned again.

All stood when Judge Crispin, looking irritated from his virtual house arrest, took the bench. The gallery sat down with a collective *whoosh*, and the judge delivered his rules of decorum to a new set of spectators. No one could doubt him when he said, "Outbursts will be dealt with by immediate removal from this courtroom."

I sat in a middle row between two strangers. Richie was seated a few rows ahead to my right. Elena Sierra sat behind the defense table, where she had a good view of the back of her husband's head. A white-haired man sat beside her and whispered to her. He had to be her father.

The jurors entered the box and were sworn in.

There were five women and nine men, including the remaining alternates. It was a diverse group in age and ethnicity. I saw a range of emotion in their faces: stolid fury, relief, curiosity, and a high level of excitement.

I felt all those emotions, too.

During the judge's address to the jurors every one of them took a long look at the defendant. In fact, it was hard to look away from Kingfisher. The last time he was at the defense table, he'd cleaned up and appeared almost respectable. Today the King was patchily shaven and had flecks of blood on his collar. He seemed dazed and subdued.

To my eye, he looked as though he'd used up all his tricks and couldn't believe he was actually on trial. By contrast, his attorney, Jake Penney, wore his pin-striped suit with aplomb. DA Leonard Parisi looked indomitable.

All stood to recite the Pledge of Allegiance, and then there was a prolonged rustle as seats were retaken. Someone coughed. A cell phone clattered to the floor. Conklin turned his head and we exchanged looks.

Kingfisher had threatened us since the nasty Finders Keepers case last year—and *still* he haunted my dreams. Would the jury find him guilty of killing Stone and Whittaker? Would this monstrous killer spend the rest of his life inside the high, razor-wired walls of Pelican Bay State Prison?

THE TRIAL

The bailiff called the court to order, and Judge Crispin asked Len Parisi if he was ready to present his case.

I felt pride in the big man as he walked out into the well. I could almost feel the floor shake. He welcomed the jury and thanked them for bearing down under unusually trying conditions in the interest of justice.

Then he launched into his opening statement.

CHAPTER 32

I'D NEVER BEFORE SEEN Len Parisi present a case to a jury. He was an intimidating man and a powerful one. As district attorney, he was responsible for investigating and prosecuting crime in this city and was at the head of three divisions: Operations, Victims Services, and Special Operations.

But he was never more impressive than he was today, standing in for our murdered friend and colleague, ADA Barry Schein.

Parisi held the jury's attention with his presence and his intensity, and then he spoke.

"Ladies and Gentlemen, the defendant, Jorge Sierra, is a merciless killer. In the course of this trial you will hear witness testimony and see video evidence of the defendant in the act of shooting two innocent women to death."

Parisi paused, but I didn't think it was for effect. It seemed to me that he was inside the crime now, seeing the photos of the victims' bloodied bodies at the Vault. He cleared his throat and began again.

"One of those women was Lucille Stone, twenty-eight years old. She worked in marketing, and for a long time she was one of Mr. Sierra's girlfriends. She was unarmed when she was killed. Never carried a gun, and she had done nothing to Mr. Sierra. But, according to Lucy's friends, she had decisively ended the relationship.

"Cameron Whittaker was Lucy's friend. She was a substitute teacher, volunteered at a food bank, and had nothing whatsoever to do with Mr. Sierra or his associates. She was what is called collateral damage. She was in the wrong place at the wrong time."

I turned my eyes to the jury and they were with Len all the way. He walked along the railing that separated the jury box from the well of the courtroom.

He said, "One minute these friends were enjoying a girls' night out in an upscale nightclub, sitting together at the bar. And the next minute they were shot to death by the defendant, who thought he could get away with murder in full sight of 150 people, some of whom aimed their cell phones and took damning videos of this classic example of premeditated murder.

"I say 'premeditated' because the shooting was

conceived before the night in question when Lucy Stone rejected Mr. Sierra's advances. He followed her. He found her. He taunted her and he menaced her. And then he put two bullet holes in her body and even more in the body of her friend.

"Lucy Stone didn't know that when she refused to open her door to him, he immediately planned to enact his revenge—"

Parisi had his hands on the railing when an explosion cracked through the air inside the courtroom.

It was a stunning, deafening blast. I dove for the floor and covered the back of my neck with my hands. Screams followed the report. Chairs scraped back and toppled. I looked up and saw that the bomb had gone off behind me and had blown open the main doors.

Smoke filled the courtroom, obscuring my vision. The spectators panicked. They swarmed forward, away from the blast and toward the judge's bench.

Someone yelled, "Your Honor, can you hear me?"

I heard shots coming from the well; one, then two more.

I was on my feet, but the shots sent the freaked-out spectators in the opposite direction, away from the bench, toward me and through the doors out into the hallway.

Who had fired those shots? The only guns that could have passed through metal detection into the Hall had to belong to law enforcement. Had anyone been hit?

As the room cleared and the smoke lifted, I took stock of the damage. The double main doors were nearly unhinged, but the destruction was slight. The bomb seemed more like a diversion than a forceful explosion meant to kill, maim, or destroy property.

A bailiff helped Parisi to his feet. Judge Crispin pulled himself up from behind the bench, and the jury was led out the side doorway. Conklin headed toward me as the last of the spectators flowed out the main doors and cops ran in.

"EMTs are on the way," he said.

That's when I saw that the defense table, where the King had been sitting with his attorney, had flipped onto its side.

Penney looked around and called out, "Help! I need help here!"

My ears still rang from the blast. I made my way around overturned chairs to where King-fisher lay on his side in a puddle of blood. He reached out his hand and beckoned to me.

"I'm here," I said. "Talk to me."

The King had been shot. There was a ragged bullet hole in his shoulder, blood pumping from his belly, and more blood pouring from a wound at the back of his head. There were shell casings on the floor.

He was in pain and maybe going into shock, but he was conscious.

His voice sounded like a whisper to my deafened ears. But I read him, loud and clear.

"Elena did this," he said. "Elena, my little Elena."

Then his face relaxed. His hand dropped. His eyes closed and he died.

CHAPTER 33

JORGE SIERRA'S FUNERAL WAS held at a Catholic cemetery in Crescent City, a small northwest California town on the ocean named for the crescent-shaped bay that defined it.

Among the seventy-five hundred people included in the census were the fifteen hundred inmates of nearby Pelican Bay State Prison.

It was either irony or payback, but Elena had picked this spot because her husband had asked to be imprisoned at Pelican Bay and now he would be within eight miles of it—forever.

The graveyard had been virtually abandoned. The ground was flat, bleak, with several old headstones that had been tipped over by vandals or by weather. The chapel needed paint, and just beyond the chapel was a potholed parking lot.

Several black cars, all government property, were parked there, and a dozen FBI agents stood in a loose perimeter around the grave site and beside the chapel within the parking lot with a view of the road.

I was with Conklin and Parisi. My partner and I had been told that Sierra was dead and buried once before. This time I had looked into the coffin. The King was cold and dead, but I still wanted to see the box go into the ground.

Conklin had suffered along with me when Sierra had terrorized me last year, and even though justice had been cheated, we were both relieved it was over.

The FBI had sent agents to the funeral to see who showed up. The King's murder inside the courthouse was an unsolved mystery. The smoke and the surging crowd had blocked the camera's view of the defense table. Elena Sierra and her father, Pedro Quintana, had been questioned separately within twelve hours of the shooting and had said that they had hit the floor after the blast, eyes down when the bullets were fired. They hadn't seen the shooting.

So they said.

Both had come for Sierra's send-off, and Elena had brought her children to say good-bye to their father.

Elena looked lovely in black. Eight-year-old Javier and six-year-old Alexa bowed their heads as the priest spoke over their father's covered coffin at graveside. The little girl cried.

I studied this tableau.

Elena had many reasons to want her husband dead. But she had no military background, nothing that convinced me that she could lean over the railing and shoot her husband point-blank in the back of the head.

Her father, however, was a different story.

I'd done some research into Mexican gangsters and learned that Pedro Quintana was the retired head of Los Toros, the original gang that had raised and trained Sierra on his path to becoming the mightiest drug kingpin of them all.

Sierra had famously disposed of Quintana after he split off from Los Toros and formed Mala Sangre, the new and more powerful drug and crime cartel.

Both Elena and her father had motive to put Sierra down, but how had one or both of them pulled off this shooting in open court?

I'd called Joe last night to brainstorm with him. Despite the state of our marriage, Joe Molinari had background to spare as an agent in USA clandestine services, as well as from his stint as deputy to the director of Homeland Security.

He theorized that during the power outage in the Hall, a C-4 explosive charge had been slapped onto the hinges of Judge Crispin's courtroom doors. It was plausible that one of the hundreds of law enforcement personnel prowling the Hall that night had been paid to set this charge, and it was possible for a lump of plastic explosive to go unnoticed.

A package containing a small gun, ammo, and a remote-controlled detonator could have been smuggled in at the same time, left where only Sierra's killer could find it. It could even have been passed to the killer or killers the morning of the trial.

Had Elena and her father orchestrated this perfect act of retribution? If so, I thought they were going to get away with it.

These were my thoughts as I stood with Conklin and Parisi in the windswept and barren cemetery watching the lowering of the coffin, Elena throwing flowers into the grave, the first shovel of dirt, her children clinging to their mother's skirt.

The moment ended when a limo pulled around a circular drive and Elena Sierra's family went to it and got inside.

Rich said to me, "I'm going to hitch a ride back with Red Dog. Okay with you?"

I said it was. We hugged good-bye.

Another car, an aging Mercedes, swung around

the circle of dead grass and stone. It stopped for me. I opened the back door and reached out to my baby girl in her car seat. She was wearing a pink sweater and matching hat knit for her by her lovely nanny. I gave Julie a big smooch and what we call a huggy-wuffle.

Then I got into the front passenger seat.

Joe was driving.

"Zoo?" he said.

"Zoooooooo," came from behind.

"It's unanimous," I said. "The zoos have it."

Joe put his hand behind my neck and pulled me toward him. I hadn't kissed him in a long time. But I kissed him then.

There'd be plenty of time to talk later.

EPILOGUE

CHAPTER 34

THE LIMO DRIVER WHO was bringing Elena Sierra and the children back from a shopping trip couldn't park at the entrance to her apartment building. A long-used family car was stopped right in front of the walkway, where an elderly man was helping his wife out of the car with her walker. The doorman ran outside to help the old couple with their cumbersome luggage.

Elena told her driver, "Leave us right here, Harlan. Thanks. See you in the morning."

After opening the doors for herself and her children, Elena took the two shopping bags from her driver, saying, "I've got it. Thanks."

Doors closed with solid thunks, the limo pulled away, and the kids surrounded their mother, asking her for money to buy churros from the ice cream shop down the block at the corner.

She said, "We don't need churros. We have milk

and granola cookies." But she finally relented, set down the groceries, found a five-dollar bill in her purse, and gave it to Javier.

"Please get me one, too," she called after her little boy.

Elena picked up her grocery bags, and as she stood up, she saw two men in bulky jackets—one with a black scarf covering the bottom of his face and the other with a knit cap—crossing the street toward her.

She recognized them as Jorge's men and knew without a doubt that they were coming to kill her. Mercifully, the children were running and were now far down the block.

The one with the scarf, Alejandro, aimed his gun at the doorman and fired. The gun had a suppressor, and the sound of the discharge was so soft the old man hadn't heard it, didn't understand what had happened. He tried to attend to the fallen doorman, while Elena said to the soldier wearing the cap, "Not out here. Please."

Invoking what residual status she might have as the King's widow, Elena turned and walked into the modern, beautifully appointed lobby, her back prickling with expectation of a bullet to her spine.

She walked past the young couple sitting on a love seat, past the young man leashing his dog, and pressed the elevator button. The doors instantly slid open and the two men followed her inside.

The doors closed.

Elena stood at the rear with one armed man standing to her left and the other to her right. She looked straight ahead, thinking about the next few minutes as the elevator rose upward, then chimed as it opened directly into her living room.

Esteban, the shooter with the knit cap, had the words *Mala Sangre* inked on the side of his neck. He stepped ahead of her into the room, looked around at the antiques, the books, the art on the walls. He went to the plate-glass window overlooking the Transamerica Pyramid and the great bay.

"Nice view, Mrs. Sierra," he said with a booming voice. "Maybe you'd like to be looking out the window now. That would be easiest."

"Don't hurt my children," she said. "They are Jorge's. His blood."

She went to the window and placed her hands on the glass. She heard a door open inside the apartment. A familiar voice said loudly, "Drop your guns. Do it now."

Alejandro whipped around, but before he could fire, Elena's father cut him down with a shot to the throat, two more to the chest as he fell.

Pedro Quintana said to the man with the cap, who was holding his hands above his head, "Esteban, get down on your knees while I am deciding what to do with you."

Esteban obeyed, dropping to his knees, keeping his hands up while facing Elena's father, and beseeching him in Spanish.

"Pedro, please. I have known you for twenty years. I named my oldest son for you. I was loyal, but Jorge, he threatened my family. I can prove myself. Elena, I'm sorry. *Por favor.*"

Elena walked around the dead man, who was bleeding on her fine Persian carpet where her children liked to play, and took the gun from her father's hand.

She aimed at Esteban and fired into his chest. He fell sideways, grabbed at his wound, and grunted, *"Dios."*

Elena shot him three more times.

When her husband's soldiers were dead, Elena made calls: First to Harlan to pick up the children immediately and keep them in the car. "Papa will meet you on the corner in five minutes. Wait for him. Take directions from him."

Then she called the police and told them that

she had shot two intruders who had attempted to murder her.

Her father stretched out his arms and Elena went in for a hug. Her father said, "Finish what we started. It's yours now, Elena."

"Thank you, Papa."

She went to the bar and poured out two drinks, gave one glass to her father.

They toasted. "Viva Los Toros."

Their cartel would be at the top again.

This was the way it was always meant to be.

JAMES PATTERSON
BOOKSHOTS

HEIST

WITH
REES JONES

HEIST

BY JAMES PATTERSON
WITH REES JONES

CHAPTER 1

THE THIEF'S GLOVED FINGERS beat against the steering wheel, a rhythm as hectic as the young man's darting eyes.

"You're doing it again," the woman beside him accused, rubbing at her face to drive home her irritation.

The thief turned in his seat, his wild eyes quickly shifting to an angry focus.

She wouldn't meet the stare, he knew. She never did, despite the fact that she was five years his senior, and tried to order him about as if she had the rank and privilege of family.

"Doing what?" He smiled, his handsome face made ugly by resentment.

The woman didn't answer. Instead, she rubbed again at her tired eyes. Her name was Charlotte Taylor, and anticipation had robbed her of any sleep the previous night. Instead she had lain awake, thinking of this day. Thinking of how failure would condemn the man she loved.

Charlotte tried again to hold the gaze of the man beside her, but she couldn't meet his eyes— she saw the past in them.

And what did he see when he looked at her? That a once pretty girl was now cracked from stress and sorrow? That her shoulders stooped like a woman of sixty, not thirty? Charlotte did not want to feel that scrutiny. That obnoxious charity she had suffered from family and strangers for nine years.

"It's OK if you're scared," she baited the thief, knowing that aggression would be one way to distract her from her niggling thoughts.

"Me? I'm excited," the younger man shot back.

And he was.

Today was the day. Today was the day when years of talking, months of planning, and weeks of practice would pay off.

Lives were going to change, and it would all start here.

"I'm excited," the thief said again, but this time with a smile.

His name was Alex Scowcroft, an unemployed twenty-five-year-old from northwest England's impoverished coast. Today the thief was far from home, his white paneled rental van parked beneath a blue October sky on Hatton Garden, the street that was the heart of London's diamond trade.

Charlotte was not excited. In truth, she was sick to her stomach. She had never broken the law—not in any meaningful way, anyway—and the thought of being caught and convicted turned her guts into knots. And yet, the thought of failure was infinitely worse.

As she always did when she needed comfort, Charlotte pulled a blue envelope from the inside pocket of her worn leather jacket. The letter was grimy from oily fingers, and teardrops had smudged the ink. The blue paper was the mark of military correspondence, given to soldiers at war so they could write to their loved ones.

Hoping to take strength from the words, Charlotte looked over the faded letter.

Catching sight of the "bluey," Scowcroft stopped his fidgeting. "Was that—"

"His last one."

"He never wrote me any letters." Scowcroft smiled. "Knew I couldn't write one back."

Charlotte folded the letter away, replacing it into the pocket that would keep it closest to her heart.

"You're his brother, Alex. You two don't need to

put words on paper to know how you feel about each other."

Uncomfortable at the sincerity in her words, Scowcroft could only manage a violent nod before turning his gaze back out of the window, his chest sagging with relief as he saw a man approaching.

"Baz is back."

Gaunt-faced and stick-thin, Matthew Barrett entered the van through its sliding door and pushed his bony skull into the space between Charlotte and Scowcroft.

"Same as it's been every day," he told them in a voice made harsh by smoking only the cheapest cigarettes. "The shops are opening. No sign of any extra security. If he sticks to the same pattern again today, our man should be here in ten."

Scowcroft exhaled hard with anticipation. "Get your gear on."

Behind him, Barrett changed from the street clothes of his reconnaissance into a similar style of assault boot and biker jacket worn by his two accomplices. Finally, he pulled a baseball cap tight onto his head, and brought up the thin black mask that would obscure his features. Eyeing himself in the mirror, Barrett thought aloud: "Assume that we've been spotted as soon as we pull off. Don't try to be stealthy. Maximum violence. We get out. We shock. We grab. We extract."

"I know the plan," Scowcroft grunted.

"I know you do, mate," Barrett told him with the patience of a mentor. "But there's no such thing as going over it too many times. Five minutes," he concluded, looking at the van's dashboard clock.

Scowcroft turned the ignition, and four minutes passed with nothing but the throb of the van's diesel engine for distraction. It was Charlotte who broke the silence.

"If they get me, but you two pull this off, I don't want Tony to see me in prison. I don't want him to see me like that."

Barrett reached out and placed a gloved hand on her shoulder. "Since when does anyone tell Tony what to do? He loves you, Char, and when he's back to us, he'd be seeing you on Mars if that's what it took."

Charlotte eased at the words and rolled down her balaclava, her piercing blue eyes afire with righteous determination.

"For Tony, then."

"For Tony," the two men echoed, voices thick with grit and love.

Barrett looked again at the van's dashboard. "Five minutes is up."

In the driver's seat, Scowcroft's fingers began to beat against the steering wheel once more.

"He's here," he told them, and put the van into gear, pulling out into the lazy traffic of a Friday mid-morning.

A few pedestrians, mostly window-shoppers, ambled along the pavements, but Scowcroft's eyes were focused solely on a burly skinhead who looked as if he'd been plucked from a prison cell and clad in Armani. More precisely, Scowcroft focused on what was in the man's hand—a leather duffel bag. A leather duffel bag that would change their lives.

The big man's stride was slow and deliberate. Scowcroft reduced the van's speed to a running pace and glided close to the curb.

The moment had come.

"Go!" he shouted, overcome by excitement.

Then, as they had practiced dozens of times, Charlotte threw open the heavy passenger door so that the metal slammed into the big man's back, the leather duffel bag flying free as he collapsed onto the pavement.

"He's dropped it, Baz! Go!" Scowcroft shouted again as he stood on the brakes. Barrett threw himself from the van's sliding door, his eyes scanning for the bag and finding it beneath a parked car.

"I see it!" Barrett announced from outside, but Scowcroft's eyes were elsewhere. And widening in alarm.

"Shit," he cursed.

He'd expected to see pedestrians flee the scene. He'd expected to see a brave one try to interfere. But what Scowcroft had not expected to see was two motorcycles coming at them along the pavement, the riders hidden ominously behind black visors. With gut instinct, Scowcroft knew that the bikers were coming for the contents of the bag.

"Shit!" he repeated, then spat, because years of talking, months of planning, and weeks of practice were about to come undone.

So Alex Scowcroft formulated a new plan. One that any Scowcroft would have made.

He reached beneath his seat and pulled his older brother's commando dagger from its sheath. Charlotte saw the blade the moment before she saw the incoming bikers, and grasped the implications. She looked to Scowcroft for leadership.

"Would you die for my brother?" he asked her.

She nodded, swallowing the fear in her throat.

"Would you kill for him?"

Her eyes told him that she would.

"Then get out and fight."

CHAPTER 2

SCOWCROFT AND CHARLOTTE FLEW from the van's doors like fury, adrenaline coursing through their veins.

"Baz!" Scowcroft shouted. "Leave the bag where it is and get over here! We've got a problem!"

"Leave the bag?" Charlotte questioned aghast, a ball hammer in her shaking hands.

"They'll snatch it and go. We need them off those bikes."

With no sign of the duffel bag, the black- helmeted riders slowed their pace. Scowcroft could feel their gaze now falling on him and his two accomplices from behind the tinted visors.

Barrett came running up beside the others.

"The bag's by the front-left wheel arch. I can grab it quick, but what about them?" he asked, then took in the sight of Scowcroft's commando dagger. For a moment, Scowcroft thought Barrett would tell him to put the weapon away. Instead, Barrett drew an identical blade from a sheath on his lower leg.

"Just remember, drive the blade, don't slice," Barrett encouraged the younger man, brandishing his own dagger in an attempt to scare off the riders and avoid bloodshed.

It didn't work.

The bikers had their own weapons—five hundred pounds of metal, and that metal could reach sixty miles per hour in the time it took to close the gap to Scowcroft and his companions.

The bikes revved hard, leaving rubber on the pavement. Side by side, they came forward in a cavalry charge of steel.

Barrett and Charlotte darted left and pressed themselves into the cover of a shallow doorway, but Scowcroft dived for the duffel bag beneath the wheel arch, the bikers aiming for the easy target of his exposed body. They saw the chance to cripple the man as he grasped for his prize, and engines roared louder as throttles were held open.

Then, as his accomplices waited for the dreadful moment of impact, Scowcroft pressed his body down into the tarmac, squeezing himself beneath the car, and flung the duffel bag into the face of the closest rider.

The bikers had taken the bait, and now they paid the price. Traveling at sixty miles per hour, the rider was hit by the light leather bag as if by a baseball bat, whipping his neck and sending both bike and rider skidding across the pavement. With great skill, the fallen rider's partner was able to avoid entanglement, but it brought him to a stop.

"On him!" Scowcroft shouted, rushing to collect the bag.

Charlotte and Barrett broke from the refuge of the doorway and sprinted towards the second biker. The rider tried to twist on his seat, reaching down for a blade concealed in his boot, but Barrett was quicker and hit the rider with a rugby tackle, his own dagger flying free in the collision. The two men and the bike crashed to the floor, Barrett crying out in pain as his leg became pinned beneath the hot metal of the engine, and grunting in agony again as the rider head butted him with his helmet. As the pouring blood soaked his balaclava, Barrett was forced to remove his mask.

"Charlotte!" he gasped. "My dagger!"

Charlotte looked around desperately for the

blade, but when she saw where it was, the discovery caused her to go rigid with panic.

The blade was in the hand of the bag's courier. Recovered from the initial ambush, the big man was on his knees, aggressively turning the van's tires into husks of useless rubber.

Without thinking of her own safety, Charlotte charged towards him, but Scowcroft beat her to it and drove his blade into the man's shoulder. The big man roared in agony and tried to turn his captured dagger towards Scowcroft, but the wound had severed muscle and the arm hung limp and useless by his side. Scowcroft kicked the blade from the man's hand and followed by planting his steel toecap into the man's jaw. Barely conscious, the burly man slumped backwards against the van, leaving a smear of blood against the white paneling.

Pinned beneath the bike, Barrett and the rider continued their own struggle, the helmet crashing again into Barrett's broken nose.

Scowcroft and Charlotte arrived to haul the bike off the pair. Then Barrett pulled himself clear as Charlotte threw herself at the rider, her furious punches wasted against the protection of his helmet and thick jacket.

"Get off him!" Scowcroft called out. Barrett gritted his teeth and dragged Charlotte back by her shoulders, leaving Scowcroft free to push the bike back on top of the sprawling rider.

"I've got the bag," he panted. "But the van's done."

Barrett looked over his shoulder, blood bubbling from his shattered nose. A few curious heads were poking out of windows, but most of Hatton Garden's diamond traders had bolted their doors at the first sign of trouble.

"Get the backpacks out the van," Scowcroft told them. "Come on, let's go!"

"There's no sirens," Barrett observed as Charlotte handed out the small backpacks, each one unique in design and color. "Where the hell are the coppers?"

"Who cares?" Scowcroft countered. "We got what we came for. Let's get out of here!"

Without waiting for agreement, Scowcroft made for the nearest alleyway. Charlotte and Barrett followed in his wake, leaving three groaning bodies on the pavement.

Not one of them saw the pinstripe-suited gentleman in the window of Swiss Excellence, a specialist diamond jeweler. If they had, perhaps they would have noticed that the man's manicured hand was shaking as it picked up a telephone from its cradle. Perhaps they would have assumed that the pinstripe-suited gentleman was finally calling the police.

They'd have been wrong.

"Hello, sir," the jeweler began, with deference born of fear. "I'm afraid..." He swallowed. "I'm afraid that someone has stolen your diamonds."

The line clicked dead.

CHAPTER 3

DETECTIVE INSPECTOR ANDREW HILL was sitting behind his desk in Scotland Yard.

"Well, technically I'm FaceTiming you from the office," he told his wife of three weeks. "It's bloody purgatory, Deb. I've got no cases. All my paperwork is done. I'm like the ghost of a young girl who was murdered in a Victorian manor. My soul can't find peace, and all I have to look forward to is jumping out on you when you use the bathroom."

"I told you I'd stab you if you do that again." Deb laughed on the phone's screen. "Now stop being a melodramatic ass and find something to do. Get working on the business."

"I'm not allowed to work a second job until I get the redundancy," Hill grumbled.

"Yes you are."

"Well, OK, yeah, but it's frowned upon. I don't want to rub anyone up the wrong way before I leave. You never know who's going to be useful for business," the detective protested through a smile.

"I'm just hearing a lot of gas. Anyway, some of us do have to work. I'll see you tonight, babe. Love you."

"Love you, too."

His call ended, Hill checked his emails and texts for the tenth time that hour. Entering his podcast app, he scrolled through a dozen shows on entrepreneurship and business management. Hitting refresh, Hill searched in vain for a new episode.

"Bloody purgatory," he groaned under his breath. He reached for his briefcase and opened it, pulling a sheaf of bound papers from within.

These were Hill's business plans, drawn up over the past two years, and he spent the next hour poring over them, even though every detail was ingrained in his memory. As a regular gym-goer, and former center for the national police rugby team, Hill had been looking for a way to turn his passion for fitness into a career. Two years ago, he'd finally found it.

Hill wanted to create a national chain of gyms, but he also knew that 80 percent of independent gyms failed in their first five years of business. Hill didn't intend to become one of those failures.

Instead, he would buy those that did fold, streamline them, and so grow his own chain of twenty-four-hour, low-cost fitness centers.

All he needed was money.

He had scrimped and saved what he could, but living in central London sapped even a detective inspector's fifty thousand a year. Deb had insisted on the finest ring and wedding, and soon she'd want a family. Both in their mid-thirties, that day would have to come sooner rather than later, and with it the bills. Always the bloody bills.

So Hill had snatched at the opportunity for voluntary redundancy that the police budget cuts had mandated, and the package would almost give him enough money to buy the first of the failing gyms. It was a small step in what he saw as the beginning of an empire. Having studied the markets and gone over the figures until he saw them in his sleep, Hill was now desperate for the day of his redundancy and the beginning of his new life.

Until then, he was bored. Frustrated and bored. So he went in search of something to occupy him.

He found it in the form of Detective Inspector David Morgan. The Welshman was a drinking partner of Hill's after a long day or a trying case.

"You look like someone pissed in your tea, Mo," Hill greeted his friend. "What's up?"

Morgan was pulling his winter coat over his thick shoulders.

"Got a right stinker of a job, mate. Just about to call it a day for the weekend, and they shaft me with a bloody robbery in Hatton Garden." Morgan sniffed, gesturing at the notes on his desk.

"Diamonds?" Hill asked with interest.

"Take a look."

Hill picked up the notes, flicking quickly through.

"So this wasn't called in by a jeweler's, and none of them have reported anything stolen?" Hill assessed, eyes narrowing.

"That's right. The robbery was a snatch and grab on the street. Except it was more like a Royal bloody Rumble than a snatch and grab, by the sounds of it. The witnesses' details are in there."

"Who the hell does a street robbery in Hatton Garden?" Hill posed, puzzled. The high-end area was awash with CCTV. "And the uniforms didn't get there until everyone had vanished?"

"Exactly. Hence why I'll be in all bloody weekend. This one's got organized crime written all over it. It should be the NCA's case, but they won't touch it unless there's something tangible. So it looks like I won't get to watch Wales smash the French."

"You go, mate. I'll take the job," Hill said, shocking the Welshman.

"Bollocks, man, it's your last week."

"It'll be my last week on the planet if I don't find something to keep me busy. And this has got something to it, I can tell."

Morgan was unconvinced, so Hill came clean.

"You know what the last case I closed was, don't you?" he asked his friend.

Morgan knew. Everyone knew. It was one of those stories that circulated around the station like wildfire.

A young woman had been murdered. Hill had been close with the grieving family for weeks, and then had discovered that the blood was on the victim's husband's hands. Before the man could be brought into custody, he'd taken his own life. The reason was money—two lives cut short by bankruptcy.

"I don't want to look back on this job and re-member that as my last case," Hill told him with honesty.

Trying to lighten the mood, Hill put out his hand.

"And twenty quid says I'll have it wrapped up by the time you get back from watching the French kick your Welsh asses."

"I suppose I could just sign it back from you

next week," Morgan conceded. "And you can keep your twenty quid when you lose. Rugby's priceless."

"Right then. You clear it with the guv and I'll get on my way to Hatton Garden."

"Don't be shopping for Deb while you're on the clock, mind," the Welshman laughed.

"Bit out of my price range," Hill replied, smiling to himself.

CHAPTER 4

AS THE TUBE RATTLED into King's Cross Underground station, Scowcroft raised his gaze from the carriage floor and met the eyes of Barrett amongst the other passengers.

This was their fourth and final station on the Underground, the multiple legs taken as a way to lose tails. As part of their escape, the trio had changed clothing in an alleyway with garments pulled from their backpacks. There, Charlotte had done what she could to clean up Barrett's battered face, but baby wipes and a baseball cap did little to hide the destruction of his nose.

"It's the London Underground," Barrett had comforted his accomplices. "No one points fingers or talks to strangers. I'll be fine."

Hoping that he was right, they had boarded the westbound train from Chancery Lane to Bond Street. There they'd changed trains and lines for Waterloo, doing the same again to Leicester

Square and then taking the Piccadilly line to King's Cross. Having emerged from the Underground, the thieves once again changed clothing in the mainline train station's public toilets. In the privacy of the stalls, secondary bags were pulled from within the original backpacks, which were then stuffed inside their replacements. Barrett had suggested that precaution, knowing that disposing of a bag in a train station was likely to raise an alarm in a city wary of terrorism.

Scowcroft stepped out onto the concourse and scanned the faces of those who stood waiting for their trains. He saw nothing that raised his hackles. He looked over his shoulder, seeing Charlotte and Barrett in position behind him. He wasn't worried if they should lose him in the crowd—they both knew the rendezvous point.

He kept his head down, fitting in amongst dozens of commuters and tourists and looking at the phone in his hand. The screen was locked, but it was the perfect excuse to keep his face from the cameras. Behind him, Charlotte and Barrett did the same.

Scowcroft took an escalator up to the champagne bar. He waited there patiently until his two accomplices appeared on his shoulder. The trio was now complete, and aside from Barrett's nose, they resembled respectable tourists.

"I've got a reservation," Scowcroft told the young hostess, who smiled at the handsome man in front of her as he gave a false name. "Ashcroft. Sorry I'm a bit late."

"That's no problem, Mr. Ashcroft," the hostess told him, pushing her hair back from her face. "If you'd like to follow, I'll show you to your table."

"Thank you," he replied, wishing for a moment that he truly was an innocent tourist. His fantasy was cut short as he caught sight of the shock on the young woman's face when she took in Barrett's shattered nose.

"He's a cage fighter," Scowcroft shot in quickly. "We both are, except I'm a lot quicker than him."

"Not too quick, I hope," the hostess replied with a smile and swiftly left.

The table was at the English end of the champagne bar, and offered excellent views over the station below—if there was trouble, the thieves would see it coming. They all knew the location of the fire escapes, and their emergency rendezvous at St Pancras Gardens, but this was doing little to calm their fraying nerves as the adrenaline of that morning was being replaced by a bone-crushing weariness.

"Be nice if we could remember why we're here,

instead of you trying to shag anything with a pulse," Charlotte scolded Scowcroft as they took their seats.

"I know why I'm here," he shot back, his mood shifting from arousal to anger in a split second. "I'm here because Tony's my brother. I wasn't the one who tried to run out on him when he came back like he did."

Charlotte's first retort died as an angry choke on her lips. The second was stalled by Barrett's intervention.

"Easy now, Alex. We're all here because we love Tony. Doesn't matter if it's by blood, marriage, or mates. We're all here for him."

"I'm not having her talk to me like that," the young man grumbled, showing the immaturity behind his confident facade. "You're not my family," he told her, the words quiet but resonating.

"I'm *his* family," Charlotte hissed. "I'm his family, in a way you can't even imagine."

"We'll see about that when he gets the full story," Scowcroft told her. "We'll see who's family when my brother wakes up."

CHAPTER 5

HILL STEPPED OUT OF the unmarked police BMW and looked at his shoes.

"Good start." He smiled, his toecap poking into a patch of congealed blood. "Now, where's the rest of it?" he mused, looking about him.

His eyes were drawn to the deep scratches in the pavement and scraps of rubber in the road, but there was no sign of how either had come about. Save for the patch of blood, there was nothing to indicate that a crime had taken place here only two hours ago.

Hill looked at the case notes Morgan had given him: a uniformed officer had arrived on the scene seventeen minutes after the call from a witness, but the report made no mention of any suspects or vehicles. The officer had initially written off the call-out as a hoax, but a second eyewitness came forward and corroborated the story of a street fight, seemingly over a bag. Hill searched the notes again, hoping he'd somehow missed the photos that the first responding officer should have taken. Finding none, Hill cursed the ineptitude of the constable.

Something had happened here, Hill was sure. But what?

He walked slowly to the address of the second eyewitness, scanning the pavement as he went. Besides some burned rubber, there was nothing to draw his attention.

Hill pushed open a door and entered a glass-fronted coffee shop. The lunchtime rush was in full effect, and several queuing customers protested loudly as Hill eased his way to the front.

"Police," he told the groaning line over his shoulder.

"Can I help you?" the shop's manager asked.

"Looking for Emma Pell," Hill told her.

"She's one of my baristas," the manager replied, pointing a finger towards a young woman who was frantically handing out fanciful concoctions of caffeine. "You can't talk to her now. Look how busy we are."

Hill smiled and pretended to care. "Yeah, but you see, this badge says that I can."

"Ass," the manager muttered beneath her breath.

Hill joined the patrons waiting at the end of the long counter for their coffees.

"Emma," he gently called to the barista.

"I don't have an order for Emma," she replied without looking up.

"No, Emma, I'm Detective Inspector Hill. I've come to speak with you about what you saw today."

"Oh!"

The girl looked to her manager for permission. The woman gave her assent with an angry nod, her eyes staring daggers at Hill.

"Take me to where you saw it happen," Hill said, and Emma took him back out through the coffee shop's front door.

"It was down there," she told him, pointing in the direction of Hill's BMW and the congealed patch of blood.

"And you were here when you saw it?"

"Yeah, I was just coming in for my shift and I heard the bikes, so I stayed to watch."

"Bikes?"

"Motorbikes. They were riding down the pavement, heading straight at this group of people, and then it just turned into a massive fight."

"How many people?" Hill pressed gently, taking notes.

"Three or four, and the two bikers. I thought

it was some kind of TV thing at first, but then I didn't see any cameras so I guessed it was real. Was it?"

Hill resisted the temptation to tap the young woman's skull to see if it was hollow.

"It was real. Did you call the police?"

"I didn't," the girl admitted, shifting her weight on her heels.

"That's OK," Hill told her. "Were you worried they might come after you if you did?"

"Nah, it's not that," she said, laughing. "I was using my phone to film it. Then I put it on Insta and Snap. I was gonna call the police when I'd finished, but by then you guys were already here so I just popped across to tell them what I saw."

"And you gave them the video?" Hill asked, incredulous that this evidence hadn't been included in the case file.

"No," the girl told him, her cheeks turning ruddy. "I forgot."

"But you remembered to put it on all of your social media?" Hill laughed, thinking about how much he was actually going to miss his job. "You have it saved on your phone?"

The girl blushed a further red and shook her head. "Deleted it. I don't have the space."

"Don't worry about it, Emma," Hill smiled. "What's your Instagram account?"

CHAPTER 6

SCOWCROFT PUSHED OPEN THE door to the champagne bar's bathroom. A sideways look in the mirrors confirmed that he had entered alone, his only company a rotund businessman wheezing at the urinal. Scowcroft dismissed him quickly as no threat and stepped into the stall.

The stall door stretched from floor to ceiling and fitted snugly. Scowcroft had the privacy he needed.

He opened the bag and pulled the crushed leather duffel bag from its depths. The bag's zippers were padlocked, so Scowcroft used his brother's commando dagger to cut through the leather. The blade had no struggle in cutting open the bag, spilling its bubble-wrapped contents onto the floor: a dozen golf-ball-sized packages.

He reached for the closest. A flick of the dagger was enough to cut the tape and open the wrapping like a flower. Seeing what was in his hand,

Scowcroft's heart beat faster. He took hold of the next bundle and opened that, then the next, then the next, his heart beating faster all the time. Finally, he looked down at what was in his hands.

A dozen diamonds, and none below six carats. In the bathroom stall, Scowcroft held three million pounds' worth of precious stones.

But it was more than that.

Alex Scowcroft held his brother's life in his hands, and knowing that made him feel more powerful and more terrified than he ever had in his entire life.

For a fleeting second, an image pushed its way into the young man's mind of what could be. A life in the sun. Beach houses. Yachts. A never-ending supply of women of every shape and color.

Scowcroft rejected the image. Better the family's terraced house with his brother than all of the superyachts and women in the world.

He placed the diamonds in a small leather pouch that was suspended from a chain that held two metal discs: his brother's dog tags. Then he wound duct tape about his chest to hold the small pouch securely in position. It created a visible lump under his T-shirt, but nothing that would be noticed beneath his winter jacket. Scowcroft took deep breaths to ensure that the tape would not restrict his breathing—he knew that they were not out of danger yet.

Finally, the diamond thief performed a solemn task.

His brother's commando dagger could not follow him on the final leg. Carrying such a weapon would draw unwanted attention from customs. So, after wiping it down thoroughly, Scowcroft reluctantly placed it into the walled cavity of the toilet's plumbing, vowing that he would return for the blade his brother had endured hell to earn.

Remembering to flush the toilet so as to avoid suspicion, Scowcroft left the bathroom and rejoined the others.

"I ditched his dagger," he told them with sorrow.

"Never mind a bloody knife," Charlotte replied, earning herself a scowl. "What about the diamonds?"

"On my chest."

"We're supposed to split them up," she stated, trying to master her temper.

"They're on my chest," Scowcroft said again, challenging her to struggle for them in the busy bar and doom their mission. "I'll split them when we're closer to the target," he pressed on. "Our train's in forty minutes. We should go and clear passport control."

"We've been talking about that, Alex," Barrett interjected with calm. "Something's really been bothering me, mate. I think we should let this train go and wait for the next one."

"Why would we wait?" Scowcroft asked with a frown.

"The absence of the normal," Barrett told him, then explained. "Before me and Tony went to Iraq, they used to tell us to watch for the absence of the normal and the presence of the abnormal. In other words, you see something out of the ordinary, it probably means that bad stuff's gonna happen. And if you don't see something you should, that also means bad stuff's gonna happen."

"What's that got to do with us, Baz? We're not in Iraq."

"What was missing this morning, Alex?" Barrett posed.

"Police," Scowcroft answered.

"Robbery and a street fight on Hatton Garden, and no police? I don't know why that is, mate, but it's definitely not normal."

"And it's more than that," Charlotte added. "Those bikers were after the exact same thing we were."

"Coincidence," Scowcroft shrugged.

"Maybe," she conceded. "But then you look at

the police not showing up, and it doesn't feel right."

"It doesn't," Barrett agreed. "My gut tells me something is wrong here, Alex. I've had my eye on the news since we got here. Nothing. No stories. No coppers. There's another train in an hour and a half—let's just get that. We've come too far to half-ass this now."

It wasn't in a Scowcroft's blood to sit and wait, and the youngest of the trio balked at the thought. He may be outvoted, but he was the one with the diamonds.

Scowcroft wanted to leave now. He wanted to charge. He wanted to see this through and restore his brother's life not one minute later than he could. But he also knew that Barrett, a best friend to Tony since they were boy soldiers of seventeen, was the reason that his brother had been able to come home at all. Barrett's training and instincts had rescued Tony that day. Scowcroft hoped that those instincts would not fail them now.

"We wait an hour and a half," he told them. "And then we go to Amsterdam."

CHAPTER 7

HILL CONSIDERED SOCIAL MEDIA to be an essential part of any business, particularly in the fitness industry in which he was determined to thrive, so he was an active user of all platforms and earned a look of admiration from Emma as she received a follow request from Hill's Instagram account.

"You've got eleven thousand followers!" the barista said in awe. "And amazing abs," she cooed, scrolling through his pictures.

"Thanks, but let's concentrate on your video."

They did, and what the detective saw astounded him—two motorbikes charging down a group of three pedestrians, who somehow turned the tables on their assailants and overpowered them. For reasons unclear in the video, the trio then bolted by foot, rather than using the van that Hill assumed was theirs.

"The tires," Hill said aloud, thinking of the

scraps of rubber beside the blood. "Someone slashed the tires."

Thanking Emma for her time, Hill took a moment to stand alone outside the coffee shop, his eyes working the length of Hatton Garden.

Two bikes, two riders, and a van, all vanished. How? How was it possible to clear that carnage before the uniforms had arrived on the scene? Neither Emma nor her video had been able to shed light on how or when the area had been cleared. She had been inside the coffee shop, busily uploading the video online.

Hoping the witness who'd called it in could help solve the puzzle, Hill walked along the pavement and found her in a jeweler's named Heavenly Diamonds.

"Mrs. Underwood?" Hill asked a tall, nervous-looking woman in her sixties as the reinforced door closed heavily behind him.

"I am," she replied, and seemed to brace herself as Hill held out his police identification.

"I believe you reported a crime, Mrs. Underwood."

"So what if she did?" a man's voice challenged from the back of the jeweler's.

Hill turned his head and caught sight of a gray-haired man he presumed to be her husband.

"Mr. Underwood?" Hill asked.

"So what if she reported a crime?" the man asked again, ignoring Hill's question and taking a stand behind the thick glass counter. "A fat lot of good it does."

"What do you mean?" Hill posed, earning a contemptuous tut in reply.

"I mean, someone tries to do the right thing, and where does it get them? Don't bother to answer, and don't bother to ask any more questions either. My wife did her bit. How about you do yours?"

"I'm trying, Mr. Underwood, but it would make my job a lot easier if I could talk with your wife."

"No," Mrs. Underwood answered for herself.

"Well, OK then," Hill conceded, knowing a brick wall when he saw one. "I'm sorry to have taken up your time."

He made for the door, but Mr. Underwood wasn't done.

"You want to talk to someone about what happened, talk to that bastard across the street."

Hill paused at the open door. "And which bastard would that be, Mr. Underwood?"

"Him," the man spat, pointing a finger towards the opposite side of Hatton Garden. "The owner of that sham."

Hill followed the angry stare and read the

jeweler's name above the tinted windows: Swiss Excellence.

An alarm bell rang in Hill's mind. A trip wire to a case five years ago, where a jeweler had loudly reported extortion and harassment, before finding himself facedown in the Thames.

Hill turned back to the shop's owner, his tone lowered. "You don't need to tell me anything, Mr. Underwood. I believe I understand the predicament you're in. It would help me, however, if you could nod in the right places."

After a few moments of thought, the man agreed with a look. He then unlocked the counter, placing several rings atop the glass. Hill played along with the ruse, pretending to inspect the jewelry.

"Swiss Excellence. That's now owned by Marcus Slate, isn't it?"

The older man nodded, though a tremor of fear made it seem more like a twitch.

"He bought it after the previous owner died?"

"Was bloody killed," Underwood mumbled beneath his breath as he nodded, confirming the story that Hill had recalled.

"The fight today. It seemed to be over a bag. Did it come from that jeweler's?"

Another nod.

"I assume you have CCTV here. I don't have to take anything away with me, but could I watch it?"

This time the jeweler shook his head. "You're not the first visitor we've had today, Inspector. All our hard drives have been taken." His wife seemed to shrink at the memory.

"Someone came here before the police?" Hill asked, provoking a bitter laugh from the man.

"Before them?" Underwood spat.

Hill could see that the man knew he shouldn't talk, and was struggling to contain his words, but resentment drove them from his mouth.

"Let me rephrase that for you, Detective Inspector Hill. You're not the first *police* visitor we've had today."

CHAPTER 8

HILL WAS SHOCKED BY the accusation. In truth, he refused to believe it.

But then he visited the other jewelers whose CCTV may have covered the incident on the doorstep of Swiss Excellence. No one would talk. No one had footage that they'd hand over. In more than one instance, Hill saw a tremor of fear in the face of the shop owner as he announced himself as a police officer.

Finally, it was time for Hill to visit Swiss Excellence itself.

"How can I help you, sir?" a gentleman in a pinstriped suit welcomed him, putting forward a manicured hand in greeting.

Hill took it, enjoying the man's discomfort as he held his tongue.

"Sir?" the man finally managed, and Hill let go of the hand with a smile.

"Detective Inspector," Hill stated. "There was an incident outside here today, Mr. . . . ?"

"Winston, Detective. There was? What kind of incident?" the man stammered, badly feigning shock.

"The kind that people like to cover up, it seems." Hill smiled, catching Winston off guard with his directness. "Why didn't you report the stolen diamonds?"

"What diamonds?" Winston protested, taking an involuntary step backwards.

"You were here this morning," Hill asserted, closing on the man but still flashing brilliantly white teeth. "We have your voice on the call," he bluffed. "Your call to Marcus Slate. You were telling *him* what had happened instead of the police."

Hill had interviewed enough liars to read their eyes, and Winston's screamed that Hill had hit a hole-in-one.

"Listen, Winston, I'm not interested in who you tip off, or who you're laundering for. What I want to know is, who cleaned up that mess outside your window?"

Winston held his tongue. Then, as Hill inched his face closer, Winston saw something in the detective's eyes—it was the same single-minded drive that shone in the face of Marcus Slate, and Winston knew there was no option but to confess to this man.

And so he told Hill what he wanted to know.

CHAPTER 9

WITH TWENTY MINUTES UNTIL the Eurostar's departure, it was time for the trio of diamond thieves to make their move.

"There's been nothing on the news," Scowcroft confronted his accomplices. "We got away with it, all right? Let's just get the train and meet Baz's buyer. I don't get what's wrong with you," he pressed. "Tony's relying on us. He's waiting on us."

"Which is exactly why I don't want to mess this up, Alex," Charlotte retorted. "We went over every single possible scenario we could think of for this, but did we ever plan that there'd be a no-show from the police? We didn't. *That's* how strange it is. Something's going on here."

"You're just nervous."

"I'm cautious."

"Well, what do you think, Baz?" Scowcroft pressed the gaunt-faced veteran.

It was a long time before he replied.

"Something that we don't know about is going on behind the scenes, but the fact is, we can't stay here forever. I say we get the train and make for Amsterdam."

"You see?" Scowcroft laughed, his bitter eyes on Charlotte.

"Hang on, Alex. I wasn't quite finished, mate," Barrett told him gently. "I think we should get the train, but divide the stones and split up. We can meet up again in Amsterdam, but at least this way, if something does happen, one of us should get through."

"One of us is enough for Tony," Charlotte agreed. "We should go different ways. One on the train, one on the ferry, and one flying."

"Are you off your head?" Scowcroft yelled.

"Keep your voice down, mate," Barrett warned the young man, seeing heads turn in their direction.

Scowcroft did lower the volume, but his tone was as harsh as ever as he laid into his brother's fiancée. "You ran out on Tony with nothing," he hissed. "You think I trust you to stay when you've got a million quids' worth of diamonds in your pocket?"

Charlotte stood quickly and raised her right fist to bring it crashing into the side of the petulant boy's skull, but Barrett caught her wrist.

"Everyone calm down," he urged. "People are looking. Do you want to bollocks this up now?"

"Of course I don't," Charlotte replied with heat.

"Alex?" Barrett asked, but was ignored. "Alex?" he asked again.

But Scowcroft's attention had left the group, and the argument. Instead, his gaze was fixed on the escalators that carried patrons to the champagne bar.

And there, wearing a fresh suit and with his arm in a sling, was the big man that Scowcroft had stabbed only hours before.

Barrett and Charlotte followed the young man's gaze.

"Staircase," Scowcroft told them. "We all get the train, and we get it now."

This time there were no arguments.

CHAPTER 10

IT TOOK HILL ONLY two minutes to drive to Snow Hill police station, the location from where Police Constable Amy Roberts had responded to the call of the Hatton Garden incident.

"Why only her?" Hill pressed the stoat-faced desk sergeant.

"Wasn't a crime in progress, and we're on a tight budget. Big area to cover and not enough coppers. She was just there to take reports."

"And where did she respond from?"

"Here, on foot. Budget," the desk sergeant explained again.

"She arrived seventeen minutes after the witness called," Hill said, his voice hard. "It's a five-minute walk."

The sergeant merely shrugged.

"Where can I find her now?" Hill asked, tiring of the silence.

"I can call her in."

Hill shook his head.

"She's on her patrol route around the Stock Exchange area. You'll recognize her easy enough. Tall and blonde. Wasted in this uniform, to be honest. Sooner she gets a plainclothes gig the better."

Hill didn't bother to reply and left the station on foot.

The London Stock Exchange was close, and as Hill walked down Newgate Street he caught glimpses of the magnificent dome of St Paul's Cathedral between the buildings. Hill had been born and raised in the city, and the image of that cathedral standing tall amongst the fires of the Blitz had always provoked an intense pride within him. Now that his own grandparents were gone, it was almost as if the iconic architecture of the old city had taken their place as the guardians of Hill's heritage.

"Bugger it," Hill thought aloud and took a side street towards the cathedral. He knew that starting a business would consume his time for months, perhaps years to come. When would he get the chance to sit and stare in awe at the striking lines and the subtle beauty of a place like St Paul's?

The case could wait twenty minutes.

Hill entered through Paternoster Square, taking

his time to admire the space that so brilliantly trapped the autumn sun. Passing through a narrow archway, and squeezing by a group of eager Chinese tourists, Hill came out at the rear of the cathedral.

There was a cafe to his left and Hill took a seat, ordering coffee and a chicken sandwich. Then he pulled his earbuds from his pocket, connected them to his phone, and opened an app that had become part of his daily ritual.

After years of training his body for optimal performance, Hill had finally been convinced by Deb of the need to train his mind. The app centered on a form of meditation known as mindfulness, the calm voice guiding Hill through his breathing exercises and helping him to put order into the scattered thoughts that bounced around inside his mind. In central London, a man with his eyes closed was not enough to draw attention or comment, and when Hill finished the seven-minute session, feeling revitalized and energized, a coffee and a sandwich sat in front of him.

But before he had reached for either he saw her.

PC Amy Roberts was on the opposite side of the square, giving directions to a pair of grinning backpackers. Thanking his luck that he wouldn't have to pace the area endlessly to find her, Hill picked up his lunch and walked towards the police constable.

As he drew near, and the backpackers went on their way, Hill saw that the desk sergeant had been right: Hill was six-two, and Roberts was easily his match. She was also strikingly beautiful.

"No wonder they all come to you for directions," Hill smiled, then took a deep bite of his sandwich.

"Excuse me?" PC Roberts asked, her beautiful face drawing into the haughty mask that she used to drive away unwanted male attention.

"Don't worry about it," Hill replied through a mouthful of bread and chicken.

"Can I help you, sir?" Roberts asked, forcing herself to add the title.

"Actually, you can," Hill said, swallowing the mouthful. "You can tell me how much they paid you to cover up the Hatton Garden robbery."

Roberts froze, but her eyes widened in alarm.

"Are you a reporter?" she finally managed.

"Afraid not, Amy. I'm from Scotland Yard." Hill dropped the words as casually as he tossed a corner of his sandwich to the pigeons. "But I'm not with internal," he added.

"Who the hell are you, then?" the constable asked, regaining some of her composure and fire.

"Well, that depends on what you tell me. I can be the guy who ends your career, and sees you do a nice stretch inside, or I can be the guy who conveniently forgets to include certain things in his report, and nobody cares because the case will be solved, and someone else will be going to prison. How's the second option sound to you?"

"Like I have a bloody choice. The same as I didn't have a choice this morning."

"Go on."

"Look at me. I can't blend in. I can't hide. They know where I am, and they know we patrol alone now since the cuts. Why do you think I'm standing in the middle of this sodding square giving directions?"

"Because you're scared," Hill answered with empathy.

"Because I'm fucking terrified," she hissed, her eyes backing up her words. "They stopped me on my way there. Told me what I had to do."

"And that was?"

"Turn a blind eye while they cleared the scene. There was no one there, just two bikes on the pavement and a van with slashed tires. I had to wait for the tow trucks to come, and then they sent me to gather the CCTV."

"Where's that now?"

"In the Thames, I'd imagine. One of them came

with me, pretended to be a plainclothes officer, but I could see that the owners of the stores knew better. There's a racket going on there, and they all know about it."

"Marcus Slate?"

She shrugged. "Maybe. There's been a big guy parading up Hatton Garden every morning. Catches a taxi from the end of the street. I saw him on my rounds a couple of times. I thought he looked out of place, a right thug in a nice suit, but then when I saw him come out of the shop that Slate owns, it made more sense."

"What are they running out of there?"

"Diamonds, and I'm not going to die because two gangs were fighting over them."

"How do you know it was diamonds?"

"It's Hatton Garden—what else can it be?"

"OK. Look, I understand why you did what you did. I know it's not black and white on the streets."

Hill watched as Roberts balled her hands into angry fists, no doubt wishing she could take revenge on the men who'd threatened her and forced her to turn her back on the job and service that she no doubt loved.

"I feel like a piece of shit for it," she said with anger. "But these guys are serious, and I did what I had to do."

Hill had nothing to say and simply handed her his card.

"I really hope you figure it all out," Roberts told him, and Hill could feel her sincerity. "But figure it out quickly, because someone's going to die for those diamonds."

CHAPTER 11

SCOWCROFT PULLED A WEDGE of twenty-pound notes from his pocket and waved them at the waiter to catch his attention, before dumping them on the table—the last thing the thieves needed was to be chased by the bar's security for running out without paying their bill.

"Follow me," he told the others, and took them to the stairwell at the opposite end of the bar from the escalators, where the gorilla of a courier was now scanning the tables.

"How did he know where to find us?" Charlotte asked as they pushed through a fire escape. There was no alarm on the door, and the stairs led down into the main station.

"Not a question for now," Barrett told her, his nose throbbing in agony as they bounced down the steps.

"There's the train," Scowcroft told them as they reached the ground floor. "Platform two. Don't split up too far, but don't walk in a bunch."

The trio moved across the bustling concourse, Scowcroft resisting the urge to shoot a glance up at the champagne bar terrace. To keep his eyes rooted downwards, he pulled his phone from his pocket and pretended to type a text message.

"I don't see anyone else," Barrett whispered as the men were pushed closer together through a turnstile and headed towards the passport checks of the French police. "And they only saw *my* face. If it comes to it, I'll bolt and draw them away."

"Bollocks to that," Scowcroft hissed. "They weren't the cops, Baz. If they get any of us we're done. No suicide missions."

"If they see me, I'm running," Barrett insisted.

"Fine, but me and Charlotte will run with you. That what you want?"

The thieves showed their passports to the French police officers and moved swiftly through to the platform, where they waited to board. Scowcroft was frustrated at being forced to stand in the open, but the press of other travelers about him gave him some measure of comfort. Reversing the camera on his phone, Scowcroft used it as a mirror to look over his shoulders. The action drew no attention from the other tourists, many of whom were taking selfies as they documented their travels, and Scowcroft saw no sign of the courier.

But he did see something else.

Twenty yards behind Scowcroft was a muscular, thickly bearded man in his thirties. He carried no baggage and appeared to be alone.

Perhaps these indicators alone Scowcroft could ignore. But why was the man looking up at the champagne bar?

"Baz. The stacked bearded guy behind us. I reckon he's with them. Where's Charlotte?" Scowcroft hissed, seeing no sign of her.

"She boarded," Barrett explained. "Next carriage."

"Bollocks. We need to stick close."

"Get into this one. We'll join her through the carriages."

Scowcroft nodded, and the pair climbed aboard the Eurostar, Barrett pausing to help an elderly lady lift her baggage onto the rack.

"Thank you, dear," she smiled. "Oh! But what happened to your nose, you poor thing?"

"Bike accident, love," Barrett grinned through missing teeth. He turned to Scowcroft. "I didn't see the beard get on."

"Must be waiting for his mate in the champagne bar. Where the hell's Charlotte?"

"Over here, boys," the two men heard, finally spotting their female accomplice amongst a horde of lager-swigging men.

"This is Graham," Charlotte explained, pointing to a slightly overweight man in his late thirties.

"Pleasure to meet you, lads," Graham slurred, before remembering that he was dressed solely in a leopard-skin bikini. "It's my stag party," he added by way of explanation.

"Graham's been kind enough to invite us to join them for drinks," Charlotte explained, having found an excellent way to disguise her and the other two for their journey.

"Yeah! Come get pissed with us, boys!"

Warm cans of lager were shoved into Scowcroft's and Barrett's hands, the men recognizing quickly that there was safety and camouflage in numbers.

They pushed themselves into the throng of revelers.

"You got your dagger?" Scowcroft whispered.

"Dumped it with yours," Barrett told him. "There's glass bottles on that table if it comes to it."

Scowcroft nodded. As a nineteen-year-old he had suffered a wound from a bottle himself and had the scars to remember it by.

"All right, then." Scowcroft forced a smile, knowing their backs were against the wall. "Cheers!"

CHAPTER 12

FROM BEHIND THE WHEEL of his unmarked BMW, Hill hit speed dial, making his second call in as many minutes. This one was to his superior, Chief Inspector Vaughn. The first had been to the offices of Marcus Slate.

"You can't just go turning up at Marcus Slate's place, you idiot," his boss told him on the phone, Hill picturing how Vaughn's freckled face would be pressed into his hairy hands.

"That's why I called ahead, boss."

"You know what I mean, you ass. You've already got your redundancy. Why the hell are you pushing for disability on top of it?"

"So there are people above the law now, Chief Inspector? Is that what you're telling me?" Hill poked with levity.

"You know damn well that's not what I mean, but Slate has political clout as well as business. You rub him up the wrong way, Hill, and you can forget about ever opening a business in this city."

"That thought had occurred to me," Hill told him with honesty. "But here's the thing, boss. I'm actually a big fan of Slate's. As far as British entrepreneurs go, he's up there with Branson."

"You know damn well that Slate's not clean."

"Ouch. I hope that wasn't deliberate, boss. And I'm not stupid, but I do want to meet the guy."

"You're lucky it's your last week," Vaughn told him, though there was no malice behind the threat. Like every superior officer Hill had served under since joining the force, Vaughn had nothing but good words to say about him.

"I know, boss, I know," Hill placated. "Now something's occurred to me about this robbery. Three of them bolted from the scene on foot. Can we pull footage from the local Tube and train stations? Say a half-hour window?"

"Yeah, I'll get the tech guys on it."

"Cheers."

"And you're sure this visit is just to blow smoke up Slate's backside?" Vaughn asked finally.

"Nothing but smoke," Hill assured him.

"Well, I'll see you back at the office, then."

"See you at the office, babe," Hill replied, and cut off the call before Vaughn could berate him.

Ten minutes later, Hill pulled up outside the

Chelsea property that served as the offices for Slate's business empire. The building was high-end but subtle. Like the man who owned it, the property hinted at money and power, but the secrets of its wealth were kept within. Slate was not an entrepreneur who was about to launch a podcast, hold seminars, or write a memoir.

Hill had heard the rumors, but his admiration for good business had led him to study Slate's path to riches closely enough to separate the facts from the fiction. As he stepped out of the car, he prepared for the meeting by running through what he knew of Slate.

Growing up in London, Slate was the son of an East End mechanic. The story went that at fourteen Slate junior had dropped out of school and helped transform his father's failing business from a repair shop to a spare parts supplier. Within a year the business had been profitable. Within five, Slate had opened a further three sites across London. Within ten, he'd owned twelve nationally.

And then the internet had become a part of everyday life, revolutionizing the way people shopped. Twenty-four-year-old Slate had seen the future, and had been one of the first to offer spare car parts online. He'd bought out the competition, and three years later he'd made the

Forbes list as one of Britain's wealthiest young men.

The story was inspirational: a young boy who rescued the family business and, with the vision few people possess, saw the way his industry would evolve in the future.

But that was only half the truth.

Slate had not dropped out of school—he had been expelled for repeatedly assaulting his fellow pupils and teachers. In the ten years before he'd opened his internet stores and marketplaces, Slate had seen the inside of a courtroom on several charges. His final appearance, for grievous bodily harm, had earned Slate six months in prison. Ironically, it had been there that he learned of the emerging possibilities of the internet, taking all the IT courses available through the prison reform programs.

As Hill stepped into the plush lobby of the mogul's office, he smiled at the thought that the taxpayer had given Slate the education and time to exploit such a gap in the market.

"Detective Hill," he told the three beauties behind the desk. "How many of you does it take to answer the phone?" he couldn't help but add, earning a smile from two and a look of contempt from the third.

"Mr. Slate is expecting you. Please follow me,"

the sour-faced secretary told him, her tone as sharp as her eyes.

They came to a pair of thick mahogany doors. Along the corridor, Hill saw two men sitting behind a desk that was home to only mugs of tea and a television. The muscular men gave him a dismissive look and turned back to their talk show.

"That the concierge, is it?" Hill asked the secretary.

She ignored the jest and knocked at the door.

"He's a very busy man, Detective, so please keep it short."

"But of course." Hill smiled, thick-skinned from years on the force. Compared to being spat at and beaten as a uniformed bobby, a few narrowed eyes and dismissive glances were no sweat.

Hill stepped into Slate's office, and the door clicked shut behind him. In the next instant, adrenaline and panic coursed through his body.

Because the room was empty.

CHAPTER 13

NOT A DESK. Not a chair. Not a single family photo. Save for the plastic sheeting on the floor, the room was completely empty.

Hill spun on his heel, grabbing for the door handle.

It turned. It opened.

And Hill found himself staring into the face of Marcus Slate, who had something in his hand.

Tea.

"Hold the door then, mate. Sorry, Detective Inspector," Slate corrected himself with a smile. Hill obliged after a pause to reset the chemical actions of his fight-or-flight defense.

"Sorry about the room," Slate said. "I'm a private person, Detective, and I can be a pretty messy one, so I don't like having people from outside of the business in my office where I have all kinds of documents lying about. I've just had this room redecorated, but we're still waiting on the furniture. Still, I'm glad to be on my feet and away from the desk for a change, if I'm honest with you. Here you go." Slate handed Hill a mug.

"Thanks."

"Soy milk and no sugar, right?" Slate smiled, and Hill's mouth dropped.

"Watching my figure," Hill replied, hoping he didn't appear rattled.

"Yeah, I saw your Instagram. You're something of a fitness fanatic." Slate's white teeth flashed like a wolf's. "And you follow some interesting people, Detective."

Hill tried to feign calm by sipping at the tea, but it did little to melt the ball of ice that was formed in his stomach.

"Some young lady on there. @emslondon, I think her username was. She had some really fascinating videos."

"She did? Tea's great, by the way."

"Isn't it? Sri Lankan. And yeah, she did. I'd show you, but looks like she deleted the account, which is a shame."

Hill cursed himself for leaving a trail to Emma, his coffee-shop witness, then remembered that she had already been compromised by the actions of PC Roberts.

If Slate wanted to play the game, then Hill would oblige.

"People spend too much time on social media," he told Slate. "People don't talk anymore, and that can be a problem. Lucky for me, I think of myself as a problem-solver."

"Do you, now?" Slate asked, feigning a smile.

"I used to love doing jigsaws as a kid, Mr. Slate. My older brother liked to upset me by hiding the pieces around the house, but I'd hunt them down, one by one. When I got bigger, I stopped having to look for them."

"Grew out of playing puzzles, did you?"

"No, Mr. Slate, but instead of looking for the pieces my brother was hiding, I'd just beat them out of him."

For a moment Slate had no retort. Behind the facade of calm, Hill knew the man's anger would be bubbling over. Police officer or not, he was walking a fine line.

"Diamonds, Mr. Slate. Your diamonds, stolen this morning."

"It's a crime to be a victim of crime, Detective?"

"No. But it's a piece of a puzzle. A large one. And when the pieces of this puzzle are put together, it's not going to be a steam train in the Scottish Highlands, Mr. Slate. It's going to be a long stretch inside."

Hill looked into Slate's eyes. There was danger in them, a lot of danger, but Hill had faced intimidation before and knew how to deal with it. Both men had made their threats with insinuation and subtlety, but now Hill sensed the moment to be direct.

"I'm going to expose your diamond heist," Hill told the man who could have him killed. "I'm going to expose you, Mr. Slate, and then you're going to prison for a long, long time."

CHAPTER 14

HILL SLUMPED INTO THE driver's seat of his BMW.

"Fuck." He exhaled heavily, his fingers tingling with adrenaline.

He sat there for a moment with the engine off, hands in his lap. He told himself the delay was to show Slate, who he was certain would be watching, the demeanor of an ice-cold detective. In truth, Hill didn't trust his shaking hands on the wheel. He had walked a very fine line, and he was lucky to still be in one piece.

In one piece for now, at least.

After a moment to catch his breath and steady his nerve, Hill pulled out of the automatic gate and into the Chelsea traffic.

Taking a few more deep breaths, and noting that the trembling was almost gone, he called his boss.

"How'd it go with your idol?" Vaughn asked.

"You know what they say about meeting your idols, boss."

"I wouldn't know. Mine are Brian O'Driscoll and Rory McIlroy. Can't say we move in the same circles."

"Slate set up his diamonds to be stolen," Hill stated, getting to the point. "They've been parading them outside the jeweler's he owns for weeks. One guy, one bag, no other security. The guy walks to the end of the street, gets a taxi, and comes back at the end of the day the same way."

"And where's he going between those times?"

"Slate tells me it's to show the diamonds to prospective buyers. I've got a list."

"And I'll bet a cross-check of them shows they're friends or associates of Mr. Slate."

"Exactly, boss."

"So what's in this sham for him?" Vaughn mused.

"I'm guessing at the moment, but I think it's insurance."

"Insurance? But what's the point in that if he loses the diamonds? He'd just be getting back the value of the stones he'd lost."

"Not if *he* stole them," Hill explained. "Slate stages the robbery, keeps the diamonds, sells them on the black market, and gets the three million they're insured for. As far as the insurers are concerned, Slate's courier and jeweler were following the same pattern that had been safe every other day, and then got unlucky. What Slate didn't see happening was another gang spotting an easy meal, and swooping in before his own guys could."

"Bloody hell," Vaughn sighed. "So who are this other lot, and where are they now?"

"I don't know, boss, but wherever they are, they're dead men walking."

After exchanging good-byes Hill hung up and began to type Scotland Yard into a traffic-beating app on his phone. He was about to hit Enter when an incoming call flashed onto the screen—Vaughn.

"Boss?" Hill asked, puzzled.

"St Pancras station," Vaughn told him, excitement in his voice. "The techies pulled three faces from Chancery Lane Tube station and the three flashed again on the facial recognition software. They're at St Pancras."

"Where are they going?" Hill asked, hitting a hard right turn.

"If they haven't left already, then there's one at the platform with a final destination of Amsterdam."

"Amsterdam?" Hill replied. "I can't think of a better place to offload the diamonds, can you?"

Vaughn couldn't. As with many of the city's vices, Amsterdam's thriving diamond trade had a reputation for turning a blind eye.

"Departure time?" Hill pushed.

"Forty minutes ago. Trouble in the Tunnel again. I've got uniforms on their way there now."

"Tell them to wait for me."

"You're on borrowed time, Hill."

"I want to close this case, boss. Email me the shots of their faces."

Hill hung up, then hit the blue lights and sirens that were concealed behind the BMW's grille.

He raced through central London's streets, his mind full of visions of how he could end his career in glory.

"Just stay where you are," he prayed, and hoped the thieves would listen. "Just stay where you are and make me a hero."

CHAPTER 15

SCOWCROFT FIDGETED IN HIS train seat and looked out the window. By now the train should have been inside the darkness of the Channel Tunnel, well on its way to Europe.

Instead, Scowcroft looked up at the magnificent wrought-iron ribs of St Pancras station's roof.

"Why the hell are we still here?" he hissed at Barrett beside him.

Barrett shrugged. "Conductor says it's a problem on the line."

"Here," Charlotte spoke up, handing them her phone—it was showing the BBC News app. "They've had refugees trying to get on the trains coming this way. Says that one of them's dead."

"Well, how long will that hold us up?" Scowcroft pushed, but no one had an answer for him.

Surrounding the thieves, Graham's stag party were raucous, outlining in detail their hedonistic plans for Amsterdam and its red-light district.

"I'm gonna go take a piss," Scowcroft told them, standing. "See if there's any sight of the big lad or the beard."

"Don't wander off," Charlotte said, earning a contemptuous tut in reply.

Scowcroft left the carriage and tried the toilet door. It was locked, and sounds of retching came from within—the first casualty of the stag party.

He ran through the events of that morning in his mind. At no point had his face been revealed to the big man or the bikers, and he had been well clear of the scene before dumping his mask into the backpack. Of average height and build, Scowcroft was just one more twenty-something male in a city that held tens of thousands of them, so he considered it safe to walk the train. If he was on board, the courier was sure to be made conspicuous by his size. Likewise, the bearded man wouldn't blend in amongst the increasingly irritated businessmen and parties of tourists.

Scowcroft moved from one carriage to the next, finally coming to one that served as a dining carriage. Scowcroft bought half a dozen sandwiches and bottles of water. The cost made him balk,

and then the young man laughed, remembering that three million pounds' worth of precious
stones were taped to his chest.

"You can keep the change, love," he told the
server with a smile, and moved back to rejoin the
others, the sound of the stag party reaching him
long before he entered the carriage.

"Long time for a piss," Charlotte snorted.

"I got these," Scowcroft explained, dumping
the bag into Charlotte's lap.

"Shit," Barrett groaned.

"What? You don't like ham and cheese? It's all
they had, mate. Bloody French."

"No." Barrett shook his head, his face turning
pale. "That."

Scowcroft followed the man's gaze, and the
bread turned to ash in his mouth.

Two British policemen appeared to be casually
walking the platform, but with a soldier's instinct Barrett had recognized their fleeting
glances at the train's windows, and the hands
that rested ready on the hilts of their extendable
batons.

"They're looking for us," Barrett almost sighed.

"How can you be sure?" Charlotte pressed, desperate for him to be wrong.

"The insignia. Those aren't transport police.
They're the Met."

"Bollocks," Scowcroft hissed. "Over by the escalators. There's another one there. That must be why the big lad and his mate have done one."

"They're putting the nets out," Barrett assessed.

"So what do we do?" Charlotte asked.

"We get off the train," Barrett answered, and Scowcroft nodded in agreement.

"But first..." the younger man said, tapping his chest to still their questions.

Scowcroft left the carriage and moved to the closest toilet. It was open, but splattered with vomit. The thief had no time to notice. The sight of the police had sent his heart beating fast against the stones. He knew the time had come to divide them. He took eight from the pouch, placing four in each of his trouser pockets. He was about to retape the remaining four to his chest, but another idea came to him.

Scowcroft would swallow the stones. If the big man and his friends were to catch him, then they'd have to gut him before Scowcroft failed his brother.

He swallowed, washing down the diamonds with handfuls of water from the washbasin.

"Here," he told Charlotte and Barrett when he got back to their seats, handing them the diamonds beneath the table. "Swallow them. Right now. Don't mess around."

Neither did, knocking back the small rocks with bottles of water.

"Christ!" Charlotte gasped.

"Hey," one of the stag party grinned, his voice conspiratorial. "Is that Mandy?" he asked— meaning ecstasy.

"Travel sickness pills," Scowcroft replied. "Sorry, mate."

"Oh," the man said sadly, before his eyes brightened up. "Guess I'll stick to the coke then." The size of his grin suggested much of the powder had already been consumed.

"This is the best place you found for us to sit, yeah?" Scowcroft whispered to Charlotte.

"You don't have to be a Scowcroft to make a decision," she replied. "If trouble comes, you'll be glad I did. You'll see."

"Wait. You feel that?" Barrett cut in, smiling. "The table's vibrating! We're ready to go!" The conductor's whistles on the platform were closely followed by cheers from the stag party.

"Thank God," Charlotte sighed, seeing the police making no effort to board. "We're clear."

She couldn't have known about the man entering the station, and how desperate he was to prove her wrong.

CHAPTER 16

DETECTIVE INSPECTOR HILL sprinted across St Pancras station's concourse, the uniformed sergeant beside him struggling to match the pace.

"Can't they stop it?" Hill demanded of the man as the pair flashed identification at the border officials.

"We've got no cause, sir," the sergeant told Hill for the third time. "Three robbery suspects is not enough to hold an already delayed international train. We're not even sure they're on there."

"They're on there," Hill declared, trusting his gut and pushing his way through a group of startled tourists.

"Where are your officers? How many are on the train?"

"Well, none, sir," the sergeant told him, fighting for air. "They can't go to the Continent."

Hill swore beneath his breath, scanning the

scene about him. Whistles rang along the platform. Hill knew the train's doors would close in a
second, and with them his chances of catching the
thieves.

"My car's pulled up across the front!" he
shouted at the sergeant, tossing him the BMW's
keys as he leapt through the open door and onto
the train. The closing door cut off the sergeant's
shocked reply.

"You can't do this, sir," Hill lip-read. He smiled
as he waved the man good-bye.

The train lurched forwards. There was no turning back now. Either he would come out of this a
champion or a disgrace. He knew he was placing
his redundancy package—and therefore the future of his business—in jeopardy, but Hill believed in bold strokes, and he trusted his gut. The
thieves, and Slate's diamonds, were on this train.

After a few moments to collect his thoughts,
Hill pulled out his phone.

"Now, don't get angry," he said into it after
Vaughn answered, "but I'm on the Eurostar."

"Yes, I just bloody heard from the sergeant!
What the hell are you doing, Hill? Get yourself
off there at the first stop. If you're lucky, maybe
we can keep the IPCC out of this."

"I'm going to Amsterdam, boss, but I'll be back
tomorrow."

"You've got no jurisdiction to operate on the Continent, you stupid idiot!"

"I know that, boss. That's why I'm calling you to let you know I'm taking tomorrow off as leave. Pretty sure I've got a couple of days left in the bank, and I was already pushing into overtime today. This is just an above-board day break across the Channel."

"Right, but all that goes to shit when you find these thieves of yours."

"Exactly. *When* I find them," Hill smiled. "These thieves scream amateur to me, boss, and they've bitten the hand of one of the shadiest men in London. If I don't find them before his crew does, then we'll have an international murder inquiry on our hands."

"Christ. OK. I'll call ahead to a friend of mine in Amsterdam. I'll write it up as a familiarization visit."

"You're a good bobby, boss," Hill told Vaughn, and meant it.

"Save the ass-kissing, Hill. Just find those thieves before they're corpses."

CHAPTER 17

OPENING THE EMAIL VAUGHN had sent him, Hill once again studied the faces of the three thieves he was tracking. State-of-the-art, antiterror surveillance software had matched the images, but to a human eye the photo stills were distorted and blurry, and there was little Hill could gain from the photos except the knowledge that he was tracking two men and a woman. Luckily for him, he'd spent the last thirteen years of his life spotting people breaking the law, and he had come to recognize the signs. The thieves would make a mistake, or somehow show their hand, he was sure of it.

So Hill began a slow inspection through the carriages. He had to assume his suspects would have split up for the journey, so anyone who could match their description had to be studied. Hill knew the trio had been fit and able enough to beat off the attack of the bikers, so he kept his eyes peeled for healthy but potentially bruised individuals.

Hill's searching drew several comments from passengers, but the detective let them wash over him. He may be causing some slight offense, but he hoped he was doing nothing to attract the kind of attention that would jeopardize his search.

He was wrong.

"Sir?" A conductor stopped him in the passageway between carriages, the man's English accented by French. "May I see your ticket, please?"

Hill's eyes were drawn through the glass door to where a rowdy stag party were bawling football chants.

"Sir?" the Frenchman pressed.

"I don't have one," Hill confessed, reaching for his wallet. "Amsterdam, please. One way."

"Sir, I'm afraid you cannot purchase a ticket on board the train. You should not have been allowed to board without one. May I see your passport?"

"My passport?" Hill asked, incredulous. "You don't have that authority."

"Then please accompany me to the police officer at the front of the train, sir. They do."

"*I* am a police officer." Hill spoke quietly, discreetly showing his badge.

"Are you on duty?" the Frenchman asked.

"I'm not, no."

"Then I must ask you to accompany me, sir. You will be required to pay a fine."

At least comforted by the knowledge that his thieves had no way of leaving the train before him, and not wishing to cause a scene that could draw attention, Hill turned to follow the conductor.

Then, as he stepped out of the gangway connection, Hill heard the flushing of the toilet, and its door unlocked. With the overactive senses of an officer, Hill turned to look as a man emerged from within.

A man with a broken nose.

"All right," the Englishman said, catching Hill's eye.

"All right," Hill replied, attempting to control his compulsion to act.

He succeeded, and after an awkward pause the broken-nosed Englishman stepped into the stag party's carriage, and Hill stepped into the other. Then, losing the battle with his twitching muscles, Hill finally smiled.

Because he'd found his thieves.

CHAPTER 18

"WAKE UP." BARRETT prodded Scowcroft. "Amsterdam."

Scowcroft opened his eyes and saw the Amstel river—from which the city of Amsterdam takes its name—stretching out beside the tracks.

"You didn't sleep?" Scowcroft asked, rubbing at his eyes as the train slowed into the city center rail hub of Centraal station.

"Kept my eye on things," Barrett replied, not wanting to admit that he was rattled. Though he couldn't place a finger on what was bothering him, the trip wire of his veteran's instinct had been triggered. "We're all good," he said aloud to reassure himself.

The Eurostar came to a final stop and the stag party let loose a mighty roar that drowned out the bilingual Tannoy announcements.

"About bloody time!" one of the party shouted. "We're out of drink!"

"You coming with us?" another of the men slurred at Charlotte.

"Course I am, babe," she smiled back, before whispering to her partners, "We can use them as cover to leave the station. It'll be easy enough to ditch them outside."

Barrett liked the idea, but Scowcroft kept silent, reluctant to admit that Charlotte had found them a brilliant disguise for their journey from London.

"Let's go!" shouted the best man, the bikini-clad groom draped over his shoulder.

The thieves followed, pressing themselves into the group. As they stepped onto the platform and Dutch soil, Charlotte and Barrett put on big smiles, acting every part the traveling British lager louts. Scowcroft scowled.

This was usual for him, the young man full of fire and bitterness, but at that moment Scowcroft scowled because of what he saw ahead of them.

Dutch police officers. A pair at every exit.

His heart beat faster.

"They can't be here for us," Barrett whispered, keeping up his smile. "Look who they're stopping."

Scowcroft did, and saw that the police were stopping mainly young people in gaudy neon outfits.

"They're looking for drugs," Charlotte assessed, relief in her voice.

"No." Scowcroft shook his head. "You don't bring drugs *into* Amsterdam. Even the bloody police have to know that. It's a cover, so they don't spook us."

"It's not. Just be calm, mate. It's fine." Barrett was trying to reassure the younger man, noticing the sweat beading on Scowcroft's forehead.

"I'm gonna do something," Scowcroft suddenly declared.

"Alex, don't," Barrett pleaded.

"Don't you fucking dare," Charlotte hissed, her eyes ablaze.

But he did.

Scowcroft had already seen his chance—a loud-mouthed member of the stag party who was strutting along the platform as if he had bales of hay under his arms. Scowcroft moved forwards and shoved a businessman hard in the back, and the middle-aged man slammed into the drunken Brit, who spilled lager on his white sneakers.

"Prick!" the lout shouted into the business-man's face, rounding on him and shunting him backwards.

The businessman tried to open his mouth, but before he could protest his innocence, the Brit threw what was left of his beer into the man's face. Then the businessman surprised even Scowcroft by replying with a quick right hook into the loudmouth's jaw, sending him reeling.

At that moment, the platform turned to anarchy as the rest of the stag party jumped on the businessman. The police were forced to bolt from their positions to intervene, leaving the thieves an open exit into the city.

They took it.

And at the end of the platform, one man watched it all.

CHAPTER 19

DETECTIVE INSPECTOR HILL HAD been in no rush to leave the train. He'd seen the police waiting by the exits—why, he didn't know, but he wasn't about to question good luck—and he was certain his thieves would try to lose themselves in the crush of passengers.

So Hill had stepped from the train, walked to the back of the platform, and made a call.

"Hello, babe."

"I thought you were dead," Deb replied. "My phone hasn't been going off every two minutes. At least not from you, anyway," she teased.

"That's because I don't want a horrific phone bill. I'm in Amsterdam." Hill's eyes scanned the passengers that began to emerge from the train's doors.

"What? Why?"

"Calm down, Deb. I had to deliver some confidential docs."

"You're not a bloody postman," Deb moaned.

"I'll make it up to you," Hill promised, eager to be off the phone before his wife's temper took over. "Listen, babe, I've got to go, but I'll call you tomorrow, OK? Love you."

"Love you too, but stay away from red lights, or I'll cut your bits off."

Shaking his head, Hill hung up the phone and readied himself to move.

This was the time.

A steady flow of passengers was coming down the platform now. The police were searching the bags and persons of young adults, causing a bottleneck at the exits. Hill guessed the police action was an antidrugs gesture, though why anyone would bring their own drugs with them to Amsterdam was beyond him. Doubtless a politician or high-ranking officer had thought it a great idea.

Hill now saw the stag party amongst the mix, the men launching into a lewd chant that Hill was well acquainted with from his rugby-playing days. Perhaps it was due to someone taking offense at the obscenities that a fight suddenly broke out, and in the space of one breath the platform turned into a mess of flying fists and chaos.

Then amongst all that chaos, Hill saw them.

He saw his thieves.

CHAPTER 20

"LEG IT!" SCOWCROFT SHOUTED, grabbing his partners by the arms and tugging them clear of the melee. "Come on!" he hustled as the police entered the fray. "The exit's clear!"

"You stupid ass!" Charlotte chided him as they passed through the exit and onto the busy pavement.

"It worked, didn't it?" Scowcroft snarled.

"We should walk," Barrett cut in. "It's one thing running clear of a fight, but we should walk."

Around them, other passengers who had run from the trouble had slowed their pace to breathless gaits. Amongst them, Barrett saw the old lady whose bags he'd helped place into the train's overhead storage.

"Are you all right, love?" he asked her, seeing her face was flushed. "Come on, I'll carry your bags to the taxi for you."

Scowcroft glared as the woman gave her

thanks, but Barrett ignored his younger accomplice and turned to pick up the lady's suitcase.

And that's when he saw him—the man who'd looked into his eyes outside the toilet. The man who had studied his face, his broken nose. The man who, Barrett now knew, was the reason his soldier's survival instinct had been triggered. Whoever he was, the athletic man glided around the side of the melee at a slow trot, avoiding the flying fists and police batons with ease. Clear of the fight, he didn't slow down.

He was coming straight for them.

"I'm sorry, love!" Barrett shouted the apology as he hurled the woman's baggage into the man's path. It didn't collide with him, but it sent other travelers scattering. The fast-approaching man crashed into a young woman, sending them both sprawling to the ground, the woman crying out in pain.

"Go! Go!" Barrett shouted, but the others were already running.

Barrett chanced to look over his shoulder. He saw the man leap to his feet, unharmed, but the woman lay prone, and Barrett could see his pursuer was torn between tending to her and continuing his pursuit.

"He's police," Barrett said as he caught up with the other two. "He stopped to help that girl."

Slowly, above their heavy breathing, the thieves became aware of the sound of bass and cheers in the distance. Mastering their temptation to run, the trio pushed off at a fast walk. The sound of music and cheering soon grew louder, as did the steady stream of ravers making their way in the direction of the party.

"What's going on?" Scowcroft asked a young girl whose face was painted with dots and swirls of neon.

"It's the Amsterdam Dance Event," she told him in accented English that hinted at Italian. "It's a five-day music conference, and party."

"Outside?"

"Outside, inside—it's taking over the city." She beamed at him.

Scowcroft smiled his thanks, and turned to his accomplices. "How did we not know about this?" he hissed.

"We came here to sell diamonds, not to go clubbing," Charlotte reminded him. "Now make friends with that girl. Ask her to paint our faces."

Scowcroft hated being told what to do by Charlotte, particularly when she was right, but the incident at the station had shaken him and the chasing man could still be on their heels.

"OK," he relented.

HEIST

Five minutes later, their faces painted neon and backpacks deposited into waste bins, the diamond thieves pushed their way into a crowd with their new friends, and were swallowed up by the party.

CHAPTER 21

"THEY GOT AWAY," Hill said into his phone. "Bollocks!" he spat, hating to lose.

He was standing back from the streets that were a riot of noise and color, the Amsterdam Dance Event in full swing. Hill was the only one present without a smile.

"Tell me you have a bone, boss," he pleaded, pressing Vaughn for the reason that he'd called.

"I do," Vaughn replied, and Hill could tell from his tone that his superior was becoming as invested in the case as he was. "The CCTV images from the stations have come up with a hit on the facial recognition databases."

"Well, that's bloody good news!" Hill beamed.

"Good and bad," Vaughn admitted. "One of them is Matthew Barrett. He served with the Commandos on three tours of Iraq, including the invasion. Made the rank of corporal, but was discharged for drug abuse a year after his final stint out there."

"A Commando?" Hill asked, relishing the challenge. "What did he do when he left? Any priors?"

"He's been living on welfare benefits since they kicked him out. The forces were his last employer."

Vaughn paused. When he went on, Hill could hear the conflicting emotions in his voice.

"This was a good lad, before he went bad, Hill. Sounds like he's got balls enough for ten men, and if he was a Commando, he has the skills to back it up."

"Don't worry about me, boss." Hill grinned, looking out at the sea of partygoers. "I know where he's hiding."

CHAPTER 22

THE STREETS POUNDED WITH sound and throbbed with the movement of thousands of ravers.

"They'll never find us in this," Scowcroft shouted against the noise. "It's insane," he added with a smile, a young man after all.

"Head in the game, mate," Barrett warned, attempting to bring Scowcroft back to earth. "I'm gonna text the buyer."

Scowcroft leveled out at the mention of the anonymous buyer. The search for a prospective customer for the stolen diamonds had been Barrett's child in the operation, and had involved months of feeling out old military contacts— men who made their living by selling their skills to the wealthy, the greedy, and the crooked. To find such a connection took time and trust, but Barrett had finally found their go-between.

The connection was a former Commando

known to Barrett from his deployment during the invasion of Iraq. The veteran—whom Barrett had sworn he would not name to his accomplices, or vice versa—had left the forces for the private sector, and was now bodyguard to an Arab prince. An Arab prince who coveted diamonds no matter their source, so long as the price was good.

Barrett had agreed to two million pounds for the dozen stones that were valued at three. The money would be enough for Tony, and that was all that mattered. Barrett hadn't turned to crime for his own benefit.

Now he took a cheap phone from his pocket and turned it on for the first time. Entering a number from memory, he sent a simple message: "SEND."

"Now what?" Scowcroft asked, the neon paint on his face doing little to disguise his anxiety.

"We wait, mate," Barrett told him. "Come on. Let's go find some food." He led the trio into the narrow alleyways that ran from the densely packed streets.

"You want Charlie? Ecstasy?" they were asked by shady men in hoodies.

Scowcroft was wary of the criminals. "They could be cops out to sting," he whispered.

"Look at his eyes, mate," Barrett schooled him. "He's off his face."

Partygoers came and went in the alleyways that fed the main party, but away from the crowds the group's camouflage was diminished.

"I'll keep a look up the street," Charlotte volunteered, and Barrett led Scowcroft into a kebab shop with Arabic lettering on its sign.

"*Marhaba,*" Barrett greeted the graying owner, before going on to order the meals in the man's native language.

"Bloody hell," Scowcroft said with admiration. "I didn't know you could do that."

Barrett shrugged. "After the invasion, it wasn't a bad place for a while. We'd patrol around, get some food and some tea. It was all right," he said, casually dismissing some of the most momentous times of his life.

"So why my brother?" Scowcroft asked, after a pause to catch his nerve.

It was longer still before Barrett replied.

"It all went to shit, Alex. Don't ask me the how and why, but it went to shit."

The conversation was uncharted territory for the two men. Scowcroft had always yearned to know more about his brother's service, but the thought of Tony in his younger years, strong and vital, caused the younger man much pain to reflect on it.

As for Barrett, he had kept the memories of

those days pushed down in his mind, weighted there by drugs, but the memory of his best friend would never let him be.

Perhaps it was seeing his brother's salvation at hand that let Scowcroft finally ask the questions that had burned inside him for almost a decade.

"Did he like it?" He pushed carefully. "My bro. Did he like Iraq?"

"He loved it." Barrett smiled. "But he missed you. And he missed her," he added with a nod towards the door. "He never shut up about the pair of you."

Their conversation was cut short as the restaurant owner placed their trays of food on the counter.

"Was he happy?" Scowcroft finally asked, taking great interest in the salt shaker. "The day it happened. Was he happy?"

Scowcroft stole a glance out of the corner of his eye, and saw the older man's jaw twitch before he answered.

"Right up until that last moment." The phone buzzed in his hand. "Must be my guy."

The message was from a Dutch number that Barrett had never seen before, doubtless bought to send that single text before it would be discarded: Get drinks with my British friend Pete at midnight. Table to the left of the DJ booth. Club Liquid.

"We got our place," Barrett said, taking his food from the counter and turning towards the door and Charlotte.

He was stopped by Scowcroft's hand.

The veteran met the young man's eyes.

"Thank you," Scowcroft told him.

"It's just a kebab, mate." Barrett attempted to laugh, uncomfortable with the admiration.

Then, as he turned away from the young man, Barrett wondered how Scowcroft would have thanked him had he known the truth.

That every day since the insurgent's bomb had blown their vehicle apart, Barrett had hated himself for saving the life of Tony Scowcroft.

CHAPTER 23

"DETECTIVE INSPECTOR HILL?" Hill was asked by a Dutch giant of a man.

"That's me."

"Sergeant Corsten. Please follow me and I'll show you to the control room."

Hill followed behind the Dutchman's huge strides. They were in a mobile operations center set up at a city-center police station, the building providing a control point for the policing of the Amsterdam Dance Event.

"My chief tells me that you are here to see if there is something you can learn for the policing of festivals in London this summer?" Corsten asked, repeating the fabricated story that Vaughn and Hill had concocted.

"That's right, Sergeant. They get bigger every year, and the police force gets smaller."

"Maybe that is why they send a detective to observe?" Corsten questioned with a knowing look.

Seeing that the sergeant had spotted the visit as a charade, Hill was content to smile and let him know he'd scored a point.

"Here is our CCTV room," Corsten told him, pointing to banks of TV screens monitored by a mixture of police and private security personnel. From the look of a hard bearded man in the corner, even the Dutch special forces had their eyes on the event.

"Terrorism," Corsten explained, catching Hill's gaze. "But it makes our job easier, in a way. We wouldn't have half the number of these cameras and equipment if it wasn't for the terrorism budget. If you want to see the number of crimes prevented or responded to today, I can bring you the papers."

"Sure." Hill smiled, playing along. "Until then, you mind if I take a seat? Oh, and do you have a Wi-Fi connection I can use?"

"Of course," Corsten replied, and wrote out the memorized network and passcode for the detective before taking his leave. Hill didn't expect to see any paperwork. Corsten knew that Hill's familiarization was a sham, but police officer to police officer, he was happy enough to look the other way.

Hill quickly cast his eyes over the TV monitors, seeing the same thing repeated over and over—

DJs and revelers bouncing to a beat lost to the soundproofed control room. He knew that looking for individual faces in the sea of ravers without some direction was a pointless task. As he had on the train, Hill put his faith in the fact that the thieves would slip up, but this time Hill would not be denied his prize.

Connected to the internet, Hill now opened up his phone's web browser and began to dig the thieves out from hiding with the one connection he had—the name of Matthew Barrett, and his service as a Royal Marine.

It was only moments before Hill had his first result. It was a BBC News article from 2008, listing Barrett as being awarded the Military Cross for his actions in Iraq the previous year. Further searches led to local news websites, where Barrett was lauded as a hero for saving the life of his hometown friend Tony Scowcroft, who'd been crippled in an explosion.

Now Hill had a second name, and he entered it into the search engine.

"Bloody hell," he muttered, seeing a long list of results. All of them were fund-raising campaigns aimed at getting Tony the medical support he needed not only to recover, but to survive—his body was intact, but Tony was brain-damaged, seemingly beyond repair.

Scanning through the web pages, Hill saw that the latest plea had been posted on justgiving.com only three months ago, and aimed to raise the $2 million it would take for Tony to be accepted into a groundbreaking medical trial in America. If successful, it would give the man back his life.

But the campaign had raised barely $50,000.

"Bollocks," Hill breathed, sitting back in his chair, because the reason behind the diamond heist had become abundantly clear, and the consequence of the thieves failing caused his stomach to turn.

"If I catch them, he's dead," he whispered, and dropped his head into his hands.

CHAPTER 24

DEPOSITING THE LEFTOVERS OF their takeaway meal into an alleyway bin, Scowcroft pressed Barrett for information on the buyer's location.

"He's told you twice already, Alex," Charlotte cut in, her patience thin, but Barrett calmed her with a look and gestured to his smartphone.

"It says on here that it's a high-end club about a mile away, mate," he told Scowcroft.

"What's high-end?"

"It means it's expensive," Charlotte answered. "It means we can't go in there dressed like this." She gestured at their neon faces, jeans, and sneakers.

"Well, the bags are gone, and we're all out of clothes, so how the hell are we going to get into a place like that?"

"I'll look and see if there's a twenty-four-hour store," Charlotte proposed, taking out her phone. "Are we expected at this guy's table?" she asked Barrett, who shrugged. "It would help getting in if we are," Charlotte told him.

"You seem to know a lot about this kind of club," Scowcroft muttered, knowing that Blackpool's drinking and club culture was anything but high-end.

"I did have a life before your brother," Charlotte replied without thinking, instantly regretting her words. "I didn't mean it like that."

"Fuck you," Scowcroft said, his voice flat and cold.

"I..." Charlotte tried to backtrack, but Scowcroft's eyes simmered with anger, and she knew it would be useless. Instead she concentrated on her phone.

"Here," she pointed, her voice a shadow of its usual strength. "We can get the clothes from there."

Barrett knew Charlotte's words hadn't been meant literally, but even he was subdued at the implication in them.

"OK," he finally uttered.

Charlotte moved to put her phone away, but an alert flashed onto its screen with a loud ping.

"It's the BBC News update," she told them as she opened the app. And then she wished she hadn't.

Because Barrett's face was spread across her screen.

CHAPTER 25

IN THE POLICE CONTROL center's CCTV room, Detective Inspector Hill's guts churned as he watched over the monitors.

"Are you hungry?" Sergeant Corsten asked, noticing Hill's hand on his stomach.

Hill told him he wasn't and moved the hand away. In truth he was sick. Sick at the implications that his own success would have on a man who'd been crippled and brain-damaged while serving his country.

He rubbed at his eyes and tried to visualize a future where his decisions would concern buying a new piece of gym equipment, and not the life-and-death struggle of a brave man.

The detective's phone buzzed, and he saw the message from Vaughn: "BBC just ran Barrett's picture."

Hill opened the BBC News app, seeing that the

newly released story was one of the top trending items on the site. He scanned the short article, which simply stated that Matthew Barrett, a former Royal Marine, was wanted in connection with a violent crime, and that his nose was badly broken. Above the text, the proud photograph from Barrett's military record sat alongside the grainy image from London's Underground.

The article was light on detail, but that was how Hill had wanted it. The news report was the beater that would flush Barrett and his friends into the open, he was sure of it.

"Look at this." Hill heard Corsten address him on the second attempt, the Dutchman pointing a finger towards the room's CCTV screens.

Hill stood and let out a deep breath to clear his mind.

"Here," Corsten jabbed with his index finger. "And here."

Hill followed the finger and saw what the eagle-eyed Dutchman had seen.

Something wasn't right in the colorful pictures of ravers. Two men—no, three—were combing their way through one of the stage's crowds, their thick shoulders and shaven heads marking them out as obviously as a tractor cutting through a field of hay.

"They are not there for the party," Corsten

observed, and Hill found himself nodding in agreement.

"You mind if I use your bathroom?" he asked.

"Of course." The Dutchman smiled, knowing that Hill would not be coming back.

CHAPTER 26

BARRETT LOOKED INTO THE faces of Scowcroft and Charlotte. Their wide eyes reminded him of his battle-shocked comrades in Iraq.

"You can't go," Scowcroft finally murmured.

"Of course I can." His mentor smiled. "I'm not charging an enemy machine gun, mate, I'm just going to draw the police away from you two. Just remember, the buyer doesn't know you, or your names. You may have to win him over. Show him the news article. Here, give me one of your phones."

Charlotte handed him hers, and Barrett flipped the phone's camera so that the screen showed himself and his two sullen accomplices. "These two are with me, mate. You don't need to know who they are, and they don't know who you are. Deal with them. Out."

"Pete's not his real name?" Scowcroft mumbled.

"No real names." Barrett shook his head.

"Where will you go?" Charlotte asked, beginning to accept the inevitable.

"Your meet with the buyer is at the top end of the city center. It's mostly waterways to the east, so I'll go south or west. I'll find a way of letting them see me, but keep enough cover that they can't catch me."

"Baz," Scowcroft pleaded, "you'll go to prison."

A genuine smile broke across the veteran's features. He couldn't tell his partners how his mind had been imprisoned and tormented since the moment he'd seen Tony's mangled body by an Iraqi roadside. He couldn't tell them that the four walls of a cell would be heaven to him, if only he knew that his best friend was restored.

"Since they kicked me out of the Marines, I've been living in shitholes worse than I ever did in Iraq," he told them instead. "I'll have a roof over my head, and food. I'll even have a gym." Barrett smiled.

"We can't let you go," Scowcroft insisted.

"Don't worry about it, Alex. I'll probably even run into some of the old unit inside. God knows they're in and out of the system enough. Just think of it as me being back in the barracks at Taunton, but no marching, and no pay."

"You're a knob," Scowcroft managed, trying to put on a brave face.

"Here." Barrett pushed something into the young man's hand.

"Your diamonds?" Scowcroft said, shocked.

"I didn't swallow them. I got spooked on the train. I thought it would come to this, eventually. My good looks make me stand out too much."

"Stop trying to make jokes and give me a hug, Matthew," Charlotte told him suddenly, pulling her friend into a tight embrace.

At the display of affection, Scowcroft swallowed the ice-like lump in his throat. No Scowcroft was known for voicing their emotions, as Barrett and Charlotte well knew, but the young man tried his best.

"Baz," he began, "I'm not a soldier, but I'd take a bullet for you. I know you're Tony's brother as much as I am."

Barrett simply nodded, not trusting himself to speak. Instead, he put out his hand. Scowcroft took it, his grip like a vise.

There was only one thing left to say.

"Good luck," Scowcroft told him.

And Barrett walked away. When he had put some space between himself and his two friends, he tossed his cap down onto the pavement and lifted his face up to Amsterdam's camera-filled streets.

CHAPTER 27

HILL STEPPED OUT OF the police control center, but was stopped instantly by a commanding voice.

"Detective Inspector Hill!" He turned to see Sergeant Corsten approaching. With a sinking feeling, Hill considered that he'd misjudged the man.

He hadn't.

"Here's my number," Corsten told him, handing over a piece of paper.

Hill's eyebrows rose in question.

"My priority is the safety of the people here," Corsten explained. "Including you, and whoever it is you're looking for. Who those men are looking for," he guessed with a veteran officer's insight.

Hill paused before his next move. He could see no reason why the Dutchman would set him up to fail, or to fall foul of the local police force, and so he took his phone from his pocket and entered the number, texting Corsten a link to the BBC News article and Barrett's pictures.

"I need to find this man, and take him quietly home before somebody gets hurt," Hill told him.

"Is he a threat?"

Hill shook his head without needing to think. All the evidence suggested that Barrett was a brave and selfless man. His actions may have been illegal, but they were noble.

"The people looking for him are," he added.

Corsten gave a curt nod of acknowledgment and turned back to the control center. Hill saw the ebbing tide of ravers coming to and from the stage, and followed his ears in the direction of the driving bass.

"Trance stage?" Hill shouted. A blank-faced steward pointed lazily ahead.

Hill pushed on through the crowd, and was funneled into a circus-sized tent, his senses overloaded as soon as he set foot within. Lasers and lights criss-crossed the air above the hands of a thousand joyous clubbers.

At the far end of the tent stood the main stage, where the image of a leather-jacket-clad DJ was cast up onto a huge array of screens.

"Amsterdam!" the DJ's British voice came across the twenty-foot speaker stacks. "Make some fucking noise!" The crowd replied with a roar that fought to drown out the drop of a pounding bassline.

Hill held his position at the rear of the tent and cast his eyes over the mass of bodies ahead of him. The thousands of moving limbs and the flashing light made it almost impossible to make out detail, and he wondered how he would find his target.

He pulled out his phone, and texted Corsten: Anything?

The reply was instant: No sign of your man. I see you.

Hill quickly texted back: What about the men looking in the crowd? Where are they?

This time there was a slight delay, and Hill ground his teeth as he waited impatiently, praying that the men had not slipped away. Push down the left-hand side as you face the DJ. Thirty meters. Big guy on the edge there. Alone. Not dancing. Seems to be watching.

Hill kept his phone in his hands and followed the instructions, spotting the man when he was ten meters away. Hill could see that he was a formidable build, muscular and bearded. The man seemed to be taking no interest in the music, only the crowd.

He remembered the bearded man in the police

control center and texted: You sure he's not one of yours? Special forces?

There was a pause, where Corsten must have checked with the soldier, then: Not ours.

Hill didn't move any closer, but kept the man in his sight. The detective was certain that Slate would have more men scouring the event. Having been burned once by the thieves, Slate's men would surely call in reinforcements before springing their attack, and so Hill would watch this man, and let him lead the way.

"I wanna see every one of your hands up!" the DJ called, the crowd cheering themselves as their fingers reached for the sweeping lasers.

And not wanting to give himself away to Slate's henchmen, Hill threw his own hands up with them.

CHAPTER 28

BARRETT STOPPED BESIDE A canal to get his bearings. Taking stock of his surroundings, and seeing that the locals outweighed the few ravers, he decided that he had found himself in the no-man's-land between stages of the Dance Event.

The ex-Commando knew that his part in the heist was drawing to an end, but Barrett intended pulling the police into as long a chase as possible. Out here on the quiet streets, hemmed in by canals and tightly packed properties, he was a sitting duck.

He walked up to a Scandinavian-looking couple worn out from a day of drugs and dancing. "Excuse me. Do you speak English?"

"Sure," the man replied enthusiastically.

"Are there any stages around here?" Barrett asked.

"Right down the street, man. The trance stage. It's banging!"

"Thanks. What time does it finish?"

"Like, six?" the man guessed.

Barrett thanked him as he went on his way and began formulating a simple plan—he would lead the police to the stage and lose himself in the crowd. Should he evade them until dawn, he would slip out with the masses and attempt to take public transport to Belgium. If the police picked him up via their CCTV network—and Barrett hoped they would—then the press of bodies at the stage would give him the best chance for prolonging the chase.

He found the trance stage easily enough and entered to see a British DJ jumping up and down on top of the booth, exhorting the crowd to new levels of energy.

Seeing the smoke and flashing lights, Barrett was sure the crowd would make a maze in which the police would have to follow, but before he could let himself be swallowed by its depths, he turned his head up to the gloom of the canvas and hoped the police were watching.

Someone was.

Barrett saw him coming from his left, his soldier's instinct registering the man traveling at an angle that was opposed to the other ravers, who pushed as one towards the DJ at the head of the tent.

Barrett swore, plunging into the crowd and wishing he had more time. He pushed and weaved his way into the densest section of the dance floor, any chance of keeping track of his pursuers lost amongst the raised hands and writhing bodies.

Then, as if a giant switch had been thrown, all light and music was cut away, the stage cast into a pitch-darkness that was pierced only by the whistles and shouts of the crowd.

"Do you want more?" the DJ's voice echoed in the blackness.

The crowd roared that they did. Barrett prayed silently that his eyesight would adjust quickly to the dark.

"Do you want more?" the DJ screamed again, and the crowd matched his intensity.

"Then let's fucking go!" the DJ boomed, and the bass pounded through Barrett's chest, the lights coming up like a solar flare.

And in that flash of light, Barrett saw that his pursuers were almost on top of him.

As the music blared and the DJ hosed the crowd with champagne, Barrett pushed and shoved his way forwards, finally hitting the railing at the front of the stage. He thought to leap it but saw a line of security between himself and the DJ booth, so he followed it to his left, bumping and bouncing off the ravers. The drunk clubbers berated him, the drugged ones ignored him, but Barrett had no time to think about either and he finally came loose of the bodies in the giant tent's corner.

And there he saw a fire exit.

Barrett ran for it, ignoring the steward who called on him to stop, and barreled out into the cold October air. He kept running, and heard more calls behind him—the police were on his heels.

The veteran turned right, seeing an assembly of artist and production trailers at the rear of the domed stage. What he didn't see were the thick cables running to and from them, and as Barrett chanced to look back over his shoulder, it was these that ended his flight.

He tumbled to the tarmac, feeling the skin scrape from his cheek and elbows. After a split second the agony of his already ruined nose began anew, but Barrett had no time to reflect on his pain.

Rough hands gripped him by the throat.

He was caught.

CHAPTER 29

A **SUBDUED SCOWCROFT** and Charlotte walked out of the twenty-four-hour store, a bagful of fresh clothing in each of their hands.

"We need somewhere to change," the young man said. "There's Portaloos around the raves. We can ditch our old stuff in them too."

Charlotte shook her head. "I need light and a mirror for my makeup," she told him, and caught the young man's look of frustration. "It's a high-end club, Alex. If we're going to fit in, I need to look the part."

Scowcroft relented with a shrug, and pointed out a nearby hotel. "Let's try that."

They did, but the city center hotel was fully booked. So were the next four they tried.

"We're running out of time," Scowcroft grumbled. "I can change in the street and go in alone."

"They won't let a young guy in on his own.

That kind of place, you need a one-to-one ratio at least."

"Ratio of what?"

"Women to men," Charlotte explained. "Guys don't pay five hundred quid a bottle to be surrounded by other men. Besides, I have an idea."

That idea led them to a part of the city where the windows pulsed with red light and the silhouettes of writhing bodies.

"Over here," Charlotte instructed the wide-eyed Scowcroft, leading him through the door of one of the more decrepit-looking brothels. Scowcroft was assaulted by the scent of bleach and cheap perfume.

"Hello." Charlotte smiled at the establishment's madam. "I'd like a girl please, and he'd like to watch."

The woman didn't bat an eyelid at the request.

"One hundred euros."

"OK," Charlotte agreed. "And I'd like a woman, not a young girl."

The madam shrugged and led them into a corridor washed with red light.

"What are you doing?" Scowcroft hissed into Charlotte's ear.

"Trust me, Alex."

The madam pulled aside a heavy curtain, and

the pair entered a shoebox that was home to a single bed, a toilet, and a shower cubicle.

"In there." She pointed first at Scowcroft and then at the shower.

"OK," he stammered as the madam slid the curtain closed behind them.

A moment later, a curvy brunette glided her way in through the fabric, the cracks around her eyes deepening as she smiled an introduction. "I'm Eva," she whispered.

"Eva, I'm Charlotte." The thief pushed a thick wedge of euros into the prostitute's hand. "We need this room."

Eva needed no more explanation. "Anything you want," she cooed, sitting down on the bed and groaning in mock pleasure as she counted her windfall.

"This is so messed up," Scowcroft said, shaking his head.

"It's about to get worse," Charlotte told him, pushing a small bottle into his palm.

Scowcroft looked at the label.

"Laxative?" he asked, shocked.

"Unless you want to cut the diamonds out," Charlotte answered plainly. "Put your T-shirt in the toilet bowl. Come on, don't make this any worse than it has to be."

The next few minutes were a low point in the

lives of the thieves. Save for a wry smile between moans, the prostitute appeared unmoved. No doubt she assumed the pair were drug mules.

Grateful for the presence of a shower, Scowcroft changed quickly, at all times keeping his back to Charlotte—he did not want to catch a glimpse of his brother's fiancée, no matter what intimacy he had just been privy to.

Pulling on a dark dress, Charlotte cast her eyes over her accomplice, approving of his well-fitted gray suit.

"Beautiful." The prostitute beamed her own approval, as Scowcroft carefully pulled a coat over his shoulders—Barrett's diamonds rested within its thick pockets.

"Whatever happens, don't let me forget my coat." He tried to smile.

"How do I look?" Charlotte asked him, finishing her makeup.

"Amazing," he said honestly, before he could catch himself.

The pair weakly smiled their thanks to the prostitute, who stopped her moaning and pushed the money into the depths of her corset.

"Have fun." She waved as Charlotte and Scowcroft slipped out of the brothel and onto the street, Charlotte's heels ringing on the cobblestones. The air coming off the canal was tinged with ice, and Scowcroft pulled his coat across his body.

"All right, love?" a drunk British tourist slurred at Charlotte. "How much for a go around?"

"Hold my hand," Scowcroft told Charlotte, surprising her. "If they think I'm with you, they won't bother. We can't afford to draw attention."

Charlotte took his hand.

"I'm worried about Baz," she confessed.

"Me too," he replied. "Since what happened to Tony, he's been like my brother. I only just realized that today."

"We'll see him soon," she said, though she didn't quite believe it herself.

"I hope so," Scowcroft breathed, then surprised Charlotte by coming to a stop, his hand like a vise on hers.

"I've got to ask you something." His voice became hard again. "Before this last bit, I've got to ask you. I've got to know."

"Go on then." Charlotte had been expecting this question.

"My brother. Did you want to leave him?"

"Yes," she said without hesitation. "Yes, I did, Alex." She broke into a flood of tears.

Despite her words, despite his once furious anger towards her, Scowcroft pulled Charlotte close, his own tears coming.

"Why?" he sobbed. "Why would you leave my brother?"

It was a minute before she could speak, but eventually Charlotte mastered her emotions.

"It wasn't after he got hurt," she told him. "It was before that. All the deployments. All the worry. All the stress. It was too much, for both of us. It was too much, but he was in love with the Marines as much as he was with me. I knew he'd never leave it. And so one day I told myself it was over, but I wouldn't tell Tony until he was back in the UK and safe. I didn't want that in his head if…if…"

"If the worst happened," Scowcroft finished for her.

"And I feel like a bitch. It wasn't until I saw him in that hospital that I knew I'd wait for him forever if I had to, through a million wars, but by then it was too late, and he's never going to know."

As Charlotte's tears began anew, Scowcroft pulled her closer.

"He's going to know, Charlotte. Because of what we're doing right now, he's going to know. Tony's going to get his life back."

CHAPTER 30

BARRETT'S WORLD WAS BLACK.

A hood had been pulled over his head and the former Commando recognized the dank, musty smell of wet burlap. It was a sandbag that was hiding his captors from his eyes, and Barrett could almost laugh at the irony that he'd pulled the same bags over the heads of dozens of Iraqi men.

But Barrett wasn't laughing.

He was scared.

Since when did the police hood the men they arrested? Could it be that he'd somehow fallen foul of an antiterror operation?

Perhaps Barrett would get his answers, because suddenly the hood was whipped away, his eyes quickly adjusting to what appeared to be the gloomy interior of a van. There was no sign of his captors. He tried to turn, but his feet were in shackles, his hands tightly bound behind his back.

He became aware of a presence behind him. He could hear the man's breathing. Minutes passed while Barrett waited for his captor to say something or make his move. Finally, he felt compelled to fill the eerie void.

"Look, I know we broke the law, all right? But you can't go tying me up like this. You're violating my rights."

Silence.

"Don't you want to ask me anything? I'll talk. I'll tell you about how we got forced to do this, because the government won't look after its own. How it bleeds its soldiers for oil, then throws them away when they're broken. I'll tell you about that!" Barrett was shouting, his anger and bitterness growing.

His captor still said nothing.

"What would you do if your partner was put in coma, and your government just left him to rot? Well? You're a police officer—you think that's justice?"

And then Barrett felt the presence of the man lean in from behind him, his words a chilling whisper against the captive's ear. "I'm not a police officer."

CHAPTER 31

"IT'S ALMOST TIME," Scowcroft told Charlotte, looking at his watch as if mesmerized by the passing seconds.

The pair stood on the street opposite the entrance to Club Liquid. A line of would-be patrons stretched back along the block. When the doors opened to admit the lucky few, the pounding of house music pumped out from within.

Charlotte ran her eye over the line, seeing well-heeled twenty-somethings. It was certainly a different crowd to the street parties taking place at the Dance Event.

"We should go in," Scowcroft said. She followed alongside as they headed directly for the door, bypassing the line.

"We're at Pete's table," Scowcroft told the beautiful hostess, who looked the pair up and down.

"OK," the local shrugged after a moment, her eyes lingering on Scowcroft's handsome face.

"You can both come in, but tell Pete no more guys."

"Sure," Scowcroft answered, and smiled his thanks at the colossal bouncer who held open the door.

Inside, the pair were accosted by the throb and blare of music. The dance floor was a tangle of bodies, but Scowcroft's eyes were drawn to the sectioned-off tables that ran along its edges. There, the most beautiful women in the club danced with each other, the men at the table content to sit back and watch, safe in the knowledge that their connections or wealth would see at least one of the girls going home with them.

Scowcroft again had a vision of what could be with the diamonds in his possession. It could be him buying tables at high-end nightclubs. Him surrounded by beautiful women.

But no—Scowcroft only wanted to be surrounded by his family. Tony, Barrett, and, as he looked at her beside him, even Charlotte.

Even Charlotte. If nothing else came from this whole endeavor, at least Scowcroft could take comfort that his brother was adored.

"You should wait here," he told her, suddenly protective. "I'll go to the table with the diamonds."

"We're both going," Charlotte replied, calmly but firmly.

"What if it's a sting? They're going to catch Barrett, Charlotte. If they catch us too, then who's left for Tony?"

"What choice do we have?" she said plainly. "This is it. It's all or nothing."

Scowcroft knew she was right.

All or nothing.

"Then let's do it."

CHAPTER 32

THE BUYER'S TABLE WAS easy enough to find, sitting in the prominent position to the left of the DJ box. The single man sat behind it swarmed by half a dozen beautiful women.

"I thought the girl at the door said no more men to this table?" Scowcroft shouted above the noise of the music.

Charlotte shrugged in reply. "I guess they left."

"Or they gave us the wrong place to meet."

"They didn't," she told him, and prayed that she was right. "Just look like you belong." They cut along the edge of the dance floor and towards the front of the club.

"Hi." Charlotte smiled at the bouncer watching over the table, breezing straight by him up the couple of steps to the table that allowed the people at it to see—and more importantly, be seen from—anywhere in the club.

"Pete?" Scowcroft asked the lone man on the couch.

"That's me," he answered in a British accent. "Girls, give us some space." Scowcroft was intoxicated by their perfume as they wafted past him and down the steps.

"Take a seat," the man offered, and Scowcroft obliged. Pete was a handsome, athletic-looking man in his thirties. He looked every bit how Scowcroft expected a former Commando turned lucrative contactor to appear.

"Where's Baz?" Pete asked.

"Broken nose. Didn't think it would be a good idea to draw attention," Scowcroft answered. "He gave us a video."

Pete smiled and waved the gesture of the footage away.

"I saw the news. I'd told the staff on the door not to let him in. At least this way I won't have hurt his feelings. Drink?"

Scowcroft shrugged in answer, and Pete gestured to a server. The stocking-clad blonde poured four large vodkas.

"I'll take Baz's," the buyer told them. "To those who can't raise a glass."

The three of them knocked back the vodkas.

"Another one?" Pete asked. "It goes for ten grand a bottle here, so enjoy it."

"Business first." Charlotte smiled. "It's been a long day, Pete."

"Of course it has," the man allowed, doubtless no stranger to long days himself. "Let's go over it, then. My car and driver are outside. The money, for obvious reasons, is in there."

"We're not driving anywhere to do it," Scowcroft cut in, his voice calm but forceful.

"Of course not." Pete shook his head. "My driver will get out. As a measure of trust, one of you can get behind the wheel. The other will get in the back with me, where we can inspect the goods. Once we're both happy, you guys get out with the money, I come back in here to the company of these beautiful ladies, and the driver takes the stones to my employer. Sound good?"

"Works for us," Scowcroft announced after sharing a look with Charlotte. "Thanks for meeting with us."

"Not a problem. Anything for a good cause." The man beamed.

"A good cause?" Scowcroft asked, his heart beginning to beat faster than the club's bass.

"Your brother," Pete explained, still smiling. After a moment the grin slid from his face.

Because he knew he'd slipped.

Scowcroft knew it too, and trapped between

the press of dancing bodies and the table, there was only one thing he could do.

So he slid the store-bought kitchen knife from the sleeve of his shirt and prodded the tip into the man's belly.

"Who are you?" he hissed in the imposter's ear.

"You think you're the only one with a knife?" the man sneered. "I've had mine pointed at your femoral artery since you sat down." Scowcroft felt the press of a blade against the flesh of his thigh, his body shaking with the re-leased adrenaline of his fight-or-flight survival instincts.

"Scared?" the man mocked, feeling the shaking muscles through the blade. "Just hand over the diamonds."

"Who sent you?" Scowcroft challenged, his eyes burning with fury, desperate now that the heist had fallen at the final hurdle.

"Marcus Slate," the man growled, his own eyes equally alight with determination. "Marcus Slate sent me, and I'm taking him back his diamonds."

Scowcroft fought for control of his muscles, because the thought of flight had passed, and he knew there was only one thing left to do—fight.

So he did.

"Fuck you," the thief spat as he drove the knife deep into the stomach of Slate's henchman.

"Fuck you," he shouted again as he drove the knife into the stomach of Detective Inspector Hill.

CHAPTER 33

HILL HAD NEVER BEEN stabbed before, and for a hundredth of a second he almost marveled at the brilliant-white pain that shot through his entire body.

And then, on instinct, he drove his own blade forward.

He felt it part flesh as it cut into the young man's thigh. He felt the spit on his face as his adversary howled in pain, the scream lost to the bass and revelry of the club. He felt the hot blood spurt over his hand as he pulled the blade free.

It was the blood on his hands that shook Hill from his instinctive reactions and brought him the realization of what he had suffered, and what he'd done. Hill knew the gushing wound would kill the young man within minutes. There was no reclaiming the situation—he was committed now.

No, he realized. He'd been committed since the

moment he'd told Slate he'd recover the man's diamonds, and avoid any trial that would cast a shadow over Slate's enterprise. He'd been committed to this end when he'd sold his soul to Slate for a million, the dream of his own business empire, and a better life for himself and Deb.

Hill had never thought he'd have to kill for it.

The woman was pulling the young man away and half carrying him down the few steps that led out onto the dance floor, the dancing girls shooting angry stares as she barged by them.

Hill hesitated to follow—surely someone would see the blood? Surely someone would stop them?

But the club was dark, and the dying thief looked like one more drunken idiot. Seeing that they were already moving to the exit, where they would become someone else's problem, the bouncers did little more than roll their eyes and turn their attention back to the girls.

Hill saw his prize slipping away. And he knew what Slate would do to him if he didn't get those diamonds.

Everything had gone perfectly up until then. With the right kind of persuasion, Barrett had talked. Hill had then handed him over to Slate's men, to what end he didn't know, but he could guess. Then it had simply been a case of meeting the buyer, showing his police identification, and kindly telling the man to forget everything related to the sale of the stolen diamonds. "Pete" had been more than happy to escape so lightly.

Now it had all gone to shit. Hill moved to stand, pulling his jacket closed across the wound. The knife had torn the muscles of his abdomen, each step causing pain to shoot through his body, but he would worry about the damage later. First he had to catch the thieves.

He had to catch them, and then he had to kill them.

CHAPTER 34

"NOT THROUGH THE FRONT!" Scowcroft groaned through gritted teeth, seeing that Charlotte was leading them towards the club's main entrance. "Security will stop us," he managed, knowing that out on the street there would be no hiding the blood that flowed from his leg.

"We have to stop the bleeding!" Charlotte's eyes were wide as she pushed him into a dark recess amongst the club's shadows. "Put your hands on it!" she shouted. "Apply pressure!"

Scowcroft tried, but he was already weak from blood loss. He felt Charlotte free the belt from his trousers and pull it tight around the top of his thigh.

Then, as the blood slowed to a trickle, the agony built to unbearable. Scowcroft squeezed his eyes shut and cursed. "I can't take it, Charlotte! Take it off!" he cried.

"No! You'll bleed to death!"

"Charlotte!" he pleaded. "Take it off!"

Charlotte ignored the cries. Instead she punched Scowcroft in the stomach.

"Think about your brother, Alex," she hissed at him. "Man up!"

The savage tone of Charlotte's voice forced Scowcroft to try, clenching his jaw against the agony. She helped him up and over towards the club's toilets. Looking over her shoulder, Charlotte saw their assailant following through the crowded dance floor. The man moved slowly, not wanting to draw attention to himself, but his eyes were fixed on them.

The thieves staggered into the passageway that led to the toilets. Free from the crowd of the dance floor, individuals began to notice and go wide-eyed at the sight of the bloodied young man.

A suited gentleman stepped forwards and spoke to Charlotte in Dutch. She presumed he was offering to help, and did her best to show a carefree smile.

"Ambulance is coming out there, thank you," she replied, using her free hand to point to the nearest fire escape.

"I will get it," the man said in English, then trotted ahead to push open the door, cold air rushing into the corridor.

"Thank you," Charlotte said, then slammed the door behind them. Letting go of Scowcroft, she quickly wheeled a heavy dustbin across the entrance to block the doorway, and then followed it with another.

"I've got to lie down," Scowcroft said weakly and dropped heavily to the ground.

Charlotte heard banging against the fire escape, but the large bins held.

"You need a hospital. I'll get an ambulance."

"No, they'll bring the police," he groaned.

"A car then."

"No. Just take them," Scowcroft implored, pushing the diamonds into Charlotte's coat pocket. "Take them. Find another buyer."

"No," Charlotte stated firmly, then threw her eyes up at the fire escape—the banging had stopped.

Scowcroft, weak as he was, also became aware of the silence. It was time to run.

"We can't both get away, Char, but you can," he told her calmly. "It's you and Tony making it, or you and me dead. Even I can do that math. Come on. Get the fuck out of here."

"I'm not leaving," she promised, clutching the young man's hand. "I'm not leaving," she said again, as tears began to roll down her cheeks.

Because she knew he was dying.

Alex Scowcroft knew it too.

"I let him down," he sobbed weakly, struggling to keep Charlotte's face in focus. "I let Tony down, Charlotte. I couldn't finish this for him."

"You've done everything a brother could do and more, Alex," she told him, putting her hand against his graying face.

Scowcroft's eyelids shuddered as he tried to stay awake. He tried to fight, because he still had so many things he needed to say. Needed Charlotte to hear. That he was sorry. That she was, and always would be, the true guardian and soulmate of his brother.

But Alex Scowcroft could only gasp.

And then he slipped into the darkness.

CHAPTER 35

HILL PUSHED THE heel of his hand against the knife wound in his abdomen. He knew the pressure would slow the bleeding and help the clots to form, but he hoped the pressure would also take away the pain he suffered with every step. Not wanting to draw attention in the club, he had taken his time in pursuit, but the blocked fire escape had meant he was forced to exit via the club's main entrance.

Luckily for him, Hill's dark suit hid most of the bloodstains, and with his hands pushed deep into his pockets, he was able to keep his face neutral as he walked by the bouncers. Clear of the club's front, Hill then tried to break into a run to its rear, but the pain in his stomach almost caused him to scream, so he was forced to continue his chase at a walk. Despite the restriction, Hill at first took comfort in knowing that the thief would be in a worse condition, but then the cold realization hit home that it was his own hand that had doomed the man, and he was racked by a wave of nausea born of guilt.

"Too late now," he hissed, trying to convince himself.

The detective turned another corner, working his way between the stacks of empty beer kegs to the club's rear fire escape. With the young man's wound, they couldn't have got too far ahead—but then Hill saw that the young man hadn't got anywhere at all, and the longtime police officer knew from one look that the youngster was dead.

And so Hill was a murderer.

"Jesus Christ," he groaned, then reminded himself he was a man with no time for remorse. Hill had made a pact with the devil, and if he didn't deliver on his end of the bargain, then he had no doubt his own skin would be as gray and waxen as that of the thief who lay before him.

"You got yourself into this, you stupid bastard," he hissed at the corpse as he dropped to his knees and began to rummage through the boy's pockets. "Sometimes shit things happen to the people you care about!" he went on, defending his actions. "Life isn't a movie, you dumb piece of shit! There are consequences! Your actions have consequences!" Hill said to dead ears, before sitting back heavily.

Because he had found something in the pockets—a hard object, wrapped tightly in tape.

Hill used his knife to slit open the packaging, and then, dropping the blade to his side, he hastily unwrapped it with his bloodstained hands.

And he saw the diamond sparkling in the moonlight.

Hill swallowed, overcome by what the stone signified. Yes, it was beautiful, but it was also his future. The future he'd always wanted, for him and for Deb.

"Thank you." He spoke aloud, though only Hill knew to whom the words were intended.

His final words.

Caught up in his own exoneration, Hill hadn't heard the fall of soft footsteps behind him. He hadn't heard the soft scrape on tarmac as his blade was plucked from the ground.

But he did feel it pierce his spine.

It was the last thing he'd experience in his life.

EPILOGUE

Two years later

CHARLOTTE LOOKED UP FROM the pile of laundry placed in front of her, and ran her hands through her frayed hair. On days like this she hated the mundane routine that her life had become. Part of her—a part she hated—almost wished that Tony still needed her care and total dedication.

But Tony was his own man now, at least in body, she reminded herself sadly. In mind, he was consumed by grief and guilt. The thought of it was too much for Charlotte to bear, and as she did every day, she tried to lose herself in her mundane tasks, meticulously folding each item of laundry so that there wasn't a single wrinkle present.

An hour passed before there was a knock on the highly polished door.

"Hello?" a woman called from the threshold.

She had the city look about her, Charlotte

noticed. Well spoken, and with a hairstyle that was yet to grow out. She was new, Charlotte decided.

"How long have you been inside?" she asked her fellow inmate.

"Here, only a week, but I've been moving around a bit." The woman blushed. "I'm supposed to help you."

"So help." Charlotte shrugged, two years in prison having blunted her manners.

And no wonder, because it had been a hard two years. For stabbing a police officer, Charlotte had suffered at the hands of every bobby and prison guard she'd come across since her arrest in Amsterdam.

"What can I do to help?" the fresh meat asked, but Charlotte was a world away now. She was back in the courtrooms, a sideshow of the media circus.

Charlotte wanted to puke when she thought of how Hill had become the darling of the tabloids—the hero who'd taken on a dangerous case in his final week of service. Scotland Yard was as happy as the media to take that line, glossing over coincidence. Only the keenest on-lookers noted that Chief Inspector Vaughn, Hill's superior, had resigned his post at Scotland Yard and had been relocated to a small station in England's hinterland.

"You're the one that did in that detective, right?" the woman pushed, cutting into Charlotte's thoughts.

She wasn't surprised to hear the question. Amongst the criminal fraternity of prison, Charlotte enjoyed notoriety.

"Yeah," she answered. "That was me."

Charlotte shrugged, going back to her task of folding sheets and thinking of how her vengeance had capped a story of crime and love that had gone viral across the world, attracting the attention of a generous benefactor who'd been moved to cover the costs of Tony's treatment.

"I read about it in the paper," the woman said, struggling to fold her own pile of clothing. Charlotte noticed that her tiny hands were shaking. Funny, she thought, how people's attitudes had changed towards her.

"Leave the clothes," Charlotte said, trying to sound pleasant. "I'll just have to do them again anyway."

"I'm sorry," the woman said quickly.

"No. It's fine."

"I'm just a bit nervous," she explained. "My husband, he's not well. He's quadriplegic, actually. I don't know how he's getting on without me."

"I'm sorry to hear that," Charlotte told her, her prison mask slipping. "I know how that must feel."

"I know. I read the stories. About you and your husband. That's why I asked them to put me with you, down here."

"Oh. How long are you in for?"

"They gave me a couple of months, but I think it's going to be a lot longer than that," the woman whispered.

"A couple of months?" Charlotte asked, confused—her prison catered to long-term inmates only.

"I knew some people—through my husband—guards, judges. They made it happen."

"You wanted to come here?" Charlotte asked, taking a half-step back.

"Because I said I'd do something really bad."

"What's your name?" Charlotte asked, suddenly uncomfortable. "I'm Charlotte Scowcroft." She tried to smile, putting out her hand.

"Deborah." The woman grinned back, lifting her own hand from her pocket. "But my husband called me Deb. Deb Hill."

Too late, Charlotte saw the blade.

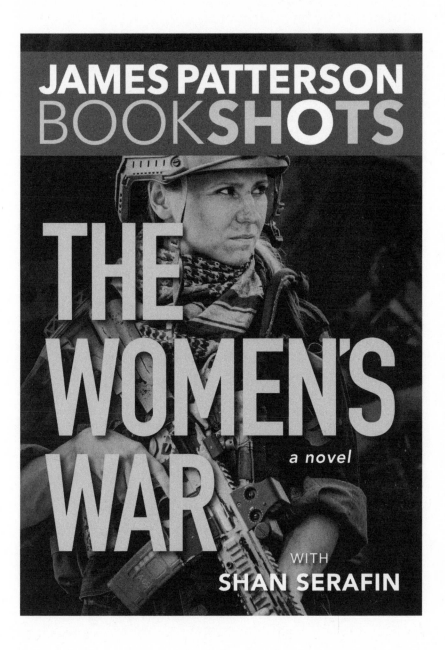

JAMES PATTERSON
BOOKSHOTS

THE WOMEN'S WAR

a novel

WITH
SHAN SERAFIN

THE
WOMEN'S
WAR

BY JAMES PATTERSON
WITH SHAN SERAFIN

CHAPTER 1

Two years ago

WHILE ALL THE OTHER girls in kindergarten would doodle pictures of ponies and rainbows, I would draw myself parachuting out of helicopters and landing on dictators. My little stick figure would karate-kick twelve other stick figures, somehow making them explode in the process, and then I'd aim my portable missile at the obvious target: a dragon.

Nearly thirty years later, I'd be a Marine Corps colonel riding on a Huey. The only difference between the girl in my crayon drawings and the real me is that I didn't have a parachute, I'd use rope. And the dragon caught in my crosshairs wasn't a big lizard with wings—he was a little lizard with total dominance over the US–Mexican narcotics trade.

His name was Diego Correra.

We were midflight, northwest of Diego's location, which was a compound tucked in the outskirts of a Mexican town called Matamoros. It was nearly midnight. Dark. Hot. Damp. Eighteen members of my platoon were riding in three separate Bell Huey helicopters. Flying low enough to read road signs and fast enough not to bother.

I scanned the terrain below using the scope on my M16. The goal was to spot anyone who might be on a rooftop with heavy weaponry. Was I scared? No. Was I lying to myself about not being scared? Yes.

We'd been hunting Diego Correra for three years. I personally had been assigned to six different raids on his drug fields and had been introduced to his legendary "business etiquette" firsthand. Yet I never got the pleasure of introducing him to my M16.

Our helicopters banked left. We were avoiding the city's population. It was a sizable town but not sizable enough that the growl of a chopper would go unnoticed.

The entirety of our intel came from an anonymous source who divulged only a single detail about himself: his name was the Fat Man. We knew nothing else about him. We had no idea if he was a defector from Correra's cartel or if he was the governor of Maine. *Fat Man?* I pictured a bloated, balding car salesman with crusted mustard on his tie, running to pay-phone booths with borrowed quarters to call me.

This morning he gave us the best news we've ever had. "Correra is in Matamoros. Tonight."

Two hours later, we were airborne. I kissed my kids good-bye and tried super hard to seem like a normal mom.

I'm not, though.

There are three main things that can go wrong while jumping out of a helicopter. You could get shot before you jump. You could get shot while actually falling. You could get shot after you complete your fall.

On this mission, we didn't anticipate there would be a fourth thing that could go wrong: your enemy kicks your teeth in.

I had on heat-protective gloves, but I let my boots absorb the majority of the work. I pinched the cord with the arch of one foot against the instep of the other. I don't know how the friction didn't cause a small forest fire, but, honestly, my boots have never shown signs of burn. Credit the US Marine Corps for that. Or me eating salads.

The ground greeted me like a speeding truck. *Wham.* Release, roll, get to position, crouch, aim, hold. Lieutenant Rita Ramirez hit the field second, taking front watch. She was my no-nonsense assistant team leader, so she'd be the caboose once our human caravan got going. Sergeant Kyra Holmes, the best navigator and the best shot, led on point as our sniper. My allies; my two best friends.

I'd never had less intel on a situation, and it was making me an anxious wreck, but my job as colonel was to win the Academy Award for seeming nonwrecked. The shrubbery up ahead was starting to afford us a view as we approached it. I could see the backyard of Diego's compound in front of us.

Showtime.

In general, this hombre used two to three roaming guards even when he was the visitor to a location. I'd have loved to believe these men would be his worst troops: the ones who drew the short straws and had to take the graveyard shift by obligation, the majority of their thoughts on whatever discount porn they might be missing out on.

But that's a dangerous assumption. These could be his best soldiers.

We divided into our three teams: two to engage from the sides and one to come over the back wall. Alpha Team, Bravo Team, Charlie Team.

Rita and I took Alpha toward the driveway.

Quiet and invisible. Those are the golden adjectives. We moved with as much silence as our boots would allow. No scuffling. No talking. Moving along routes that yield as much visual cover as possible. Bracing ourselves for the most complicated phase.

The entry.

Ideally, you fast rope directly onto a target, but Diego had used RPGs in the past: rocket-propelled grenades. So, no, the prospect of hovering in the air like a noisy piñata while angry men with rockets watched you from below was not desirable. Fifteen seconds up there would be an eternity. Too much potentially bad luck involved. No thanks.

My platoon didn't like bad luck. My platoon didn't even like good luck. We preferred drawing up two hundred different football-style diagrams with X's and O's, staring at maps and sketches, and letting everyone verbally shoot holes at our plans until we found one plan that seemed logistically bulletproof.

We passed quietly through the gate. And we arrived in the courtyard.

Already? Wait a second. This breach took no effort.

Oddly, this was the first sign that things were about to go horribly wrong.

The place was fully abandoned. From above, the compound looked like a normal set of buildings, but here at ground level, you could see this interior was hollow. Literally hollow.

Another group had already met us from the far end of their horseshoe-shaped journey. Bravo Team. We were all kind of staring at each other through a very empty structure: just some pillars and an old house with zero furniture.

"Bravo clear," said the Bravo Team Leader from a back room.

My heart sank.

"Charlie clear," said the Charlie Team Leader. Charlie had already arrived from the middle.

Is this over?

"Alpha clear," I said, barely able to hide the disappointment in my voice. I wasn't getting nominated for that Oscar anytime soon. My platoon quickly began to scour the complex. There was nobody here.

Was the Fat Man lying?

And then Kyra found the first sign of what was to come: Blood. Lots of it.

I was thinking we had just executed the biggest failure ever. I was wrong. The failure was just getting started.

CHAPTER 2

DIEGO CORRERA WAS MUCH more evasive than our mission budgets could handle. Some of our top Pentagon brass said he's just not qualified to be a priority, but during his rise to glory he butchered nearly twenty-nine hundred human beings, most of them innocent citizens, many of whom were children, with the worst aspect being *how* he did it.

It's a process he lovingly calls El Padron.

The first time I saw photos of El Padron, I threw up. I thought I'd seen it all. I'd been on over fifty missions in twelve years and led combat action in five different nation states, but I'd never seen anything as harsh as El Padron. It's like the guy was setting a world record for the most disturbing usage of pliers.

And there in that empty compound in Matamoros, I was about to get my first personal taste of it.

"Fat Man, this is Spider Actual. Do you copy?" I tried my radio on the off-chance that the Fat Man was patched in. "Fat Man, you there?"

He wasn't.

Kyra had blood on her sleeve from brushing up against a dark wall that was absolutely drenched with it. Fresh, bright red.

I began making my way to the roof of Diego's compound. Something was wrong here. Very wrong. Yes, it's possible that Diego was tipped off ahead of time, but, beyond my annoyance at being evaded, there was a growing unrest in me. How can this place be literally empty?

"Fat Man, do you copy?" I said again as I climbed up the courtyard wall, grabbing a rain gutter to pull myself up to the roof of the compound. My goal was to scout the town from a high position. There would be a decent vantage point up there. I needed to at least "feel" the visual, to satiate my nagging need to see that there was nothing to see.

There atop the second story, I raised my M16 and scoped the horizon with its sight lens. "Fat Man, come in." I was hoping to snoop around whatever was visible a half mile down the main road.

I wouldn't need to look that far.

El Padron.

It was on our front porch.

The "message" was set up for us in front of the compound. At first I saw only one. But then I saw another and another. And by the time Rita joined me, there were twenty-three to behold.

Police officers.

All dead.

Two dozen Matamoros police officers, murdered, left in the street like confetti. Killed for no other reason than to tell us, tell my platoon, who we were dealing with. We were being warned.

"How can you be sure this is for us?" asked Rita.

"It's for us," I said, wishing it weren't.

"Colonel!" yelled Kyra.

She was calling me from below. She was already on the street, investigating. The other platoon members were slowly, quietly elbowing each other, calling attention to the spectacle out front. Kyra was the first one to the center and she had found something she wanted me to see.

I went down. And I saw.

Each of the dead bodies was mutilated with an extra type of signature. It was known as Diego's Cross. He would etch it into the flesh of his victims. The wounds were fresh, the blood still trickling. His violently sarcastic artwork had taken place just minutes ago.

Minutes ago.

That meant our entire arrival was logged on their evening agenda. I grabbed the radio handset off our radio man. No more audio protocol.

Rita tried to slow me down. "Wait, Colonel." She was going to tell me there's no connection, no listener, no rational reason to bark what I was going to bark. But it didn't matter: I had already begun shouting into the void. "Fat Ass, I swear to God, do you have any idea what's on the street in front of—?"

"Tango, eight o'clock!" Kyra called out, dropping to her knee and aiming her M27 directly at the shadows behind us.

We all instantly spun around, took cover, and aimed, waiting for the silence to usher in a shit storm of trouble.

None of us lit up, though. Our potential tango, as in potential target, as in potential enemy, as in we're about to reduce you to burger meat, was a little girl.

"Hold your fire!" shouted Rita.

"Hold," I reiterated to my platoon. *We're not here to kill kids.* "Hold!"

The child was about nine years old. Unarmed. Alone. A local. She was emaciated but there was a raw energy to her eyes. She was driven by something deep inside.

She stood in the middle of the street and looked right at me, eye to eye. She knew I was in charge and I could tell she would deliver her message only to the one in charge. Undaunted, unabashed, she faced me directly, then raised her index finger and gradually pointed in my direction.

Slowly, viciously, she pointed at her own throat. She made the cross sign.

"Ya tenemos usted," she said with a carnivorous smile.

Then she walked away. Her words hung in the air.

We already have you.

CHAPTER 3

ARRIVING BACK HOME IN Archer, Texas, usually felt good. It had been only a two-day jaunt, the Matamoros fiasco, but that's enough to feel like forever.

You miss everything when you're away. Everything. The traffic, the radio, the mini-malls, even the trash on the street. Why? Because that trash is hometown trash. That trash is made up of scraps of daily life. My daily life.

But nothing compares to the first glimpse of your front door. Both of my daughters love Halloween more than they love their own birthdays, so at this point our porch was covered with pumpkins and skeletons and Disney witches. Even though it was mid-September.

They were expecting me tomorrow morning, which technically was still five hours away, so I didn't want to wake them. I didn't even want to wake my husband. I just wanted to slide under the poofy sheets and reverse spoon him. To disappear into his dreams. True stealth.

He was a heavy sleeper. His fantasy football app would be the last thing on his phone besides one or two naughty texts from yours truly. He'd be out cold. Our hallway floor always creaked, so I took my time with each step. Nothing seems louder than walking to your kitchen at 2:00 a.m. I could even hear the fabric of my pants slide against itself.

I gently pushed open our bedroom door. We always sleep with it slightly ajar. Tonight was no exception. He'd learned over the years—the years and years of unpredictably long or short missions—that his sexy colonel could potentially saunter in at any hour of the night, and if he played his cards right, he could get that "she outranks me" sex he bragged to his buddies about. Though, on this occasion I was already spent, already shell-shocked from what my platoon had seen. *We already have you.* Drained from a day and a half without sleep. Tonight I'd be using him as a slab of warm comfort. He has his back to me. Curled in a fetal position. Perfect.

I crawled onto the bed.

And then my hand squished into a swamp.

A wet area of the mattress.

My first thought was that our eight-year-old

was just here, napping, and probably had wet the bed. She'd probably left, stayed quiet, and thereby Daddy never knew. My second thought was that my husband had a fever and he was sweating out what had become a lagoon.

My third thought wasn't a thought. It was professional opinion.

My husband is dead.

I finally saw it. Bullet holes through his shoulder and through his temple. Heavy sleeper—they shot him in his dreams. His head was half gone. He'd been dead for at least three hours. *Who's they?* My legs were already carrying me down the hall. It wasn't even an instinct. It was like I was watching myself appear ahead of me. Fast. Inexorable. *Who's they?* Already bursting through their bedroom door. Already flicking up the light switch, already prepared . . .

To scream.

The training manual says to arrive at a violent situation and execute your training with dispassionate precision. Don't yell out your reaction. The enemy could still be nearby. Don't gasp. The enemy could get the first attack.

Don't let anyone know what emotional state you're in.

Keep quiet. Watch exits. Assess the scene. Keep your weapon up.

I did none of that.

My daughters were dead.

Both of them. Within several feet of each other. I grabbed my limp babies. The manual says to flee a situation where there is clear and present danger and insufficient intel. That's Chapter Nine.

What chapter is the chapter that says how to carry your dead daughters over to your dead husband? And place them in front of you, in a futile group hug, so that God could see that he might have made a mistake? That there is an undo button somewhere at his console he can press?

God didn't press it.

Diego's Cross was permanently etched on my family's flesh.

I made the only phone call my hands and my spinal cord were capable of making. I called Rita. I didn't speak. I couldn't. I couldn't make my mouth emit words. But she could hear my throat cracking in the air. She could hear all she needed to hear to know that this isn't Amanda's normal communication. And so Rita was gonna do what Rita would then do.

"This is your home phone?" she asked without expecting a reply. Calm. Decisive. Bankable. "Be there in four minutes."

CHAPTER 4

Present Day

THAT WAS THE BEGINNING. That was what led me here to this freeway underpass, parked under a tree just beyond it, eighty miles east of El Paso. A million miles south of paradise.

Waiting. Watching.

I was in a sedan, waiting for the arrival of a particular truck. Rita was parked five miles away, watching from a small hillside. Page one of that manual I mentioned earlier says that heat is a state of mind. You can decide to be uncomfortable. You can decide not. I stopped feeling things entirely. It had been two years since I became a person without a family. At this point in my life, my skin doesn't feel. My skin merely assesses.

"Badger Three to Badger Eight."

I was talking to the Fat Man. I was using identification codes that intentionally misrepresented the size of our team. When your numbers are small, you want your enemy to think you are large. When you are large, you want them to think you are small. So says Sun Tzu.

I was no longer an active Marine. I was free-lance.

"How's the road?" asked the Fat Man.

"Empty."

"What about the temperature?"

"Hundred and five," I replied. "About to get hotter."

Rita's voice then came on the radio. "Eyes on tango, Badger Three. Point-eight klicks. Barrel-assin' your way."

I looked up. I saw the truck. A big rig. Un-marked. Driving well over the speed limit, heading toward my position.

Time to rock.

"Good luck," said the Fat Man.

"Don't need it," I told him.

CHAPTER 5

I PUT MY POLICE beacon on the roof of my sedan, flicked on the siren, and stomped on the gas. The enemy was on eighteen wheels and moving fast.

You never know how someone's going to react to getting lit up by the law. Most normal people freeze mentally and pull over erratically slow. They cooperate almost to a fault. But this guy could have warrants out. He could have paperwork issues. He could have a girlfriend who just told him she cheated on his ugly mug. He could have whiskey in him. Brass knuckles. You never knew.

He pulled over as soon he cleared the bend. This picnic was just getting started.

His big rig took a half minute to slow to a stop. I had to assume this was sufficient time for him to radio his contacts, his pals, his boss, his muscle, his mom, whomever. And I, of course, had to assume he was leaning over to his glove box and getting, what would be my guess, a Glock. I had my own Glock. Making for a Glock-on-Glock fight.

I don't like those odds. I don't like a fair fight. Ever. That sort of macho B.S. might work on a TV show, but in real life I never want a level playing field. I want the upper hand in every possible category. If you have a black belt in jujitsu, I want a knife. If you have a knife, I want a gun. If you have a gun, I want a missile. A missile that shoots smaller missiles from its side missiles and that bleeds acid. I want surprise on my side. I want backup. I want a sniper covering my six. I want my enemy drunk, sitting on a toilet, asleep, when I find him.

But that's a perfect story that never gets told in the world of Amanda.

There's always one fun detail that jacks things up a bit.

I was walking up along the left side his trailer. I would have loved to stay in his blind spot but truck mirrors pretty much cover all angles.

I knocked on his door and he opened up. *Game on.*

"Do you know how fast you were going?" I asked him.

"*¿Cómo?*" he replied. Accent thick. Mexican.

"I got you doing eighty-four in a seventy zone."

My goal was to keep him off track. Confuse him. Have him think I'm a cop initially.

"*Lo siento pero no hablo Ingles.*" But maybe he was the one confusing me. "*¿Es usted la policía?*"

"Keep your hands where I can see them."

He didn't. His hands were roaming.

"Your *hands.*" I gestured to indicate the obvious.

"*¿Mis manos?*" he asked, seeming to barely, just barely, understand me. "*No hay una problema.*"

He was reaching for his center console. Slowly. As if his slowness would go unnoticed.

"*¡No te muevas!*" I shouted at him. "*Tus manos.*"

"*¿Mis manos?*" Was he really thinking he was going to grab his weapon before I could react? Yes, he was.

Five tenths of a second later, he was pointing a .38 Special in my general direction and I was already firing three quick shots at his hand.

I missed my first but the second and third bullets both nailed him in the arm, ruining his chances for a response.

There was a second guy in the cab, the wingman. I hadn't yet seen him from my vantage point. He was getting ready to join the party, but Rita was lightning-quick to yank open his passenger door and get the muzzle of her Glock on his rib cage.

She had capitalized on the previous distraction.

"Damn, lady, what the hell's your problem?" yelled the injured driver.

"Get out of the cab!" shouted Rita. "Both of you. Now!"

They were slow and grumpy about it, muttering all sorts of hateful gems under their breath. *Bitches. Putas. Lesbians.* Trust me, coming from your enemy, these are all compliments. Every last syllable. The best part is they were cooperating, bless their little cotton socks, they were moving along, hands interlaced behind their sweaty heads, exiting, and separating themselves from our eighteen-wheel trophy.

"You're gonna run down the road," Rita told them. "Directly down the center line. And if you turn your head back...I shoot you."

They started to trot away from us.

"If you run slow, I shoot you," she declared.

They increased the speed of their trot by a billionth of a percent.

Rita fired a shot through the flannel shirt flap of contestant number two. Didn't hit his body. Just hit his shirt. From a field goal away. On a moving target. She's that good.

They started to sprint.

"If you drift to the side, I shoot you!" she yelled.

They ran so dead center it was almost comical.

And soon the heat waves from the asphalt drowned them from our sight. And soon we were going to work. Barbecue time!

We had backpacks full of C-4, my favorite way to end the life of a large vehicle. Fuse detonation. Lightweight. Very stable. Rita cracked the padlock off the back with the butt of her gun and swung open the trailer doors. The cargo bay was mostly empty except for a pyramid of sacks piled up against the front end. Sacks of cocaine? Yes. Sacks of meth? Yes.

Sacks of them.

Not a bad haul. I'd say a quarter of a million's worth, as a guess.

Leaving our backpacks nuzzled down in the heart of the matter, fuses lit, we scrambled out of the trailer top-speed. We both got in my car and spun around, fishtailing it, gravel flying, hustling to flee the scene as fast possible, just as—*boom*—a concussion blast of ten M112 bricks of plastique shattered that truck into last Tuesday.

Diego Correra isn't going to like this.

CHAPTER 6

NOR WAS HE gonna like this....

Within a twenty-mile drive from the previous raid, we had located the second of Correra's big rigs. A Peterbilt. We were tracking the driver on a desolate stretch of Highway 285, waiting for him to be truly alone. The question was whether or not he had been warned by the last guy.

He pulled over as soon as he saw my police beacon light up.

As far as we knew, the last thing his buddy would've announced is that some asshole cops were detaining him. We made sure they didn't take their phones with them on their involuntary hike. So, yes, they might have broadcasted that the law was stopping them but, fine, that was a much better bulletin than, *Dios mío, some crazy bitches just blew up our truck.*

When we got the Peterbilt driver to open his

driver door, he was more angry than surprised. Almost indignant.

"Do you know whose shit this is?"

I looked over at Rita. He was engaging us as if we were bribed cops, as if we were on Diego's payroll. What do we say to this? Play it cool? Play dumb? We didn't look like cops. At best, we looked like immigration patrol. But this was the type of bandit who wouldn't care regardless.

"Do you know whose shit this is!" he asked again.

"I guess it's mine." I had to speak up. My mouth does that. And then it added, "As of today."

"This is the property of Diego Correra, you dead pig. You know who you're dealing with?"

"Not really. Is he nice? He seems nice. Does he give you dental benefits? Because you could use some."

"And you just wasted your time," he said, pointing to his trailer, "because this shit is empty." He started laughing, his yellow teeth gleaming in the sun. "I already made the drop."

Rita and I traded a look. This would really suck. An empty bed. It would mean Diego had one-upped me. Again. The driver seemed excited that we were escorting him to the rear of his vehicle, that we were about to open up his trailer's doors and witness his hilarious joke.

"Open the gate," Rita said to him. *"¡Muévelo!"*

He led us to the back and started to unlatch the door. Squeaking the bolt like crazy. The pride in this guy's demeanor—I was cringing at the thought that his truck would be bare.

The door opened up and, here we go, two of his pals were right there, AK-47s all set, immediately unleashing a spray of bullets right at us. *Ambush!*

Rita and I both dove for the ground, tumbling as tightly as we could, to roll forward, into the protective cover of the truck itself. Wheels, metal, axles, anything. My only thought was to get behind a barrier, any possible barrier, because if these guys had the sense to shoot directly downward through their floor, they'd have a good chance of shredding us.

And I hate chances like that.

I was just getting to a crouch and soon enough a rain of high-caliber bullets came streaking down around us. Rita was on the far side of the combat zone, already in the ditch, just off the road, scurrying for some rocks. Smart *muchacha.* She would have a great angle of attack once they emerged from the tailgate.

The thing is, now all three of them were armed.

I was listening to their footsteps above me. They had emptied out their magazines on us and a reload might give me just enough time to roll out from the wheel well and unleash one mediocre flurry of upward shots. Glocks versus AK-47s. Not fun. Never bring a slingshot to a missile fight. The creaking floor above indicated my enemy was doing the same thing I was. Positioning. The driver stayed still, I think, but his two pals headed toward the exit. He must be staying home to guard the goods. Or to come over to where I was, by the wheels. I let loose three quick shots. Fifteen degrees apart.

I heard him gasp.

Payday. I must have at least nicked him. The other two guys started whispering to each other. I think they were deciding to leap out and surprise me because what happened next was a one-woman greeting party by my favorite lieutenant.

Rita took them out from her hiding place in the ditch. Two quick shots. And two quick dropped bodies.

"Two out!" she yelled.

"Trailer!" I yelled back. She needed to know we had a third of our enemy still on the menu.

"Compadre," she shouted to the third guy. "We have you trapped! Throw the gun out! Then come slowly into my sight!"

I could hear him shuffling around. I must have

grazed him in the leg or something nonvital. He had strength and energy. I could hear him prepping for his epic finish.

"Last chance!" I shouted. "Or we're gonna blow your ass to burger meat."

"*Ultima vez!*" shouted Rita. "*Tenemos plastique.*"

She was hoping the threat of our explosives would convince him to behave. We made our decent offer. Would he take it?

A tiny moment of silence settled over the desert. We were alone. Possibly for miles. A slight breeze came and went. Then suddenly a storm of bullets squirted out of the trailer's side wall. The guy was probably praying he could somehow hit Rita without knowing where she was.

I shoved my second bag of C-4 directly into the belly of the trailer. Rita dashed up and tucked her own bag near the trailer hitch. Because we couldn't operate directly on the interior of the target, we'd have to compensate by doubling our dose on the exterior.

This guy was about to be erased from earth.

"Fuse!" I yelled.

"Fuse!" she yelled back. We couldn't see each other but this wasn't our first rodeo: We knew our standard operating procedure was to default to detonation. "Three...Two...One..."

I lit my fuse. She lit hers.

We both ran for the opposite side of the highway. Toward the parallel ditch on the far side. Diving for cover. Just as our friend let out another spray of bullets through the wrong wall of his mobile fort. Within five seconds, *wham!* Our explosives lit up half of west Texas. A towering fireball.

Police sirens had already started to wail in the distance, so we had to go.

The law was coming.

And we weren't exactly on the right side of it.

CHAPTER 7

KYRA JOINED US FOR the next raid. She had missed the last two because we'd sent her to obtain more explosives on the black market. It sounds funny to say, but we ran out of things that go *boom*. She was waiting on her connection, a shady group of bikers in Lovington, New Mexico, while Rita and I executed those first two raids. C-4 is only about fifteen dollars a pound. But that's the price only if you have time to wait and if you trust your source and if you need only a small quantity and if you don't need to be an anonymous buyer.

We were absolutely none of those things.

The bikers wanted five thousand dollars.

Nobody said justice was cheap.

During the next two days, the three of us converged on every active Correra shipment in Texas. He had routes strewn all over the back roads of El Paso, Dallas, Houston, and Laredo.

Some loads were obviously his. Like the unmarked Peterbilt with serial numbers still visible for us to confirm. Some were tricky. He had a six-wheeler disguised as a Hertz rental truck, upon which his goons even went so far as to latch a bicycle on the back, just to throw off us dogs completely.

But we had the list from the Fat Man. And the list was relentlessly accurate. It gave the description of each shipment and a time frame of when it would pass a certain point. "Highway 87. Milepost 55. Tuesday evening. White big rig with blue cab."

We blew it all up like clockwork.

The quantity of C-4 Kyra obtained was phenomenal. More powerful than we expected. Sent a tower of fire and smoke high up into the clouds.

We were perched on a plateau overlooking a nice lonely stretch of Interstate 380. Kyra was using her Steiner high-power binoculars to track our prey.

"Well, I have him in sight," said Kyra. "But..."

"But what?" I asked.

"Cessna. Five o'clock."

Cessna? I looked up in the expansive desert sky. Yup. I saw a small plane circling our general area. Was it state troopers? Sheriffs? This was a problem. The police were using planes now. We had detonated enough C-4 to make national news. Nobody knew that we were the ones behind these raids, which was ideal, but the fact that there were drugs in the trucks was kept secret from almost every single article. To discourage copycat behavior, the authorities didn't want to report moral victories. Fine. I didn't want applause. I wanted Diego. But I called off our half-week rampage at target number seven.

"We're letting this one go," I said.

"Because of the plane?" she replied.

"Too much attention."

"Let's just do this one last one. We're right here."

"Negative, Sergeant. Stand down."

We had earned our rest. It was time to lie low for a bit and be as normal as possible. Diego Correra operates nearly fifteen shipments a month. We hit half of them and thereby pissed in his revenue stream to the tune of four million dissolved dollars. For men who like money, the best way to hurt them is to punch them in the money.

And I was just getting started.

CHAPTER 8

THE PLACE WE WERE heading home to was Righteous. Literally. Righteous was the name of the repair garage that Kyra and I built. She started it when neighbors kept asking her to tweak their motorbikes and lawn mowers and dune buggies. Eventually, she graduated herself to cars and trucks and even boats. All of us were comfortable with power tools. Kyra, however, was a mechanical genius. And in a town like Archer, Texas, where locals thrive on old motors, we had stumbled on the formula for contentment.

For me, going in on Kyra's repair business was simply a chance to keep my hands busy, which was a chance to keep my brain busy, which was a chance to keep my heart busy.

Not that it ever worked.

Not that I could ever find sixty consecutive seconds in a day when I wasn't thinking about my family.

Next door to Righteous the Repair Shop was Righteous the Cafe. We served miserably under-priced doughnuts and delicious everything else. On Tuesdays Rita made gumbo. Fresh sausage. Fresh veggies. Some of the locals would bring in produce from their own gardens.

It was that kind of town.

Rita and her husband had made quite a nest for themselves. The income from the cafe wasn't gluttonous but it was enough to cover its own cost. And its ten-acre setup was perfect for our needs. Base camp.

That night I was helping in the back with the dishes when Rita came to me with the mail.

"I think you should see this," she said.

It was a greasy, plain envelope addressed to me. The smudges made it look like it came from another mechanic somewhere. Clever camouflage. But it was a little too greasy. A little too carefully messed up. I knew the situation. We all did. I started to open it, with Rita giddy, as Kyra locked the door. Inside was a check for two hundred thousand dollars.

The Fat Man delivereth.

He may be a lot of things (annoying, tardy, elusive, cryptic, suspicious, allegedly fat) but one thing is unmistakable about our unknown friend: He pays.

He pays well.

Two hundred thousand dollars split into three goes a long way in a backwater town like Archer. None of us lived like royalty. We were more likely to wear Smith & Wesson than Dolce & Gabbana. We never took vacations. We never bought yachts.

Kyra held up the check for us like a title belt. We all smiled at each other knowing we did good work. For me, my share, it was sixty-six thousand dollars that simply went into a bank. Just a testament to the fact that money couldn't buy back a dead husband or two kids.

It couldn't even buy the end of Diego Correra. Or could it?

CHAPTER 9

THAT NIGHT, TO CELEBRATE the dent we put in Correra's financial shinbone, we opened up the cafe for a late-night romp. Open to the whole neighborhood. Music. Pie. Beer. On the house. We were that kind of town.

We cleaned up the garage and annexed it off as the world's most backwoods discotheque. Picture the barn dance in *Footloose* minus the barn. Domestic beer flowing. Free biscuits and gravy. Braised pork ribs worth starving yourself all day for. And, my goodness, a slice of pecan pie à la mode.

Rita and her rhythmic hubby captivated the middle of the dance floor. Kyra was getting hit on by half the locals, and I...

I couldn't be happier watching from the sidelines.

I managed to sneak back toward the periphery, unseen by the crowd. I didn't want to draw attention. There's a type of loneliness where you're just aching to be approached by someone to coax you back into the crowd. Then there's the loneliness that can't be solved by the mechanisms of this world.

I have that second type.

I miss my husband so much. I look up at the stars every night and search for his soul. I know he's there. I can feel it. I can hear him talking to me. And I know he's got both our little cherubs with him. And they're all pleasantly restless, waiting for me. But they're also looking down with understanding.

At least, I hope so.

I have the same argument in my head over and over. That I blew it. That I got them killed. That no matter what I do to Diego, it'll never address what Diego did to us.

Then I hear my family chime in. I hear them tell me I've always stood on the right side of any decision in life. That I'm not perfect. I make mistakes. But I don't make mistakes out of selfishness. I'm trying as hard as I can to contribute to this world.

To protect the kids of future generations.

"What are you doing?" came a voice from behind.

It was Gus, the honorary vice mayor. We have

an honorary vice mayor. It's that kind of town. Gus was ninety-seven years old and didn't look a day over ninety-six. Still drove a car. Still mowed his own lawn. He saw me out there in the darkness, beyond the doorway to the dance-hall garage.

"Oh...I...uh...heard a couple coyotes," I replied. "And wanted to make sure the hens were okay in the coop."

"Always on recon."

"Me? No. I'm just secretly a terrible dancer. I can't let anyone witness that."

He offered his hand. "Well, now I have to expose you." Bouncing his head to the music, he wanted to see me Texas two-step. No human being should be subjected to the sight of me dancing.

But he insisted. "You're a good person, Colonel. You deserve to wear a smile tonight."

He knew what was going on with me. I think the entire town did. When we entered the room and headed for the dance floor, they all cheered like I was a hero. It was really embarrassing, and it made me feel stupid. But I swear I could hear my kids cheering in the background as well.

And I could hear my husband's voice. I could hear him warning me.

That things were about to get rough.

CHAPTER 10

AROUND HERE IT DOESN'T take much to stick out. Archer, Texas. If all you did was get a faulty haircut, everyone would know about it within a half day. And it would be talked about. Passionately.

So when he arrived, of course he was the main topic of gossip.

I started hearing rumors that there was a stranger asking questions at local businesses, trying to seem casual about it. It raised red flags with certain friends of mine. We didn't know this stranger's name yet, but already the gaggle of ladies down at the salon were making uneducated guesses:

"I bet his name is Lorenzo. He's tall. Like Lorenzo tall."

"No, no, no, he's a Victor," said the second lady. "Those yummy shoulders."

"You're both wrong about my Derek," said the third lady.

It probably wasn't Derek. Most locals thought he was at least half Latino. He reportedly had a very slight but definite accent while doling out random questions to random people about the neighborhood. *Is it safe around here? Would this be a good place to raise a family? How well do you know your neighbors?*

He apparently had been asking around town about us without actually asking around town about us. Until the next day when he decided to stop being coy. He marched right into Righteous the Cafe and was soon joking around with the busboy and suckering him into a free round of billiards on our pool table. Kyra didn't like that. She didn't like that he skimped on paying the measly seventy-five cents for a rack.

"Excuse me, pal," she said to him. "Games ain't quite free."

But he wasn't going down easy. In fact, he wasn't even going to participate in the same conversation she started.

"So whose bar is this?" he asked.

"Bar?" said Kyra.

"Bar...cafe...I like it. You built this place yourself?" He smiled with each sentence. He had that Ted Bundy sort of charm. You couldn't help but like him, but you were also pretty sure he'd be murdering you by 9:00 p.m.

Kyra was direct. "It belongs to Rita. Me and Coll run the auto shop."

"Coll?" he asked, racking up the table for eight-ball. "Amanda Collins?"

"Are you here to play or to gossip? Because I can get some yarn and we can sit and knit. Otherwise, seventy-five cents."

He gestured to a dollar bill that was already on the table. He had indulged her fee. Without her knowing. Sly. Hot-guy sly.

She took the money as he cracked a thunderbolt break and sent three balls in three different pockets. All solids. He was here to play. In every sense of the word.

I was hearing all this firsthand. I was in the back of the diner, carrying boxes to the kitchen, shielding my face from view by my stack of cardboard. He hadn't seen me.

Until now.

Until he turned to me, calmly, knowing I was there the whole time. A cocky smile already orchestrated on his face, as if he knew I was stepping forward, as if his entire mission was this moment.

"Are you Amanda Collins?" he asked me.

Screw this guy.

"I'm not very good at pool," I replied. "So I'll make you a deal."

I set my boxes down and approached his table. "You win: I'll introduce myself. I win: you leave town immediately."

"Ouch. No kiss?"

"Deal?"

I figured I could at least scrimmage with him for a little bit and let him divulge whatever he might divulge about himself.

"Deal." He gave me a dangerously confident nod.

I've seen how these Mexican cartels send a message. When they have a true enemy, like myself, they can't just kill her. They need to make her front-page news.

"Whoops," he said, nailing his next shot nonchalantly. A combo.

How would they kill me? How would they amplify it? A severed head in front of a school? A burned body?

After two more shots, he finally missed, perhaps on purpose, and handed me the cue.

I yanked it from him, noting he had a large pistol in his jacket pocket. He was doing his best to hide this fact from me, but over the years I've gotten disturbingly good at spotting a concealed weapon, even under a puffy jacket.

I've also gotten disturbingly good at a two-cushion corner pocket shot. I kept up with his sharp shooting. We traded two rounds, then I sunk three stripes in a row and positioned myself for an easy fourth. He was better than me, but he was letting me win.

"Eight ball. Side pocket." I said. And sunk it. Game over.

"Good shot, Colonel."

I walked over to the front door, opened it, and held it there for him. "You a man of your word?"

"I am." He slowly walked over to me and stopped to get close to my face. "But I should tell you something."

"Oh yeah?"

"I'm coming back." He walked out the door. Heading to his car. And without looking at me, he added, "With friends."

CHAPTER 11

I **DIDN'T SLEEP MUCH** that night. I'm a bad sleeper in general, but that night I was staring at the ceiling fan, watching it go in circles, wasting brain cells ruminating on the fact that the blades keep slicing the same area, the same invisible circle of air, never slicing anything new, never improving their position.

I was also listening.

For him. The stranger.

By the time I finally felt slumber take hold of my thoughts, the first light of dawn was piercing my window. I slept like I was dead for an hour or so then awoke again. It was seven o' clock. I was still in bed but my mind was twisting around. Something didn't seem right. And after a half minute I realized what it was. There was no noise from the cafe kitchen.

I generally hear the assistant cooks start banging around early in the morning. Today there were some sounds from out back, but as I lay there, piecing together a sleepy recollection of the early morning hours, I realized the sounds I'd heard came from the garage, not the cafe.

The garage? Uh-oh.

I grabbed my bowie knife and headed outside to check around. This couldn't be what the Ted Bundy guy meant, could it? This quick of a return?

I crept into the garage through the backdoor and braced myself for the worst.

I didn't click on the light yet. I could see bad news the moment I stepped in. Our stuff was thrown everywhere, strewn all over the ground. The tool chests tipped over. The shelves ransacked. Everything we owned was flipped on its head.

Were they searching for something? What?

While I was standing there, mulling it over, I saw a shadow begin to creep along the wall. Someone prowling.

They were still in the room! The intruders. Whoever they were.

I ducked down behind the fender of a Chevy Tahoe and readied my knife. Terrified. Bewildered. Ready to rock.

Within seconds, I saw my enemy walking past me, well unaware of my presence. He was wearing a dark jacket and a dark hood. Six two. Probably 210 pounds. Up to no good.

I sneaked up on his backside, quick as a house cat, and instantly put him in a choke hold with the blade of my knife pressed directly onto his jugular. Checkmate, son! I had him at an absolute surrender position.

Finally in control, I was ready to ask him three brief questions, almost praying for him to give me false answers so I could have the moral green light to slit his jugular and drain him right on the spot.

And I was all set to begin question number one.

"Who—?"

But just as my mouth began to blurt out the first word, I felt the barrel of a Beretta M9 press on the base of my neck.

"Don't do it, Colonel."

It was the calm voice of my billiard opponent. He was so close I could smell his nuclear-grade aftershave. I wished I had moved more quickly and positioned myself closer to the door so that my flank wouldn't have been so vulnerable, but—damn it—shitty strategy on my part, I was cornered.

And outnumbered.

He did indeed bring his friends. In addition to

the thug under my knife, there were now two other thugs standing on both sides of me. In business suits.

I cooperated. I slowly, meekly, lowered my blade away from the throat in question.

"Who are you?" I asked him through gritted teeth.

"My name is Warren Wright," he said. "And these are my friends. We work for a fun little group called the DEA."

CHAPTER 12

AGENT WARREN WRIGHT HOLSTERED his weapon. All the guys around me then seemed to relax a bit. A very small bit. With the cat out of the bag, the fact that he'd revealed himself to me as a fed, the fact that they're *all* feds, the fact that his boring name is Warren Wright, the entire group seemed to decide I was no longer a threat to them.

Pfffff. If they only knew...

How close I came to breaking his jaw regardless. Him, with his stupid suit. And his stupid hair. And his impossibly white teeth. What they were doing here in my garage had yet to be politely explained to me. So I was impolitely furious.

Warren looked me up and down. He was smirking. He had enjoyed his words in this situation. He had enjoyed every last syllable.

"You look old up close," I told him.

"Incorrect. I look handsome. And responsible. But most of all you know what I look like? I look like the one who isn't going to jail."

"Jail," I repeated with disdain.

"Would you like me to tell you why?"

"Nope."

"Would you like me to tell you how done you are?"

"Nope."

"I wonder...have you heard anything about big rigs blowing up? On routes out of small towns? Small Texas border towns?"

I didn't have an answer for that. I didn't want to try to deny it. He obviously knew. He had half his department standing there, crammed into my Podunk garage. They weren't here for a banjo lesson, that's for sure.

"Let me repeat myself, Colonel Amanda Rae Collins, Highly Decorated Employee of the Month, have you heard anything about big rigs getting blown up?"

"N—"

"No, you haven't," he said, cutting off my *no* with his own slightly more contrived *no,* then pausing. This was him setting up his corny crescendo. (God, these government jackoffs are all the same. As if they were all issued the identical dismal sense of humor at academy graduation. The type of idiot banter that guarantees they will never have sex.) All to set up his grand explanation of world facts: "You know why you haven't heard about it? Because *we* buried the story," he replied to himself, with pride. "*We* did."

Silence.

I think it was my turn to speak. To be impressed.

"Each time?" I finally broke the silence.

"We can do that."

"Do you want me to clap? Slowly?"

Warren leaned in close. I could smell the federal on his breath. The faint odor of decaf and bureaucracy. "We're watching you and your little girlfriends. We know all about your history with Diego. The games. The felonies."

"He's more than a *felon*."

" 'I'm talking about *you*. About illegal behavior."

"Oh, yes, please keep *talking*. Let's just spend the next month *talking*. And filling out forms. And holding conference calls. And spell-checking email. Meanwhile, that bag of shit is still at large. And have you seen what he's done?"

"I've seen what *you've* done," said Warren. "So far. And I'll tell you something, we know how to *keep* you doing it."

"What?"

He didn't answer.

There's no way he could be saying what I thought he was saying—was he giving us his government-issued blessing to continue our crusade? "Keep me doing what?" I asked again.

He had turned away and was about to exit the garage but he stopped. This was his patented move. He was going to savor this moment.

"Doing...nothing," he said.

I had to stand there for a moment and absorb it. *Keep me doing nothing? How could he think we weren't accomplishing anything!?* He looked over at me, smug about his little zinger. Then he nodded for his nerd clan to pick up a few items of mine: to gather two of our trunks and a couple of our duffel bags, holding our only six rifles, plus our only stash of ammo.

"That's our only chance!" I protested, referring to the weapons. "That gear was *not* easy to get, you need to leave all that here."

"Sure, Amanda, as soon as you show me a permit." His posse then funneled behind him as he exited. *"Hasta luego."*

I watched him leave. (More like smelled him leave.) I was fuming. "Oh, the *luego* is coming, you bastard. Just you wait."

CHAPTER 13

CHURCH WAS FULL ON Sunday. Church is always full in Archer. Part of it is pure piety. Part of it is Rita. Rita is one of the most beautiful souls this town has ever seen. One of the most eloquent. One of the most loved. Our pride and joy. Our pastor.

She was mid-sermon. And reiterating one particular point over and over again. "I'm so sorry," she said to the congregation.

She was talking about the DEA raids. Most everyone knew about them at this point, but she took them personally. She took them as an affront to her way of life.

"...That they would come into your neighborhoods, violating the sanctuary of the Home. That they would trample the rights and values of the very backbone of this proud community, the fundamental backbone: family."

A murmur of *amens* circulated in the room. About four hundred people were present, and aside from maybe two or three teenagers texting each other and Gus snoring gently, I daresay every single sheep in this flock was fully invested.

"I'm so sorry that our *families* were subjected to this," said Rita. "It's no secret that my busy past has drawn undue attention to you, and I beg you your forgiveness." Another murmur of support from the crowd.

My thoughts couldn't help wandering to the last remark from Agent Warren Wright. *Nothing.* Uttered merely days ago. *Amanda is doing nothing.* It wasn't the caustic attitude behind it that stung me: It was the truth of it.

I had indeed done nothing.

I had accomplished nothing. I had improved nothing. Diego was probably richer and smiling harder today than he had ever smiled before. All thanks to me and my big bucket of nothing.

Kyra was in the back. She didn't (as she put it) "subscribe to all this stuff." But she'd do anything to support one of our trio, even if it meant enduring two hours of (as she put it) "doctrine." Secretly, I was hoping one of the nice guys from the fire department in the third row would turn around and ask her to, I don't know, roller skate

with him, or something. But Rita was too capti-
vating up front.

It was poetic and inspiring. And I was so
caught up in it, her quotes from the Good Book,
the way she ushered us into hymnals, that it took
me a few seconds to realize she was about to
shatter my Sunday morning.

"Amanda, would you do us the honors?" she
said.

What?

She was looking at me. Me? Honors? What?
Why was she suddenly mentioning my name in
the middle of the sermon?

Rita had just asked me, in front of everyone,
to come up and share my views on "hope." She
had asked me about it yesterday. But I thought
she meant to write my dumb thoughts on someone's greeting card or something. I had no idea
she was going to make me say it out loud in front
of hundreds of people.

The entire church turned to look at me sitting
there. I swear an entire minute passed. I was
stunned. Gus soon leaned over and whispered to
me, "She wants you to go up front." I guess he
wasn't asleep after all.

Um.

I started to make my way to the front of the
room.

There were warm nods from various towns-
people. Dentists. Moms. Dads. Janitors. The
wondrous slice of diverse American pie that any
serving of Texas can offer. And, good gosh,
they were all expecting me to say something
amazing.

I slowly made my way to the front. I have
spoken quite often to large groups, to my
troops, but I did so as a colonel. I'd stood
on platforms under a large military tent. I
commanded the Fifth Regiment. As a *colonel*.
That's 1,227 Marines under my assignment,
allowing me to design their life or death
struggles.

I got to the altar.

I'm not a colonel these days.

Rita held me in place for a moment. I dread
this stuff. Seriously dread it. "We all know about
so much of Amanda's efforts out in the field," she
said to the crowd. "But what most of us don't get
to see is how much courage she displays in her
day-to-day affairs."

Oh, my God.

"She is determined," continued Rita. "She gives
100 percent."

Oh, my God. We all get through our day, whatever that day may bring. We all face it. We all
battle it. I'm not special. The room was spinning.

I hated standing up there. Rita finally finished and gave me a nod along with a graceful gesture that the podium was now mine.

When I talk to troops I'm not Amanda. I'm a colonel. And that colonel got sealed in an imaginary envelope when my husband died. I didn't have her inside me anymore. She was gone. So I was capable only of being 100 percent regular me at that point. And as I looked out at the sea of expectant faces, regular me freaked out.

I glanced over at Rita, who remained at my flank, the perfect position for an assassination. She smiled warmly, having no clue that she was setting me up for pure failure.

I mustered all my courage and conviction and emitted the following.

"...Uh..."

And that stupid-ass syllable, amped by the church's brand new 110-decibel sound system installed by gleeful Kyra, sounded like the belch of a dragon.

My hands started to shake.

"...Um...The...R-Rita...She wanted me to say a few words about taking a...Taking a... s-stand."

Good Lord, that sentence was the worst thing that ever came out of my mouth.

"Taking a stand...is...is hard."

My breath was gone. I could hear my voice quiver. Some people started to shift around in their seats.

"But it's only hard when you forget the one thing that matters most," I said. "The people you're standing up for."

There. I managed to get one thought out. It was a cliché at best, but at least it almost seemed like a decent point to make.

Looking out at all those eyes looking back at me, I was so far in over my head that I decided, *Screw it.*

Rita's face froze as she saw the look on my face. She was thinking I was about to implode.

I wasn't. I was finding my stride. I was starting to make sense to myself. Not easy to do.

"See, I've faced the working end of a Kalashnikov," I continued, "stepped over Syrian land mines, been trapped in a collapsing bunker in Korea. But I've managed to find hope even in the most hopeless nightmares thanks to one thing: I always knew that I was doing it for my people. Without that thought, I definitely would have tumbled."

I felt like I was making sense to them. The congregation. I paused, feeling the room.

"You brought this on us," came an angry voice from the back.

Which was the last thing in the world I expected to hear. It was this guy who worked at the local dive bar. Phillip, I think was his name. A decent man. Vocal.

"You know we just like to mind our own business here," he continued. "This town doesn't need to go kickin' on a foreign hornet's nest."

A lot of the congregation instantly rallied in my defense. "Amanda is amazing." "Quiet, Phil!" "Don't say stuff like that!"

Phillip continued. "We got our own problems. Vandals. Gangs. Shootings."

"Sit down, Phil!" said a number of people. "You're out of line!"

But I disagreed with their disagreement. I was hearing my own words, echoing in my ears, realizing how hypocritical I'd be to ignore the truth.

"He's right," I said, and the room suddenly quieted. "Phillip's right. I have no business making this town a second priority."

I thanked the crowd and walked back to the pews. Amid silence. It was awkward, no question. But I had figured something out. Phil had helped me see it: I can't just attack Diego and watch him attack me and my people back, us attacking each other back and forth, again and again like the two of us were in a boxing match.

I don't care what the excuses are at this point; I have to finish him.

CHAPTER 14

HOW DO YOU FIGHT a war without weapons? Answer: You don't. The first battle is to prepare for the battle. Which means we needed to get *new* weapons.

DEA interference was just a bump in the road. I couldn't whimper in the corner about how tough I had it. I needed to move forward. I needed to treat every phase of the preparation like it was part of the grand battle.

We'd been fighting with low-budget guns on both sides of the equation, but it was a guarantee that Diego would refortify his drivers immediately—as in, he'd increase their fire power. I could imagine he'd also add secondary vehicles as escorts, maybe a guy on a dirt bike, maybe a guy in a sport pickup, a technical.

Rita found a headline on a Mexico City news site that gnawed at my soul. "Nineteen People Dead in Ranchita." Diego had retaliated against us. Against me. He was ravaging small villages in Mexico that had shown support for US intervention in the past.

"And look at this second article," said Rita. She knew this would get my attention. This update was even worse: The people who were killed were kids. Nineteen girls from an all-girls kindergarten.

My hands were shaking. I was ready to fight the entire planet at this point. I was so sick of hearing about psychotic dickheads doing mass damage, I had to make a move. *We* had to make a move.

The biggest gun store in Archer was run by two brothers from Arkansas. Arm & Arm Gun Depot. In addition to overcharging for every item in the store and boozing on the shooting range, these gentlemen had both been convicted of assault on a disabled kid. Truly not the pride of Archer, they would sell weapons to minors and violate just about every law invented, given the chance.

Which meant Rita, Kyra, and I felt comfortable obtaining weapons from them in our own special way.

It was 2:15 a.m. We were on the outskirts of town, standing in front of Arm & Arm.

"We should make sure—"

Smash!

Before Rita could even finish her brilliant sentence on the importance of being subtle, Kyra sailed a brick through the front window. She was already entering the premises.

"My gosh, our fingerprints will be all over," said Rita. "There's gonna be video. Surveillance."

"No, there won't," I told her.

"How do you know?"

"Because we're gonna burn it down."

CHAPTER 15

WE ENTERED ARM & ARM Gun Depot and ransacked every nook, obtaining the key weaponry we needed for our quest. If you want a short-muzzle compact machine with kick, may I suggest the MP5, easily modified to automatic fire? Picture Tom Cruise running around in *Mission: Impossible.* Now add my face and subtract his cinematic grin. I rarely grin while blasting up a warehouse.

That's the MP5. I love it. And Kyra knows I love it. So we got two.

Rita took a shotgun, double barrel, eight concussion grenades, and an Eickhorn combat knife. Those blades are nasty. You can cut the base of a streetlamp with one. (If you're ever sitting around feeling super angry at streetlamps, I guess).

Kyra started the ignition on our getaway minivan. We had doused the place with gasoline, added some sloppiness so it didn't look like the handiwork of the three most obvious bitches in town and, *whoomf,* we set the place ablaze—

Just as Kyra ran back inside.

What was she doing?! We tried to grab her but she squirmed out of our clutches, disappeared through the door, and, within seconds, emerged toting an SR-25 sniper rifle.

"Christmas in July!" she said.

"It's December," said Rita.

"I know, but nobody says Christmas in December."

CHAPTER 16

A FEW DAYS LATER, we were standing across the street from La Sombre Fashion Boutique, a fancy dress shop in town, at 1:45 a.m. We had been debating which unlucky spot would be our decoy, and this was it. When you're doing multiple break-ins, you have to confuse the pattern a bit, just in case a bunch of sheriffs were in front of a wall map of Texas, putting colored thumbtacks in all the right places.

But something about it felt so odd.

"Are you sure?" asked Rita.

"Based on your wedding dress alone, definitely!" said Kyra. "They so overcharged you."

"It was French," I chimed in.

"I love that dress," said Rita. "I thought you did, too."

"There's no decent reason to charge a good Texas woman fifty-five hundred dollars for a dress!" said Kyra, hurling a brick as hard as she could, shattering the display window. Helluva shot from this far away. She was a pitcher in high school. Never lost the arm.

Within a split second the security alarm was ringing. A fancy-pants French boutique like this has pricey merchandise, so of course the only two patrol cars active this late in a town this small would soon be screeching to a halt right here. Which was our goal.

Because we were leaving.

Our first stop was the Shooter Rooter gun store located on the opposite side of town. We took side streets and drove there as fast as we could.

Skidding to a stop just at the curb, we jumped out and doused the exterior walls with gasoline with the intention to then pour as much as we could down the pipes on the roof. Inner and outer fuel.

This wasn't a necessary part of the Diego equation, but it was important to all three of us. Automatic weapons were in the wrong hands. True, the rights to defend yourself and protect your home are a vital aspect of individual, self-preserving freedoms. But the stores here in Archer had become like video game centers. Kids were coming in, bypassing paperwork, and walking out with hollow points and Armalite assault rifles. Worse, there was a growing armada of teen delinquency in town. Being a known drug stop had proliferated the usage of weaponry to solve problems. We were infested.

"Flame set!" yelled Kyra.

She was on the roof and ready to drop her pilot lighter down the pipe shaft at the same time that Rita and I were going to ignite the outside fuel. This would give us a solid chance of burning the whole thing down at once rather than some sort of half-assed beginners-grade arson.

Flick.

We ran top speed back to the car. Within moments the flames were licking up the sides of the walls.

The bonus of blazing up a gun store is the aid of all the explosives inside that are destined to go off. Heat and pressure can do that.

When it finally exploded, it was like the Fourth of July. In December.

I hated that we were committing arson, but here's what I hated more: junior high school kids getting shot by junior high school kids. So, yeah, when it comes to the lesser of two evils, I'll take this, with a cinematic grin.

CHAPTER 17

THE NEXT MORNING I woke up at 6:05 when my phone began to ring. You'd think there might be a congratulatory message for a righteous deed or two, not that I was looking for one. I couldn't really expect one without the obvious accompanying criminal charge. But the call was from a phone number I didn't recognize, with an area code that seemed two digits short.

"—Grrehhhfffolllll," I said.

When a call wakes me up in the morning, my top goal is to appear completely awake. However, my unstretched vocal cords could do nothing but roar a hello that, I swear, must've sounded like a motorcycle rev.

Didn't matter, though. Within two syllables of my caller's reply I already knew the beginning, middle, and end of what would be the ugliest conversation I'd had in quite some time.

"Amanda," said the man.

It was the voice of disappointment. He wasn't greeting me. He wasn't commending me. He was shaking his head, slowly, side to side at the other end of the phone. I could hear the muscles in his neck.

I was waiting for the tongue click sound of disappointment my mother invented long ago but he plunged ahead.

"Arson? Really?" he said.

This was the Fat Man. The one and only.

"You! You got some nerve," I replied. "I had my balls busted by the feds. *Feds*. Who ransacked my garage, stole my gear, and shat on my morality. And you...you didn't do a single thing to help us out. Nope. Meanwhile, the only word I get on Diego Correra—remember him?—is when he gets a PR parade on the evening news!"

He didn't respond. He sat on the silence for a moment.

"You're wasting your time," he finally said. "I need you ready for Diego."

No pause from me. "Listen, Fat Boy, my entire life is dedicated to ending his but I can't do *an-y-thing* with the DEA parking a car in my ass. They came to my town. My town! And they pissed all over it with paperwork from some oily loser named Warren Wright. How am I supposed to take down Diego with all this shit? I need to hit him *directly,* not just his shipments!" I was yelling now. I wasn't even mad. I was more jilted, jilted that the Fat Man hadn't called me sooner. I felt like a high-school cheerleader nagging her ex.

"Colonel Collins, I'm gonna do you a massive favor and pretend you didn't just cry about how hard the DEA is being on you. Are they firing bullets? No. Are they torturing villagers? No. Are they locking you up in a cellar? No. Stay focused."

"Listen, the last time I—"

Click. He was gone.

I hated this guy.

He paid. That's about it. That's about the nicest thing I can say about a gopher hole like him. His checkbook didn't suck.

The thing that scared me, though, all jokes aside, is the fact that my own contact didn't know what the DEA was up to. How is that logistically possible? How could they come after me and my friends without scuffling up a dust storm in Washington? What were they doing in my town? Were they still here?

Were they being bribed by Diego?

Were they *working for* Diego?

CHAPTER 18

"WE HAVE NO CHOICE," said Rita. "We have to check if the DEA is still in town."

"That could be dangerous," I replied, trying to sound profound. "You can't simply *spy* on the DEA while it's trying to spy on you."

We all looked at each other. It was one of those late nights in the garage. Kyra was all greasy from arguing with an engine's intake manifold and I was elbows-deep in a dead Buick. Rita had brought us clam chowder, which we drank from mugs. We three ladies do a terrible job of being dainty.

"We can't launch a war if they're sitting in the backseat waiting to yank the wheel," I said, as I took my arms out of the engine.

"Why not?" said Kyra.

"Because the next time we raid a convoy, they could put us in jail."

"No, *why not* as in why not spy on them?" clarified Kyra.

"What do you mean?" Rita set her mug down. It was one of those set your mug down types of proposals.

"We don't know if they're still here. I mean, if they're gone, if they're not even paying attention...then...then..."

"Then their entire visit was fake," concluded Rita. Which silenced us for a little bit.

Fake?

Later that night, Kyra and I ventured out to a few sketchy motels around town. Let the games begin.

We found one clerk idling in his office, watching shark attack videos on his laptop. The trick was to pretend we were the type of ladies who wanted to meet "dudes in suits." Which was doable because Kyra is blessed with the following problem: She looks like Audrey Hepburn. She looks so much like Audrey Hepburn, she spends most mornings dressing up to not look like her.

Except tonight.

Tonight she was doing recon. Civilian style. And she was wearing a cocktail dress and altitude shoes and talking like a bimbo. "Are there, are...y'know...eligible guys who might be...at the pool tomorrow...being eligible-y?" she said to the clerk.

This man was helpless before her. He said there was a ton of such guys. Smiled, pulled the toothpick from his mouth, and was delighted to try to pimp out his friends.

"No, no, no, more like, y'know...guys in suits...types," said Kyra. "Are there...that?"

"You wanna wrangle a fella in a suit?" The toothpick went back in the mouth.

"Does that type come in here?" I asked.

"Naw. Last June, we had some gents from the fishing expo. But they was bearded 'n' such. You like beards?" He stroked his beard.

"She doesn't." I pulled Kyra away.

Mission accomplished. No DEA there.

And the next two places would go exactly the same way. Some dude in flip-flops, feet up on the counter, telling us he hadn't seen a "suit" since last March, or since Reaganomics, or whatever.

Three hours later, we moved up a notch on the social spectrum and canvassed the hotels, too.

Obviously, this took a bit more ingenuity. You can't flirt with a desk manager who's young and busy and female and straight, who stands as merely one of three possible managers rotating shifts during any given week.

Nevertheless, we had to try.

"By any chance, have you seen either of these two gentlemen in here lately?"

We showed her, the desk manager, a photo on Kyra's phone of the billiard prince known as Warren Wright.

"Oh, I would've definitely recognized *him*," she said, ovaries on alert. "But, no, he wasn't here, sadly." She seemed to be telling the truth.

Five hotels and five conversations later, we were in the clear.

To go to war, of course.

CHAPTER 19

IMAGINE WALKING OUT TO your backyard in your otherwise normal, Plain Jane neighborhood, stopping by a wall just beyond the garage, moving a bush to the side, exposing a hatch in the dirt, looking around to make sure no one is watching you from down the street, or across the street, or anywhere at all, and opening the hatch to expose a dark, underground cavern.

Took us three shovels and a mini dozer, but we dug a tunnel.

Two days earlier, Rita had the idea that we needed a subterranean passageway. We got the inspiration from a busted mission she had led years ago. We were in Barranquilla, Colombia, chasing several bandits into a dark hut when, mere seconds later, the bandits vanished. They fled down a tunnel that crisscrossed their main boulevard underground, so that our teammates on the perimeter at street level could be evaded. It was annoyingly brilliant. Those bastards dug the passage with enough twists and turns at just the perfect angles to thoroughly shield their entire escape. Their layout created a very rough journey for anyone unfamiliar with the serpentine darkness. Yet for them, the *narcos,* it was like a second home.

We hated it. And loved it.

The day the DEA raided our garage and stole our most difficult-to-obtain weaponry, we became desperate for a plan B.

So now, we kept our stash eleven feet underground, buried along subterranean walls.

"Did you know Paris has underground tunnels?" said Kyra. "Full of bones and shit? I dated a Parisian once. He hated that I didn't smoke."

"This top area needs a buttress," said Rita. "This is where cars drive when our parking lot is full."

Rita was pointing to an area just beyond our heads. We had buttressed the tunnel entrance and the exit but this middle section was quite a task—to brace loose dirt to withstand the weight of six thousand pounds or more. That takes real engineering.

Kyra's brain could handle it. And did.

We even had a place to duck into in case both

ends of the tunnel got breached. We built it at the vertex of the V-shape in the tunnel. This allowed us to fire on enemies from both directions, should we need to. This was worst-case scenario Armageddon-type thinking, but it's worth being overprepared.

So then the obvious question was, What's this tunnel really about?

This morning, we got the call we'd been waiting for. I was down the hole within minutes, heading for the far side. Rita and Kyra were both already there, gearing up. Strapping on Kevlar, lacing up boots. True, you need the very best gear when you're a three-person army. But today we were more than three, and we were in full kit.

We emerged from the tunnel into a copse of pecan trees about a quarter mile away from the café and the garage. We walked out onto a clearing two miles beyond the back hills. A secluded area. This would be a tough place for anyone in the vicinity to hear our noise.

Helicopter noise.

Three Bell Huey 600s sat whirling on the deep grass, awaiting us.

The best part about shiny packages was what's inside. Two of the pilots were from the Matamoros mission. Quiet and competent. They had a cargo of eighteen willing Marines. They'd heard of our exploits and wanted to help out. The Fat Man had arranged it, finally agreeing with my plea to really hit Diego where it hurt.

They saluted me. They saluted all three of us.

Kyra wiped tears from her eyes. She's all heart. Rita hides her emotions well, yet this stuff got to her, too. Me? I was mushy as custard inside. But I was a colonel again. And these troops needed me to be razor sharp.

This was the night Diego would never forget.

"Platoon," I shouted over the rotor noise, "let's make some history."

Oorah.

CHAPTER 20

AT AROUND 1:00 A.M. our choppers crossed into Mexico. The US border at certain points is fairly nondescript. You might not even realize that the two nations had swapped underneath you. But soon you start to see it. Even in the dark, you see it.

You ain't home no more.

The street lights are different. They're more randomly laid out. American towns tend to be a grid. Right angles and rows. Mexico is like a colony of lamps.

I was situated as a gunner. Seated at the handles of the .50 cal. For those who don't know, these bullets are massive, like mini-torpedoes that can rip through concrete at a rate of six hundred rounds per minute.

Normally the sniper takes the point, but I know this terrain better than anyone. And seeing as how this was an ill-advised, ill-conceived, illegal mission, it was crucial we didn't falter on any detail. Not one.

Tonight we were hunting something new.

Crops.

And I just spotted the first landmark on the way. Pitch black up ahead. "NV on," I called out to my gang via the radio headset. We flipped our night vision goggles on. Everything then became monochrome and anonymous. You have a range finder in the bottom of your view, telling you that that tree up ahead is seventy-nine meters away, telling you that the dope field on the right is seven hundred meters.

They're hard to spot from a distance, these crops, because the trees shield them from sight. But once your visual angle is correct, you can tell that up there on yonder hill lies a three-million-dollar crop of Diego Correra's finest herb.

And it would be a shame to just leave it by its lonesome.

CHAPTER 21

WE LET LOOSE ON six AGM Hellfire missiles. The dope field had no chance. The power of a Hellfire is unreal. Think of the impact of a monster truck barreling through a pillow fort in the middle of a freeway.

Overkill.

My favorite type of kill.

In the time it takes to spell the words *absolutely wrecked,* we absolutely wrecked about 150 acres of Diego's lifeblood. Lit it up like a backyard barbecue. Hillside gouged. Foliage fried.

"Platoon," I said into the radio. "Breakfast is cooked. Let's move on to lunch."

We coded our targets as follows:

"Breakfast" was the cluster of dope fields located thirty-five miles west of the Sierra Madre Occidental line, tucked just inside the Mexican border. Those fields were, *ahem,* gone now.

"Lunch" was a row of meth labs on the edge

of a small town called La Resaca. This place was located twenty miles beyond the first fields. The trick was that it was nestled in between an elementary school and a pediatrics hospital. Not kidding. A school and a hospital. Thank you, Diego, for being the predictable douche we needed you to be.

"Dinner" was pure coca leaves. An entire crop of Colombian-grade cocaine located near the Gulf Coast. Diego's pride and joy. No other cartel on the continent had the technology to grow good coke this far north. Diego spent four million bucks to create the crops. His opus. And it would be last on our evening's raid menu.

But, en route to lunch, we encountered something we didn't think we'd face. "Contact left!" screamed Rita.

"Tangos on ridge, seven o'clock!" shouted the pilot.

A hailstorm of bullets whizzed past us. Lance Corporal Kagawa, a nice kid from Delaware, great sense of direction, terrible at karaoke, got his upper thigh ripped open by one of the random shots. "Ggggnnnnphhhhhh." He cringed.

I quickly slid over to his side of the helicopter. He was strapped in, there was no way he could fall out the open door, but a bullet hole is a bullet hole and I needed to stanch his bleeding ASAP.

"Man down," I called out into the radio.

We had a medic on our team, but the medic was in one of the other birds.

Yet that was about to be a very secondary concern. "RPG INCOMING!" my pilot yelled at the top of his lungs. You could hear what sounded like a jet engine whining in the distance, climbing the notes of a Doppler effect as it approached us at the terrifying pace of 650 miles per hour. An RPG hitting us would ignite our entire world in a huge midair explosion. Blades flying. Body parts soaring through the air. Flames singeing us at five thousand degrees. No thanks.

The first chopper dove left and downward. Smart pilot, Heather. She knew to fly into and askew from the oncoming RPG trajectory: A textbook move, but it's not easy to actually defy every survival instinct you have and turn *toward* an oncoming death projectile. The second chopper, my chopper, had to split in the other direction, which was obviously undesirable—the maneuver meant exposing ourselves to a wider arc of vulnerability.

Luckily, or fatefully, the bandito who shot the first rocket at us severely underestimated that thing called gravity. Everyone does.

So he missed.

And the third chopper was well clear.

But the problem with in-air combat is that shooters who miss their first shot usually nail their second. Why? Because the RPG lights up the night sky with a lingering trail, so the shooter now knows exactly how to adjust his next trajectory.

Another problem was that an additional shooter might already be locked and loaded and waiting for us up ahead. Like the way you position two border collies to herd sheep into each other. There was a strong chance this potential second shooter would be up ahead in the ravine, prepared to take an easy shot at a slow-and-low bird.

Damn.

We were zipping down out of the sky, racing for airborne cover.

I took a kneeling stance, to aim out the door.

"Jack 'em up, Colonel," Kagawa rasped.

I readied my tiny little M16. A peashooter at a distance like this. The helicopter banked the opposite direction from my view, so, with our severe tilt upward, I had to pretty much aim down across our landing gear. I was scoped and ready to unleash a burst before I even knew where I was targeting.

"Gotta change speed," said the pilot.

I took a wild guess that Shooter number one

would be higher than potential Shooter number two, so I aimed at a dark patch on the hillside.

Yup.

There he was, the clever chump. About to blast us to hell at pointblank. I let loose on three of the worst shots I'd ever shot. Hoping that my instincts about the same gravity that hurt his RPG would now *help* my return of fire.

Tap, tap, tap. Nailed him.

I'm lucky sometimes. Rarely. But sometimes.

"Nice shot, Coll," said the pilot.

But things were just getting started. Corporal Kagawa's upper leg was crooked and oozing blood. The second bird was alongside us. I could see the medic looking over at me and my wounded friend from his perch in his bird's doorway. The good news was that we had a chance to stabilize him on our own. The bad news was that there were more RPG shooters up ahead and a small plane on the horizon.

If we were going to dust the next target, we were going to have to do it on the run.

"Condor Two to Condor Five, advise descent to one-five meters," said my pilot. He was calling out the new altitude to fly at. Fifteen meters. Fifteen teeny little meters. We were descending below the tree line so that visual detection was as hard as possible for our enemies.

Up ahead were the lights on the children's hospital, which were shining across from the soccer field for the elementary school. Sandwiched in between, in the dark buildings, was the meth lab. I was mounted with my trusty M16. Kyra was now on the .50 cal. Rita was coming over to me to try and stop the blood gushing out of Kagawa's leg.

"Small plane, fifteen miles north by northeast," said my pilot. "Approaching fast."

Kyra was now on point surveying the upcoming groundwork, laying out her assessment of our tactical options for me: "We can either scrap target two and race these guys to three, or we get as low as possible to hit the labs. Your call, Colonel."

It was indeed my tough decision. We were facing a small Beechcraft Bonanza plane on the horizon, which didn't have missiles but certainly had the ability to blitz our choppers from above by dropping random items onto our blades.

Would that work?

Very possibly, yes. Helicopters don't like to have their dainty little private parts touched. Not by you, not by me, not by their boyfriends, no one. They will literally rip themselves apart in self-hate if the rear rotor gets out of sync with the main rotor. The torque is maniacal. The birds go down. Hard. Ugly.

So, yes, that plane rapidly approaching us on the horizon—that little bugger was the potential kiss of death.

But it wasn't here yet.

I got on the radio to tell the platoon my decision, to tell them exactly what they were praying to hear.

"Time for lunch."

CHAPTER 22

THE TRICK WITH A quick bombing run is to be as comprehensive as possible during the one pass you make. Instead of doing multiple passes, you want to do one, just one. And it needs to count.

Ironically, to speed things up, you need to slow things down.

We were originally planning for fifty-mile-per-hour attack patterns. Straight routes. Repeated three times.

Now, instead, we were going to fly zigzag. One pass. "Slow," I said to the pilot. "Slowwwww. Slower than a bureaucrat." I wanted this win badly. I couldn't risk a clumsy attack.

Over the next crest, we'd find the small orchard we'd use as a landmark. Then beyond that would be the outskirts of La Resaca.

"I'm really s-sorry," mumbled Corporal Kagawa. He was writhing in pain but also trying to prevent his lower half from squirming too much. He didn't want to draw attention to himself.

"You're good, bro," I said, readjusting his compress. "Just imagine how much ass you're gonna get thanks to this."

"I'm...picturing that one chick in the 304th," he replied. "Asking her to marry me an' shit." And then, after some more writhing and moaning, "Sorry I messed up."

There's nothing worse than feeling like you let your teammates down. I knew his pain all too well. And it got me losing focus a bit. It's the bone-crushing guilt trip that I'd already been cultivating inside my soul, watering it, fertilizing it, nurturing it into a huge treelike thing. A guilt forest, actually. The knowledge that I'd led my crew on mission after mission and we had yet to stop Diego. That I got my buddies into danger. That I lost my entire family. That Corporal Kagawa now had a splintered upper thigh and was bleeding pretty bad.

"Does he need immediate aid?" I asked Rita.

He wouldn't let her reply. "Don't you dare turn us back, Colonel."

"He can hold out," said Rita, "but he's leaky."

She was right—the gauze she kept refreshing for the wound was getting soaked disturbingly quickly.

"Don't," said Kagawa. "Don't, Colonel. Please?"

I know that face. I know that plea. It would positively destroy this youngster if I turned us around because of his injury.

I grabbed his hand. An assurance. From here on out, this was for him. This was for faith in the team. *Got your back, little brother.* "Okay," I said to him. "But I order you to cease bleeding."

He laughed at my cheesy line. It was the first time his face stopped wincing.

"Banking hard right," said the pilot. We were about to emerge into plain view of the target. And we were about to be in range of their turret. Yes, they had a turret.

"Technical. Far corner," said Kyra, spotting enemy armament. When a bandito mounts a big-ass gun to the back of his dinky-ass Toyota, that's called a technical. One might think this is slumming it and that it's trivial, but banditos live and die by this crap. Little pickup trucks with nasty-ass weapons on back. They're mobile and they shoot hard.

"Platoon," I said into the radio. "Friendly reminder: We don't touch the school, we don't touch the hospital. Target is the dark row of buildings in the middle."

Our two birds diverged into the woods. Just above the treetops. The obvious move was to torch the fields from the far side, but our goal was to do the exact opposite of what was expected.

"Cleared hot," I told my pilots, meaning anyone at any time could open fire.

Condor Five banked over the outer edge of the crop. My bird, Condor Two, was coming up on the rear of the hut.

"Castle in range," said the pilot "*Eyes on* at 150 meters and closing."

"Tech! Small road!" shouted Kyra, immediately firing at a technical speeding along our right side. The dude in the back was on a mounted PK machine gun. Pointed at us.

He didn't stink at aiming. He managed to spray a good amount of bullets right at our belly, and, since we didn't know how close he was, his salvo caught us off guard.

But Kyra is no slouch in bed. With a second barrage, she massacred the front of the Toyota and, yes, flipped it on its side, throwing the guy in back deep into the bush.

Now our co-pilot was going to work on the meth lab. "Target acquired. Firing away."

Both pilots then clicked that little red switch just under the right thumb, the one that first needs a clearance toggled from the main console, the one that was cleared half a minute ago, the one that sends about eight hundred pounds of fireworks forward from the bottom of the chopper, and, holy shit, pulverizes a goddamn meth lab.

Every crevice of that compound went up in flames at once. A white volcano. Bright as hell. Loud as God.

It's like I got to kick Diego in his favorite nut.

CHAPTER 23

THE METH LAB AT location two was a roaring inferno. We had served breakfast and lunch. We had finished the easy part.

Word would have already gotten to the ranch hands at location three, dinner, by the time we were en route, a thirty-five-minute journey. Enemy trucks were already on the way to intercept us along with that small plane creeping up on our rear.

Corporal Kagawa was bleeding like crazy, which meant his body defied my official orders to coagulate, but he found enough strength to clamp down on his wound on his own. Rita didn't want to let him be the one to do it, but I told her she had to.

Why?

Because the kid needed to feel like he had something to do. Even if he was doing a worse job than she would. His body needed the feeling of responsibility so that his immune system could fight harder inside him. The potential stress of him knowing he was depriving Rita of her combat assignment would've probably eaten him alive.

"Two klicks and closing," said our pilot. "Firing on your mark."

"Copy that, Condor Two. On your flank. Evasive will be down and left."

"Down and left, affirmative. Will mirror."

The two pilots were agreeing on what path of rapid evasive maneuver they would each take in the event they were both surprised and had to scurry. Two helicopters accidentally touching in any way is about as desirable as getting dental work done in the middle of a rodeo. A helicopter is the most delicate contraption ever invented, and it operates amid a hurricane of force—let's just say it's super damn jealous of other helicopters.

"Firing away." Once again the pilots unleashed the Hellfire missiles, and the world in front of me exploded. We had crushed the entire crop into a massive cloud of heat and fury. We had won.

That was my thought for about a fraction of a second. Then came a rather strange problem.

"Horses," said Kyra.

"What?" I said.

"Horses, ten o'clock," Rita was pointing to the

center of what was a large, quickly shrinking doughnut of fire.

I looked down and saw it. We were set to bank hard back toward the hillside and get the hell home, we were officially done—but there were three horses in the middle of the burning field.

Protocol says you can't risk soldiers to save animals. But my crew was rabidly fond of horses.

"Can't leave 'em, Coll," said Kagawa.

"No way," agreed a couple of other troops, including Rita.

There was a path through the circle of confusion that would allow the mare and her foals to head directly out of the fire. But the three animals were absolutely terrified and unable to recognize salvation. To be honest, if I were down there at ground level, I doubt I'd see it either. Those poor things would have to gallop across a football-field's worth of flaming cocaine before they could be safe.

Why in God's name someone tied three horses in the middle of a coke field I'll never know, but the reason really didn't matter. The hope was that they weren't tethered.

"Contact hillside!" said the pilot. And of course we were now getting peppered by AK-47s, a group of banditos shooting from the edge of the forest hill.

Our bird, Condor Two, was about to rip them to shreds, but Condor Five was hovering too close to our line of attack. One of the horses was trotting tragically toward the heart of the fire and the troops aboard Five were trying to deter it. Just as bullets were coming at us from more AK-47s. This shit was insane. We had never been this scattered.

I blamed myself for pushing dinner without proper recon.

Rookie mistake.

The Condor Five pilot leveled his bird out, giving us a trajectory, and my second gunner and second assistant team leader unleashed about seven hundred rounds of ammo toward the far side of the field.

We had herded the horses a bit. The first two made it across the path. The third one was on fire, literally on fire, thanks to the cloth blanket on his saddle, and was about to leap over the gap, too. We were so inexplicably excited about this. All of us. Going nuts. Like watching a running back break loose on a game-winning touchdown.

"Go, homeboy!" shouted Kyra. "Go!"

He was about to cross. He was about two strides from completion. And the banditos shot him.

Shot him dead.

An intentional barrage hit his head and torso as the animal buckled and tumbled into an ugly heap, sliding across the dirt. We freaked out. All of us. He still had some zest in him. He knew where his safety zone was now. And he was trying to drag the back half of his magnificent body toward the promised land.

But his limbs couldn't do it. His front hooves were clawing the dirt. He was pulling hard. There was no quit in that little muchacho. But the physics were against him. Christ. If there ever there was a way to piss on your enemy's morale in the midst of battle, this was it. There was zero tactical reason to shoot the animal. Zero.

"Permission to vacate," the pilot said to me.

Not sure what would be waiting for me back home in Texas: what kind of self-inflicted mood would be lurking in my subconscious. Would I be happy? Relieved? Proud? Stuck on a horse? We had consumed all three meals but as I looked across to the faces in the other two helicopters, looking past the sullen faces in our own cabin, I could tell that this entire platoon was fixated on the animal.

"Mission over," I replied. "Take us anywhere but here."

And we headed out.

It's hard to savor a vague victory. Did we win? Did they win? If they would shoot down their own horse just to spite us, how much damage did we really do to them? How much closer was I to Diego's capture?

To answer my original question, yes there was something waiting for me back in Archer, Texas, that's for sure. I found out as soon as I settled inside my house.

I was about to be kidnapped.

CHAPTER 24

THE TASTE OF VICTORY was short lived. Whatever ground we just gained only sought to re-
mind me that we hadn't gotten him yet.

When I come home after a mission, I like to
take a hot shower. Sounds trivial but there's something about the steam and the acoustics. You can
sing anything in there and you feel like a rock
diva. Plus you get cleaner. Plus your muscles relax.
Plus it's a way of procrastinating whatever long-ass
litany of crap you have on your to-do list, like item
thirty-seven: Kill stupid Diego Correra. Still.

I had been under the shower nozzle for about
half my usual epic stay, shampooing and just beginning a full-body soap down, when I heard the
first squeak.

I turned off the water and stood there. Listening. Did I seriously just hear something in my
house? A noise?

Unlike the cute visit to the garage by the DEA,

this whatever-it-was noise wasn't quiet. It sounded as if someone's shoulder bumped into a wall, the wooden beam behind the plaster contorting under instant pressure.

I stood there, naked, not breathing, my hand still on the shower knob.

I instantly realized it was better for me to keep moving around—silent inaction would alert anyone in the house, any intruders, that I knew something was up. I wanted them to think I knew nothing.

I stepped out of the shower. I had two towels ready to go, folded neatly on the sink counter. Way over there. By the time I had taken two steps toward the towels, I heard a door shut.

My heart started racing. *Shit.* This wasn't my imagination. This was an actual intrusion.

I needed a weapon in my hand. Across the hall I had a Walther PPK stashed. Yes, that's the James Bond gun. Yes, it's small. And amazing. If I could just turn off the bathroom lights and dart across the hall and arm myself, I could make a mad dash for the guest bedroom and get out through the window, assuming they had both doors guarded.

But before I could even start to consider how long this would all take, the bathroom knob started turning. On its own. Slowly.

It took about three seconds max, but it felt like super slow motion every step of the way. The knob turned, and I lunged forward, went low to duck under any line of fire, to intercept the opponent rather than retreat deeper into the bathroom where I would be weaponless and easy to shoot. I'd love to claim that I grabbed some perfume and a BIC lighter and made a blowtorch or that I ripped the shower curtain rod from the stall and wielded a Martha Stewart spear, but I'm not that clever. Besides, I don't wear perfume. And is that crap really flammable? My bathroom, as I noted in that millisecond of combat prep, was sadly lacking in sharp objects. I had a bar of fragrant soap. That was it. From a crouched position, still midstride, I let the door open just enough so I could access my enemy's weapon. Utilizing Krav Maga techniques, I could snatch it.

The first thing I saw through that door was, yes, a gun. But that's when the lights went out.

And so I was in the dark, weaponless, grabbing at a Glock from the grip of what I came to discover was a 240-pound ogre, while I stood with wet feet on a slippery floor.

Naked.

I punched at his ribs. The ogre. I wanted to grab a handful of torso skin and just twist the hell out of it, twist and pull downward, but he had on a big poofy jacket. We grappled for a long, silent, respectable four seconds. But he was on a mission. And his mission was completed rather quickly. Before I could strike even one blow, my neck was jabbed with a needle by another assailant. His partner. And, within seconds, precious seconds, my ability to struggle expired. And my hands and legs were cuffed. And a hood came over my head. And the darkness got even darker.

CHAPTER 25

ANYONE WHO'S HAD THE flu has had those weird-as-hell vivid dreams. You get this whacked-out mixture of reality and surreality. You come in and out of being awake. Sweating. Feverish. Unsure whether anything that just happened in your mind happened for real. This, my friends, is exactly what it's like to be drugged and hooded.

Hood on, obviously I couldn't see much. The first sensation I had was hearing something. It was murmuring coming from the far corner of the room. Two males. Middle-aged. Whispering. Stopping every minute or so, as if to glance over at me. I heard snatches of their strange conversation: "...or before the other one checks in..." and then "...sure if the other doesn't..."

I couldn't tell where these guys were from. To tell the truth, I didn't even recognize the accent, or whether they even *had* accents.

Suddenly, I was approached by a guy whose knuckles smelled like kerosene.

Offering me a drink of water, he removed my gag and lifted my hood—just enough for me to look down across my cheekbones and across the room. I tried to take a mental photograph so I could study it in my head after I glimpsed it:

1. On the far side of the room were two guys in track jackets. They had guns. An M24 and an M5.
2. The room was big and bare. Not much furniture.
3. There was a doorway, and through it I caught a glimpse of a tire. The tire of some kind of vehicle.
4. The tire was mounted on an airplane wheel.

It took me a split second but I quickly realized that I was in a hangar.

The hood was yanked back down over my face, and Kerosene Hands stuffed the gag back in my mouth. I heard some whispering behind me. And then I heard a yelp from what sounded like another room. A female voice. Muffled. Crying out. I didn't know for sure it was Kyra, but I certainly suspected it. Then I heard some more whispering and a large metal object clanging against something.

Goddammit, you dogs. Don't hurt her.

That's what I tried to say. Those six words. But I was gagged.

I assumed six hours had passed since they put the gag on me.

But I have no idea if it was six or three. Or sixteen. Or sixty. The hood ensured that I couldn't see any daylight. You can learn a lot from daylight. The height of the sun in the sky. The apex of its arc. The fact that it's out, at all. The difference in angle fifteen minutes between glances, if you're lucky enough to get a second glance, can tell you where north is.

Every little bit of info counts.

I wasn't going to get that far, though. I could already hear what sounded like a hierarchy of conversation. Somewhere off to my left I detected what was distinctly a verbal command: not two guys talking but one guy telling another guy what the hell to do.

There's my fulcrum.

I made up my mind that the next time they came to give me water or raise my hood or take a look at my sulky disposition I was going to spit out the gag and bite the hand that reached in. I was going to bite the damn thing as hard as possible and see if that little oral *hello* could get them to change their plan.

Because I was now convinced Kyra was tied up in the next room and was being ordered onto that plane.

And if that plane was going to Mexico, death would be a luxury.

CHAPTER 26

THERE REALLY IS NO way to escape a situation like this. Not if it unfolds as planned. The plan, their plan, was that I'd be cuffed to my chair. Hooded. There were armed men in the room. They knew where I was. I didn't. They knew what they intended to do with me. I didn't. They knew who they were. I had no clue.

That meant I'd be worse than dead if I let their plan unfold.

I had to derail it somehow.

Even if it was just a tiny hiccup in their agenda. I had to prod the tissue of their intentions with a surgical instrument: to see how it responds, gain an edge. Because if I bite the ideal guy's hand, he will want to beat the living shit out of me. And if he's not *allowed* to do that yet, then I might cause a conflict between him and whoever *is* in charge.

But that's not how this day would go.

"I don't care, just get it done," said the voice in charge.

My hood got lifted off. And before I could bite the guy who was lifting it off, I saw his face. And you know whose face it was?

Warren Wright. I should call him El Warren. Warren Wrong. I don't know how he slipped his allegiance from the DEA to Diego Correra, but he must have. The shit-sucking brickhead.

"Colonel," he said. "I need you to keep your mouth shut. Just do as you're told and you won't get hurt."

I wanted to say the following: "Pretty much whatever you tell me to do, I'm going to do the opposite." But I was gagged, so it sounded like "Heehee muh heheheh hoo." And I gave up half-way through.

"Stop moving," said Warren.

If I could just get him in a choke hold, maybe get my hand around his voice box and threaten to yank it out, I could get his minions to let me bargain for Kyra's life.

But my handcuffs were tight. Too tight.

"Stop moving!" barked Warren.

I moved even harder.

"STOP!" he shouted, then added, "Trust me."

I stopped.

Not because he told me to stop and certainly

not because he told me to trust him. *Trust you, you little bitch? I'd rather trust a garbage fire.* But because I heard something in the background that was an absolute game changer.

The plane was starting its engines.

CHAPTER 27

I MUST HAVE LOST consciousness again, because the next thing I knew I was on that plane, with a pounding headache. They put silencing-headphones over my ears so I couldn't hear anything. Hooded, gagged, and cuffed, I could barely tell if I was sitting or standing. The only sensation I felt were changes in altitude, which, let's face it, with all my other senses deprived, made me wanna puke up everything I had eaten in the past year.

At this point I was barely maintaining the combat initiative. They won, whoever they were. They owned the day. I was being taken to where they intended me to be taken. The only thing I had control of was my thoughts. And I couldn't even control those. Certain unwanted images kept floating relentlessly to mind. Namely, my youngest daughter.

"Trust yourself," she said.

Myself? How? Why?

The word *trust* was popping up because Warren had said it. I reminded myself that my sensory-deprived brain was just misfiring its synapses, bringing random memories to the forefront, blending new memories with old ones.

I'd failed, as a soldier. I managed to get my ass abducted. All because I simply *had* to take an ill-advised shower. I didn't have the good sense to check my house before getting naked and vulnerable, before separating myself from my weapon. A cardinal sin. And I had committed it.

"Mommy, you can do this," said my implausible daughter.

Do what? Was I hallucinating? She hadn't aged—my vision of her. It had been two years, but she wasn't any taller. Sensory deprivation is guaranteed to fry you into mental anguish. No one survives it.

"Stay awake, Mommy."

"I am awake, munchkin. I'm just sort of losing the battle right now. Don't look at Mommy. Look at the sunrise over—"

Wham! Somebody hit me with a baseball bat. Aluminum. Hard as a slugger.

Here in this plane.

No, not a bat. It was a rib of the aircraft cargo area. I was lying down. This was the metal support, the curved girder that braces the fuselage.

I felt a pair of large hands move me back to whatever position I was in. I think we hit turbulence. Nobody hit me, actually. It was the air. The air hit us all.

Or, no, wait a minute.

We were landing.

CHAPTER 28

I WAS IN THE middle of a warehouse. In a chair. Cuffed. Muffed. Hooded. When the blinders finally came off, I had to squint. My vision was blurry. Everything was so bright. I couldn't tell if it was the next day or the next week. There were two guards posted at the main door to the warehouse. I could hear some footsteps echoing in the distance. They were coming from behind. My captors. The boss of my captors. I didn't even turn. My final middle finger. Let them look at the back of my uninterested head.

I want to say I could smell his aftershave or his stench, but I couldn't. I could only just hear him. Warren.

Warren Never Wright.

"I'll need your full attention, Colonel," he said.

The thing is, based on yet another weird exchange of murmurs I caught just now, I realized it wasn't Warren who was in charge of this abduction. I heard a pair of high-heeled feet approaching. I'd recognize those shoes anywhere. Patent black leather asexual heels. Retail cost $69.99 at the naval base store. We ladies all had to buy a pair. And she was wearing hers.

General Claire Dolan.

She stood in front of me in full uniform. She had enough brass on her chest to outshine a pride parade.

"Sorry about the methodology, Colonel," she said to me in her standard bludgeoning tone. One doesn't get to the rank of general without tapping into one's inner mega-bitch. But she might not necessarily be here to ruin my life. "I hope you're physically undamaged."

I didn't say yes.

"I hope you're mentally undamaged," she added.

I'd worked under her Fifth Battalion six years ago. She was tyrannical, ruthless, and played her favorites, but she absolutely positively always got her job done. Something that's been hard for me to relate to lately.

"I'm here to ask you about your informant," she said. "Where are you getting your information from . . . about Diego Correra?"

I wasn't going to answer anything until she assured me that Kyra and Rita were all right. If she was worth even one stripe on her rainbow scoop of medals, she'd quickly tell me that my two spiritual sisters were fine.

"Who is your leak?"

I didn't answer.

She pulled up a chair really close to me and sat down. She took out a ballpoint pen from her coat pocket. I started to get the feeling that they'd ask me this question over and over until I gave in.

She started to whisper really close to my ear. "I know you've done a lot for your country. I know what happened after Matamoros. I know the price you've paid. Prices." She leaned in even closer, talked even quieter. "You have my condolences. You have my sympathies. You have my prayers to the God of your choosing. But you *don't* have my patience. *Who. Is. Your. Leak?*"

If I knew, I still wouldn't tell you.

I sat unmoved. She took a deep breath in. She hovered her pen near the canal of my ear. Not in it. But around it. Hovering. She could poke my eardrum. Tidy. It would be easy for her to deny it afterward, easy to say it got punctured on its own. Perforated. It would be easy for her to deny touching me. Perforated eardrums hurt like crazy.

"You rose through the ranks pretty damn quick," she said, launching one of those *here is your dossier, you soon-to-be-dead tramp* monologues. "Almost as quick as my royal ass. You paid your dues. Got the desk job promotion with the privilege of staying in the field. You did what any good rookie does, you made male officers jealous. Now, I don't want to have to ask this one more time..."

"Who is your leak?" yelled Wright.

His voice echoed in this warehouse. If General Dolan seemed annoyed, Agent Wright seemed downright enraged. Not sure how I could be the source of his intense exasperation, given that I'm the one who sat under a hood for a day. Maybe he just hated that he was being dragged alongside me. Locked in this trash dump of a warehouse, wherever the hell this was.

"I'm not gonna keep waiting for an answer," said Warren.

Luckily for us all, Dolan finally said the magic words. "Sergeant Holmes and Lieutenant Ramirez are fine."

So I spoke up.

"I want verification," I said to her. "I want to be treated like a human being."

"Then act like a colonel."

"I'm not a colonel anymore," which was a fine thing to say, but then I stumbled right into what was clearly her verbal trap. "I was discharged two years ago."

"Yet you prance around…all around the continent…shooting villagers and setting shit on fire."

"Villagers?" I had to correct her. *Murderers!*

"You don't raise your voice at us!" said Warren, who at this point was fuming, who stood up and kicked his metal folding chair across the room. "Not us!"

I'm guessing he'd promised Dolan I'd cooperate instantly. It started to seem more and more likely to me that they had already questioned me while I was drugged and that maybe I didn't say jack to them. Even while drugged. High five to Drugged Amanda and Her Stubborn-as-a-Morgue Mouth.

Warren kept yelling and was clearly ready to take over the whole interrogation. "You put the lives of hundreds of agents in jeopardy."

Yes, sir, I did.

"Compromised US–Mexico diplomatic relations."

Yes, sir, I did.

"Committed enough criminal acts to be tied up in a box for life."

"You have no proof of any of that," I said to him. Loud. Turning to give him the direct eye contact he probably didn't want. Bully. "If you did, we wouldn't be talking in a warehouse."

He leaned in. "You better hope there isn't some sort of Geneva Convention thing you're relying on in your head right now, thinking, *hoping,* that we don't get out some power tools and Guantánamo you into a more cooperative bitch."

"If Rita and Kyra are in the next room, then prove it to me," I said.

He stood there. Unflinching.

"If all you want is the name of a leak," I continued, "I don't *have* the name of a leak. This conversation is over, so take us home."

"No," said Dolan.

"Well, then we'll just stay here for a really long time and trade beauty tips," I said. I'd lost my cool at this point. "Who does your beehive? When was the last time you rechiseled it? Was it here? In this room? And by any chance are you gonna tell me where the hell this shit hole is?"

General Dolan stood up, a sneer forming on her face. "You're in Mexico City, babe. You wanna leave?" She tossed the pen in my lap and added, "Find your own way home."

CHAPTER 29

"FIND YOUR OWN way home?" questioned Rita. "That's what she said to you?"

"Let's not worry about it," I replied.

"I hate that whore," said Kyra. "Always have."

The three of us were literally standing on a street corner in what felt like, by American standards, a back alley, but what was really, by Mexico City standards, an actual street. Quaint, with little colorful stores and square houses all sandwiched together. The whole thing would be lovely if it weren't so run down. This was the bad part of town in Mexico City, Distrito Federal.

"That's north," said Rita, pointing eighty degrees to the right of the setting sun.

"Find your own way home," repeated Kyra. "How about my boot finds its way up your ass?"

"That would be fun but you're not wearing boots," said Rita.

None of us were. They had left us in almost nothing worth wearing outdoors. We barely had the clothes on our backs. All jokes and wardrobe malfunctions aside, we had a more horrific problem looming over us now. We had literally nothing. No weapons. No car. No bikes. No phones. No cash. No credit cards. No food. No water. I had on a pair of prison-issue overalls and sandals, which was only *slightly* better than the towel I was wearing when they brought me in. Kyra was in yoga pants and a T-shirt. Rita was rocking mom jeans and a turtleneck sweater.

"We can't stay in one place," I said, adopting command mode. "We have to keep walking."

"Yes, ma'am," said both of my best friends, snapping into soldier mode.

I pointed across the street and we crossed. We began our hike. "Are either of you hurt?"

"My everlasting love for the Marine Corps is hurt," said Kyra. "But, no, other than that, my body is a flawless temple and that temple is ready to do some really un-Zen things."

"I'm fine," said Rita, "physically and mentally. They didn't torture us. Are we really gonna walk to Texas?"

She was only 38 percent kidding.

I didn't answer her. I honestly had no idea how

we were going to get back. This situation would be hard enough for normal people to undo, but for the three of us, who were high-profile targets for every kind of bad intention from every kind of a bad-intending person, we were in for a long night.

Dolan didn't get promoted to general based on her sagging tits. She was a ruthless witch, who out-ass-kicked in every ass-kicking contest she entered. And she entered all of them. If she felt a mission needed to be done a certain way, she would destroy whoever contradicted her. And she would get that mission done. Had to tip my hat to that. But she hated me. Not sure why. I had never spoken to her face-to-face before today, but I'd hear things around the base. She wanted me erased from the Corps.

She couldn't kill me. But technically she could certainly find a situation to let me die in. Here. In Mexico.

And would Warren Wright stop her? Apparently not.

"Do you think we'll see any hostiles?" asked Rita.

"Affirmative," I replied.

"What exactly should we be on the lookout for?" she asked.

"Them," I said, pointing across the street.

There were four guys standing at the far end of the block. Locals. Mean-looking.

It would be better if they just wanted to *do* us. We could repel that sort of thing. But they didn't have that sort of "do" in mind.

CHAPTER 30

"THEY COULD BE DRUNK," said Kyra.

At this point we had walked several blocks in a tangential path that took us away from whatever barrio our four enemies spawned from. We would stop to point at shit in store windows so that we could yap with each other like giggly little tourists, so that we could happen to glance to our rear without looking like we were glancing to our rear.

This is how we could monitor them. This is how we confirmed that, damn it, they were still there.

"They're following us way too well to be drunk," replied Rita.

Indeed, they were. We picked up the pace. We fast-walked down the tiny streets, turning abruptly, turning again, crossing, crossing back. Not exactly in a full-fledged sprint to evade them, no. We didn't want to take it to the next level just yet, not without further information, like whether they were armed, what they were armed with, whether they had friends up ahead of us. We didn't even know if they were using cell phones.

Every time we turned, we'd lose them for about a half block, and then we'd see them come around the corner right behind us. Still on track. It was eerie.

"They might have eyes above," said Kyra.

Yes.

Overwatch. A situation with one of those old ladies, a native, pretending to reel in her laundry line, *squeakity-squeak,* while actually scouting the three of us from her third-floor window. The majority of the neighborhood was two stories, so anyone with any kind of additional height could see us gringas from a mile away.

"Turn here," I said, as we then ducked behind a tight alley. "Definitely caught sight of a handgun on the pudgy one. I'm guessing the others have knives."

The fastest-moving of the four guys was a youngish looking chap, maybe twenty years old. He looked agile. Probably good at parkour. Probably just dying to impress his buddies and get extra violent with me and my lady friends.

"Do you think they're connected to Diego?" asked Rita.

I quickly peeked my eye around the edge of the wall and took a brief look at each one.

"Worse," I replied. I was starting to realize we were in for a rough trip. "I think they're cops."

I needed to take us into the smallest possible area. The problem with cops is they'd have a very close network of radio communication. Probably the best in town. I was already dismayed by the presence of four dudes tailing us—but then there was the prospect of another, let's say, *ten* joining in...

"I dunno that we can ditch 'em," said Rita, "here in their own backyard."

"This place is like a maze," agreed Kyra.

"We're not trying to ditch 'em," I replied.

I repositioned the ballpoint pen in my clenched fist. The one General Dolan dropped in my lap. The one I now had gripped like a dagger.

"We're about to start the party," I said.

CHAPTER 31

WE ROUNDED THE CORNER into a narrow alley, wide enough for maybe one horse or one cow or moose or whatever-the-hell transport animal this stupid ghetto was founded on. It was narrow as shit. One horse on a diet. There were stoops and inset doorways. Those were perfect for us. We readied ourselves in three separate positions. Rita and I tucked ourselves into two different doorways while Kyra kept walking toward the deep dead end in plain sight.

Visual bait.

I could hear some commotion just around the corner. The four men were approaching. We had no weapons except my pen, but we had the element of surprise. What we wanted was the first guy to be well ahead of his pack. He would then round the corner alone, and we could ambush him and take his gun or knife. Then do the same thing to the next person.

I was calming my breath. Listening. Staying loose. I was planning to deliver a swift pen stab to the clavicle.

But that clavicle never arrived.

Whatever lone-vulnerable-pursuer-Disney-perfection-scenario I'd envisioned did not come to fruition at all. Kyra was correct. These guys knew their backstreets like the back of their hand. Instead of us trapping one of the four guys in these tight quarters, those four guys had trapped us in a small city alley.

I could hear the pudgy one yell to his buddy down the block. Something about "staking" it. They were positioning themselves at the four sides.

Kyra finally checked back over her shoulder to see how we were doing. She saw the cancel signal from Rita and quickly returned to us. No talking, no making sounds—we signed each other the following:

Four enemies. Surrounding. We run. That way. One mile.

That was it.

That was our entire plan. We were going to improvise the hell out of this. Because I had no idea if those four guys were packing machetes or if they all had firepower. We braced ourselves. And then I nodded.

Let's do this.

We all three ran through the back door of a small taqueria in a dead sprint and emerged onto another street. It became instantly clear that I was wrong about there being only four guys.

Now there were twenty-four.

And they had submachine guns. And they were using them.

CHAPTER 32

WE RAN AS LOW as we could with as much zigzag as efficiency would allow. We were dodging every kind of third-world-Kalashnikov bullet they had in stock, from seemingly every direction.

We ran hard, directly into the first open door we could find, a laundromat, with zero time to assess anything at all, just banking on the possibility there might be a back door and that, through it, there might be another tiny alley like the previous one.

There was.

We ran down the alley, and I skidded to a stop along the gravel to try to open the first back door that looked accessible. It wasn't, and neither was the second, but the third—the door to a dive bar—was, and I burst it open just as Kyra and Rita ran in behind by me, just as a wash of thirty more bullets embedded themselves in the wall where my head had been merely two seconds prior.

We were back out on the streets.

At this point there was no way to survive by continuing to flee. Soon, very soon, statistics would catch up with us and the law of mathematical probability would dictate that a random round from a random gun fired by a randomly aiming shooter was going to find its way into one of our torsos. That is, *if* we kept exposing our torsos to submachine-gun fire while running in a straight line away from young men who have memorized every straight line in the neighborhood.

I was desperate to recreate the setting for the failed ambush we tried earlier but I was too scared to sacrifice our current velocity. After about five minutes, I think we'd seriously traveled one entire mile. You'd be shocked to learn just how damn fast you can run when guns are behind you. We had emerged out of the heart of one of the most dangerous neighborhoods in the world: Iztapalapa, a barrio of Distrito Federal. Poor, run-down. A virtual playground for criminals.

"If we can cross into the center of the city," shouted Rita as we sprinted, "I seriously doubt they'll follow us."

"No, no, no," yelled Kyra. "They'll go anywhere. They're not allowed to lose us. That's their pride."

"So we have to square up with them," I yelled back.

"With all twenty? All twenty of these guys?" shouted Rita.

"No," I replied. "The first four. The cops."

We were running down a gradual hill. To our right was the legendary Cerro de la Estrella, a national park with a small, remarkable mountain of history. Actually everything around here is charming to look at if you simply subtract the poverty, misogyny, oppression, depression, pollution, corruption, and daily violence.

None of the locals would help us. Doors were closing ahead of us. We could see curtains being drawn. Cars turning away from our direction. Pedestrians ducking into shops.

As soon as anyone saw us, fear governed their next move.

I don't know how fast word can spread in a city of sixteen million people, but this neighborhood had its own little ecosystem. Its own self-sustaining misery. *Welcome to Iztapalapa: Three Days Since Our Last Lynching.*

"The last corner on the left," I shouted to Rita and Kyra.

Still sprinting, we rounded yet another corner. I think we had logged three miles in fifteen minutes. We were close to Avenue Río Churubusco, which meant we were on the way to downtown. To "civilization." Close to exiting the Iztapalapan war zone.

But instead of finding an area to trap our captors, we found ourselves trapping ourselves. Again. In a dead-end corridor. With no alcoves or inset doorways for cover. Not even a cardboard box.

Ladies and gentlemen, the world's cleanest damn back alley.

And I managed to find it. And I managed to lead Rita into it and somehow managed to lose Kyra at the same time. We weren't together! Jesus.

And then, finally, as if on cue, at the worst time possible, those first four bastards showed up. Guns ready. They were looking to shoot the living shit out of us. In tight quarters.

Perfect.

CHAPTER 33

"HANDS UP!" YELLED Officer Whatever-The-Hell-His-Name-Was.

"¡Los manos, puta!" said his sidekick. *"¡Levante los manos!"*

Rita and I were cornered.

There was obviously a huge reward paid to whoever captured us, but something sinister, something ulterior, could be seen growing in the eyes of officer number three. Let's call him Señor Sleazy, muscling his way to the front row. He had some stripes on his sleeve, so I guessed he was the local captain and the three guys around him were his sergeants and fluffers.

"On your knees," said Captain Sleazy.

Rita and I traded a look. We knew what this one meant.

"On your knees, *puta*," he said again.

The guy behind him, let's call him Officer

Double Chin for obvious reasons, started murmuring some inaudible crap into his radio. They
were telling the rest of their gang to do whatever.
I didn't like the sound of it—directions to hang
back. I hadn't seen Kyra since two blocks ago.
If these slimy reptiles had their hands on her,
a pretty girl like her, I can't even imagine what
they'd already be doing.

"*Estamos solo turistas,*" I protested. *We're just
tourists.* "*Queremos visitar,* er, the museum."

Wham, I felt a kick into the back of my knee,
which sent me down onto the pavement in a
forced kneel. Double Chin didn't like my Spanish conjugation.

Rita immediately knelt alongside me. Cooperating. She knew that defiance was my preroga-
tive, not hers. She knew to follow my lead. We
were down, execution style. Would they do it
right there? I was the political prize, I'm sure,
but would they maybe shoot Rita right in front
of me? Was she expandable? Collateral? Had they
already shot Kyra?

This was scary. If they were connected to Diego
Correra, which, c'mon, how the hell could they
not be, there's no way the bounty on my head
wasn't astronomical. These bastards were willing
to shoot my eight-year-old daughter in bed. In
Texas. In the United States. So I seriously

doubted there would be any sort of moral hesitation about destroying lives out here.

"Take off your clothes," said Captain Sleazy to Rita.

I knew it. He had a few minutes alone. A few minutes before his police chief would arrive. He knew his bounty was already in the bank, and he wanted to get the most out of this rare assignment.

"Your pants, bitch," said the Captain.

"Don't do it," I told her.

"I'm going to count down from five."

He clicked the hammer on his revolver and aimed it at the back of my head. His leverage against Rita.

"Take off your clothes," he said to her again.

"Don't do it," I told Rita again. "He's bluffing."

"Five."

I just wanted to picture my daughters. Just them. Just to tell them I was about to be with Daddy really soon.

"Four."

I pictured the old living room. The one Christmas when the tree fell over and we all started laughing because the star landed in a bowl of oatmeal. But my daughter—she was now saying something to me. In my head.

"Three."

She was saying, "Not yet."

"Two."

Not yet.

"One..."

And just as, I swear to God, I saw his finger begin to tighten on the trigger, a door swung open.

Kyra.

And she grabbed Sleazy's muzzle.

And, *bam,* the gun of Double Chin went off and fired a bullet at the left shoulder of Lieutenant Rita Ramirez. Within two steps Kyra had broken her opponent's neck with a judo move, had pulled someone down, flipped him forward, and his body along with his head hit the unforgiving pavement at such an incredibly wrong angle, he was done. Forever.

And we were just getting started.

I rolled backward, trying to move in whatever way my enemy least anticipated, and grabbed the leg of Sergeant Double Chin while still on my back. My foot cocked under his left kneecap just before kicking upward along his thigh as hard as I could, dragging the arch of my foot along his leg, taking his kneecap along for the ride.

He gasped in pain.

His day was over.

Kyra had already grabbed the revolver from the captain and aimed it the throat of the third guy as the fourth guy was trying to wrestle it from her. She was fighting two men at once.

I finished Double Chin with as many forearms to the nose as my controlled rage would allow, which soon rendered him inept so that I could turn to help Kyra, who had already finished off both of her assailants, freeing me to help Rita. So we could get the hell out of there.

Rita didn't look good. Her shoulder was pretty much a half-serving of lasagna thanks to the horrendous gouge of the gunshot. But she was focused. Maintaining her breathing. And was already up on one knee. Ready for me to yell the cue.

"Move out!"

We got up underneath Rita's good arm, her right one, and helped her rise for what just might be our final sprint. I grabbed a pistol from one of the unconscious hombres, and then we were dashing back through the doorway that Kyra emanated from. A small house. Heading out through the owner's front stoop, *muchas gracias*, where we now had at least a one-minute head start on the rest of the gang. There was nobody in front of us. Nobody behind us. A three-person hydra—we were running our six-legged asses off.

Then I looked over at Rita.

She was smiling.

Not ear-to-ear. But a slight smirk. Smiling.

Kyra and I traded the *uh oh* eye contact. Was she delirious? Losing consciousness?

No.

Rita had something in her hand. Something precious that I forgot to grab from the alley in my adrenaline haste, something that was going to revolutionize our situation for good.

She had Double Chin's cell phone.

CHAPTER 34

ON THE MOVE, RUNNING, sprinting, losing a little speed (because, let's face it, we're not goddamn Terminators, although Kyra's a suspected candidate), we were now covered in Rita's blood, some of my blood, and a whole lot of blood from the four inert hombres back in the alley.

It was time to make the call.

I took Double Chin's cell phone and dialed the only special number I had that might function outside the United States. "Bakery Blue Three," I said after the line connected, then paused and slowly stated the following, "The wedding should be held in Mexico City."

We were still running. I was doing my best to enunciate.

"Repeat...the wedding should be held in Mexico City."

This was the evacuation code. It would supposedly—if it worked, which would be a

424

certified miracle since the goddamn number was issued to me two years ago—identify who I am, how many people needed rescuing, and where that rescuing needed to happen. It would thereby elicit an immediate one-time no-questions-asked response consisting of either a ten-thousand-dollar cash deposit to the nearest Western Union, or a ride in a Learjet.

I was waiting on the reply. *The wedding planner has to check on the budget.* That means money is coming. *The wedding planner has to check on the weather.* That means the jet. It's an SOS call that I was never supposed to make. It represented the last favor I could ever ask of anyone at the Pentagon. I'd earned it, trust me, years ago, but the person who felt I'd earned it was probably not at the same desk anymore. Probably didn't answer the same line. In fact, I didn't even hear either one of those code phrases stated back to me.

Instead I got a long pause and then the following:

"Rooftop. Hilton. Nineteen minutes."

It was a man's voice. Meek, almost. Definitely not jolly. Definitely not open to a chat. And then the call ended.

Of course, I tried to dial it back. You're not supposed to, but I tried. And of course my efforts got me the infamous *number is no longer in service* message. In Spanish.

"The Hilton?" questioned Kyra.

There could be two million Hiltons in Mexico City. Or three. Or *ocho*. Or...I don't know. This town is, after all, the second largest damn city in the Western Hemisphere. Why would there be just one stupid Hilton?

"Nineteen minutes," said Kyra, glancing at the clock on the phone. "Eighteen," she corrected herself, as we apparently just spent a full minute worrying about how many minutes we had.

"Gotta be the downtown," said Rita. Her last gasp of verbiage before slipping into delirium again. She was losing blood.

"We need a cab," I said.

No cab would stop for us. Fortunately, we did have enough mileage laid behind us to be within running distance of the downtown hotel location, which meant, yup, more running.

With two minutes to spare, we limped into the hotel's lobby. We were promptly greeted, or should I say, intercepted, by the concierge, who took one look at our triple serving of bad news and already wished we were pre-deleted from his average Tuesday.

"I need roof access," I told him.

"Uh...roof...?" questioned the concierge,

before telling me, "I'm sorry, señora, but there is a private party on the terrace right now and the only way to access the roof is to walk through the—"

My gun pressed into his dick. Secretly. So no one else could see. Just me and him, near each other. With my gun. Quietly aimed. And everyone still smiling that fake vacation staff smile.

"*Aquí está mi pistola*," I said all calm and ex-wifey. "So let me tell you again. Tell you. Not ask. *Tell*…you…I need roof access."

He was already sweating. Poor kid. I bet he's from a nicer part of town where guns and shit aren't the local currency. He seemed gentle, like an avid computer user or someone who played piano in college. "Uh," was his response.

"And make sure we aren't stopped…because if we're stopped…the first thing I'm gonna do is remove your *pito*."

"*Claro*," he said.

"Ninety seconds," I informed him. "I want to be up there in ninety seconds."

And he immediately led the three of us past his security group.

I had let him glance down and see my gun. That it was there. I let him see that it was pointing toward his *pito*. I did not let him see that it was out of bullets. That wasn't important now. We were marched through the lobby into an elevator. The four of us. He wisely tried to shoo away a couple of security guys who wanted to sniff around our odd aura. The thing about nice hotels in financially challenged regions of the world is they have a ghastly armada of obsequious service staff, grinning and attentive, gawking at each step you take. Rita's blood was everywhere. On her. On me. On Kyra. We looked like a car accident.

"Is there something wrong?" said one of the security guards.

Our clever concierge spoke without hesitation. "They're doing a Shakespeare...uh...show...for the party upstairs. *No hay problema.*"

The elevator doors closed. We were alone. Thirty seconds.

We might have fooled the lobby staff with the *Macbeth* thing, but, walking through an elegant dining room on the twenty-sixth floor, with classical music piped in and a five-course meal clanking around while snooty tourists looked over at us was not going over well.

I didn't care.

We crossed to a third set of stairs and started walking up to the roof.

"I want your landing pad lights on," I said to our concierge.

"My what?" he replied.

"For the helicopter."

"Ten seconds," said Kyra.

"We don't have a landing pad," he said to me.

"What?"

The door opened. And, yup, there was the roof. The roof, with mostly gravel and some giant air-conditioner units and giant fans.

And that's it.

No landing pad. No landing *area.*

"Rope," said Kyra, announcing that this was gonna be one bitch of an extract.

Rita was passed out at this point. Were they going to lower a harness to us, whoever they were?

Right at the nineteen-minute mark, a *Noticias 6* helicopter emerged from behind another skyscraper, growling with its noisy blades, pulling up to a hover above our roof, to present us with a glorious sight for sore eyes. Our escape vehicle.

The pilot probably had no idea who the hell we were but I'm guessing what he did know was that his boss owed some kind of mafia-type favor to my boss, whoever *that* might be at this point. Didn't matter. Orders were orders. He looked at us, knowing he was obligated.

The rope ladder descended. Yes, a rope ladder, like, to climb a tree fort. And Rita roused from her drowsy delirium to gather her strength for one last surge of effort. She's such a trooper. Kyra climbed alongside her, two rungs behind, cupping her upward with her body as they both ascended, grip by grip, the fifteen rungs to heaven.

I was about to go next but I stopped to shake my concierge's hand: "I appreciate this more than you know...I uh..." Tired and worn out, I couldn't think of jack shit to say to him so I stated the only sagacious thing I could think of. "Stay in school. And don't do drugs."

Once inside the 'copter, the pilot flew us directly east. I had been on the verge of unconsciousness for many hours now, barely having a sense that, yes, east was toward the main airport, that, yes, this was the extraction we were counting on, that, no, I would not get a chance to pass out because, no, things were not about to get any simpler for the world of Amanda.

Not at all.

CHAPTER 35

I WOKE UP WITH a three-year-old girl staring at me. Rita's daughter. In Rita's living room. I was on Rita's couch. Her little imp was pointing to my phone. "It keeps winging," she said as she got my attention and walked off, her mission accomplished.

I squinted, looking for whatever she was talking about, thinking at least someone was accomplishing missions in my peer group. I saw my phone. Thirty-seven missed calls, thirty-three of which were from the same number. The Fat Man.

I dialed him right away. He answered right away. Uh oh.

"Colonel Collins, welcome back."

"Listen," I said, groggy, but ready to verbally obliterate him.

"No, wait," he interrupted. "Sorry, no, there's no time. Diego is making moves. We have a known location on him. A banquet."

Silence.

I sat there trying to figure out what to say. I'd

been gone for, what, one single nap? This was after sprinting through the streets of the most violent city in North America, sprinting, not jogging, *sprinting,* after being borderline tortured by my former employer, after torching three drug crop fields, after the ransacking of my garage, and after the DEA threat to lock me up.

I barely had a sense of who was who anymore, as in who's actually on my team.

"We wanna make a move," said the Fat Man. "Now. This evening."

I still didn't say anything.

"I really shouldn't get into it but..." He hesitated, then he mumbled to himself, "Fuck my fucked-up life." He was already regretting what he was about to say next. "I'm sure you got random presumptions going through your head right now, wondering who the hell I am, whether my intel is legit, why the hell I haven't pinpointed Diego before, why the hell I stay hidden while you're out there in the field get—"

"I'm in."

Silence.

"What?" he replied. He wasn't ready for those two words.

"You had me at 'fuck my fucked-up life,'" I told him. "I'm in."

Minutes later I was standing across the kitchen

counter from Kyra. It was a short phone call with the Fat Man so it only took me several seconds to tell her all I knew.

Her response wasn't nearly as enthusiastic as mine. "Are you serious? Total no."

"This could be our only chance," I replied.

"The the Fat Man? Yeah. I ain't buyin' what he's sellin'."

"He said Diego is reactionary. You know what that means? You know what Diego's being re-actionary to? Us. Our little waltz through Izta-palapa. We rattled him. *We* did."

"Is that what the Fat Man told you? The same Fat Man who probably sent us there in the first place? Almost got Rita's arm blown off? She's fine, by the way."

I stood there, formulating in my mind the most reasonable explanation I could think of for what was a very unreasonable hunch about him.

But Kyra didn't let me continue.

"Y'know what, it doesn't matter," she said, tone shifted. "If you trust him, I trust him." She saw something in me. Or maybe she just saw me being me, standing there. "I don't need to know what's going on in there." She pointed to my head. "Just tell me where to aim and feed me an MRE."

She turned to head back to her bedroom. She needed what sleep she could get.

CHAPTER 36

ALREADY LATE FOR THE mission prep, I did
something I never let myself do before a combat
outing. I drove my truck out to Serenity Mead-
ows. Yes, that's a cemetery here in town. You
can always tell when something's the name of a
cemetery. It sounds like someone tried to put a
couple of nice words together in reference to the
saddest place on earth.

I don't usually do this before missions. Visit my
family. I don't usually kick my heart around like
that. But I had something to say I hadn't said before. A question, really.

Their gravesites were near a nice elm tree at the
far end of the knoll. I had a box of chocolates
for my older daughter. A box of crayons for my
younger. And a bottle of A.1. Original Sauce for
my husband. Our running joke. Or my running
joke. He loved the stuff. Practically drank it.
Which repulsed me when he was alive. But now

I miss it. I miss the label. I miss the smell. I miss him.

"I…uh…I didn't come here for a good-bye," I said, standing across from his headstone. "I…uh…I just want to just make sure nothing is left unsaid."

I'm not much for communicating beyond the grave and so forth, but I tell ya, there's something real about it. Whenever I need a response from him, I swear, the wind will rustle every tree on the hillside. He speaks to me through the country. That's who he was. Is. A quiet, natural man. And I just needed to find out one last thing from him.

Did you know I was doing this for you?

"You were my favorite person of all time," I said to him. "And…Sorry I brought this tornado upon our family. But I just need to know…if *you* know…that I did it because I wanted to be…to be the person you always admired."

I wanted to be a good Amanda.

My husband's wife.

I needed him to know that. Because there was a strong chance I would never have this conversation again. I could get killed on this one. Not just based on the high danger level, but because I was starting to get careless during battle. I was starting to be less self-preserving. I glimpsed it in Mexico City: a willingness to die. Which is fine,

I guess, but the deeper issue was starting to loom on my peripherals: *I don't know if they send souls of people like me upward or downward.* What's in the cards for a former mother who runs around the Western Hemisphere killing people? Shooting enough people to elicit retaliation against her own family? I don't think my soul goes to heaven for that.

So I seriously doubt I'll get reunited with my family up there. But that's fine. I just need my husband to know that when I don't show up, it wasn't for lack of trying. Which sounds like a pity party, table for one, but it's not. I just need them never to wonder how much I loved them.

I put the steak sauce on the base of the stone. I looked up toward the clouds in the distance, felt the breeze rise across one of those spectacular cloud-filled sunsets that looks like the portal to divinity.

"Dear Lord," I said out loud in prayer, "I don't have the proper words to say all this but I pray that you forgive me what I'm about to do." And then I added, "I'm about to finish my life story." And then, "One way or another."

I leaned down and placed a kiss on top of each gravestone. The wind did come up. But it didn't drown out my final whisper.

"Good-bye, my darlings."

CHAPTER 37

BACK IN THE SUPPLY tunnel behind our garage, I was prepping my new HK416. Rendezvous was at 6:45 p.m. And the birds were on time. Whatever dread I had that Fat Man might screw me over was entirely dispelled when I emerged onto the field. Two Bell Huey helicopters were there. That was expected. But what was truly a shock, what brought tears to my eyes, and I'm not a crier, is what was *in* those helicopters. My crew.

My crew.

Nearly half my original platoon was suited up. Locked and loaded.

"What Diego did to you is beyond criminal," said the radio operator. Marcus. My first friend from basic training. "We can't let it go unchecked."

The others nodded in agreement.

I had a lump in my throat. I was already beyond emotional. Then, when I got in, I saw Rita there, shoulder bandaged, hobbling, barely able to get her fatigues to fit. She looked like a medical training video. I couldn't hide the disapproval on my face.

But she wasn't interested in my face. "Can't keep me out of this fight, Colonel."

"No, no, no," I said, ready to begin orating my commonsense dissertation on the importance of health and safety. "You need to stay here so that—"

She cut me off, "You can't keep me out." And with that, she yanked the door hatch shut, closing us all in the cabin to make her point. And then stared at me with enough impenetrable stubbornness to change my mind on the spot.

"No, ma'am," I agreed. "I can't."

CHAPTER 38

WE WERE ROARING ALONG at 110 miles per hour back into Mexico. I might as well buy a condo there. Feels like my second home. No, wait, first home. I spent more time there than I did in Texas. In my head, anyway.

After an hour of chitchat among the crew, we began to quiet down. Mission protocol was to start focusing mentally on what was ahead for each of us. Focusing on the execution of the basics.

"All right, platoon, listen up," I said over the radio. "The intel on the compound is that it's occupied by both hostile and neutral persons. But I'm not interested in being morally correct on this one. I'm not interested in you fine folks losing life or limb. The ROE on this op is fire away."

"Drop zone in sight," said the pilot. "Range to target six clicks."

My crew started murmuring to each other in reaction but I kept talking. "Expect every single thing in that place to want you dead on arrival. Even the chef'll throw his fork at you if he can. Shoot to kill."

And that's exactly what we did. Ten minutes later, we hadn't even commenced our fast-rope insertion, and we were already embroiled in an air-to-ground gunfight. We were firing on their watchtower. They were firing on our broadside.

We were at war with Diego.

Fast roping works best when you can destroy whatever is shooting at you before you drop down next to it and cuddle. In our case it was a genuine watchtower. Two enemies with M24 rifles. Mid-conversation, mid-smoke, they looked up, saw us on the horizon, and shot us up. We saw them and returned service.

The ROE, the rules of engagement, were wide open for us. My teams had been so battered by Diego over the years, they were now playing the feud game. Scars were deep. Memories were long.

Show up and shoot.

I slid down the rope and greeted the ground along with a flood of bullets from the patio. Some douche decided to buy himself a Gatling gun and mount it by his pool. That's what was now besieging me and Marcus as we were the first on the ground.

However, with two quick shots from her rifle, Kyra had pierced the guy's skull open from high up in the doorway of our helicopter. That's my girl. Allowing me to crouch down, take point, and fire as many rounds into the gazebo as possible.

They weren't precise shots. I was aiming for where I expected soldiers to be. The entire picnic crowd was scrambling. We definitely had caught them with their pants down. There wasn't one single guard who looked ready for a fight. Their own intel, if they even had any, was that skies were clear, weather was balmy, and the roasted pork was lightly salted.

The bad news for us, though, was that the whole place was crawling with families.

Kids.

Ugh. My team was cleared to shoot at will but none of us was willing to blast at a crowd of kids. Even with all the enemy guards ducking down and running back into the shadows among the scattering families, we still didn't have the stomach to shoot into a civilian throng. Which, *ahem*, was a recipe for a difficult afternoon.

"Pressing forward," I yelled. "Condor Five, gimme cover on the patio."

The gunner in the Huey fired his Vulcan 20mm, which is a big weapon that makes a big noise and desecrates everything it sees, spitting out the kind of big bullet hailstorm that devours concrete. He lit up the pool deck as a show of force, as a poker move, to intimidate enemy shooters who were hiding in the family crowd and motivate them to take deeper cover rather than hold a line. Those enemies weren't, after all, 100 percent sure we *wouldn't* fire into them. (We wouldn't, but they didn't know that.) Which meant we now had about ten solid seconds of hesitation on their part when we could rush inside the hacienda.

"PRESS!" I yelled.

And I darted along a pinball path of whatever items of cover I could find. A lawn chair, a lawn table, the buffet itself, a cart, some garbage cans, a moped. Aiming my gun to take any precise shot possible toward the cluster of enemies, but not finding a single clean target, given that each thug was eclipsed by a screaming nine-year-old or a terrified nanny.

Where the hell is Diego?

As my platoon scurried into better positions, covering one another, taking out stray guards who couldn't retreat fast enough, I began to scan the area for the Holy Grail himself. Our radio code name for him was quite fitting, by the way.

"I have no visual on Dickbag," I said into my radio. "Condor Two, make sure he doesn't have wheels."

"Copy that," replied the pilot.

My primary Huey ascended up out of its hover and flew about a hundred yards down the hill toward the mansion's parking lot, where a bunch of Escalades and Mercedes were parked.

Wham! Not anymore!

One by one, each vehicle was blown to Neptune by our guy in the sky. Hellfire missiles will do that to your morning commute. Which, however, still didn't bring me my Dickbag.

Where was he?

I now stood in the hacienda's living room, searching among the cowering faces for any sign of my nemesis. Please God, tell me this S.O.B. is actually here. I kept thinking to myself I can't do this again. I can't drag my comrades into hell, burn them in combat, drench them in foreign and domestic blood, then send them back home, baked and bruised, only to sit by a fireplace years from now and say wistfully, *Yeah, whelp, we did our best, tough racket.*

Erase that thought, Amanda.

A cartel bandito in a cowboy hat spun from

behind a wall with a 12-gauge aimed right for my chest, just as I squeezed the trigger on my HK first, downing him.

Close call.

I pressed forward even more, entering the middle rooms of the massive ranch. I think this place was actually one of Diego's seven mansions. Seven.

More bullets flew past my head, screaming their airy little trajectories, as I barely ducked in time. I couldn't believe how distracted I was getting. This particular shooter was on the far side of the room—a dude with a superb nickel-plated .45. Must be nice to be rich. I spun up and hammered three quick shots at him, catching his face all three times. Which scared his buddy, who was already having second thoughts about loitering in public during a Marine invasion.

I entered the main dining room.

And finally found myself dwelling in a moment I'd salivated over and dreamed about, craved and feared and loathed and talked about, for nearly a decade.

Him.

I had come around a large wooden pillar, moving low, moving while crouched, in case anyone was anticipating where my *cabeza* would appear.

"*Ten cuidado,*" said Diego Correra.

He looked different from what I imagined. I almost didn't perceive him as him. And you know why? This is going to sound weird. Because he looked exactly like his pictures. I never expected it to be so real. So vivid. Like seeing a celebrity. An evil superstar.

It was a bit surreal and robbed me of my focus for a moment.

"Slow!" he said.

He had a hostage. He had a girl by the throat. I had discovered him before he even had a chance to reload a gun. We were in a standoff. He had a jungle knife and was holding it against the jugular of a tall, skinny adolescent.

"Drop the blade!" I yelled at him.

He didn't. He repositioned himself so she became his full armor. He knew his angles. My guess is he's done this before. She literally blocked every square inch of his body I could've had a shot at.

I kept my aim at a small sliver of nothingness lurking just outside the edge of his neck, on the off chance the girl squirms even a tiny bit sideways and exposes a lethal target for me.

She didn't. But she could. She might.

And there we stood.

I doubt I meant as much to him as he did to me, but I could tell this wasn't an ordinary encounter for Dickbag Correra. He was sizing me up. Finally getting a chance to put the face to the name.

"Be careful how you aim, Amanda, you might hit *me*."

I had to think of a way to lull him a bit. Defuse the tension on his end. "Let's just relax, Diego, I don't want you dead," I lied.

"Drop the gun, or I cut her open right in front of you."

Dear God, please tell me that's not his own daughter.

"I'll poke the bottom of her brain," he said. "Right in front of you. And her coma will be on your conscience. Forever."

"My orders are to bring you in alive, Diego. You're no good dead. Let's just walk out of here. Both of us. No harm."

He didn't respond.

"What do you say," I said to him. "Deal?"

There was a ton of gunfire occurring behind me. My estimation is that most of the families were taking deep cover at this point, which meant my platoon would be trying to overtake the fight. I could hear our HK submachine guns and I could hear enemy AK-47s. Everyone shooting at everyone.

Diego was growing skittish in front of me. He could tell his hombres outside were losing. I could see it on his face. Which meant he was becoming a man of desperation. Which was not ideal. For either of us.

"Drop the knife!" I yelled at him.

"Wait."

"Drop the knife!"

"Listen!"

And just when I thought I might watch a grown man crumple, he did the unthinkable. He plunged the blade into her throat. Up her chin, into her head, twisted the blade so the hole became a cross. He did it because he knew I would stutter for just that one split-second as my chess opponent committed a move I just didn't think professionally possible, and then he, Diego, descended down an entrance to a wine cellar, disappearing from the room, just as I let three bursts from my gun smash uselessly against the wall above him.

Dear Lord.

The girl slumped forward.

Rita came running in. "Medic!" she called out, hurrying over to tend to the girl. As Kyra ran right for the wine cellar entrance, driven by killer instincts, knowing exactly what had just happened without even seeing it, firing into the dark entrance, then turning back to check on me.

She called into the radio headset. "Condor

Five, I have positive ID on Dickbag, heading into a wine cellar on the southwest corner."

Kyra saw me frozen there. She knew I was having a moment.

"Colonel, form up?" she asked me.

She was waiting for me to organize a posse, to form up. You don't want to just ram yourself down into a dark tunnel alone with a psychopath. Going in solo would certainly mean getting shot or walking into explosives.

"Colonel, can we form up?" Kyra asked again, flipping her night vision goggles on. Diego was running as fast as he could down along a tunnel that was guaranteed to lead him wherever we didn't want him to be.

But I didn't wait for that posse. I didn't even call it in. I ran straight down into the darkness. Straight after him.

Now or never.

CHAPTER 39

THERE WERE LOTS OF kids down here. And moms. And maids. And chefs. It was unlit. It was one of those tunnels we hated to raid. Chaotic. Confusing. Dark. Wrong.

I was in kill mode. Bearing a heightened sense of detail. Whenever one of the bandits ahead of me, hidden among the sporadic pockets of cowering civilians, would rise up and point a gun at me, I would end him. One shot. Forehead. Bam. Dead.

Heightened sense.

I kept moving. Kept pursuing. I'd entered Hades itself. Small torches here and there. The pervasive sounds of various women crying in fear set against a backdrop of eerie silence. I could hear my own breathing. Like jogging laps on the track back at Pendleton. Just hearing myself inhale. Just finding the calm in the respiratory rhythm. Exhale. I descended a few stairs to enter a deeper corridor, this one intermittently lit by bare bulbs, creating darkness punctuated by semidarkness punctuated by darkness again. I could see a few women up ahead fleeing from my oncoming presence but no sign of Diego.

Then, bam, another shot from my gun, piercing another one of the thugs who was crouched among the kids.

Heightened.

"Colonel! Slow down!" called Kyra from way behind.

I had vastly outpaced her, violating mission protocol, letting my emotions get to me, opting for a dangerous tactic, but I was in a different consciousness right now. My value system had been inverted. I didn't care about my own safety. I just needed Diego down. More than I needed my own life, I needed his. I needed to possess it.

I emerged into a room, a sort of cave or antechamber, with three women huddled on the floor off to the side in an anonymous clump. They had their faces buried, their long dresses covering their bodies and their limbs.

He had to come through here. He had to. But I couldn't see him in the next stretch of passage. And it was a long stretch.

There's no way he sprinted that fast. That would be two hundred meters in under ten seconds.

That's faster than the Olympics. And while I was standing there, overanalyzing, overcalculating, overthinking, as Amanda always does, it happened.

I heard a pop.

The front of my chest poofed with red air. Red spray. Like I'd been hit from behind by a sledgehammer.

I had been shot. From the rear.

By one of those women.

By someone who was *dressed* as a woman.

By Diego. In a dress.

I could hear him reload. Shotgun blast. The only reason I was still standing was because he fired too close behind me, missing my heart but hitting my shoulder instead. Shotgun shells hurt. I could now answer that question whenever someone asked me at parties. *Hey, does that shit hurt?* Yes, it goddamn does. While he reloaded, while this eternal split-second continued to elapse, I spun around and one-handedly rifle-butted him in the jaw with my HK. His head snapped back, then he lurched forward and bear-hugged me in a full tackle. The women shrieked. They must have been his wives or sisters. Or both. We started to wrestle. Clawing at each other. It wasn't the cinematic fistfight you'd pay twenty bucks to watch at the IMAX. No. It was two people scraping their talons at each other's everything, trying to get any kind of physiological advantage. Him dead-tired from sprinting, me dead-tired from being alive the past decade.

And that's when the first ray of dawn smiled upon my cloudy life.

I cracked his wrist bone backward making him yelp in pain, then bent his elbow backward, hyperextending it. Then broke it. Broke his arm.

And broke him.

He was done.

Rendered inept. Fight over. He was thoroughly at my mercy, as I stood there maintaining my superior leverage on his fractured elbow, leaving him now gasping on his knees.

He was waiting for me to fire my pistol at him. I had a sidearm. Available. But I hadn't even taken it out of my holster.

I had him.

When he saw this, saw what was not happening, he did something I didn't expect. He started laughing. And after a half minute of this, this genuine amusement, this borderline inexplicable joy, I had to know.

"What's so funny?" I asked.

"Hahaha..." he petered out, to collect himself, to say the following. "I kill your friends, I kill your husband, I kill your ugly daughter, her ugly sister...I do all that...and you don't have the balls to do anything back."

"I'm above you," I said to him. "I'm above your world. I'm putting you in jail."

"I own the damn jail, you lonely cunt!" He spat blood on the floor. Proudly. "I'm already free. While you stand there! Frozen like a statue. Like a statue commemorating my power. I'm already free. That's how untouchable I am! Because I am to your people the most precious thing your country could ever want. I am *stability,* you gaping cow." He stood up, gathering Socratic steam. "Your bosses...and your bosses' bosses...will never let me die. In fact...I'm gonna tell them that they should take you by the hair and—"

BAM!

He dropped to the floor. Dead.

Shot by Kyra.

Smoking gun in her hand. She didn't move for a moment. She stood there catching her breath. Then she leaned over to whisper to the bloody pulp of his skull: "Amanda Collins is a lawful person...but I'm not."

And there we stood. She and I. With Diego on the floor.

We got him.

Each in our own way.

We got him.

EPILOGUE

THAT WAS ELEVEN months ago. That was also one pregnancy ago. Rita, the baby machine, got busy with Mr. Rita several weeks after that mission, and cranked out another baby girl. Gorgeous enough to earn her the name Kyra Jane. She was born right in their house because Rita's womb was either too efficient or too lazy to wait for the hospital ride.

Kyra, the original version, started dating one of the firefighters from church. Theoretically it was a courtship, but they were going on those ambiguous non-date dates where nobody in the equation is sure if they're actually on a date or not. And that fog has lasted six weeks now. Welcome to modern social combat. I don't miss it.

Me, I was sitting on the porch, clutching two wrenches while arguing with a carburetor. And that's when a pair of government feet creaked onto my wooden front steps.

There stood Officer Teeth himself.

Warren Wright.

To be honest, I wasn't even mad. The closure on Diego's case was handled in such a deft way that my name was kept out of every single news article and military document. That was my deepest wish. Anonymity. And I know Wright's department, deep within the bowels of his behemoth administration, must have made that happen.

"Colonel," he said. His greeting.

"Agent Wright," I said back. Trying to sound cool.

He stood there a moment, probably intending to conjure up small talk to disguise his real purpose, whatever that would be, and looking shy about it. For the first time ever. Shy. "You managed to locate the number five guy on the North American Most Wanted list. And you managed to take him down in the middle of his own army. Never got a chance to say thanks."

"And?"

"And...it was impressive. You must've had help."

Oh, so that's it. "Look, slick, if you're here to try to..."

"No. I'm not here to ask that question."

I heard a familiar rasp in his voice. A twang. Something I couldn't place. He was staring at me.

His smirk etched on his face with God's permanent marker. Then I started thinking a thought that just couldn't possibly be true, a thought that occurred to me once a long time ago but got instantly dismissed.

"Then what are you here for?" I asked.

"Well, it's certainly not to get you to betray your source. That would be lame." He sighed. "Fuck my fucked-up life."

I knew it!

"I'm here to buy you a beer," he said.

"You're the Fat Man," I quietly exclaimed, scrutinizing his face, his body, his tailored suit. Refusing to believe it. "No...there's...if you...no..."

And so he came clean. "Third time you and I ever talked on the phone I was trying to think of a decent code name for myself and literally had no idea what to tell you. So...since I had just eaten two pints of Ben & Jerry's...and felt bloated...I figured..." he presented himself, arms outstretched. "Fat Man." He patted his gut for reference, his six-pack. Proud of his irony. "I know it's a bit ironic—"

"No, I can see it."

He stopped. Almost hurt for a second, then saw my deadpan face and infinite sarcasm and started laughing. Then he shifted gears. "Sorry about Mexico City. I had to cooperate with

General Claire 'The Hair' Dolan, otherwise she'd sniff me out."

We paused for a moment. We worked well together. It's a shame I had to say no to what I already knew he wanted.

"I'm here to offer you a job," he said.

"I'm retired," I replied.

As usual, Warren Wright wasn't really listening to me. He continued talking as if I hadn't just said whatever I just said. "We have a situation," he informed me. "In Europe. We can't take care of it with proper channels." He cleared his throat. "You're the improper one. You're the one we need."

"You know I'm gonna tell you I'm out. You know I'm gonna tell you my whole career has been a hunt for one man and now that this one man is done, I'm done."

He smirked. Wider.

"Which you're not even hearing," I said, realizing it. I put the carburetor down. I stood up. "Fine. One beer."

"So you're in?"

"No. But I'll let you have the privilege of arguing with me."

"Good," he said, opening the passenger door to his truck for me. He met my eyes and smiled. "I've earned it."

STORIES AT THE SPEED OF LIFE

JAMES PATTERSON
BOOKSHOTS

Little
Black
Dress

Slip into something...
irresistibly sexy.

WITH **EMILY RAYMOND**

LITTLE BLACK DRESS

BY JAMES PATTERSON
WITH EMILY RAYMOND

PROLOGUE

I SPOTTED IT ON the Bergdorf sale rack: see-through black chiffon layered over a simple black sheath, cut to skim lightly over the hips and fall just above the knee. Paired with a thin gold belt, there was something Grecian, even god-dessy, about it.

It was somehow subtle yet spectacular. Not a dress, but a *Dress*.

When I tried it on, I was no longer Jane Avery, age thirty-five, overworked editor at Manhattan's *Metropolitan* magazine and recent divorcée. I was Jane Avery, age none of your business, a card-carrying member of the media elite, a woman who was single and proud of it.

Even at 40 percent off, the Dress was a minor fortune. I decided to buy it anyway.

And that purchase changed everything.

CHAPTER 1

IN THE OPULENT LIMESTONE lobby of the Four Seasons New York, I handed over my Amex. "A city-view king, please." No tremor in my voice at all. Nothing to betray the pounding of my heart, the adrenaline flooding my veins.

Am I really about to do this?

Maybe I should have had another glass of rosé.

The desk clerk tapped quickly on her keyboard. "We have a room on the fortieth floor," she said. "Where are you two visiting from?"

I shot a glance over my shoulder. *Honestly? About twenty-five blocks from here.* My knees were turning into Jell-O.

Behind me, Michael Bishop, a thumb hooked in the belt loop of his jeans, flashed his gorgeous smile—first at me, then at the clerk. "Ohio, miss," he said, giving his muscled shoulders an aw-shucks shrug. His eyes were green as jade. "Mighty big city you got here, darlin'," he said, a drawl slipping into his voice.

"Oh—Ohio," the clerk repeated, like it was the most beautiful word she'd ever heard. She looked like she was unbuttoning his shirt with her eyes as she handed me the room key.

Very unprofessional, if you ask me.

But then again, how professional was it to check into a hotel with one of *Metropolitan*'s freelance writers—who, by the way, had obviously never even *been* to Ohio?

If he had, he'd have known they don't talk like cowboys there.

Michael Bishop lived on the Lower East Side of Manhattan; I lived on the Upper West Side. We'd known each other since our first years in the magazine business. Today we'd met for lunch, to go over a story he was writing for *Metropolitan*. The café, an elegant little French place with fantastic *jambon beurre* sandwiches, was close to my office.

It was also close to the Four Seasons.

We'd laughed, we'd had a glass of rosé—and now, suddenly, we were here.

Am I really about to do this?

"If you want tickets to a Broadway show or reservations at Rao's, the concierge can assist you," the clerk offered. By now she'd taken off Michael's shirt and was licking his chest.

"Actually," I said, "we have other plans." I grabbed Michael's hand and pulled him into the elevator before I lost my nerve.

We stood in front of our reflections in the gold-mirrored doors. "Really?" I said to mirror-Michael, who was as gorgeous as the real Michael but yellower. "*Ohio?*"

He laughed. "I know, Jane—you're a former fact-checker, so the truth is very important to you," he said. "I, however, am a writer, and I take occasional *liberties* with it." He stepped closer to me, and then he slipped an arm around my waist. "Nice dress, by the way," he said.

"Do you also take occasional liberties with your editors?" I asked, trying to be playful.

He shook his head. "Never," he said.

I believed him—but it didn't matter either way. This had been *my* idea.

It wasn't about loneliness, or even simple lust (though that obviously played a part). I just wanted to know if I could do something like this without feeling weird or cheap.

I still wasn't sure.

The hotel room was a gleaming, cream-colored box of understated luxury. A bottle of Chardonnay waited in a silver wine bucket, and there were gourmet chocolates arranged on the pillows. Through the giant windows,

Manhattan glittered, a spectacle of steel and glass.

I stood in the center of the beautiful room, holding my purse against my body like a kind of shield. I was charged and excited and—all of a sudden—a little bit scared.

This was new territory for me. If I didn't turn tail and run right now, I was about to do something I'd barely even had the guts to imagine.

Michael, his green eyes both gentle and hungry, took the purse from my hands and placed it on a chair. Straightening up again, he brushed my hair away from my neck, and then he kissed me, gently, right above my collarbone. A shiver ran down my spine.

"Is this okay?" he asked softly.

I remembered the way he'd kissed my fingers at the café. I remembered how I'd said to him, *Let's get out of here.*

I wanted this.

"Yes," I breathed. "It's more than okay."

His lips moved up my neck, his tongue touching my skin ever so lightly. He traced a finger along my jawline and then slowly drew it down again, stopping at the low neckline of the Dress.

I waited, trembling, for him to slip his hand inside the silk.

But he didn't. He paused, barely breathing.

And then he reached around my back and found the slender zipper between my shoulder blades. He gave it a sharp tug, and the black silk slid down my body in a whisper. I stood there— exposed, breathless, thrilled—and then Michael crushed his lips to mine.

We kissed deeply. Hungrily. I ran my palms up his strong arms, his broad shoulders. He reached under me and lifted me up, and I wrapped my legs around his waist. He tasted like wine.

I whispered my command: *"Take me to bed."* Then I added, "Please."

"So polite," he murmured into my hair. "Anything you say, Jane."

He carried me to the giant bed and laid me down on it. His fingers found my nipples through the lace of my bra, and then my bra, too, seemed to slip off my body, and his mouth was where his fingers had been.

I gasped.

Yes, oh yes. I'm really doing this.

His tongue teased me, pulled at me. His hands seemed to be everywhere at once. "Should I—" he began.

I said, "Don't talk, just do." I did not add *Please* this time.

I wriggled out of my panties as he undressed, and then he was naked before me, golden in the noon light, looking like some kind of Greek demigod descended from Mount Olympus.

I stretched up my arms and Michael fell into them. He kissed me again as I arched to meet him. When he thrust himself inside me, I cried out, rocking against his hips, kissing his shoulder, his neck, his chin. I pulled him into me with all my strength as the heat inside me rose in waves. When I cried out in release, my nails dug into Michael's shoulders. A moment later he cried out too, and then he collapsed on top of me, panting.

I couldn't believe it. I'd really done it.

Spent, we both slept for a little while. When I awoke, Michael was standing at the end of the bed, his shirt half buttoned, his golden chest still visible. A smile broke over his gorgeous face.

"Jane Avery, that was an incredible lunch," Michael Bishop said. "Could I interest you in dinner?"

I smiled back at him from the tangle of ivory sheets. As perfect as he was, as *this* had been, today was a one-time deal. I wasn't ready to get involved again. "Actually," I said, "thank you, but I have other plans."

He looked surprised. A guy like Michael wasn't

used to being turned down. "Okay," he said after a moment. "I get it."

I doubted that he did.

It's not you, I thought, *it's me.*

After he kissed me good-bye—sweetly, longingly—I turned on the water in the deep porcelain tub. I'd paid seven hundred dollars for this room and I might as well enjoy it a little longer.

I sank into the bath, luxuriant with lavender-scented bubbles. It was crazy, what I'd done. But I'd loved it.

And I didn't feel cheap. *Au contraire:* I felt *rich.*

CHAPTER 2

I SWIPED A FREE Perrier from the office fridge—
one of the perks of working at *Metropolitan*—
and hurried to my desk, only to find Brianne, my
best friend and the magazine's ad sales director,
draped dramatically across its cluttered surface.

"You took the looooongest lunch," she said ac-
cusingly. "We were supposed to get cappuccinos
at Ground Central."

"I'm sorry," I said distractedly. I could see the
message light on my phone blinking. "My meeting...um, my meeting didn't exactly go as
planned. I'm going to have to work late tonight."

"Oh, *merde*." She gave a long, theatrical sigh.
"Pas encore."

I couldn't help smiling. Brianne was one-quarter
French; the rest of her was full-blown New Jersey.
On a good day, she was funny and loud, as
effervescent as a glass of Champagne; on a bad day
she was like Napoleon with lipstick and PMS.

"Can we do it tomorrow?" I asked.

Bri still looked sulky. "You realize, don't you, that you stay late because you're avoiding your complete lack of a social life?"

"I stay because I care about my job." I tugged discreetly at my bra. Somehow I'd managed to put it on wrong.

"So do I," Bri said, "but you don't see me here at nine p.m. on a Friday."

"You're in a different department," I said, unwilling to admit that she had a point.

She took one of my blue editing pencils and twisted her pretty auburn hair around it, making an artfully messy bun. "I was going to set you up on a date tonight, you know."

"We've gone over this, Bri," I said firmly. "I'm not interested."

Bri lifted herself from my desk and stood before me with her hands on her hips. Five inches shorter than me, she had to crane her neck up. "I know how much you love your Netflix-and-Oreo nights, honey. But it's time you got back into the game."

I *did* love those nights, even though I'd be the first to admit that too many of them in a row got depressing. "I'm not ready to date, Bri. I like the sidelines."

Bri held up a manicured finger. "First of all,

you've been divorced for almost a year and a half."

"Thanks for keeping track," I said.

Bri held up another finger. "Second of all, this guy's practically perfect."

"Then you date him," I suggested. "You're single now too. Aren't you? Or did you fall in love again last night?"

Bri giggled. She gave her heart away like it was candy on Halloween. "There's the *cutest* guy in my spinning class," she admitted. She drifted off into a dreamy reverie for a moment. Then she shook her head and snapped back to attention. "Hey. You're changing the subject. We're talking about you and your nonexistent sex life."

A blush flared hot on my cheeks.

Bri immediately widened her eyes at me. Her mouth fell open, and then she nearly shouted, "Oh my God. You got laid last night!"

I looked wildly around. "Shhh!" I hissed. My boss's assistant was five feet away at the Xerox machine. She didn't seem to have heard Bri's accusation, though. Turning back to my friend, I made an effort to keep a straight face. To look serious and professional. "I did *not* get laid last night," I said.

I got laid an hour ago.

Bri's merry brown eyes grew narrow. "The more

I look at you, the more I think there's something different about you today," she said.

I shrugged. "Well, I'm wearing a new dress." I gave a little twirl. "Isn't it fantastic?"

Bri's skeptical expression softened—but barely. "If you weren't the most honest person I've ever met, I'd swear you were lying to me, Jane Avery."

I smiled. "I'd never lie to you, hon," I said.

But I might stretch the truth.

"Are you sure you won't go out tonight?" she wheedled. "I want you to find a good man."

I sucked in my breath. My mood suddenly shifted. "I thought I had," I said.

Bri looked at me sympathetically. "I'm sorry you married a bastard, Janie. He fooled us all," she said. "But one error shouldn't ban you from the playing field."

I rubbed the spot where the big diamond ring used to be. James had loved me, he really had— but he'd also loved his ex-girlfriend. And her sister.

"Enough with the sports metaphors, Bri," I pleaded.

Bri mimed a baseball swing. "You gotta step up to the plate," she said, smirking, just to annoy me.

"And *you've* gotta get back to your own desk," I said, laughing. "I have work to do."

Bri walked reluctantly to the door and then

turned back around. "Don't you want to know who your date was going to be?"

"Not really." I picked up my phone and pressed the messages button.

"Michael Bishop," she said as she walked away. "He is soooo handsome."

The receiver fell to my desk with a clunk.

Step up to the plate, Bri? I thought. *I did—and Michael Bishop was my home run.*

CHAPTER 3

WALKING INTO AL'S DINER at 90th and Columbus after work that evening, I inhaled the familiar smell of grease and burned coffee—and underneath that, the subtle whiff of good olive oil, salty feta, and ripe heirloom tomatoes. My mouth watered as I slid into my familiar booth. Al's Diner looked like just another greasy spoon, but I knew its secret: *kolokitho keftedes* and *dolmades*— aka zucchini fritters and stuffed grape leaves— so delicious you'd swear you were on Santorini.

Al Dimitriou spotted me and lumbered out of the kitchen, wiping his hands on his stained apron. "Janie, *koreetsi mou*," he said. *My girl.* "It's late! Either you already ate and you're here for baklava...or you worked too long and you're starving."

"Door number two," I said, smiling at him.

Al shook his head at me. "You work too hard, Jane-*itsa*," he said. He turned and hollered, "Veta, Janie's here!"

"I know, I know!" Veta, Al's wife, came hurrying

over with a basket of pita and a bowl of baba ghanoush. It took all my self-control to say *hello* and *thank you* before I started shoveling it into my mouth. Veta patted my head and gave me a quick maternal once-over. "You look very pretty tonight, Janie," she said. "Although the table manners..." She nudged me affectionately.

"Sorry," I mumbled. "Famished."

Al looked at me more carefully. "You got a date after this?"

Why does everyone in New York City care about my dating life?

"No such plans," I said, my mouth still full of warm pita and smoky eggplant.

Veta, who was as quick and petite as Al was big and slow, swatted him on his giant shoulder. "Just because she looks extra beautiful tonight doesn't mean she's going to see a man," she scolded. "Don't be so old-fashioned."

Al shrugged good-naturedly. "I was just making conversation."

"Just sticking your nose in a lady's business," Veta countered. She turned to me. "Don't mind the big lug," she said.

"I don't mind him," I said. "I love him."

At that, Al got slightly red and excused himself, saying something about needing to check on some fava beans.

Veta sat down across from me. She grinned. "So—do you?"

"Do I what?" I asked. I was having a hard time concentrating on anything other than the rich, delicious *meze*. I found an olive and popped it into my mouth.

"Have a date, you goose."

"No, Veta!" I exclaimed. "Why on earth—"

She ducked her head in embarrassment. "Sorry, sorry," she said. "I guess I was hoping."

"You don't need to hope for me," I said. "I'm happy."

And I was *very* happy right now. My God, the baba ghanoush...

Veta gazed thoughtfully out the window, where a flock of pigeons feasted on a discarded loaf of Wonder Bread. Then she turned back to me and said, "So, my happy Janie, do you want the lamb or the octopus?"

I laughed at her matter-of-factness. "Chef's choice," I said.

She patted my hand. "We'll take good care of you," she said.

"You always do," I said, because it was true.

It might have looked like I was sitting alone in a diner on a Friday night, but as far as I was concerned, I was having dinner with friends.

CHAPTER 4

BY THE TIME I said good-bye to Al and Veta, night had fallen. Metal grates covered the doors of the Laundromat, the shoe boutique, and the store that specialized in four-hundred-dollar throw pillows. But cars and cabs still swept by on Columbus Avenue. Couples on dates strolled along, the women tottering in high, uncomfortable heels.

One of the benefits of being 5'8": you can just say no to stilettos.

As I stood on the corner, waiting to cross, I could see the light in my third-floor kitchen, burning small and yellow and alone.

Netflix and Oreos, here I come, I thought.

Just then, the wind caught the skirt of the Dress. The black silk seemed to swirl away from me, like there was a different direction it wanted to go in.

And why *should* I go home? I didn't have a dog

or cat—I didn't even have a fish. The most I'd had was a cactus. (By the way, don't believe the hype about cacti: you *can* kill them, and it's not even hard.)

A little way down the block, the Teddy's Piano Bar sign blinked invitingly. The tiny watering hole had been there since the 1920s, when it was a speakeasy full of smoke and music, fueled by bathtub gin.

I'd never gone inside. But tonight, I walked straight toward it.

The walls were covered in abstract murals painted by some famous, long-dead artist. At the piano, a silver-haired man with a truly enormous nose played Gershwin. Couples chatted at small, cozy tables, and candlelight flickered on the murals, turning them into swirls of color and line.

I ordered a French 75 and sank into a banquette.

"Summertime, and the livin' is easy," sang a black-haired beauty who'd joined the old man on the bench.

I smiled; I'd always loved that song. But I couldn't carry a tune in a Kate Spade handbag, so I hummed along quietly.

At the table next to me, a man sat alone with an unopened book and a glass of amber liquid. He'd taken off his tie and tucked it into the breast pocket of his gray linen suit. His fingers tapped along to the music.

I noted the lack of a wedding ring.

He had a good profile—deep-set eyes and a strong chin. I watched him out of the corner of my eye.

Should I? I thought. *I definitely shouldn't.*

But then I changed my mind.

I waited until the song had ended, and then I slid from the banquette into the chair next to him. "Is this seat taken?" I asked.

The man looked up, startled. His dark eyebrows lifted. He smiled at me—a slow, almost shy smile. "I guess it is now," he said.

"I'm Jane," I said. "Hi."

"Hello, Jane, I'm Aiden," he said. He nodded toward my glass. "I'd buy you a drink, but you seem to have one already."

I clinked my cocktail to his and took a sip of the bubbly liquid. "You can buy the next round."

He laughed. "What if I bore you before that?"

I gave him my best mock-frown. "Don't tell me you have self-esteem problems, Aiden," I said. "You don't look the type."

He shrugged. "Let's just say I wasn't expecting a beautiful woman to sit down at my table tonight," he said.

Please, I'm not beautiful—that's what I almost

said. But then I glanced down at my perfect, elegant Dress and felt a surge of confidence. What if, in calling me beautiful, Aiden was actually *right?* I smiled, sipped delicately at my drink, and made a new rule for myself: *If life hands you a compliment, take it.*

"This is a nice place," I said, looking around the dim, inviting room. "Do you come here often?" Then I felt like kicking myself for delivering such a cliché of a line.

Aiden swirled his whiskey and the ice clicked in the glass. "You could call me a regular, I guess. The guy at the piano is my uncle."

I looked at the homely silver-haired player again. "Hard to see the family resemblance," I said skeptically.

Aiden said, "Really? I think we look exactly alike."

"Aha! You *do* have a self-esteem problem," I said.

He grinned. "You have an understanding-sarcasm problem," he countered.

I laughed. I felt slightly tipsy, but it wasn't from the drink—I'd barely touched it. It was from being out on a Friday night and flirting with a handsome stranger.

I'd already done *one* thing I never thought I'd do today. Why stop there?

"So what do you do, Jane?" Aiden asked.

I shook my head. "Let's not talk about work."

Aiden looked disappointed. "You mean I don't get the chance to tell you about my fascinating work in maritime law?"

I leaned closer. "Do you prosecute pirates—with peg legs and hooks for hands?"

"If only," he said ruefully.

"Then I'm not interested." I sat back and crossed my arms. "You'll have to come up with a better topic for discussion."

Aiden laughed. "And now the beautiful woman makes conversational demands," he said.

I giggled. But I didn't let myself apologize.

And so this handsome stranger told me the story of his former cycling career, including the time he crashed on the Giro d'Italia, Italy's version of the Tour de France, and finished the day's race with a face dripping blood.

I liked the way he moved closer to me to tell it, the way he kept his voice low so he wouldn't disrupt his uncle's playing.

The song was "Memory," from *Cats,* and half the bar was mouthing the words.

I was allergic to cats. And *Cats.*

But I liked the feeling of Aiden's breath near my ear.

"—and then the race was momentarily

stopped by cows in the road!" he was saying. "And the guy next to me is yelling *'Porca vacca!'* Which means 'pig cow,' literally, but also means 'damn it'—"

His face shone with the memory. He looked so happy and alive that before I knew what I was doing, I'd put my hand on top of his.

He stopped talking immediately. His eyes met mine, dark and questioning.

The room at the Four Seasons was mine until tomorrow at 11 a.m.

I knew that Aiden would go wherever I asked him to. Do whatever I wanted him to do.

He'd tell me cycling stories all night. Or serenade me while his uncle played John Lennon's "Imagine." Or he'd slip the Dress from my shoulders and make love to me until I was cross-eyed.

Wait a second: was I absolutely *insane?*

"Jane," he said, his voice suddenly husky.

I gazed into his dark eyes. My heart was thumping wildly.

I made a decision.

I said softly, "It's been so nice to meet you. But I have to go."

And then I picked up my handbag and dashed out of the bar. As I ran down the street, the strains of "The Music of the Night" faded behind me until I could hear nothing but the wind.

CHAPTER 5

THE NEXT DAY, I decided to take a last-minute getaway. Outside the city, I could fill my lungs with clean air and my mind with clean thoughts.

My mistake was going to my sister's house in Westchester.

Mylissa was four years older than me, but ever since my divorce she'd been acting like my mother. Five minutes into my visit she told me I needed a haircut and highlights. An hour later, she tried to set me up with a divorced suburban lawyer who raced vintage cars in his spare time.

I knew she was trying to help, but it bothered me. Sure, Mylissa had a beautiful house, a loving husband, and a perfect pair of eight-year-old daughters, but none of this made her an expert on *my* life.

"You're not much of an expert on it either," she huffed.

Point taken.

We ended up having a nice weekend, eating and drinking and gossiping about her neighbors. But I had to admit I was glad to leave.

It was late Sunday evening by the time I got back to Manhattan. But instead of hurrying home to the peace, quiet, and potentially depressing solitude of my bedroom, I found myself walking into the Campbell Apartment, the upscale bar inside Grand Central Terminal.

I took a seat at the mahogany bar. As my eyes adjusted to the dim light, I wondered if I'd made a mistake in coming here. It was like Valentine's Day in June: everywhere I looked, someone was canoodling with someone else, sharing vintage cocktails, artisanal cheese plates, and deep, romantic glances.

"I'd recommend the Prohibition Punch and a bowl of truffled popcorn," said a voice, stiff with formality and a British accent.

I looked up to see a bow-tied, young bartender vigorously polishing a champagne flute.

"It's just too *sad* to eat an entire artisanal cheese plate alone, isn't it?" I asked wryly.

The bartender promptly lost his professional decorum by cracking up. "Absolutely not," he said, grinning. "You could eat anything you wanted and it wouldn't be sad." He leaned forward and whispered, "But between the two of us, the Ardrahan smells funkier than an Iowa pig farm and the Époisses has the bouquet of well-used gym towel."

Now it was my turn to laugh. He was cute *and* funny—like a blond Eddie Redmayne, accent and everything. "In that case, I'll have the popcorn," I said.

"Excellent choice, miss," he said, taking a step back and clearly trying to regain his gravitas.

I raised an eyebrow at him. "Please, don't get stuffy again. I tip better when I'm entertained."

"I shall dispense with the straight face," he said solemnly. "And I would be most honored to entertain you." And then he offered me a huge, goofy grin. "Wanna see my Arnold Schwarzenegger impression?"

I most certainly did. He looked quickly around—checking for his boss, no doubt—and then he cocked his head, hunched his shoulders, and transformed into the Terminator as he mixed my cocktail.

I clapped. "You must be an actor," I said.

"Me and every other bartender in town," he said.

"Tough way to make a living?" I asked sympathetically.

For a second he looked slightly chagrined.

"Yeah. But just you wait," he said, brightening. "Someday you'll go to the movies and my face'll be up there, twenty feet tall, and you'll go, *I know that guy! He made me a great drink.*"

"And he forgot to put in the order for the popcorn," I added.

He flushed, embarrassed. "Wow, I'm not doing my job very well, am I?"

"Well, if part of your job is entertaining a single girl in a couples' bar, then you deserve a raise," I said.

"Single, huh?" he said, raising an eyebrow.

I shrugged, as if to say, *Maybe not for long.*

Because I had the sudden idea that he and I would make a great couple.

For about two hours.

You don't even know his name, Jane! said the small voice of my sanity.

So ask him, and then see when he gets off work, said a different voice entirely.

When he put the popcorn in front of me, we both took a big handful. But suddenly we were both too shy to speak.

Then I said, "I think—" at the same time that he said, "Do you want—"

We laughed awkwardly. It was like being in seventh grade again.

We were saved by a pearl-bedecked waitress,

who appeared by my elbow with a cheese plate. "Kitchen made an extra," she said to my English bartender. "You guys want this?"

I grinned at him. "Eau de barnyard," I said. "And I don't even have to eat it alone."

"You never know when you're going to get lucky," he said. Then, obviously feeling more confident, he flashed me a rakish grin. "Right?"

The double entendre was extremely clear. I smiled back at him, imagining all the possibilities. For one thing, no one had talked dirty to me in an English accent before.

But the small voice of my sanity was trying to make itself heard. *Go home and go to bed,* it said. *Alone,* it clarified.

I picked up the parsley garnish and nervously ripped it into green confetti.

What am I going to do?

"Hey," he said, "Earth to—"

"Jane," I said. "And you are...?"

"Thom," he said. "With an *h*."

"Thom," I said quickly, "can I get your number?"

He looked confused. But he scribbled it onto a napkin and handed it to me. I tucked it into my purse. Then I laid down fifty dollars and blew him a kiss.

"I'll call you," I said.

Even though I knew I wouldn't.

You're a coward, Jane, I thought as I hurried down the steps to the train station.

No, you're very smart.

CHAPTER 6

I HAD A *METROPOLITAN* editorial meeting at
10 a.m. At eight, though, clutching a takeout
coffee half the size of my torso, I strode into
the office of my therapist, Alex Jensen, PhD, and
blurted, "Do you think I'm crazy?"

Dr. Jensen looked up at me and smiled. He was
fortyish, attractive in a bookish way; he squinted
whenever he wasn't wearing his glasses, which
was most of the time. "Good morning, Jane. And
no, not especially," he said, still smiling. "Do *you*
think you're crazy?"

I shrugged. "Yes. No. I don't know."

He leaned back in his chair and regarded me
thoughtfully. I'd been pouring my heart out to
him every Monday morning for nearly two years
now, but I'd never flopped down onto the couch
and demanded his take on my sanity.

I sighed. "You want me to talk about why I

asked you that, but I don't know why. I just feel...sort of amped up."

"All right," he said gently. "So why don't you talk to me about that feeling?"

I opened my mouth and then shut it again. For once, I wasn't sure where to begin. I wanted to tell Dr. Jensen everything—that was what he was there for, right?

On the other hand, I didn't really want to admit my...recent extracurricular activities. Therapists might claim that they don't judge, but honestly: *everyone* judges.

Well, Dr. Jensen, I had a nooner at the Four Seasons, like it was some Hell's Kitchen flophouse.

Then I hit on some strangers.

And I kind of wanted to sleep with them.

Actually, take back "kind of."

He'd think I *had* gone crazy.

"I saw my sister over the weekend, and she tried to set me up with someone again," I said, shifting the subject—subtly, I hoped.

"And how did that make—"

"It made me feel annoyed," I said. Dr. Jensen had heard a lot about Mylissa over the years; such feminine perfection was a tough act to follow. "I don't know why she doesn't believe me when I say I don't want to date anyone."

"Why do you think that is, Jane?"

"Why don't you tell me?" I said, suddenly feeling ornery. "You're the expert in human behavior."

Dr. Jensen steepled his fingers together under his chin and gazed at me steadily. Affectionately, even. But he didn't answer the question.

I squirmed uncomfortably on his couch. I couldn't tell what he was thinking and it was driving me crazy.

I had the sudden and irresistible urge to fluster him. "Would you ever want to have sex with me?" I asked.

Dr. Jensen blinked rapidly. For the first time ever, I'd actually surprised him. But before he could answer, I backed off. "I'm kidding," I said. "Really. It was a joke."

Great—now I've got to get out of here, I thought.

Better to run away than explain why I'd asked him. Better to waste the appointment than admit to Dr. Jensen—and to myself, for that matter— that I probably had a crush on him.

Just a little one.

I was about to stand up, but then Dr. Jensen started to laugh—as if what I'd said was actually funny. He didn't say, *Why did you make that joke, Jane? Is this something we need to talk about?* Instead, he acted like I'd just told him the joke about the guy with the twelve-inch pianist.

Relief washed over me. I hadn't blown this—currently my only close relationship with someone of the opposite sex.

But, on the other hand, I wondered if Dr. Jensen ought to start talking to me about erotic transference or something. Didn't that seem like an obvious topic of conversation? *It is not uncommon for patients to experience romantic feelings for their therapist…* Blah, blah, blah.

Did Dr. Jensen know what I was thinking? If not, why was I paying him two hundred and fifty dollars a session?

I shook my head. I was obviously a little bit crazy.

Dr. Jensen was still smiling at me. Come to think of it, he'd been smiling at me the entire time I sat here.

And I had to wonder for real: *did* he want to sleep with me?

There was one way to find out.

But no, I wasn't *that* crazy.

Not yet.

CHAPTER 7

AFTER A WEEK OF begging, Brianne finally convinced me to go out with the brother of her current crush. A single date wasn't going to kill me, I reasoned, and since I'd just finished binge-watching *Homeland,* my Thursday evening was wide open.

And maybe, just maybe, I was a little bit lonely.

Nervously I approached Reynard: this would be my first date in six years. Then I saw the man who must be Nolan Caldwell waiting under the awning, eyes scanning the street.

He was very tall and slender, with black hair and eyes almost as dark. Every inch of him projected unwavering confidence, from the sharp jut of his chin to the expensive Italian loafers on his feet.

When he saw me, he hesitated. He looked me over carefully, like I was an expensive sweater he'd ordered off the Internet that he wasn't sure would fit.

Awkward.

"Nolan?" I said. "Hi, I'm Jane." I smoothed the shirred waist of the Dress nervously. "Jane Avery."

I must have passed his test, because he strode over to me and kissed my cheek, and then he gave me a dashing smile. "So good to meet you, Jane," he said, placing his hand at the small of my back. "Ready to go in?" But he was already steering me inside.

At a cozy corner table, Nolan reached for the wine list. "Not many Burgundies," he said, a note of reproach in his voice.

I had no response to that. If it was red and wine, I would probably drink it.

He eventually picked a bottle for us and said, "You're not vegetarian, are you?" He was ordering steak tartare before I'd shaken my head. "We'll share," he informed the waiter.

I looked at him in surprise. Who did he think he was, the CEO of blind dates? After he finished ordering things for me, would he ask me about synergy and leveraging my core competencies? Would he worry about his ROI for this fancy dinner?

As I sipped my wine—which was so expensive it practically tasted like money—I inspected him the way he'd inspected me. He was handsome, and obviously rich: two checks in the plus column. But on the minus side, he'd already racked up cocky, presumptuous, and snobbish.

"So how well do you know Brianne?" I asked.

"Never met her," he said.

"Oh," I said, surprised. "I guess I thought…"

I guess I thought she'd talk to a guy before she made me go out with him?

"My brother and I don't run with the same crowd," Nolan said. "He's a gym rat. He even does MMA."

"Is that some kind of performance-enhancing drug?" I asked.

Nolan laughed—which surprised me, since he seemed deficient in the humor arena. "It stands for 'mixed martial arts.' Basically it amounts to rolling around on the floor with some muscular, sweaty, and half-naked meathead." He tucked his napkin into his lap as he shook his head in disapproval.

Hmmm, really? Rolling around on the floor with a muscular and sweaty half-naked…

"Jane?"

"Oh—what?" While my mind had seized that image and taken an R-rated run with it, Nolan was apparently still talking to me.

"I was asking if you liked the wine. I met the vintner last summer, when I vacationed in France."

"It's wonderful," I said. "I'd love to hear about the vineyard."

Nolan obliged me, as I'd guessed he would. Which meant that I was free to nod and smile...and to pay no attention at all to what he was saying.

Instead, I thought about Michael Bishop.

Actually, that's not right. I thought about the afternoon itself: the heat of Michael's hands, the tender urgency of his mouth, the sublime friction of skin against skin. There'd been no need to talk to each other because our bodies had known exactly what to do. Those hours, stolen from our regular lives, had been electric. I'd never felt that free before. That afternoon was a ten.

Or at least a nine.

I smiled to myself at the memory.

Nolan, of course, assumed that my expression was for whatever boring, pompous anecdote he was currently sharing, so he began to talk more loudly.

Let the cocky bastard think I care, I thought. *As soon I see the bottom of this wineglass, I'm out of here.*

And I was.

CHAPTER 8

I EDITED MICHAEL BISHOP'S article on the New York City Ballet the following morning. It didn't need much work; he was a great writer.

He was an even better kisser, though. And a truly memorable fu—

God, Jane! I shook my head to clear it. This was *ridiculous*. I needed to be thinking about *Metropolitan's* next issue, not replaying the afternoon with Michael for the two hundredth time, my body tingling at the still-vivid scenes.

I decided to take a walk; maybe the fresh air would restore my focus.

Stepping into the summer sunlight, I donned my big Burberry sunglasses and inhaled deeply. New York was beautiful today—the sky a brilliant sapphire, the clouds like enormous downy pillows. It was lunchtime, and people spilled out of office buildings all along Park Avenue South: women in floral dresses, men in button-downs and linen pants or dark tailored power suits.

I watched a cute, slightly scruffy guy fist-bump the doorman of his building, who grinned and said something that made the guy laugh. I could hear it from where I stood: a happy, infectious guffaw.

I was drawn to it. And, okay, I was also drawn to the guy's lean, athletic body.

When he started walking toward Madison Avenue, I followed him. He wore a plaid short-sleeved shirt and skinny jeans, and he sported a tattoo on each forearm.

I wondered if he had other, hidden ink and what it would look like.

I imagined unbuttoning his shirt and running my hands across his smooth chest. I thought about what it would feel like to touch those strong shoulders. I was deep in a delicious daydream when he stopped short—and I almost collided with his back.

I also nearly barreled into the pretty young woman who'd just come up and wrapped her arms around his waist.

He kissed her passionately on the mouth, and, arm in arm, they went to have lunch.

Or maybe they were hurrying off to have a nooner—which was obviously what I was looking for too.

So much for the walk clearing my mind!

But instead of heading back to the office, I kept walking toward Madison Square Park.

The Shake Shack line was a mile long, as usual. The benches lining the pathways sagged with the weight of people talking, reading, and eating takeout.

Not ten feet away sat a man on his lunch break, unwrapping a Shake Shack burger from its wax-paper sleeve.

He had sandy hair and high cheekbones, and he reminded me of someone I'd gone to high school with—a guy we'd voted most likely to become a TV weatherman.

He must have felt my gaze, because he looked up and gave me a curious half-grin.

I almost turned away—but I didn't. "You must've gotten in line at ten a.m. for that," I said, nodding at his lunch.

"Yeah, approximately," he agreed.

"So was it worth it?"

He looked at his burger thoughtfully. "I don't know yet." He held it out. "Want to try?"

"No!" I took a step backward, like he was about to force-feed me a sample.

"It was a joke," he said, grinning. "I don't share my lunch with strangers, even hot ones."

"No, of course not," I said, now feeling ridiculous. "That would be weird."

The irony didn't escape me: I'd been sizing him up for a nooner, but I wouldn't take a bite of his hamburger?

He nodded. "I like weird, but you gotta draw the line somewhere, right?" He took a bite. "Mmm. It's really good, though."

I sat down on the bench next to him. "Do you work around here?"

He gestured toward a stone building on the north side of the park. "In that one," he said. "You?"

"Over on Park Avenue South," I said. "I'm an editor at *Metropolitan* magazine."

"Cool, I have a subscription," he said. "I'm in grad school. Philosophy. Currently making ends meet as a marketing writer for a pet food company." He held out his fries, offering me a taste, and this time I took him up on it. They were hot, salty, and delicious.

"Have you seen that one where the dog goes, 'Your eyes are so beautiful. They're like meatballs'?" I asked. "I love that."

He looked at me proudly. "I wrote it."

I widened my eyes at him. "You're kidding. That billboard's in my subway stop!"

"Nope, not kidding," he said.

"You're obviously an unsung genius of promotional writing," I said. "Are you sure you want to keep studying Hegel or whoever?"

He grinned. "I'm in way too deep to ponder *that* philosophical conundrum," he said. "Which reminds me—" He glanced at his watch. "Shit, I've got to run to class." He got up, somehow simultaneously hurried and reluctant, and then he turned back to me. "You're a mad fox," he said. "I would love to get your number. But I'm sorry to say I'm engaged."

I gave him my best vamp's smile—which was also my first. "Are you sure your fiancée wouldn't let me borrow you, just for an afternoon?" I asked.

He looked shocked.

"I'm kidding," I said. "I don't have sex with strangers. Even hot ones."

Not yet, anyway, I thought as I watched him walk away.

This definitely wasn't what Bri had in mind when she urged me to get back in the game. Because this, honestly, was crazy.

But I didn't want to stop.

CHAPTER 9

"HOW'VE YOU BEEN, JANE?" Dr. Jensen asked as I settled into his overstuffed couch.

"Oh, I'm good," I said. "Everything's perfectly fine. Nothing to report. Life's totally, *completely* normal."

"Really? Well, I'm glad to hear that," he said. His tone conveyed what he really meant, which was *Tell the truth, Avery.*

But I still wasn't ready.

Did other women feel the way I did, though? Did they dream—and daydream—about getting it on, no strings attached? I really needed to know.

Luckily, there was an expert in these matters sitting right across from me. "Dr. Jensen, you must get told all kinds of secrets," I said.

"That's what I'm here for," he agreed. "Why they pay me the big bucks." He smiled.

"Tell me about it," I said, momentarily flashing

on my none-too-large bank account. "I have a question for you. What do other women have to say about sex?"

His eyebrows nearly disappeared under his hair. I'd surprised him again.

"Look, sex used to be the only thing my friends and I ever talked about," I explained. "Who'd done it, and who they'd done it with. But now we've all grown up, and no one ever mentions it. Is it because we're adults and we've outgrown dirty secrets? Or is it just less exciting to talk about, now that we're not doing it in the back of our dad's station wagon? Not that I ever did that, mind you."

Dr. Jensen smiled thoughtfully. "What do you think, Jane?" he asked.

I groaned. "I don't care what I think," I said. "I want to know what other women tell you."

He hemmed and hawed, saying something about confidentiality and psychology's code of ethics.

I looked at him slyly. "Maybe you can't tell me because your clients don't feel comfortable enough to talk to you about that kind of thing," I said.

That was Manipulation 101, and Dr. Jensen knew it. "My clients tell me everything," he said.

I know one who doesn't, I thought. But I said, "Great! I want to hear about it."

"Jane, this is your time to talk about—"

"If it's my time, can't I use it the way I want?" I asked. "Sorry I interrupted you," I added.

Dr. Jensen looked at me carefully and seemed to come to a decision. "You understand I can't tell you anything that would allow you to identify another client. And everything I say is classified."

I snuggled deeper into the couch and mimed zipping my lips closed.

He took a deep breath. "All right, Jane. You asked for it, you got it. One of my clients talks about wanting to have sex with someone other than her husband." He paused. "And she wants her husband to watch."

"That's a tough thing to bring up over the salad course," I said.

"I have another client who's very wealthy," he said. "She's a patroness, and her life is one benefit luncheon after the other. Sex is only pleasurable for her if she's lying on fur." His eyes bored straight into mine. "Preferably lynx," he clarified.

"Because she's so rich?" *Kind of cliché*, I thought.

He shook his head. "Most of her life, she has to be as proper and poised as a marble Venus. The fur makes her feel both primitive and wild. It reminds her that she's an animal, too."

I was against fur—unless it was on a living mammal—but that almost made sense to me.

"Can you tell me a fantasy in more detail?" I asked.

"Jane, again: this is your time to talk—"

"I think it would be therapeutic for me," I said. "Sorry, I interrupted you again."

He gazed out the window for a moment. Then he turned back to me and said, "All right. There's a woman I'll call Marie. She likes to imagine that she has bound her breasts and disguised herself as a young man. In this costume, she finds work on a transatlantic ship. When another sailor catches her bathing and discovers her secret, she's terrified. He threatens to tell the captain unless she...pleases him. And so she does. At first it's against her will. But then she starts to enjoy it very much."

"Interesting," I whispered. This was a new one for me. Maybe I wasn't the only sex semimaniac in town.

"And then she ends up pleasing *many* of the sailors on the ship."

I felt myself blush. "That sounds...strenuous," I managed.

He said, "That's just the tip of Marie's iceberg."

"I'm listening," I said.

"I can tell," he said.

And for the rest of the session, I didn't say another word.

CHAPTER 10

IN SLING-BACKS AND MY black Dress, I inched my way through crowded, neon-lit Times Square. It was slow going, because I had a giddy eight-year-old on either side of me.

Grace, my niece, squeezed my hand happily. "I'm so glad you could come see *Aladdin* with us, Aunt Jane," she said. "Daddy was supposed to, but then he had a meeting."

I turned and gave Mylissa a mild but unmistakable little-sister scowl. "You told me this little Broadway adventure was a girls' night out," I said.

She glanced up from reapplying her scarlet lipstick. "What does it look like?" she asked.

"It looks like I'm here because your husband couldn't make it," I said.

"Ah, but *you could*," she said, blotting her lips with a tissue as we entered the theater.

"But—"

"I mean, really, Jane," my sister said. "Did you have something better to do?"

I sighed. Among Mylissa's many wonderful talents, there was also the unfortunate one of making me feel lame and inadequate.

It wasn't always this way: when I was married to James, with a two-bedroom in the Village and a new promotion at *Metropolitan,* my life had seemed enviable to her. It'd looked pretty great to me, too—until the day I caught James in our bed with Tracy, his ex, and everything fell apart.

The usher led us to our seats, which were excellent. One of the perks of having a brother-in-law with gobs of money, I guess.

Before the curtain rose, Grace laid her head on my shoulder. "Can we have a sleepover next weekend? Pleasepleaseplease?" she asked.

"Yes, may we, Aunt Jane?" said Charlotte, smiling prettily. She was the older twin by five minutes, and she liked everyone to know it.

I was flattered they wanted to spend the night in the city with me—and slightly chagrined that they, too, seemed to know I wouldn't have other plans.

"I love that idea," I said—and I really did mean it. "We can make popcorn and watch movies and paint our nails, and in the morning I'll make you blueberry pancakes with lots of syrup. Mylissa, what do you say?"

Mylissa turned to her daughters. "Your aunt *ought* to be going out on the weekends, girls," she said. "But she seems to relish her solitude."

"I don't know what that means," Grace said.

"It means she likes being alone," Charlotte translated.

"Yes, I do," I said. "But I like being with you two much better."

Mylissa crossed her arms. "If you'd only let me set you up with Jordan Andrews, Jane, you'd have dinner plans," she said. "Did I tell you he made partner?"

I kept my voice low and even. "I know you're trying to help, Mylissa. But like I said, it's really none of your business."

"Fine, if you want to be alone forever," she said huffily.

I was trying to be a good aunt by agreeing to host her darling children, and she was making me feel like a pathetic spinster: that didn't seem fair. But I kept my mouth shut because I didn't want to disagree in front of Charlotte and Grace, who were happily taking bets on whether or not there would be kissing in the musical and if, next weekend, I would let them watch two movies or three.

After a while, Mylissa turned to me and smiled sheepishly. "I'm sorry," she whispered over the top of Charlotte's head. "I shouldn't have said that about you being alone, and I'm sorry I didn't invite you first tonight. I'm *glad* it's you. Mike would just fall asleep."

I had to laugh, because she was right. Her husband worked an exhausting seventy hours a week: put him in a dark room and he'd sleep through the 1812 Overture, cannon fire and everything.

"I'm glad it's me too," I whispered back.

CHAPTER 11

WHEN WE LEFT THE theater, it was pouring rain. Mylissa and the girls gave me quick hugs and then dashed off toward the parking garage. I was left standing on the corner, soaked to the skin already.

It was impossible to get a cab in Times Square on a normal day—in a downpour, forget it. I'd have to make a mad dash for the subway.

"Upper West Side?" called a voice. From the backseat of a taxi, a man beckoned to me. "If you're going that way, we can share."

I squinted at him through the rain. He was in his fifties, with an open face and a deep cleft in his chin. He looked friendly, not to mention handsome, in a silver-haired, Richard Gere–ish sort of way.

I smiled because it reminded me of that scene in *Pretty Woman*—except that he wasn't driving a Lotus Esprit, and I wasn't a prostitute.

You've never slept with an older man before, Jane, I thought.

Then: *Keep your mind out of the gutter, Jane!*

"You're getting soaked," he pointed out.

Getting? I thought. I already looked like a drowned rat, albeit a well-dressed one.

"Last chance," the man called.

I dashed forward, shielding my face from the slanting rain with my knockoff Tory Burch tote. Sliding into the cab, I banged it against him, showering him with tiny, cold droplets. "I'm so sorry!" I exclaimed. "And thank you very much."

"No problem, I'll dry," he said good-naturedly. "You know, if you'd waited much longer, you probably could've swum home."

"It's at least three miles! I'm not Michael Phelps," I said, smiling.

"You're not? In that case I don't want to give you a ride after all." He grinned. "Hello, I'm Ethan Ross."

I shook his warm hand with my damp, chilled one. "Jane Avery," I said. I let my hand linger in his for a moment before pulling it away.

I gave the cabbie my address, and he drove wordlessly toward Eighth Avenue. The wheels hissed on the wet pavement, and the stoplights' reflections sparkled ruby and emerald against the black streets.

I felt much better now that I wasn't being deluged. Now that I was sitting next to a handsome man with a bare ring finger.

"It's actually a pretty night," I said to my cabmate. "Assuming you've got a roof over your head, that is."

Ethan Ross peered out the window. "The city looks almost *clean,* so that's a minor miracle," he said.

"Yeah, and now I don't have to wash the car I don't have," I quipped.

He laughed, and then we sat in silence for a few blocks. It was a comfortable silence, but at the same time I worried he'd think I wasn't grateful for the ride.

I looked at him out of the corner of my eye.

He was looking at me too.

I flushed. Did Ethan Ross find me as attractive as I found him? Could a connection be that instantaneous?

There was one way to find out. I turned toward him, smiling. "Did you know that the average person will spend almost six months talking about the weather in his or her life?" I asked. Definitely not my best flirty line ever, but better than nothing.

"I had no idea," Ethan said, his eyes sparking with amusement. "Where'd you read that?"

"I don't remember," I admitted, "but after five years as a fact-checker, I'm a fount of trivial knowledge." I inched ever so slightly closer to him. I could smell his piney aftershave.

"Well, that's perfect, because I'm a big fan of random, useless facts," Ethan said, grinning. "What else do you have for me?"

I could feel his body heat warming the air between us. "Cab service dates back to the 1600s," I offered. I wanted to move still closer to him, but I restrained myself. "The cabbies drove carriages, of course, though I believe the proper term is *cabriolet.*"

"Jane Avery, you're a very enlightening backseat companion." Ethan leaned toward me a little, and his knee brushed against mine. "So tell me, why are cabs yellow?"

"It's the color most easily seen from a distance," I said. "That's easy. Now you tell me something I don't know." I gave up on being subtle; I slid toward him until there wasn't any space between us at all. He inhaled sharply. "Maybe something about you," I said.

"I'd like to buy you a drink," he said, his mouth suddenly very close to mine. "You can tell me more trivia, and I'll find it fascinating. Honestly, you seem like the kind of woman who could make a lawn mower manual fascinating."

"Columbus and 89th," the cabbie said over his shoulder.

It was all up to me what happened next. I bit my lip, deciding. Then I nodded. "Yes," I said.

Ethan's hand cupped my cheek, a gesture so gentle it took my breath away. Then he turned to the cabbie and said, "Keep driving."

Ten blocks later, in the foyer of his apartment, Ethan Ross pulled me close and whispered, "Do you still want that drink?"

"I'll give you one guess," I purred, sliding the blazer from his shoulders.

"I'm going to guess no," he said, his lips suddenly soft but urgent against mine.

I wrapped my arms around his neck as we moved, our mouths still locked, into his bedroom.

The room was dark and I could barely make out a huge bed.

"Let's get you out of these wet clothes," he said, but I was way ahead of him: the Dress was already pooling at my ankles.

I fell backward onto the bed, pulling him on top of me. His weight felt delicious. His lips met mine with passion and tenderness. His hands caressed my breasts and he moaned.

"What do you want?" he whispered, planting thrilling kisses along my collarbone.

"I want you," I panted. "To—"

His fingers, somehow both urgent and gentle, were pulling down my panties. My mind seemed to be short-circuiting.

He smiled at me as he moved lower down my body, kissing every millimeter along the way. "You're so beautiful," he said. "Tell me what to do to please you."

His mouth on my stomach was warm and soft and wet. I was too breathless to answer. He looked up and grinned at me—a devilish, delighted grin—and then his head disappeared between my legs. His tongue found its target, and liquid fire shot through every nerve in my body.

"I want *that*," I gasped.

And things only got better from there.

CHAPTER 12

I WAS EXHAUSTED AT work the next day, but I didn't care. Everything about last night had been perfect—with the exception of the 3 a.m. cab ride home.

Hoping to avoid such an unpleasant necessity next time, I decided to set guidelines for my . . . *extracurricular activities.*

At the top of a blank page, I wrote TEN RULES FOR A RENDEZVOUS.

1. Do it at lunch—or possibly right after work. (Never neglect your beauty sleep.)
2. Scout out attractive prospects in the real world: no Tinder or Snapchat or whatever apps the kids are using these days.
3. No wedding rings. (Related: Look for tan lines of wedding rings quickly removed and pocketed.)
4. Swiftly approach the target and commence flirting.

5. Do not dawdle: efficiency and resolve are key.
6. Once mutual interest is confirmed, proceed to a neutral place (i.e., not his apartment or yours).
7. Orgasm must be achieved. (Yours.)
8. There is a time limit of 120 minutes.
9. No complications.
10. No second dates.

I looked my list over with a giddy thrill. It sounded so definitive—as if I really knew what I was doing.

"Jane!" Bri, her hands on her hips, was standing in the doorway. "Hello? I've been calling your name for like, *cinq minutes* at least."

"Oh, hi, Bri," I yelped, crossing my arms over my list. "What do you need?"

Bri gave me an odd look. "I don't *need* anything. I came by to say hi. What're you covering up?"

"Oh, nothing!" I said. "Just some ideas for the pitch meeting."

She raised a carefully penciled eyebrow at me. "Jane, are you hiding—"

Just then my phone rang, and I looked at the caller ID.

I'd never, *ever* been so happy to answer a call from my boss. "Hello, Jessica," I said. "I'll be right there."

Rolling her eyes at me, Bri moved away.

CHAPTER 13

AT EATALY, AN ENORMOUS, high-end Italian market not far from my office, there were dazzling displays of cured meats, gourmet cheeses, and heirloom fruits and vegetables. But the reason I'd walked in had nothing to do with soppressata or taleggio.

Every day, hundreds of men came here on their lunch hour.

Wearing a brand-new little black dress, I scanned the well-heeled crowd. I knew I could have my pick of these men. The knowledge made me feel decadent, like I'd stepped into Saks Fifth Avenue with a Birkin bag full of hundred-dollar bills.

Who would I select? Should I approach the dark-haired businessman reading the *Times*? What about the hipster in the scuffed Danner boots, or the man with tawny skin and perfect white teeth?

I didn't feel nervous about picking up a stranger—I felt powerful. I'd come a long way from the Four Seasons, that much was certain.

Over in the produce market, I spotted my target: a man in a gray T-shirt and well-fitting jeans, with eyes the blue of a deep, glacial lake. Eyes I'd be happy to drown in.

I watched him select half a dozen persimmons, and as he carefully cupped the fruit I imagined those hands on my body. I thought about him pressing me up against the bins of melons, kissing me, not gentle anymore but hard and insistent—

I walked up to him and said, "Excuse me, can I ask you something?"

He turned toward me, and my stomach did a little somersault—his eyes were even more beautiful up close. "Sure," he said good-humoredly.

I picked up one of the rosy fruits and cupped it in my hand. "How can you tell if a persimmon is ripe?"

"Well, it depends on the type of persimmon," he said, happy to be able to help me. "This kind here, which is a Hachiya, has to be jelly-soft—otherwise it's like chewing a cotton ball."

"Okay, thanks," I said. "Can I ask you another question?" He nodded, and I dove right in. I said,

"Would you like to spend the next hour or two with me? In a hotel room?"

I can't believe you just asked him that, Jane.

Half of me was scandalized; the other half was proud.

And the tiny part of me that said *This might be dangerous?* I completely ignored.

"Wow." He blushed, embarrassed, and ran his hand through his wavy brown hair. "Wow. Do you mean—"

"You know exactly what I mean," I said, handing him the persimmon. Then I gave him a smirk and headed toward the exit. I didn't need to turn around to know that he'd abandoned his groceries and was hurrying after me.

I took him to the Ace Hotel, to a cozy room decorated with vintage furniture and a splashy graphic mural. Not that it mattered: we only needed the bed.

But not right away, as it turned out.

We kissed our names into each other's mouths—his was Nick, or maybe Mick, I didn't want to take the time to clarify. I was hungry for him.

My hands had a mind of their own, greedily removing his T-shirt, then feeling the smooth slabs of muscle and warm skin underneath. His stubble scraped my lips and neck, and when his fingers found my nipples they caused a delicious, almost electric pain.

He wasn't embarrassed or flustered now. He knew exactly what he was doing. He whispered *"You want this, don't you?"* as he took my breast in his mouth. And when I said yes, his hands went under my dress, moved over my hips and ass, squeezing and rubbing them, and then his fingers slipped inside my black lace panties. He caressed me slowly at first, and then urgently, and as the pleasure grew I hung on to him so my trembling legs didn't collapse under me.

"Now turn around," he growled, pushing my hip with his free hand.

I let him spin me around and then I saw my face in the mirror: hair mussed, cheeks flushed, lips swollen from kissing. I saw him behind me, those beautiful, lustful eyes meeting mine in our reflection. I watched as he slid my dress up my legs and pushed it over my hips. I bent forward, put my hands on the desk. Then I saw him pull down the top of my dress and cup my breasts in his hands. He slid a finger into my mouth and I sucked it.

"You're amazing," he whispered.

I was almost breathless with desire, gasping how it was time, time for him to do what he came for.

LITTLE BLACK DRESS

I heard the scratch of the zipper on his jeans, the crinkle of the condom wrapper. Then I felt him, hot and hard, pressing against me. I pushed back, grinding myself against him.

And then with one thrust he was filling me. His fingers dug hard into my hips and I gripped the edge of the desk. The pleasure was so intense I couldn't think anymore—I could barely even see my own half-naked, sweat-slicked self in the glass. But I could hear the sound of bodies coming together again and again, and a gasping moan that must have been coming from my throat.

Afterward, my legs felt so weak I could barely stand. So when it was time to begin again, we collapsed onto the bed. I stared into those glacial eyes as he called my name and waves of ecstasy crashed over me. If drowning could ever be euphoric, this was what it would feel like.

Later, when he pressed his number into my hands, telling me to *please, please call,* I slipped the little piece of paper into my pocket and told myself that it was okay to keep it.

There was something special about him—something wild but sweet, too.

Later, back at home, I unfolded the paper and smiled. *Nick Anderson,* he'd written. *Persimmon consultant.*

CHAPTER 14

ON FRIDAY, I TOOK the afternoon off and cabbed to the High Line, a narrow, elevated park on Manhattan's West Side. After treating myself to a gelato, I watched good-looking New Yorkers stroll along what had once been railroad tracks.

I hadn't been able to stop thinking about my trip to the Ace with Nick: the freedom and power I'd felt that afternoon was as good as the sex. Could I find that kind of pleasure again? Was it crazy to try?

Part of me thought I should quit while I was ahead. But that would be like putting my spoon down before I'd finished this fantastic, creamy *fior di latte*, which was so rich and delicious I shivered every time I took a bite.

I'd been celibate for sixteen months, hadn't I? That was a lot of sex not to have.

Still, maybe you should take a little break, Jane.

But what if I'm still having fun?

That was a good question. Then again, so was this: *What if I'm pushing my luck?*

When the young man with floppy blond hair and golden, sun-kissed skin sat down next to me, I took it as a sign from the universe.

As Bri would put it, I was still in the game.

"Sarah?" he asked, his voice sweet and uncertain.

I tipped up my hat and lowered my glasses. "I'm Jane," I said, smiling teasingly at him. "Who's Sarah?"

Confusion flooded his beautiful young face. He looked like Robert Redford in *Butch Cassidy and the Sundance Kid*—but younger and more fine-featured. "Um, she's my roommate's girlfriend. I thought..." He frowned lightly. "Did we meet at Noah's party? If so, I'm sorry—I was kind of drunk."

"We haven't met until right this instant," I said. I put a spoonful of gelato in my mouth, pulled it out slowly, and licked suggestively at the spoon.

His eyes widened. He held out his hand. "I'm Jake," he said.

I took his hand, and, still holding it, I stood up. "Would you like to take a walk with me, Jake?" I nodded toward the gleaming Standard Hotel, which straddled the High Line a few blocks south.

He practically leapt off the bench.

Luckily, the hip hotel had a room for us, with a floor-to-ceiling view of the Hudson River and the blue summer sky.

Jake, who'd been chattering nervously for the last ten minutes, now stood in the middle of the room—the way I had, weeks ago, with Michael Bishop—silent and awed.

I stepped up to him and put my hands on his perfect cheeks. "You're going to like this very much," I said reassuringly. "Now kiss me."

He obeyed, awkwardly at first, but he got better fast.

I put his hands on the zipper of my dress and helped him slide it down. "And now my bra," I whispered.

His expression was desire tinged with doubt—as if he thought that at any moment, he might wake up in his tiny apartment with the realization that this was nothing but an incredible dream.

I put his hands on my breasts and he sucked in his breath and said, "Ohhh—"

"Now take off your clothes," I said softly, and I smiled as he obeyed.

I admired his lean body, with its small patches

of downy gold hair: his hard, flat stomach, his long legs, his smooth arms. I pulled him toward me and nuzzled his neck.

"I've never done this before," he said, wonder in his voice.

"Had sex with an older woman?" I said, grinning lasciviously. "A MILF?"

Flustered, he blinked rapidly. "No, I mean——"

I laughed. "I don't have children, so I'm not a MILF."

"I meant..." he said. "I meant that I haven't...hooked up with someone like this."

"Mmm, me either," I murmured.

It wasn't a lie, because I'd never hooked up with anyone I met on the High Line before.

I led him to the bed. He followed, eager as a puppy.

He lay back and I bent over him, kissing his chest and stomach. Then, after teasing him for a while, I took him in my mouth.

His hands gripped the sheets. "Oh God," he gasped. "I love you, I love that."

I smiled as best I could.

When I mounted him, easing my body up and down as he gripped my hips, I felt wild, charged with thrilling life. Every nerve sang as he bucked beneath me. I closed my eyes and threw my head back and abandoned myself to the bliss.

When I collapsed on top of him, exhausted, he wrapped his arms around my damp back.

He kissed my neck, my cheeks, the palms of my hands. "Thank you," he said sweetly.

I laughed. "No, thank *you*," I said.

CHAPTER 15

"THAT'S A NICE SCARF you're wearing," Dr. Jensen said as I flopped down in my usual spot.

"Thanks," I said, touching the blue silk at my neck. I was wearing it to hide the hickey the Sundance Kid had given me. "I don't think you've ever complimented me before."

Smiling, Dr. Jensen shrugged. "It's not typically a therapist's role. But that's a good color on you. It matches your eyes."

Is my therapist flirting with me?

I was probably just being crazy again. Well, if so, I was in the right place for it.

"Have you seen Marie lately?" I asked, leaning back against the cushions and trying to sound casual.

Dr. Jensen did his best to look stern. "Jane, I don't think we should keep talking about other clients' fantasies anymore when we really ought to be talking about you."

He had a point, of course. I sighed. Maybe I *shouldn't* pretend I was still the Jane Avery I used to be: lonely, celibate, and addicted to Netflix. Maybe I should acknowledge who—or what—I'd become.

Not that there was a word for it. If I were a guy, I'd be a player. But what term existed for a woman like me? Sex goddess? Too cheesy. *Demimondaine?* Only Bri would know what it meant. An erotically empowered woman who played by her own rules? That took way too long to say.

Dr. Jensen leaned forward. "What are you thinking, Jane?"

"Do you know how long it takes to get over a divorce?" I asked suddenly.

Dr. Jensen rubbed his nose, right where his glasses would be if he ever wore them. He said, "There's no magic number of months or days."

"Actually, there is," I said, sitting up straighter. *"Sixteen and a half months."* I realized this only as I said it, but it was true. "I'm finally over the heartbreak, Dr. J. Finally over James and what he did to me. To us."

I knew I looked shocked, giddy. And I almost couldn't believe it: I hadn't longed to have James beside me in bed for weeks now. Hadn't felt broken by his betrayal. Hadn't wondered if he regretted throwing everything we had away.

I'd been too busy having the kind of fun I didn't think a good girl like me could ever have.

"I can't tell you how happy I am to hear that," Dr. Jensen said. "But this seems like a rather sudden shift. Did something happen?"

A lot of things happened, I thought, pressing my thighs together as an image of naked Nick tumbled through my mind.

"You know what they say," I chirped. "Time heals all wounds!"

"I get the sense there's something you're not telling me," Dr. Jensen said.

I stared down at my hands because I didn't want to meet his gaze. I couldn't admit anything to him yet, but nor was I willing to lie. "I've been doing some…emotional work on my own," I said. "I mean, in addition to what we've been doing here," I added. I didn't want him to feel he wasn't helping me.

"I'd like to hear about it," he said.

Yeah, well, I'd like to hear about Marie and her sailors, I thought, suppressing a smile that threatened to give me away. *Looks like neither of us is going to get what we want today.*

"Jane?" he asked.

"I'm not quite ready," I said honestly.

And honestly, I wondered if I ever would be.

He nodded. "Okay, I understand. I'm here for you when you are."

"I know," I said. "I'm glad I have someone like you. No, scratch that. I'm glad I have *you*."

I could have sworn he blushed.

CHAPTER 16

HAVE LUNCH WITH ME *today,* the text from James read. *Gramercy Tavern, noon.*

I stared at my phone in shock. For one thing, James and I hadn't spoken in four months. For another, the Gramercy Tavern was romantic and expensive: in other words, not the kind of place you take your ex.

Maybe James had somehow sensed that I was over him, and he'd decided to win my heart back.

Then he'd probably rip it out and stomp all over it, just like he did last time.

Well, there was no way I was going to let that happen. I wasn't that kind of girl anymore.

So I texted him back. *See you at 12:15.*

Then I smiled to myself. This lunch was going to be *interesting.*

James was already at the table when I arrived, and my heart gave a tiny lurch when I saw his familiar, handsome face. Dark, intense eyes, full, sensual mouth—and a girl could cut glass on those cheekbones.

Okay, maybe I *wasn't* entirely over him.

He stood and kissed me, just a millimeter from my lips. "You look magnificent, Jane," he said, letting his hand linger at my waist. "Have you been working out?"

Yes, but not at a gym. "I've been walking on the weekends," I said—which was partially true.

He pulled out my chair and then poured us glasses of rosé. "It's really, *really* good to see you," he said, his eyes still sweeping over my arms, my chest, my face.

"You too," I said, pretending not to notice his admiring gaze. I'd worn a low-cut dress after all. "It's been a long time. What's new?"

His expression quickly darkened. "Tracy and I broke up," he said.

"Again?" I said drily. She'd been his ex before I was. It was stumbling upon the two of them in flagrante delicto—in other words, she was riding him like a rodeo stallion—that had led to our divorce.

"For the last time, though," James said.

"I'm sorry to hear that." And I meant it too.

"It's for the best, really," he said. "What about you? Are you seeing anyone?"

"Me? Oh, no," I said. "No, no, no." I took a gulp of wine. *The lady doth protest too much, methinks.*

"But you've been dating," he said.

"Nope," I said. I flashed him a big smile. "No interest!"

"Oh," he said, sounding surprised. "But you just seem so—I would've thought—I mean, look at you—" He floundered.

"How's the mutt?" I interrupted, because if I couldn't talk about my sex life with my therapist, I certainly wasn't going to try it with my ex-husband.

James sighed. "He gets into so much trouble he must think his name is No, Boy! But I love him to pieces." Then James shot me a look I could only describe as mischievous. "How's the cactus?" He grinned like he already knew the answer.

Which he did.

"Gone to the great desert in the sky," I admitted.

He shook his head affectionately. "Oh, Jane," he said.

"Don't 'Oh, Jane' me." I laughed. "You can't even put your oxford on right."

He looked down. "Oops."

As James discreetly unbuttoned his shirt in order to fix it, I remembered how I used to watch him undress before getting into bed. How his chest was perfectly smooth and hairless until right above the waist of his boxers. How he'd do a sexy little hip shimmy just to make me laugh.

When we were first married, we did it every night—and half the mornings too.

I crossed my legs under the table, trying to ignore the tingling I felt between them. *This is lunch, Jane, not a booty call.*

Right?

The waiter glided over and gave us a minuscule bow. "To start, we have the beef carpaccio with a broccoli rabe pesto," he intoned.

"I ordered the tasting menu—is that okay?" James asked as the platter of thinly sliced meat was set down between us.

"Perfect," I said, my mouth already watering. "Did you know that carpaccio is named after the Italian painter Vittore Carpaccio? The red-and-white tones of his paintings reminded people of raw meat."

James shook his head and smiled. "You always know the weirdest stuff," he said. "I loved that about you."

The meat was so tender it melted in my mouth. "Thanks," I said. "And oh my God, *this is delicious.*"

"I always loved to watch you eat too," James said, sounding almost shy.

"Now you're just embarrassing me," I said, ducking my head. "Also—why?"

He shrugged. "You really appreciate good food, and you look so happy when you eat it. It's…I don't know. Charming. And sexy."

I put my fork down. What was going on here? "James," I began.

He blushed and looked uncomfortable. "I'm sorry. Forget I said anything. I was trying to pay you a compliment. Maybe…maybe now isn't the time."

But what was my rule again? *If life hands you a compliment, take it.*

I said, "If you think I look good eating carpaccio, wait until we get to the chocolate semifreddo with the salted caramel sauce."

James laughed. "I can't wait." His hand crept toward mine across the table.

But we didn't touch.

As the waiter brought us plate after plate of phenomenal food—ricotta tortellini, roasted duck breast—James hardly ate. He just watched me.

I knew exactly what he was thinking, because I was thinking it too.

His apartment was a five-minute cab ride away. We could race over there, pawing at each other in the backseat, and we could rush upstairs and fall into that king-sized bed of his. And there we could do what we'd done best.

It sounded better than dessert.

"I miss you," James said softly.

I smiled. "I miss you too," I said.

I knew that going back to his apartment would be like going back in time. Everything would be just as it had been—except for me.

I was totally different.

He reached farther across the table and finally took my hand. "Do you think..."

I let him hold my hand for a moment, and then I pulled it away. "Missing isn't a feeling you have to fix," I said softly. "It's something we can live with. We had a good thing for a while. We don't anymore. And I'm finally okay with that."

CHAPTER 17

JANE, YOU IDIOT, THIS isn't how it's supposed to work!

I paced back and forth across my parquet floor until my downstairs neighbor knocked a broom handle against his ceiling.

"Sorry!" I called down. "Stopping now!" Then I sank down onto the couch and tried to calmly consider my situation.

I had managed to turn down my ex-husband. But I had kept Nick's number—and, more important, I'd used it. I'd gone so far as to ask him to meet me on the steps of the Met, tonight at 7 p.m.

Yes, the sex had been amazing. But it was the "persimmon consultant" that got me. It was both goofy and sly—a combination I found irresistible.

I imagined us having a glass of champagne on the museum's balcony bar, high above the Great Hall, laughing, talking, and getting to know each other (with our clothes on). Then we'd stroll through Central Park, dodging Rollerbladers and bikers as we made our way toward the Conservatory Garden to admire the last of the tulips. We'd hold hands. We'd kiss under the wisteria-covered pergola.

It sounded like a perfect date.

The problem was, second dates were absolutely *against the rules.*

I glanced over at the *Dress*, tossed carelessly on the back of my reading chair. It was the only witness to the secret life I'd been living, and I desperately wished I could ask it for advice.

I thought of Nick's gorgeous eyes and his infectious laugh. Because he was *funny*—I'd learned that later, when we lay curled on the bed, his hand resting tenderly on my hip as he told me stories of his reckless youth.

He could be serious too. *I've never met anyone like you,* he'd said. *You thrill me.*

He had thrilled me too.

So what was I supposed to do? I looked at the clock; it was 6:50 p.m.

I imagined Nick already waiting for me on the steps, dodging tourists' feet as they heaved themselves up the stairs, shooing away the pigeons hunting for scraps, and scanning the crowd for a tall brunette in black.

Soon he'd start checking his phone. Start wondering where I was.

His fingers itching to touch me again.

I grabbed my purse and dashed out the door.

But instead of heading east toward the museum, I turned in a different direction.

CHAPTER 18

"JANE-*ITSA!*" AL SAID, leaning across the counter to give me a paternal kiss on the cheek. "You hungry?"

"No, thanks, Al," I said. My heart was pounding. To make it to the Met on time, I'd need a hovercraft to float over the rush-hour traffic. "I just came in for a quick coffee."

I put two dollars down on the Formica, and almost immediately, Veta appeared with a steaming cup, swirling with cream the way I liked it.

"Here you go, sweetie," she said, patting my shoulder. "You look extra pretty again. But I'm not going to say anything!" She clapped her hands over her mouth, but I heard muffled words that sounded a lot like "I hope you have a date."

Yes, Veta, I do have a date, I thought. *I have a date with someone I could actually fall for. And* that *is the problem.*

A big clock, the kind they have in every high school classroom, hung above the doorway to the kitchen. As I watched, the minute hand lurched forward with an audible click.

I felt my pulse quicken.

Rule #10. No second dates.

Don't do this, Jane.

I got up from my stool.

"Where are you going, Janie?" Veta called. "You forgot your change. Do you need a to-go cup?"

I strode out to the sidewalk where I stood, jittery with nerves, under the blue-and-white awning that said AL'S #1 DINER. When Nick answered his phone on the second ring, I said, "I can't make it tonight. I'm really sorry."

"What's the matter?" he asked, sounding worried. "Is everything all right?"

Yes, I thought. *No.*

"Everything's fine. I just—I just can't do it."

There was a silence on the other end of the line. Then Nick said, "I don't understand."

I didn't want to say it again, but I had to. "I can't go on a date with you."

"You mean you don't want to," he said.

"It's not that I don't want to," I admitted. "It's that I can't."

"Why not?" he asked. "Are you married or something?"

He couldn't see my rueful smile or the shake of my head. "Not anymore."

"Okay, well, have you been kidnapped? Are you tied up in a basement somewhere in Queens? Do you need mad ransom money? Because I've got it. Tell me where you are and I'll be right there with a suitcase full of cash."

I laughed. "I'm free," I said.

"Then come be with me," he said, his voice now low and urgent.

A teenage couple came staggering up the sidewalk toward me, the boy carrying the girl piggyback, both of them laughing hysterically. Behind them, an old man and an old woman walked slowly arm in arm, their heads bent close together.

And then there was me, alone.

And *fine with it.*

I steeled myself. "For the fifth time—or maybe the millionth, I've lost track—I just can't see you tonight," I said. "I'm sorry."

"Then another night," Nick said. "Tomorrow or the next night or the next."

He was starting to sound desperate, which was kind of sweet.

"It doesn't work that way—" I began. But then I stopped. What was I going to say? I knew I couldn't explain it to him. *I slept with you, and it was fantastic, and I might really like you—but I ab-solutely won't have dinner with you.*

He just wouldn't understand.

I didn't know if I did either.

"Jane, we really had something," Nick said softly.

"We sure did," I agreed. "And I'll never forget it."

And then I hung up the phone.

CHAPTER 19

THE DOOR TO THE Red Room was tucked away under scaffolding, not to mention totally unmarked. When I finally spotted it, I took a deep breath.

Am I really about to do this?

A laughing, good-looking couple brushed past me and entered, arms wrapped around each other. I craned my neck but couldn't see inside. Suddenly uncertain, I paced the sidewalk in my satin shift that put the *little* in *little black dress*, and wondered if I had finally and completely lost my mind.

A handful of fun trysts wasn't such a big deal, not in the grand scheme of things. Tonight, though, was something else entirely.

I, Jane Aline Avery, was about to go into a sex club.

I could feel my pulse pounding all the way down into my fingertips.

I felt exhilarated. And *miles* beyond nervous.

Maybe, just maybe, things were getting out of control.

A moment later, the unmarked door opened again, and the good-looking couple reappeared, beckoning to me. "Come on in, gorgeous," the woman said, smiling. "Don't be scared!"

I blushed, tried to stand still. "Is it that obvious?" I asked.

Her dark-haired date nodded. "You look like a kitten at the door of the dog pound, sweetie. But there's nothing to worry about. Come in with us! We'll take care of you."

I didn't even have time to answer before the woman reached out and took my hand. Her touch was delicate—and strangely reassuring.

"I'm Sasha," she said, "and this is David. We're regulars." She gave my hand a gentle squeeze.

Surprised, I smiled back at her. She seemed nice, and also perfectly normal—not a scary sex maniac. Maybe the Red Room wasn't so different from a dance club, I thought. And so, after only a moment's hesitation, I let her lead me inside.

Yes, I was really going to do this.

Candles flickered in the lobby, their light reflected in gilt-framed mirrors. To my left were a bar and a dance floor; to my right, a big room with an enormous wall-to-wall bed.

"Give it an hour," Sasha told me, nodding toward the empty mattress. "Then that'll be *writhing* with naked flesh."

I gulped. *Maybe, on second thought…*

Sasha grinned as she pulled me toward the bar and ordered us Kir Royales. "Don't worry," she said. "Everything's going to be great. And remember: you don't have to do anything you don't want to do."

But what *did* I want to do? That was the million-dollar question.

I watched a half-naked woman spin acrobatically around a pole while Sasha gave me a good-natured mini-lecture about the absurdity of sexual monogamy. David interjected with helpful information about the club, including the location of the locker rooms, the dungeon, and the late-night buffet.

"No sex near the food," he informed me. "That's pretty much the only rule."

I nodded as if none of this were surprising, but my stomach was doing somersaults.

Suddenly an attractive forty-something man was by my side, his hand on my arm. "Smile if you want to make out with me," he said.

I took a step back in alarm—this was *way* too soon.

He read my expression immediately, said, "Okay then, have a good night," and vanished.

"Whoa," I said, turning back to Sasha. "What just happened?"

"We take *no* very seriously around here," she explained. "A girl can't have fun if she doesn't feel safe."

"That's a relief," I said. I took a sip of my drink, hoping to calm my nerves. "And I obviously didn't break his heart." I pointed to the corner, where he was already making out with a pretty young redhead wearing a vinyl nurse's outfit and carrying a riding crop.

Sasha laughed and patted my hand. "I'm so glad we found you," she said. "You're a unicorn, you know."

"What does that mean?"

"It means a single girl who wants to swing," David answered. His arm curled around my shoulders—but it felt friendly, not creepy. "Do you want to go upstairs?"

I was as rare as a mythical beast? Feeling suddenly giddy, I said, "Why not?"

On the second floor, everything was red: red candles, red lightbulbs, red pedestals bearing red bowls of condoms.

Oh—and there was a couple having sex on a red leather couch not five feet away from where I stood.

This is out of control, said the voice in my head. *You are out of control.*

The couple's moans of ecstasy carried over the music.

Sasha and David watched them avidly for a moment, and they weren't the only ones enjoying the show. A topless woman stepped forward and leaned down toward them, and the woman on the couch began to kiss her breasts as the man ran his hand over her black leather skirt.

"What do you think?" Sasha asked, smiling at me.

"I don't know," I said honestly. "It's a little...overwhelming?"

Sasha linked her fingers through David's and nodded toward a small room furnished with a normal-sized bed and an armchair. "Want to come play?" she asked me. "Or, if you want to ease into it, you can just watch."

I was flattered by their attention, and I actually liked them. But I didn't think I was a voyeur or a two-at-once type. I smiled and shook my head. "Thanks, but you guys go ahead," I said. "I'm going to, uh, keep looking around."

"Okay. You know where to find us," Sasha said.

She leaned forward and surprised me with a soft, Kir-flavored kiss. "See you later, I hope."

I noticed they left the door to their room open.

Alone, still feeling the sweet tingle of Sasha's kiss, I fidgeted nervously. Was this a huge mistake?

There was really only one way to know. I tossed back the rest of my drink, straightened my shoulders, and scanned the room. I saw a man with his hands down a woman's tiny disco shorts and two naked girls fondling each other on a table. Low bass thudded in the background, and it seemed like there were more pheromones in the air than there was oxygen.

I caught the eye of a tall, dark-haired man standing near one of the private rooms. I sucked in my breath.

His gaze was so intense it was like a physical touch.

I stared back without smiling, letting the tension between us build. Then, feeling bolder, I beckoned him over.

"You're new here, aren't you," he said, giving me a sexy half-smile.

"How can you tell?" I asked, trying to sound playful. He was so tall that my head didn't even come up to his shoulders.

"You look as freaked out as I did an hour ago. I'm Dylan." When he brought my hand to his lips and kissed it, a tiny jolt of electricity shot through me. "And you are?"

"Jane, and I do not look freaked out," I insisted.

"Really," he said, unconvinced. "Then let's see how you look now." And, still holding my hand, he pulled me into the dungeon.

It was a large, dark room with dripping candles mounted in iron sconces. I saw paddles, switches, and whips, some resting on hooks and some in use. In the middle of the room hung some kind of elaborate harness, with a pale, naked girl writhing ecstatically in it. Another woman, naked except for her thigh-high boots, cracked a whip near the girl's legs.

All right, I probably looked freaked out now.

But I was turned on by this man, by his coal-hued eyes and his long-fingered hands. By the animal energy that seemed to shimmer from his smooth skin.

"What do you think?" he asked, giving me a tiny smirk.

I shrugged, all put-on nonchalance. "Whips aren't really my thing. But whatever anyone else does is their business, right?"

"To each his own," he agreed. He stepped closer to me. "Or her own." His fingertip brushed my bottom lip—a touch impossibly light, yet I felt it in every nerve.

LITTLE BLACK DRESS

The girl in the sling moaned as the woman dragged the whip along her skin. Someone began blowing out candles, and the room grew darker and seemingly hotter.

I told myself that no one here mattered but me and this gorgeous man. I said, "Smile if you want to make out with me."

He flashed me a beautiful grin, and then he kissed me. Hard. My hands slid around his waist as I pressed my body against his. He broke the kiss before I was ready, taking an ice cube from his drink and putting it in his mouth, then bending down to my neck. The heat and the cold, the tease of his tongue—they made me shiver and gasp.

But when he reached for the zipper on my dress, I put my hand on top of his. "No, no, not here," I said.

"Then tell me where," he whispered.

CHAPTER 20

WE CABBED TO MY apartment, and we'd barely gotten inside before Dylan had me up against the wall, his hands strong and urgent on my body.

I was breaking a major rule, bringing him home, but I didn't care. I'd crossed so many lines already—what was one more?

Summer heat lightning flashed outside the window, illuminating my cluttered living room. Dylan was the first man I'd ever had in my apartment, but he didn't see the mess of books and magazines and coffee mugs. He cared about nothing but me.

"I'm going to bend you over the couch," he said into my neck. "But not just yet."

"What are you going to do first?" I whispered, thrilled.

Before tonight, I'd been the one in charge— but here was a man who wanted to be in control. It was electrifying.

And just a little bit scary.

His hands squeezed my ass, hard, and he said, "Don't talk."

I groaned as he ground his hips into me, a taste of what was to come.

"Not yet," he said again. Then he grabbed my wrists and yanked them down. He held them both in one big hand, tight behind my back, as his tongue traced the seam of my lips and then pushed into my mouth.

It was a hungry, ravaging kiss, and it left me breathless.

"First," he said, "the bed." And then he picked me up and carried me into my room.

I, who hadn't felt small since I was ten, felt tiny in his powerful arms. He set me down, pulled off my dress and everything else in a matter of seconds, and then pushed me back onto the down comforter.

I felt a sense of vertigo as he knelt between my legs, still clothed.

Excitement tinged with a kind of exquisite fear: my heart beat faster and faster. His desire had a violent edge, I could sense it. But I didn't want to stop.

He reached into his back pocket and pulled out a silk scarf, and before I'd even processed what was happening he was winding it around my wrists and whispering, "That's a good girl, you're going to like this."

When he had both of my arms tied to the bedpost, he licked his way down my body as his hands pinched my nipples. I arched up and pressed myself into his mouth.

It didn't matter that I couldn't move—I didn't want to move. I only wanted him to keep doing what he was doing. My powerlessness excited me.

But then suddenly he slipped the silk from my wrists, and in one quick, fluid motion he flipped me over so I was on my hands and knees. I turned back to look at him and saw him pull his hand back. Before I could tell him to stop, his palm connected with my hip and a red, stinging pain shot through me. I gasped in shock.

"You like that?" he asked, his voice husky.

"I don't know!" I cried. I did and I didn't. It scared me.

His fingers slid between my legs and found the wetness there. "I'm sorry, Jane," he whispered. One hand caressed me—and the other delivered another slap.

I cried out. He was testing my limits. I didn't know where they were myself, pleasure mixing with pain, desire with doubt.

Lightning flickered again and I saw him taking off his jeans. "I'll try to be gentle," he said.

"Yes," I gasped.

When he pushed into me, not gentle at all but forceful, animalistic, I couldn't tell if the flash of light was in my mind or outside my window. I felt like I was shattering. It was amazing and it was terrible—

But what was that glint of *metal* I could see, half hidden under his discarded jeans?

In a rough whisper, he said, "Now we're going to try something different."

I think I might have made a big mistake.

CHAPTER 21

THE PHONE SEEMED TO ring forever before voice mail finally picked up.

"You have reached Jane Avery. Sorry, I'm not available to take your call right now. Here comes the beep. You know what to do."

Jessica Keller, publisher of *Metropolitan* magazine, slammed the phone down in frustration. Actually, she *didn't* know what to do.

Jane—reliable, punctual, hardworking Jane—was three hours late for work.

Without her, the Friday-morning edit meeting had dissolved into gossip and bickering. None of the staff writers had met their deadlines, and the fact-checkers, given no new articles to review, were staring glassy-eyed at Facebook or playing computer solitaire.

Until today, until *right this very second*, Jessica hadn't realized how desperately she needed her second-in-command.

And, though she had called her twenty times at least, Jane wasn't picking up her phone.

Agitated, Jessica strode down the hall to Brianne Delacroix's office. The petite redhead was talking animatedly into her headset about "buttressing circulation in order to make rate base."

Jessica made a slicing motion across her chin, and Bri quickly ended her call.

"Is everything okay?" Bri asked, standing up and smoothing her skirt nervously.

Jessica snapped, "Have you heard from Jane?"

Bri's eyes widened. "No," she said. "I texted her last night, but—"

"Did you hear back?" Jessica interrupted.

Bri shook her head. "No."

The two women stared at each other.

"Maybe she took a sick day," Bri whispered. "And she forgot to call in."

"Jane is the most responsible person I know," Jessica said. "That is not the kind of thing she'd ever forget to do."

Bri grew pale. Jessica clenched and unclenched her hands. *Where in the world was Jane Avery?*

CHAPTER 22

"**JANE, YOU'D BETTER NOT** be screening me, you wench," Mylissa said into her headset—half laughing, half annoyed. "Are the girls coming for a sleepover tomorrow night or what? Mike's in Toronto on business, so can I come too? I promise not to mention Jordan Andrews, or say anything at all about your pitiful social life. Whoops! Sorry, don't be mad. What I meant to say was your, um, *selective* social life. Quality over quantity, right? Like shoes. Speaking of which, I came into the city today and I'm about to buy the most amazing pair of Stuart Weitzman heels— seriously, you'll *die* when you see them."

Mylissa was well on her way to a ten-minute voice mail when another call came in and she clicked over. "Hello?"

"Who is this?" demanded an unfamiliar voice.

"Excuse me?" Mylissa asked, bristling. "Who are *you*?"

"This is Jessica Keller. I'm Jane's boss, and this is the number she listed as an emergency contact."

Mylissa gasped. "I'm her sister. What's wrong? Is she okay?" Her heart began to thud painfully in her chest, and she gripped the shoe rack to steady herself.

"I don't know," Jessica said. "She's not at work and she's not answering her phone. This is completely and totally unlike her."

Mylissa dropped the Weitzman heels and began running toward the Barneys exit. She flagged down a cab and threw herself into the back, breathlessly giving Jane's address and telling him to hurry, hurry, it was an emergency.

"Hello? Hello?" Jessica's muffled voice came from the pocket of Mylissa's handbag, but Mylissa didn't even notice.

All she could think about was her baby sister and what terrible thing must have happened to her.

CHAPTER 23

BARELY TEN MINUTES LATER, Mylissa was pounding on the super's ground-floor door and yelling at the top of her lungs.

Superintendent R.J. Dattero, obviously roused from a midmorning nap, stuck his disheveled head out the window and looked at her in confusion. "Can I help—"

"Let me into my sister's apartment," Mylissa demanded. "Jane Avery. Three A."

R.J. continued to stare, unmoving, until Mylissa's patience snapped. "Wake up!" she cried, stamping her foot the way her daughters did. "Jane's in trouble."

Saying it, Mylissa knew she was right, and her mind whirled with awful possibilities. Jane had fallen in the shower and knocked herself unconscious. She'd cut herself on a knife and was slowly bleeding out on the linoleum.

I was too hard on her, Mylissa thought. *I'll never forgive myself.*

R.J. Dattero finally mobilized and came outside. Pulling a ring of keys from his pocket, he opened the building's front door and began arthritically climbing the narrow staircase to Jane's apartment. Mylissa had to fight the urge to scream at him or even push him upward—*anything* to make him go faster.

Potential disasters continued to present themselves. *Jane contracted E. coli from that Greek diner she loves so much, and her kidneys are failing. She drank too much and got alcohol poisoning. She had a heart attack.*

When R.J. unlocked the door of 3A, Mylissa shoved him out of the way and burst into the living room.

Panic exploded in her chest like a bomb, dimming her vision, deafening her to R.J.'s shout of shock.

Clothes were strewn everywhere. A footstool was knocked over. Spilled wine, dark as blood, puddled on the hardwood floor.

Mylissa thought she'd prepared herself for what might have gone wrong.

But never in a million years could she have predicted the scene before her.

In the middle of all that mess, Jane, her baby sister, was kneeling by the radiator.

Naked.

Chained to it by a pair of handcuffs.

Mylissa rushed over and flung herself to the floor in front of her sister. "Janie, Janie, what happened?" she cried. "Were you robbed? Where are your clothes? Did someone hurt you?"

Meanwhile, she tried to cover Jane with her shawl so R.J. wouldn't see her bare and trembling limbs. "Go get bolt cutters!" she cried over her shoulder. "Hurry, you comatose old dinosaur!"

Jane was laughing and crying at the same time, mascara leaving black lines down her cheeks. "I'm fine, I'm fine," she insisted. "I wasn't robbed. I wasn't raped. Oh God, I'm so glad to see you, Mylissa." She sniffled, hiccupped, giggled. "You can't call Mr. Dattero a dinosaur, that's not nice."

Mylissa took her sister's face in her hands. "What the hell is going on, Janie?" she asked. "I was so worried! I thought you were dead. And thank *God* you're not, but why are you chained to a radiator?"

Jane tried to look away, and Mylissa watched as she grew bright crimson.

"Seriously. You'd better start talking," Mylissa said.

Jane heaved an enormous sigh and tried to

meet her sister's gaze. "You always say I don't have a social life," she eventually said. "But I do, actually. And this … well, this is what you might call a side effect of it."

"I don't understand," Mylissa said.

"I brought a man home," Jane said. "And—" She stopped and glanced over to the door. R.J. had returned.

Mylissa leapt up, snatched the bolt cutters from his hands, and shoved him back into the hall.

"Actually," Jane began, "I don't think you need those. The key—"

But Mylissa was already hacking her way through the chain. "There!" she cried triumphantly as the metal gave way.

Released, Jane stood, the cuff still dangling from her wrist like a bracelet. Then she raced out of the room.

"Jane!" Mylissa cried. *What was going on?*

A moment later, Jane reappeared in a bathrobe, smoothing her wild hair with the uncuffed hand. "I had to pee *so bad,*" she said, sounding almost hysterical with relief.

She walked over to the table and picked up something small and silver.

"See," she said to her sister, "he left me the key. Just not where I could reach it."

Mylissa, overcome by absolutely everything,

sank down onto the couch. "I think we have some catching up to do," she said.

Jane gave a small nod. "Yeah, I guess we do."

Mylissa patted the cushion next to her. "So sit your crazy self down, sis. *Now*."

CHAPTER 24

I TOOK MY BOSS a giant bouquet of apology lilies the next day, and I swore on the grave of my cactus that I'd never disappear like that again. I would not get sick, ever; I wouldn't even take vacation.

Jessica Keller's smile was warmer than usual. "Let's not go too far, Jane," she said. "The secret to success? Underpromise and overdeliver." She placed the bright yellow-and-orange flowers in a crystal vase and gave their petals a fluff. "Just don't ever get food poisoning like that again, okay?"

I nodded vigorously. "From now on, I'm just saying no to mussels."

It wasn't as if I could tell her the truth, after all. Confessing to Mylissa had been hard enough.

I've learned my lesson, I thought as I walked down the hall to my office. Last night I'd ripped up my Rules, and I'd rededicated myself to Netflix.

It was probably impossible to spend fourteen hours chained to a radiator and feel any different about things.

When I got to my desk, my message light was blinking and I had approximately five thousand new emails. The one that caught my eye, though, was from Michael Bishop. The subject line was "New Pitch."

I was proud of my reaction, which was no re-action at all: my heart didn't skip a beat, and my breath didn't quicken. I opened it, hoping only for news that he'd gotten Ned St. John, a media-shy film director, to agree to a *Metropolitan* profile. Pre–Four Seasons, we'd slated it for the October issue.

Dear Jane, the email read. *I hope this note finds you well.*

He was keeping it formal—how very profes-sional of him.

> *I enjoyed our working lunch last month, and I hope you won't consider me rude when I tell you that you are wrong about Ned St. John, whose most recent movie is good but whose personality is execrable. Do not send trees to their deaths over such a cretinous ass.*

Instead I propose to feature Kelly Todd, a young female director whose artful "Song of Sorrow" left Cannes audiences blubbering in their seats.

I would also like to say that you are wrong about not seeing me again.

Lunch? Next Friday?

Yours,
Michael B

I scooted my chair back and sighed. Obviously my resolve would be tested. But I would stand firm.

My fingers inched toward the keyboard.

At that moment, Bri scooted into my office with two donuts nestled in a paper napkin. "I missed you yesterday! Look what I got at the ad sales meeting," she said gleefully.

"You're the best," I said, and meant it. I broke off a bit of the chocolate glazed and popped it into my mouth.

"What are you doing tonight?" she asked, helping herself to the coconut cruller. "Want to hit happy hour at Coquine?"

I glanced at my in-box, my messages, and the stack of magazine proofs and groaned for effect. "I have to work, honey."

"Again." Bri sighed. Then she leaned forward and pointed to my wrist. "Hey, *ce qui s'est passé?* What happened? It's all red."

I looked down and saw that she was right. How could I have failed to notice the marks from the handcuffs? I quickly covered them with my sleeve. "Oh, that! My bracelet clasp was stuck, and I was trying to get it off. I'm such a klutz."

Happily, Bri seemed to believe me. "Dumdum," she said affectionately.

You don't know the half of it, I thought.

And at that moment, I made a new rule: *Don't live a life you don't want to talk about.*

Later, I emailed Michael and gave him the go-ahead on the new profile; we could have lunch, I wrote, in the *Metropolitan* conference room. I'd order in sandwiches from Pain Quotidien.

When I finally left the office at 9 p.m., Eddie the janitor was emptying the recycling into his giant blue bin.

"Get home safe, Jane," he called.

"Thanks, Eddie. You too."

He chuckled. "Only six more hours and I can call it a night."

I flagged a cab, but as I rode uptown I realized I wasn't quite ready to call it a night myself. So I had the driver drop me at a new wine bar just off Amsterdam Avenue.

A test.

With its pressed-tin ceiling and exposed brick lit by strings of tiny white lights, Hop & Vine felt intimate and welcoming. I took a seat at the bar and ordered a Pinot, which came in a fishbowl goblet, accompanied by sliced baguette and butter flaked with sea salt.

"Anyone joining you?" the bartender asked as he polished the bar's copper surface. He flashed a sudden grin and leaned toward me. "Or do you need a little company?"

I glanced around the room. I saw a handful of prospects, the way I so often had: two banker types, just released from work and happily guzzling bottles of red, and an attractive, studious-looking guy—glasses, professorial sport jacket—thumbing through *The New Yorker*.

But I didn't want to talk to any of them.

I turned back and smiled at the bartender. "It's just me tonight," I said.

His eyes sparked with interest. "Really," he said, topping off my wine, though I'd barely had a single sip. "A beautiful girl like you?"

I nodded. "But if you don't mind," I added, as gently as I could, "I'd like to just sit here quietly. I brought a good book."

CHAPTER 25

WALKING INTO MY THERAPIST'S office the following Monday morning felt as nerve-racking as going to the Red Room. I wore my primmest dress (black knee-length linen, with a white lace collar), as if it could balance out the hedonistic story I was about to tell.

Because it was time to come clean. Time to reveal my secret, sex-filled summer.

Dr. Jensen smiled as I sank into the familiar leather couch. "Good morning, Jane," he said. "Did you know that today is a special day?"

I nearly spit out my coffee. Had he read my mind? Did he somehow *know* what I was about to do? "Well, uh, yes, maybe?" I stammered, grabbing the nearest pillow and hugging it to my chest like a shield.

"You've been coming here for two full years," he said. "As of today."

I let out the breath I'd been holding in one

long whoosh. "Oh!" I said, relieved. "Wow. Well, happy anniversary to us." I mimed lifting a glass for a toast.

"A lot's happened in two years," he said.

"You can say that again."

How far I'd come in those 730 days! First I'd been the worried wife, and then the depressed divorcée, and then what? The naughty nympho? The term made me snicker, and Dr. Jensen seemed to prick up his ears.

"What are you thinking?" he asked.

"I wonder how many times you've asked me that in two years," I said, dodging the question.

He gave a little half-shrug. "It's a big part of the job description."

I took another deep breath and let it out slowly. If I had something to say, there was no time like the present. "I have a confession to make."

Dr. Jensen leaned back in his chair. "All right, then," he said. "I'm listening."

Quickly, before I could lose my courage, I said, "I've been having sex. Lots and lots of it. With strangers."

"You *have?*"

Dr. Jensen had always seemed so unflappable—well, suddenly he looked *seriously flapped.*

Apparently, asking him about other women's

sex lives was one thing; admitting to my own wild sex life was another thing entirely.

He put his glasses on and peered at me through them, quickly composing himself. "This seems like something we should talk about, Jane," he said. "It sounds...risky."

I nodded—yes, it had definitely been risky.

And then, in a rush of relief, everything came tumbling out: my first fling with Michael and my cab ride with Ethan; man-shopping at Eataly and cradle-robbing on the High Line; the Red Room and the radiator.

Dr. Jensen's eyes widened several times, but he did his best not to react.

"I'm sure you're judging me," I said, "even though you'll deny it. And that's okay. I'm not ashamed of anything. But I could have been a little...smarter. Safer."

Dr. Jensen shook his head. "My job isn't to make judgments," he said. "My job is to listen, and to draw you out. And, occasionally, to challenge you." He crossed his arms over his chest. "So tell me, Jane. What have you learned from these...experiences?"

"Besides check a guy's pockets for handcuffs?" I asked ruefully.

Dr. Jensen allowed himself a laugh. "Yes," he said. "Besides that."

I had to ponder the question for a minute. It wasn't as if I'd embarked on my great sexual adventure because I was hoping it'd be *educational*.

But, come to think of it, I had learned a lot: about desire, about power, and about human connection—emotional *and* physical. By taking control of my sexuality, I felt like I'd finally taken control of my life.

Dr. Jensen might be doubtful about my methods, but he couldn't argue with the results.

"You know how, at the end of Westerns, the cowboy and his girl always ride off into the sunset?" I asked.

Dr. Jensen frowned slightly. "Jane—"

"This isn't a digression, I swear. And sorry for interrupting you. What I'm trying to say is that I'm happy to spend an hour or two with a handsome cowboy. But when the sun starts to go down, he and his horse can hit the high, dry, and dusty on their own."

"Metaphorically speaking," Dr. Jensen said, trying to follow me.

"Yes. Metaphorically speaking, I'm not riding on the back of anyone's horse *ever again*."

Dr. Jensen laughed. "You certainly have a way with words, Jane."

"Thank you," I said. "The point is, I like being in control. This summer has been about what I want and what I need—not what someone else wants and what someone else needs. And I can't tell you how freeing that is."

"I'm happy for you," Dr. Jensen said. "You're not chained to the past anymore—to James and his betrayal."

"Or handcuffed, as the case may be," I said.

My therapist laughed again. "Exactly. By the way, I brought you something," he said. "For the two years."

He pushed a small cardboard box toward me across the desk.

I leaned forward and looked inside. Nestled in blue tissue paper was a tiny, spiny cactus. A pink flower sat on top of it, just like a little hat.

Delighted, I leapt up and gave Dr. Jensen a hug.

I couldn't help myself. And anyway, it wasn't like I tried to kiss him.

Okay, I thought about it.

But only for a second.

CHAPTER 26

"**WHATCHA GOT IN THE** box?" the doorman asked as he pushed the heavy glass door open for me.

The question startled me, and I looked up to see a tall, broad-shouldered young man, his navy-and-gold cap tilted rakishly on his head. I hadn't seen this doorman on my way in—or, for that matter, ever before in my life.

"Wait—where's Manny?" I asked. "He was just here."

The new guy grinned, and two deep dimples appeared in his cheeks. "Manny the Silent? He had a plane to catch. Summer vacation—you know how it goes." His voice held the faintest trace of a Brooklyn accent.

"Wow, I never realized until *right this second* that I've never heard Manny speak!" I laughed. "He just nods and smiles."

"Wait until he's off the clock," the new door-man said, leaning toward me confidentially.

"Then you'd better staple his lips together if you want him to shut up."

I looked at his shiny brass name tag and then peered up into his dark brown eyes. "I take it you know him, Anthony?"

Anthony nodded. "He's my dad's best friend. I'm filling in for him for the next two weeks." He put his hands on his hips, mock-tough, as he stood in the open doorway. "So are you going to tell me what's in the box or what?"

There was something so charming about his overgrown boyishness that I couldn't help but smile. "Have a look," I said. I held out my prickly new roommate. "It's a cactus of the *Matucana* genus, and I am absolutely not going to kill it."

He laughed. "Are you in the habit of killing succulents?"

"Not on purpose," I said.

"May I?" He took the box from me and gently touched the bloom with the very tip of his finger. "I recommend a good houseplant fertilizer with trace elements. Just dilute it to a quarter strength. Give her plenty of water now, but taper off in the fall."

I raised an eyebrow at him. "Are you a cactus specialist?"

He ducked his head modestly. "No. But I'm getting my PhD in botany."

"Wow. That's really impressive," I said.

"Manny calls me Flower Boy," he said, flushing a little.

"Well, you're a lot bigger than he is," I said. "So next time, you just go like this." I held up a fist and shook it threateningly.

Anthony laughed. "That's a terrible idea," he said.

"You're a lover, not a fighter," I said. "Right?"

"Exactly," Anthony agreed. He smiled at me. "What about you?"

I tossed my hair over my shoulder and smiled in return. "Both," I said.

As I reached out and took my cactus back, my fingers brushed lightly against his. I felt the familiar sweet jolt of electrical attraction.

"Have a good day," I added.

Then I stepped through the door and into the golden morning sunlight.

"Tell me your name at least," Anthony called after me.

I walked a few feet more and then I stopped.

Might I, someday, want the services of a cactus doctor?

I turned around, hurried back to him, and pressed my card into his hand.

"Thank you," Anthony said, flushing again. "Can I call you? Can I call you right now?"

He was already patting his pockets for his phone.

Laughing, I waved good-bye, and then, still giggling, I strode down the street.

New York looked spectacular this morning. The yellow cabs, the mirrored office buildings, the emerald-leafed street trees: everything was bright and loud and full of life. I was Jane Avery: single, thirty-five, and living in the best city on earth.

Maybe my phone would start ringing soon, and maybe it wouldn't.

Maybe I'd pick up.

And maybe I'd just keep on walking.

EPILOGUE

"ARE YOU SURE—like, really, *really* sure—you don't want to meet us at Pravda later?" Bri asked as we stepped out of the *Metropolitan* offices into the sweltering August evening. "Come on, Jane, it's Friday! You *need* a vodka gimlet."

I smiled and shook my head. "But you and loverboy *don't* need a third wheel."

"*S'il vous plaît?* You'll be a major conversational aid," Bri pleaded. "Will's amazing, but I really don't need to hear about his triathlon training again. And also..." She stopped.

"Go on," I said—even though I was pretty sure I knew where she was going.

Bri ducked her head and looked slightly embarrassed. "I told Will to bring a friend." Her eyes met mine. "For, um, you."

"I knew it!" I said. "How many times have we talked about my lack of interest in dating?"

"A million?"

"And this makes a million and one." I leaned in and gave her a quick hug good-bye. "Have a good time tonight. Ask Will about his fartleks."

Bri's eyes grew wide. "His *what?*"

I giggled. "It's a Swedish running term, and I guarantee he knows what it means," I said. "Old fact-checkers never die . . . "

She grinned. "They just watch TV at home alone on Friday nights, right?"

I didn't answer—I just waved and headed uptown. For one thing, it was a rhetorical question. And for another, I wasn't actually going home.

The truth was, I had a date.

Because I didn't want to be early, I dawdled on my way north. I window-shopped, ducked into a bodega for a Perrier, and stopped to watch a street musician at Columbus and 70th. And then somehow, by the time I looked at my watch again, I was *late*.

I half-jogged fifteen blocks and arrived at the restaurant flustered and sweaty. Pausing outside to catch my breath and smooth my now-frizzy hair, I spied my date through the window.

Anthony, wearing a dark button-down shirt open at the collar, was sitting in a cozy little booth—waiting for me. A server came over and placed a tall glass of beer in front of him, and

I watched as Anthony looked up and smiled a bright, boyish smile of gratitude.

There was something so sweet in that look. Something so...*open*—like he was ready to love just about anyone.

And right then, I realized my mistake. Dating someone so young and enthusiastic and affectionate would be like dating a *puppy*. Albeit a puppy who could nurse my cactus back to life, should the prickly little thing ever require it. (But hey, so far it was doing *just fine*.)

And that's how I found myself turning on my heel and hurrying away, leaving Anthony to drink his frothy craft beer—as Bri would say—*tout seul*. All alone.

I wasn't proud of myself, not for one second. But I knew that what I was doing was right.

I was almost back to my apartment when it occurred to me that I was starving, and that my refrigerator contained only apples, pita bread, and a takeout container of Al's hummus: nothing that would make even a halfway acceptable dinner. So I ducked into a little Italian place on the corner of Columbus and 98th. Immediately I was met by the comforting smell of a garlicky, tomatoey ragù.

Most of the tables were occupied, so I took a seat at the narrow marble bar. The bartender—

black-haired, potbellied, with a name tag that said FRANCO—greeted me graciously.

"I have a beautiful Amarone on special tonight," he said, his voice a deep baritone. "Would you like a glass?"

"I'd love one," I said. I scanned the menu quickly. "And can I have the agnolotti with the taleggio and wild mushrooms?"

He gave a small smile and an even smaller bow. "Of course, miss," he said. "Excellent choice."

When the pasta came, I devoured every cheesy, mushroomy molecule of it. And then, sated, I leaned back, took a sip of my wine, and looked around the room. I noticed the lovely orchid display at the hostess stand, the pretty, faded prints on the wall, and the tiny crystal chandeliers dangling from the ceiling, illuminating everything with a warm golden glow.

How many times had I walked past this place? And I'd never noticed it before, though it had obviously been here for years.

New York City: it slowly kept revealing itself, unfolding like one of those old-fashioned accordion postcards. A person could never see half of its secrets.

When I turned back to my wine, I noticed that the seat next to mine was now occupied. By— you guessed it—a man.

LITTLE BLACK DRESS

He was a few years older than me. His dark hair was cut very short, and his eyes, behind a pair of excellent vintage glasses, were almost black. He was drinking a scotch, neat.

Was it my imagination, or did the room suddenly get warmer? I took a quick sip of ice water and pretended I hadn't seen him.

But he had obviously seen me.

Out of the corner of my eye, I watched him lean, ever so slightly, toward me. "Hi," he said quietly. "I like your dress."

I inhaled. Exhaled.

Then I slowly uncrossed my legs under the smooth black chiffon of the Dress, and I turned toward him. "Oh, this old thing?" I said, smiling.

ABOUT THE AUTHORS

James Patterson has written more bestsellers and created more enduring fictional characters than any other novelist writing today. He lives in Florida with his family.

Maxine Paetro has collaborated with James Patterson on the bestselling Women's Murder Club, Private, and Confessions series. She lives with her husband in New York State.

Rees Jones (also known as Geraint Jones) is an ex-soldier who served in Iraq and Afghanistan. He earned the General Officer Commanding's Award for Gallantry for his actions in Iraq. His first solo novel, *Blood Forest,* will be published by Michael Joseph in 2017 under the author name Geraint Jones.

ABOUT THE AUTHORS

Shan Serafin is a Los Angeles–based writer who began his career with his first novel, *Seventeen*, before adding screen work to his repertoire and eventually collaborating with James Patterson.

Emily Raymond is the co-author, with James Patterson, of *First Love* and *Witch and Wizard: The Lost*, as well as the ghostwriter of numerous novels for young adults. She lives in Portland, Oregon, with her family.

BOOK**SHOTS**

AVAILABLE NOW!

CROSS KILL

Along Came a Spider killer Gary Soneji died years ago. But Alex Cross swears he sees Soneji gun down his partner. Is his greatest enemy back from the grave?

ZOO 2

Humans are evolving into a savage new species that could save civilization—or end it. James Patterson's *Zoo* was just the beginning.

THE TRIAL

An accused killer will do anything to disrupt his own trial, including a courtroom shocker that Lindsay Boxer and the Women's Murder Club will never see coming.

LITTLE BLACK DRESS

Can a little black dress change everything? What begins as one woman's fantasy is about to go too far.

LET'S PLAY MAKE-BELIEVE

Christy and Marty just met, and it's love at first

sight. Or is it? One of them is playing a dangerous game—and only one will survive.

CHASE

A man falls to his death in an apparent accident....But why does he have the fingerprints of another man who is already dead? Detective Michael Bennett is on the case.

HUNTED

Someone is luring men from the streets to play a mysterious, high-stakes game. Former Special Forces officer David Shelley goes undercover to shut it down—but will he win?

113 MINUTES

Molly Rourke's son has been murdered. Now she'll do whatever it takes to get justice. No one should underestimate a mother's love....

$10,000,000 MARRIAGE PROPOSAL

A mysterious billboard offering $10 million to get married intrigues three single women in LA. But who is Mr. Right...and is he the perfect match for the lucky winner?

FRENCH KISS

It's hard enough to move to a new city, but now

everyone French detective Luc Moncrief cares about is being killed off. Welcome to New York.

LEARNING TO RIDE
City girl Madeline Harper never wanted to love a cowboy. But rodeo king Tanner Callen might change her mind...and win her heart.

THE McCULLAGH INN IN MAINE
Chelsea O'Kane escapes to Maine to build a new life—until she runs into Jeremy Holland, an old flame....

SACKING THE QUARTERBACK
Attorney Melissa St. James wins every case. Now, when she's up against football superstar Grayson Knight, her heart is on the line, too.

THE MATING SEASON
Documentary ornithologist Sophie Castle is convinced that her heart belongs only to the birds—until she meets her gorgeous cameraman, Rigg Greensman.

KILLER CHEF

Caleb Rooney knows how to do two things: run a food truck and solve a murder. When people suddenly start dying of food-borne illnesses, the stakes are higher than ever....

THE CHRISTMAS MYSTERY

Two stolen paintings disappear from a Park Avenue murder scene—French detective Luc Moncrief is in for a merry Christmas.

BLACK & BLUE

Detective Harry Blue is determined to take down the serial killer who's abducted several women, but her mission leads to a shocking revelation.

COME AND GET US

When an SUV deliberately runs Miranda Cooper and her husband off a desolate Arizona road, she must run for help alone as his cryptic parting words echo in her head: "Be careful who you trust."

PRIVATE: THE ROYALS

After kidnappers threaten to execute a Royal Family member in front of the Queen, Jack Morgan and his elite team of PIs have just twenty-four hours to stop them. Or heads will roll...literally.

UPCOMING ROMANCES

DAZZLING: THE DIAMOND TRILOGY, BOOK I

To support her artistic career, Siobhan Dempsey works at the elite Stone Room in New York City...never expecting to be swept away by Derick Miller.

RADIANT: THE DIAMOND TRILOGY, BOOK II

After an explosive breakup with her billionaire boyfriend, Siobhan moves to Detroit to pursue her art. But Derick isn't ready to give her up.

BODYGUARD

Special Agent Abbie Whitmore has only one task: protect Congressman Jonathan Lassiter from a violent cartel's threats. Yet she's never had to do it while falling in love....

HOT WINTER NIGHTS

Allie Thatcher moved to Montana to start fresh as the head of the trauma center. And even though the days are cold, the nights are steamy...especially when she meets search-and-rescue leader Dex Belmont.